ALVERIA DRAGON AKADEMY

The Dragon Tamer

The Dragon Sickness

The Dragon Throne

ALVERIA DRAGON AKADEMY BOOK ONE

THE DRAGON TAMER

AVA RICHARDSON

BLURB

A kingdom divided cannot stand. For those caught in the middle, it means death.

For centuries humans and dragons existed side by side in Alveria, bonded by their care of one another. But no longer. After decades with no viable eggs, humans far outnumber dragons, and the survival of the species appears bleak. The outlook for everyday humans is little better as rogue dragons raid and torment villages. Yet it's far worse for the tamers, beaten and killed simply for serving the noble dragons.

But eking by at the bottom of Alverian society isn't any easier for seventeen-year-old Kaelan Younger. Harder still when her loyalty to the dragon crown is no secret. But when her dying mother reveals a horrifying truth about her identity, Kaelan is thrust into a world for which she is ill prepared.

Faced with a new life at the proving grounds for humans and dragons alike, Kaelan must reconcile not just her past but embrace the future laid out before her. When her responsibilities as an Akademy tamer collide with her feelings for a powerful dragon shifter, it will take everything she has to prepare for the danger threatening them both. The fate of the dragons she has sworn to serve rests in her hands.

Now Kaelan is no longer an outsider.

She's the enemy.

Thank you for purchasing 'The Dragon Tamer'
(Alveria Dragon Akademy Book One)

I would like to thank you for purchasing this book. If you would like to hear more about what I am up to, or continue to follow the stories set in this world with these characters—then please take a look at:

AvaRichardsonBooks.com

You can also find me on me on
www.facebook.com/AvaRichardsonBooks

Or sign up to my mailing list:
AvaRichardsonBooks.com/mailing-list

CONTENTS

CHAPTER 1

Kaelan Younger cradled her basket under her arm as she skulked through the small, shaded market. She had to cradle it because it was full of eggs she needed to sell if she was going to buy the ingredients needed for her mother's medicine, and she had to skulk because she'd technically been banned from this particular market.

Ducking her head, she scoffed—quietly—as she wove between the vendors who were setting up shop. She was still upset about her banishment, especially since the incident that had caused it hadn't even been her fault. Accidentally break one guy's ankle, and suddenly the whole town turned against you. No one cared that she'd been stopping the jerk and his friends from pickpocketing a helpless old man, or that she'd technically done nothing more than give the boy a single light shove. He had gotten out of the incident scot-free—well, minus the broken ankle, which he'd more than deserved—while she'd been exiled to the lesser market.

Which was right next to the pigpens. In the mud. Where no customer with more than a few half-pennies in their pocket would venture. If she wanted to sell her eggs and herbs for enough money to buy the expensive, imported ingredients for the medicine her mother needed to live, she had no choice but to sneak back into the greater market.

Kaelan ducked her head and gritted her teeth, trying to concentrate on finding an unoccupied stall rather than thinking about her sick mother. Every time her thoughts ventured to the broken-down mountain cabin where Ma lay helpless in bed, Kaelan's stomach flopped over and her head went fuzzy with anxiety, and she'd need all her wits about her if she was going to get a prime price out of her goods. Not to mention avoid getting caught, which would mean the confiscation of everything she'd brought to sell.

She couldn't help the ugly and unwanted stir of resentment that always followed on the heels of her anxiety, though. The truth was, Kaelan was sixteen. She'd be an adult in a bare handful of years. She should be ramping up her studies as a healer-in-training, thinking about what she wanted to do with her life. Maybe even, if she was lucky, sneaking off to make out with some hot village boy in a broom closet. She shouldn't have to be here, risking her future and her reputation for the sake of selling a few eggs.

She shook off that last thought, ashamed, and shoved the resentment away. Ma needed her, and Kaelan would come through for her. And that was all there was to it.

She spotted a tiny stall in the very back of the market and darted towards it. It wasn't an ideal location, but it was right next to a vegetable vendor whose plump potatoes might bring a few extra customers their way. She made sure her ratty hood was pulled down far enough to hide her black hair and green eyes, and then she set her basket on the low table.

It was too early for the typical morning crowd to make their appearance yet, but she didn't have to wait long for the first trickle of potential customers. All she could see were two torsos, their heads cut off by the hood that draped over her eyes, but she could tell from the shiny buttons and fine leather that they were well-off. She pulled her hood back just a touch and worked up a charming smile which she'd practiced extensively that week since it never came naturally to her. "Good sires," she started off her sales pitch... but they'd already turned away, toward the vegetable vendor's stall.

Worry fizzed in her veins. It was still early in the morning, so she had plenty of time to make her sales, but every moment that passed heightened the risk of discovery. Maybe these customers could be swayed by a discount and she could get out of here quickly. "Good sires!" she called again, raising her voice this time and lifting her hood a little more so they could better see her hard-won charming smile.

The men—no, boys—turned away from their perusal of the potatoes and glanced at her. The worry in her veins turned to lead, freezing her in place. "You," she said, in a less-than-charming tone.

The boy in front—he was about her age—gave her an ugly smile, looking her up and down. His artfully tousled red hair bobbed with the motion. He swaggered back over to her stall and crossed his arms, probably trying to look tough, but the splint on his ankle ruined his pose.

"I thought I smelled a dragon-lover back here," he said, sneering. "I wonder, does the chieftain know you're in the greater market?"

I may be a dragon-lover, but at least I'm not a pickpocket, she wanted to reply, but didn't. The boys in town had taken to calling her that name—a slur for someone loyal to the dragon-blooded royal family—ever since her family had moved there. It didn't matter. It wasn't worth getting upset over. What she *did* have to worry about, though, was this jackass or his friend telling the village chieftain that she'd broken the terms of her banishment.

The vegetable vendor glanced over, giving Kaelan a long, suspicious look. The rest of the vendors were still preoccupied with setting up shop, but if this guy turned this into a confrontation, they'd all be on her like flies on a carcass, hoping for some juicy new gossip material. If she didn't convince the boy to move along quickly, her chances at a clean getaway would be shot.

Her mind skittered. What was his name? She couldn't recall it. All the guys were the same here, at least as far as she was concerned: a bunch of self-righteous jerks, bullies and proud of it. "Don't you have anything better to do than make trouble for me?" she tried, knowing it wouldn't work. "Surely I'm not worth wasting your time on."

The boy's ugly smile dropped. "Funny thing," he said. "Normally, I *would* have something better to do right now."

The other boy leaned forward, his sour breath wafting between them. "Knattleikr practice was supposed to be this morning," he said. "But thanks to your little stunt, Bekkr here is off the team till next season, and he was our captain. Which means the town's lost its chance at attending finals. You're now officially the least popular person in Gladsheim. So, if you ask me," he said, reaching out a finger and poking her arm hard, "making trouble for you *is* the best use of our morning."

Her heart sank, but before she could say anything in her own defense, Bekkr cut in.

"Actually," he said to his friend, "I think you do have something to do right now, don't you?"

The boy frowned, but then his eyes widened in understanding. He sent a leering smile at Kaelan before he trotted back toward the center of the market.

There was only one place he could be going—to tell the chieftain she was there. Hissing a curse under her breath, Kaelan snatched up her basket and wheeled for the side exit, but Bekkr caught her by the arm.

"Where do you think you're going, dragon-lover?"

Her temper flared and she yanked her arm away. "Stop calling me that!"

His eyes went mean and squinty, the way all her tormentors did when she lost her temper—because that was their goal. She huffed out a breath, frustrated with herself for taking the bait. She should know better by now.

"Why?" Bekkr taunted. "That's what you are, right? Well, let me tell you something, *dragon-lover*. You're not welcome here."

As if she hadn't figured that out on day one. Dragons and the dragon-blooded ruling class weren't popular in Gladsheim, nor were those loyal to them. The way these villagers looked at it, dragons used up the kingdom's resources and gave the common folk little in return. Kaelan had never agreed with that outlook, in part because she knew dragons provided many irreplaceable benefits to the kingdom. The other part of her feeling on the subject was, admittedly, due to her own fascination with the creatures.

She shook herself. She had to get out of the market before the chieftain had her goods seized. She tore herself free from

Bekkr's grip and wheeled around to face the vegetable vendor. "I'll give you a thirty percent discount on these eggs and herbs," she said quickly, evading Bekkr as he grabbed for her again. She kept her eyes on the vendor. Her offer of a discount would mean she'd only be able to afford broth for dinner again, but at least it would leave her enough to pay for the medical ingredients she needed. "You can sell them for much more than that and make a profit."

The woman squinted at her. "Don't need no eggs or herbs," she grunted, and then turned away as if Kaelan was invisible.

Kaelan groaned. What now? Should she try one or two more people in hopes of getting a sale here, or run before the chieftain arrived? Realistically, she knew she should run. It was the smart choice. She still had a chance at making a sale in the lesser market even if it made her next to nothing. But just as she turned to flee, Bekkr's hand snaked out and yanked her basket away. "Hey!" she shouted, trying to grab it back.

Bekkr smiled, holding the basket up out of her reach. Damn his tallness. "Say Queen Celede is a worm and I'll give it back."

Her blood boiled at the derogatory nickname for dragons. When the boys goaded her, it made her angry, but she was used to it. She'd be damned if she'd stand by and let him mock someone else, though—especially a descendant of the dragons she admired. "Queen Celede is a good ruler," she said staunchly. She had no idea if it was true, of course. She'd never been to Bellsor and never so much as seen the ruling family, but she was a loyalist at heart, and plus, at this point she was liable to disagree with anything this jackass said on general principle.

He raised an eyebrow, took one egg out of the basket and dropped it. She yelped and scrambled to catch it, but it hit the ground too quickly, splattering yolk all over the hem of her cloak. She fumed helplessly as he picked up another egg and held it aloft.

"One more chance," he said. "How about Prince Lasaro this time? Everyone knows he's not fit to rule, anyway. None of the royal brats are."

Her temper snapped. She took two jerky steps forward and shoved him, much harder this time than she had when she'd broken his ankle. He stumbled backward, that stupid grin slipping off his ugly face as he had to drop her basket and the egg to reach out and catch himself on a table.

She grabbed her basket and stood above him, raging. "You," she growled, "are *nothing*. All of you, including those other boys you hang out with, you're *nothing*. I don't even have to know Prince Lasaro to know he's twenty times the man you are. Now stay down before I break your other ankle."

She didn't dare look up, but she could sense everyone in a five-stall radius training their attention on her. Now that she'd made a scene and ruined all chances of escaping notice, she tucked the basket under her cloak in hopes of at least making a quick escape with her remaining goods intact. If she got out fast enough, and if there were already a few customers in the lesser market, she *might* still be able to sell her goods for maybe a third of their worth. If she was lucky.

She started to turn and nearly impaled herself on a dragon's skull.

She shrieked and leapt away from the huge thing—the jaws were big enough to fit her whole torso inside—and her basket went flying. The herbs scattered to the ground, her eggs splattering at her feet. The skull's wicked-sharp teeth gleamed in the shade of the market, its dark eye sockets staring at her as she stumbled further backward. Shock and fear flooded her system before she registered that the skull was being carried by two of Bekkr's lackeys who were now laughing so hard that they risked dropping their burden on their feet.

She whirled back around, hands shaking with her fury. Bekkr had righted himself and was laughing, too, completely unsurprised. So, this was why he'd kept her here. He'd been distracting her while his friend went to set up the prank.

"Better watch out, dragon-lover!" he said. Several of the vendors and customers around them were smiling along with him, and the rest ignored the scene and her dismay. "It could be the great Mordon come back to destroy the land! That's all dragons are good for anyway—destruction. But you would know, wouldn't you? That burn on your arm, I bet you got that from dragonfire, right?"

She wasn't looking at him, however, or even really listening. She was looking at her eggs, their yellow yolks broken and soaking into the dust. One of them had shattered against the dragon skull and now dripped down a long tooth. The money she could have made from those eggs could've made her mother well again, at least for a while. And now they were *gone*. And the boy who'd ruined her chances of making that sale was mocking the dragons, the kingdom she called home, and everything she cared about.

It was too much.

She flung her arms down, threw back her head, and roared.

The sound seemed to vibrate up and out of her skin, to wrap her up in a wall of sound, to grow and swell until it was nigh unbearable. It crackled with heat, flashing out from her in a wave, burning the boys' hands. They dropped the skull. Bekkr reeled away, covering his ears and knocking the vegetable vendor's table askew as he tried to flee. The woman shouted, keeping her own ears covered as she stared down at her scattered vegetables being trampled on as people stampeded away from Kaelan. The look in the woman's eyes reminded Kaelan of how she herself must've looked at her lost eggs just a moment ago, and, as suddenly as the roar had started, Kaelan shut her mouth and cut it off.

What had she done? And how in Hel's name had she done it?

She took a ragged breath, and the sound echoed in the sudden, ear-shattering silence.

"Freak!" Bekkr hissed at last. "You're cursed. You're... you're a *freak*."

Throughout the whole market, everyone was staring at her the same way he was: shocked. Frozen. Afraid—of *her*.

She took a step backward. Then another. And then she dropped her empty basket, turned, and fled.

When Kaelan got home, her mother was dying. She'd been dying for months, of course—but now, with Kaelan's mind still spinning from whatever had happened in the market, she was unable to ignore it the way she usually tried to. Her mother lay in bed, her hair brittle and her eyes sunken and yellowed, and barely had the energy to sit up when she saw her daughter come crashing into the house like the mountain-side itself was on fire.

"Kaelan, what's wrong?" Ardis Younger asked, alarm coloring her faint voice. Her knuckles looked knobby, the skin stretching thin over them as she grasped the side of the bed to support herself.

Kaelan took a breath, trying to un-see her mother's weakness.

It wasn't what she should be focusing on right now, anyway. She'd run home as quickly as she could because she needed to tell her ma and grandmother what had happened, and that they'd probably need to uproot themselves and move again because of it. Their business as healers depended on their good reputations with a populace that trusted them, and thanks to the rumors that Bekkr and his friends were surely spreading about her at this very moment, the town of Gladsheim would no longer fit that bill. But she didn't want to say that yet. She wanted to listen instead—to the scrawny chickens clucking outside the back door, to her grandmother humming as she harvested the little garden, and to the gentle noise of the austere mountain around them. She wanted to close her eyes so she wouldn't see her mother already looking like a corpse, and just listen to life as it should be.

As it *would* have been if she hadn't just messed it all up.

"Kaelan," her mother said gently, knowing her mind—as always. "Standing there with your eyes shut won't make the trouble go away."

The familiar words made Kaelan bite back a bittersweet smile. How often she'd heard that phrase. Her curiosity and temper always had been good at getting her into difficult situations, and she'd always preferred ignoring them to facing the music. "I'm sorry, Ma," she said, opening her eyes. "But I lost the eggs and herbs."

Haldis, Kaelan's grandma, slammed open the back door just

then. From the frown slanted across her face, she'd been eavesdropping—a skill she'd been sharpening lately now that her eyesight was failing. "You tried to sneak into the greater market, didn't you? Fool of a girl!" But the words were more exasperated than angry. "How are we supposed to afford the ingredients for the new potion now?"

The new potion. It was a reminder that they'd already tried dozens of potions, dozens of increasingly desperate treatments and nothing had helped Ardis. The wasting illness she had was a tricky strain, one they'd never managed to find a complete cure for. This new potion was a last-ditch effort, and an expensive one at that, with rare imported ingredients.

Kaelan spread her hands, not bothering to deny the charges against her, but not ready to confess everything, either.

"Mama," Ardis said, turning. "Be calm. I'm sure it's not as bad as you think."

Haldis huffed and crossed her arms. Even with her filmy blue-white eyes, she could see right through her granddaughter.

Kaelan cleared her throat, shame burning through her. "Um. Well. It… might actually be as bad as she thinks."

Haldis' stare sharpened. "And how bad exactly do I think it is?"

Kaelan winced. "I hear Skorraholt is nice this time of year?"

she ventured. Skorraholt was a village on the other side of the mountain pass.

Her mother and grandmother stared at her. "Oh dear," Ardis said faintly.

Haldis wasn't nearly so reserved. "We have to move again? What under Odin's blue sky did you *do*, girl?" she demanded.

"I was defending myself!" Kaelan protested.

"Someone attacked you?" her mother asked, sounding a little like her old self.

"Some of the village guys pulled a prank." Kaelan looked away, remembering the gleam of egg yolk on sharp ivory teeth, the herbs stomped into the dirt. And the way she'd roared at them like she had more in common with the dragon skull than with the boys holding it.

She yanked her mind away from the memory as if it'd burnt her. She was no dragon-blooded noble. She was a peasant and a healer-in-training, and very happy to be so, or at least she would have been if village idiots like Bekkr hadn't constantly been lording it over her. She had no idea what had happened earlier, but there was a perfectly good, perfectly *normal* explanation for it. Maybe the acoustics of the greater market had thrown her voice so it had sounded louder than it truly was.

"The boys were making fun of you again?" Ardis scowled, though that was a relative term. Even her scowls looked serene and soothing. Kaelan's mother was a born healer in a way Kaelan herself would never be, even though they both technically had the same healer's touch—the gods-given ability to sense what herbs would heal and which would poison, to understand with a mere touch just how bad an injury was, and to mix potions and tonics that healed people just a little faster, just a little better than those mixed by normal folk. But Ardis was patient and calming, and Kaelan was... well, less so. Kaelan might be able to make a perfect potion for spotted fever, but she was as likely to throw it at someone's head as she was to administer it correctly.

"Yes," Kaelan answered.

"And what exactly was your response that merits us packing up and skipping town again?" Haldis demanded, unmoved.

Kaelan swallowed hard, swiftly losing hope that there might be a way she could wriggle her way out of this without telling her family the truth of what had happened. She didn't want them to know, but more than anything, she didn't want to acknowledge it to herself, not yet. What if she *was* cursed? What if she was truly a freak like Bekkr said? "I told you, I defended myself," she tried one last time, avoiding eye contact with both women. "Aren't you two always telling me to be loyal to myself, not to let anyone else try to tell me who or what I am and all that?"

Neither bought it, unfortunately. Ardis' scowl shifted into suspicion, and Haldis clucked her tongue.

"What's more important?" her grandmother asked, shaking a finger at her. "Loyalty to yourself or honoring promises to others? We *needed* that money, Kaelan. We were depending on you to get it for us. You're nearly a grown woman yourself. Couldn't you have been more responsible?"

Unspoken was the fact that Haldis herself could no longer make it to the market now that her eyesight was failing. Her health was failing, too, and had been failing ever since Ardis had fallen ill—even the best healer could only keep herself going for so long, especially under so much stress—but that was another thing Kaelan refused to see.

"I don't know," she replied. "But I couldn't just stand there and let him slander the dragons." Unshed tears clogged her throat. Her words had come out thick and defensive, though she'd wanted them to sound strong, certain.

Ardis heard the change in her daughter's tone and narrowed her eyes. "Sweetheart? What are you not telling us?"

Kaelan gave up.

"I roared," she said, hating the helplessness in her voice. "I don't know what happened! The boys pulled their prank, and they were all laughing, and I'd lost the eggs and the herbs and I was so *mad*. And… I roared."

The word wasn't enough to encompass the sound, to explain the ringing in her head when it had been happening, or the way the silence afterwards had felt so absolute in comparison.

But it was enough for her family to understand what she'd done. Haldis' hands fell back to her sides and her rheumy eyes went wide with shock. Ardis took a breath and didn't let it out. The look on her face made Kaelan take a step forward, concerned.

"Ma? Are you okay?"

Ardis' knuckles whitened on the bedpost she'd been clutching, making her skin look as fragile as old parchment. She let out the breath. "Oh, Kaelan," she said, the words faint and faraway and wavering in a way that scared Kaelan more than anything else that had happened that day. "Oh, sweetheart."

Ardis took one more shaky breath. Then she closed her eyes and her grip on the bedpost loosened.

And then she crumpled to the ground.

CHAPTER 2

K aelan's hands trembled as she tore herbs ruthlessly from the ground of their little garden. She knocked a scrawny hen out of the way, ignoring the peck she received in retaliation and yanked a witch's weed seedling up from its spot. The rich, earthy scent of it filled her nostrils as dirt clumps scattered outward from its curling white roots. What else did she need? She tried to recall the details of her mother's teachings, focusing on the correct herbs for a healing tea, for waking a patient who slept too deeply.

"Redroot!" her grandmother shouted from inside the house. Kaelan scrambled over to the little flowering vines and yanked off three buds—her healer's instinct, weak as it was, at least told her that was the right amount—and then carried everything inside to Haldis. The old woman took the plants but paused before turning away. "She will be well," she said gently. "It was only a faint. Your news was disturbing. She'll wake soon."

Sagging with relief, Kaelan moved to her mother's side and lifted her, placing her gently back into her bed. She tugged the threadbare blanket up to just under her chin, the way Ardis had always done for Kaelan when she'd been small.

Tears stung her eyes again. Her mother was okay, Haldis had said, but the truth lingered unspoken... *for now*. Ardis had caught a wasting illness from a villager she'd been trying to heal last year and nothing that Kaelan or Haldis could do would help. Her mother would wake from this faint, but one day soon, she wouldn't.

Kaelan had seen how the stages of this illness went for the villagers. First, they'd waste away, getting to the point where they were hardly even able to stay upright for long. After a year or sometimes two of that, they would fall into a coma. About eight weeks later—if you could still get enough food into them to keep them alive that long—it was all over. Which was why, every time her mother had fallen asleep lately, Kaelan had lived in fear that this would be the day she wouldn't wake. And at the same time, secretly, shamefully, she knew that at least then they would know how much time she had left. The waiting, the terrible uncertainty at this point in the illness... it was grueling for them all.

"What do you mean, my news was disturbing?" Kaelan asked, turning to her grandmother. Talking more about what had happened in the market was suddenly preferable to dwelling on the thin frame tucked under the covers.

But Haldis only tightened her lips as she retrieved a mortar and pestle from the cupboard. "This tea will help, but it won't heal her," she reminded Kaelan instead.

"I know that," Kaelan snapped back.

"The energy of a dragon is the only thing that might heal her now," she went on.

Kaelan gritted her teeth. She knew that, too. They'd all known it, but it was a pointless thing to say because, fascinated by the dragon-blooded nobles as Kaelan might be, she still understood that not a one of them would bother with healing a poor peasant woman. "Much good knowing it does," she muttered tightly.

But then she thought of the roar, and the skull, and the look on her mother's face before she'd fainted. Something within her tightened and curled in on itself in fear. Suddenly, she didn't want to talk about dragons at all.

Methodically, Haldis ground the redroot buds to paste and scraped them into the tea. "Now *that* sounds like something those fool-headed villagers would say," she chided. "You of all people should know that not all dragons are bad, just as not all people are bad. Even Mordon, terrible as he turned out to be, was once an honored Master at the Akademy—one of the most powerful dragons who ever taught there."

The thing that had curled up inside Kaelan began to ease a bit. This sounded like the start of one of her beloved bedtime stories. And she could use a comforting story right now, even if it was about Mordon, the most infamous rogue dragon in history.

Truth be told, she'd always been fascinated by dragons even though she'd never gotten to see one up close. A long, scaly tail quickly blocked out by trees as one flew overhead; a gracefully sinuous neck stretched over a distant rooftop. That was all she ever saw. But every time she spotted one, every time she read one of the old fables or heard her grandma's bedtime stories about them, she got the same feeling: a trembling awe, a wondering sort of nervousness that drew her closer when she knew she should be running away. The feeling was addictive. And she wasn't a fool—she knew dragons and the dragon-blooded nobility were as dangerous as they were powerful—but she couldn't help always wanting to know more, to get closer, to feel that feeling one more time.

Kaelan sat on the edge of her mother's bed. "If he was so powerful, why'd he vanish instead of fighting back when he was named a rogue?" Dragons, who could shift into human form, and dragon-bloods, humans who had dragons in their ancestry and could sometimes shift into dragon form, tended to live longer than regular people—so it was unlikely Mordon's disappearance decades before had been because he'd died. Of course, Kaelan already knew much of Mordon's story, but she wanted the soothing cadence of her grandmother's voice.

But Haldis changed the subject yet again. "And anyway, it's not like humans are a shining example of righteousness themselves. Just look at King Lothan," she said, naming the ruler of Unger, a kingdom bordering Alveria. "And the head of his military, too, that General Marque. Always threatening war, always treating us Alverians like we're a bunch of dimwitted sheep who need herding. A king should be noble." She punctuated her complaint with the sharp rap of her spoon against the edge of the teacup as she finished stirring Ardis' tea. "And so should dragons. And many of them are, no matter what most people think."

She handed Kaelan the tea, and working as a team, the two of them carefully poured it into Ardis' mouth. The woman shifted and sighed afterwards, settling more deeply into the covers, and Kaelan relaxed a little.

But her conversation with Haldis lingered in her memory for a long time. Her grandmother, and probably her mother also, were hiding something from her. Why had Ardis fainted when she'd found out about the roar? Why wouldn't her grandmother tell her why the news had been so shocking?

She didn't know the answers, but she had a feeling she'd discover them soon—whether she wanted to or not.

Late that afternoon, Kaelan went back to Gladsheim with a new, smaller basket of herbs and eggs, giving a determined smile to each villager she crossed paths with. Every single one of them sent her darting glances and tight-lipped frowns, which meant that either her charm needed more work or the boys had already told everyone who would listen about what a freak she was. Or both.

She kept her smile firmly in place, anyway. It hurt her cheeks, but she deserved much worse than a sore face after the disaster she'd brought on her family.

"We can't afford to move again," her grandmother had told her as she'd tucked the last of the eggs—the ones that had before been reserved for their own family—into the basket. *"We've spent near everything we had on the last bout of medicines for your ma."*

Which meant they were stuck there, on the side of a mountain next to a town that now held a grudge against Kaelan—and worse, perhaps, feared her. The only thing to do now was to try to win over as many villagers as she could and perhaps grovel at Bekkr's and his friends' feet if they happened to come by her post at the lesser market. It would be humiliating, and she'd much rather hide out in her cabin forever, but this mess was all her fault. The least she could do was try to salvage the situation. She didn't have much time to accomplish that, though—it was nearing the end of the business day, and she'd be lucky if she could catch the last trickle of customers as they filtered out.

She stood in front of the pigpens with the other market exiles to one side of her and a pack of sleeping mastiffs to the other. The dogs smelled better than the pigs, at least, but when awake they tended to be aggressive which kept even more customers away from the lesser market.

She glanced at the customers. There were only three left, and two of them were on their way out already, baskets full of the wilted lettuce and stale bread they'd bought, not even bothering to look at her. It was unlikely she'd get a sale out of them. The last customer, though, looked more promising. He was scuttling past Kaelan even as he pretended to examine the pigs—probably so he wouldn't have to make eye contact with her, she guessed. It was the town baker, a big-bellied man with ruddy cheeks who always managed to look friendlier than he actually was, walking with quick, uneven steps to avoid the pig leavings. "Sir!" she shouted, lifting her skirt so she could chase him down if necessary. "I have eggs and herbs! Fresh as they come!"

He gave her a side-glance and moved faster.

Oh no, he wouldn't simply go past her, she told herself. She knew he needed eggs—he was a baker, so he *always* needed eggs—and he'd been one of her best customers in the past. There was no way she'd let him get away so easily, not when he was her last chance at making a sale today. She strode after him.

"Sir!" she called again. "I have an excellent deal for you! These eggs are half-off, today only!" *Smile*, she had to remind herself, and she tried to kick up the charm a few more notches. She must have ratcheted it a little too high, though, since he blinked and startled when he glanced back at her again, then lengthened his shuffling steps into a near-jog.

Not to be deterred, she tucked her basket under her cloak and slung herself over the pigpen fence. Time for a shortcut. She gritted her teeth behind her forced grin, breathing shallowly and trying not to think too hard about the things that squished beneath her boots. And *into* her boots, which were so old she'd worn holes in the creases of the leather.

She ducked out between the rungs of the fence on the far side. Her shortcut had paid off, and she emerged on the packed-dirt street several feet ahead of the baker. She placed herself firmly in his path. She was between him and his shop now; if he meant to turn her down, at least she'd make him do it to her face. "Good, sir," she said as calmly as she could, considering that her breathing was ragged from the chase, "would you care to buy some eggs? Forty percent off." She'd said half-off earlier, but that had been before the damnable coward had made her chase him through a pigpen and get manure in her only good boots.

He fidgeted, hemming and hawing as he glanced around.

"Miss Younger," he said at last, finally looking at her and spreading his hands, "I want to help you. I do. But my wife heard what happened this morning. She doesn't want us to buy from you anymore. She worries that you're... bad for business. She's already set up an account with some farmers on the other side of town for our eggs."

Kaelan's eyes burned. She felt like someone had struck her. If the baker had already set up another account, this wasn't a matter of waiting for the gossip to blow over. It meant she'd lost one of her best customers for good.

The baker saw the look on her face and grimaced. "Fine, fine, just this once," he muttered, flustered. He plucked a coin out of his pocket without looking at it and half-flung it at Kaelan, snatching the eggs out of her basket and hurrying off without a word.

Kaelan watched his swiftly retreating back, then lowered her gaze to the coin. A bronze quarter-weight, stamped with an outline of the Alverian Akademy on one side and a sinuous dragon on the other. It was a better price than she'd expected to get. She should have been elated.

So why did she feel crushed instead?

A cool autumn wind brushed against her hair as she stood in the street and stared down at the money. After a long moment, she dropped the coin in her pocket and straightened her spine, pushing the devastation away. She *would* be elated. This was a good start. The villagers might be afraid of her right now, but surely she could change their minds given enough time.

"Kaelan!" came a cry from the other side of the street, and she froze, her eyes darting around and looking for danger. But it wasn't danger; it was a grinning girl in a maid's dress, the freckles splashed over her round cheeks matching the red hair tucked under her cap. She was wiping her hands on her apron, leaning against the doorframe of the inn where she worked.

Gratitude surged inside Kaelan. "Reida!" she called in reply, hurrying over to greet her only friend. She hugged the other girl, pathetically happy to know that at least one person in town was apparently still on her side. But Reida drew her quickly inside, pulling her into a dim, abandoned hallway lit by smoky lanterns. Her ever-present smile faded into concern.

Kaelan sighed and slumped. "You've heard."

"About this morning? Aye, everyone's heard. Is it true?"

"Depends on what rumors those jackasses have been spreading," Kaelan replied bitterly.

"Not just the jackasses," Reida corrected her, the concern in her face deepening. Another servant passed them and Reida lowered her voice, pulling Kaelan closer to hide her identity from the older man. "Everyone's talking about it," she went on. "Saying you made some ungodly sound in the greater market this morning; that you're cursed."

"I'm not cursed!" Kaelan protested before cutting herself off. Truth be told, she didn't know *what* she was. She swallowed and shifted, looking at her feet. "Reida, please, I hope you don't—"

"Shush, you're still my friend, no matter what anyone thinks," Reida said, but she fell silent when a cook strode through.

Tears stung the backs of Kaelan's eyes. She wished she could blame the smoking lanterns, but the truth was that Reida was worried for her and worried about being seen *with* her, and Kaelan could hardly stand it. Things were even worse than she'd thought.

She caught herself rubbing at the burn scar on her arm as she often did when she was anxious, and forced herself to stop. She'd gotten it when she'd been ten—Ardis and Haldis had both caught a cold, and Kaelan was supposed to have been making them broth but had fallen asleep with it on the fire. By the time she'd woken, the hut had been aflame, and she'd barely managed to get it put out before the whole place had burned down. That had been the first time she'd failed her family. She'd hoped it would be the last.

Her lips tightened against a surge of despair.

When the cook had passed out of earshot, Reida turned back to Kaelan. "I need some herbs," she said in a hushed whisper. "Hand them over, will you?"

Reida didn't need herbs. The main cook bought all of the inn's supplies from the greater market every morning. This was a pity sale and they both knew it, but Kaelan needed it, so she handed over the herbs without question. The other girl took them without even looking and handed her a silver penny in exchange.

Again, far more than the goods were worth. And, again, Kaelan was left feeling crushed.

"Thank you," she said when she was sure her voice would be even.

"Hush, don't even mention it," Reida said, a bit of her old sunny smile returning. "How's your family doing?"

The tears stung more with the question, and Kaelan had to swallow them back before she could reply. Usually, she matched Reida's cheerfulness when they chatted, but right now, she couldn't bear to lie to her only friend—or to herself. "Not well," she said. "My ma, she gets thinner every day. I can almost see through her skin, I swear it. And Grandma... she tries to hide it, but she's not doing well, either. Her eyesight's failing and she's catching more sicknesses every winter. I think I might lose them both. Soon, I'll be on my own."

There. She'd said it. Finally admitted it, much as she wanted to keep turning a blind eye. A sob caught in her throat but she stuffed it down, too proud to let sweet Reida see her weep.

Reida clucked. "Oh no, I'm so sorry. Don't lose hope, though —there's a chance all might be well yet."

Kaelan shook her head, unable to articulate her knowledge that all would almost certainly not be well. She felt adrift, abandoned, as if she'd lost her family already.

Reida nudged her. "And anyway, I've been on my own for years, and I manage fine. It's not so bad, most days. I hope you'll get a miracle, Kaelan, but if you don't—you'll find your way. I know it."

Kaelan ran a hand across her eyes and tried to compose herself. "Thanks, Reida. I'd better be going. I need to get back before dark."

The girl nodded and stepped back, squeezing her hand. "Of course. Take care of yourself. And stop by again soon, okay? I might need more herbs next week."

It was a generous offer, considering Reida was spending her own meager earnings on herbs she didn't really need. But there was still an entire week between now and then, when Kaelan would have to make her daily sales to villagers like the baker. Would she have to chase all of them down? How long until they banned her from the village entirely? She could still sell to Skorraholt and one or two other nearby towns, but they were all more than three hours' walk from the cabin, and soon ice would lay thick over the mountains and prohibit that sort of journey. They'd still have their stores from the garden and the chickens, so they probably wouldn't starve over the winter, and Kaelan had made just enough money today to buy the last ingredient for Ma's newest potion—but if that didn't work, they'd wind up in the exact same position again soon, and if Grandma got sick, too, Kaelan would have to do the chores of three women by herself in addition to nursing them both.

She walked slowly as she headed back out to the street, trying and failing to think of any way to stave off her family's impending doom.

CHAPTER 3

When Kaelan got home, she dropped the coins she'd earned into the bowl atop the dresser. They tinkled as they fell, almost musical. She'd exchanged the silver penny and the bronze quarter-weight for copper bits before she'd left town, and the little squared-off pieces of metal winked at her, gleaming as they clinked and settled.

She could hardly look at them without thinking of the baker's fearful expression, though, as well as the pity in Reida's smile. She turned away. Tomorrow, her grandma would take the coins to the herb peddler a few towns over to buy the exotic mushroom—or was it an imported moss?—that would complete the newest potion. It was unlikely to work, since none of them ever worked, but Kaelan refused to give up hope.

"Grandma?" she called, shrugging off her ratty cloak, but

there was no answer. She must've been out gathering herbs in the woods. And Ma was still huddled under the blankets on her cot, fast asleep. That gave Kaelan some time to either catch up on her chores or go over the history schoolwork Grandma had assigned for this week. She hesitated—she should be more focused on chores, since education wasn't going to do a poor peasant girl any good, but she'd always loved learning and testing her skills. Ardis had taught her to read and write long ago, and she could do basic sums. She loved reading any histories she could get her hands on as well. Sometimes, when she'd been younger, she'd even daydreamed about attending a real school. But they moved so frequently, and most of the tiny towns that needed a freelance healer were too small to offer free schooling, especially for the daughter of outsiders.

She drifted over to the worn books on the mantle. Their family had only been able to afford a few, and every one of them was ragged and damaged in one way or another, but to her they were the most precious things in the cabin. There was a collection of fables, an outdated book of maps, a huge tome filled with healer techniques and medicines, and a book dedicated to scholarly treaties on dragons.

She ran her hand over the last one. The cover was red and frayed, its pages crinkled by countless readings. She knew everything inside it already—the different types of dragons and the elemental powers they wielded, how tamers helped their bonded dragons keep their infamous tempers in check, how dragons had helped found Alveria and how their population remained concentrated here to this day. Kaelan had never been quite sure what drew her to this book, or to the dragons themselves. Grandma was right, of course, about not all dragons being evil like Mordon—but they were simply so massive, so unfathomable, so *other* that she couldn't help but be a little bit glad she'd never met one, anyway.

But still—she couldn't help but be fascinated by them.

She started to slide the book out, but stopped at a noise from behind her. Kaelan turned to see her mother sitting up and watching her. "Ma!" she said, her voice too loud with the sudden relief. "You're awake."

Ma smiled, but her expression trembled at the corners.

Kaelan frowned, then pushed the book back into place and hurried over to her mother. "Are you well? What do you need?" She glanced to the window, looking for Grandma. She opened her mouth to shout for the old woman, but her mother stopped her with a gesture.

"Leave her be," Ma said, her voice thin but firm. Kaelan turned, frowning again—and for the first time saw the envelope in her mother's hands. Ma held it very still, like it was fragile and precious. Or, maybe, like it was dangerous. The way she was very intently *not* looking at it set Kaelan's nerves on edge.

"What's that?" she asked carefully, turning away from the window.

Ardis' smile dropped, and to Kaelan's alarm, a tear ran down her cheek.

Kaelan's heart stopped. Her mother didn't cry. And when she did, she tried not to let anyone see it. It was her only concession to pride, one of the few ways she was like her daughter. The fact that she was crying now and not even trying to hide it from Kaelan meant something terrible must've happened. And, in a blink, Kaelan knew the only thing it could be.

Ma was dying. Right now. Ardis' healer's instincts could sense the end stalking closer, a hunting cat creeping just out of sight, and any moment now Kaelan's mother would drop off into the coma.

Kaelan's feet grew roots. Her hands curled around the bedside chair. The world turned to stone. She couldn't move.

"Don't look like that, sweetheart," Ardis chided her, tilting her head. "All will be well."

"You're—you're not..." Kaelan fumbled, still unable to say the words. Her hands tightened their grip on the furniture beneath her, grounding her.

"Not just yet," her ma said lightly. And Ardis never lied, which meant she truly wasn't, in fact, dying.

The world jolted back into motion. Kaelan sucked in a breath. "What's wrong then?" she demanded thickly. Her heartbeat thundered in her ears, and her hands shook as she relaxed them.

Ardis held out the envelope. It was thick and cream-colored, much more expensive than their family could afford. "This will get you into the Akademy," her ma said simply.

Kaelan stared at her mother like she'd spoken a foreign language. She rearranged the words in her head, repeating them back to herself, trying to make them make sense. "The Akademy," she repeated. The words tasted like blocks in her mouth, thick and square and wooden. And completely *other*, like the dragons and dragon-blooded tamers who attended school there. "You mean—have I been placed there with a work permit?"

Surely, that wasn't possible. Peasants vied fiercely for positions at the Alverian Akademy, and it was tough for anyone who didn't have decades of experience and the highest of references to get a job so much as sweeping the floors there. And the city of Bellsor, home to the Akademy as well as the palace, was a full week's walk from their cabin.

Kaelan shook her head in confusion. Even if her mother had by some miracle secured her a position as a maid there, Kaelan couldn't leave her family, not like this, not when they needed her. "No," she told Ardis. "We'll find another way. I can find a job here if I need to." Maybe Reida could get her a job at the inn. It was a long shot, but perhaps if Kaelan promised to work on probation for a while and prove herself, and asked for lower wages than the other workers…

But Ardis was shaking her head now in response. "This will get you into the Akademy," she repeated, "as a *student*."

The word hung between them. Kaelan could almost see the shimmering outline of it: fathomless, impossible. "But," she said slowly, "I can't be a student. Only dragon-bloods can attend the Alveria Akademy."

"You can be a student," Ardis asserted softly and let the meaning of that sink in.

Kaelan's ears were ringing. She wished they would ring louder, too, so she wouldn't be able to hear the answer to the question she now understood she must ask. "Who?" she asked, the word choked and nearly unrecognizable as it left her lips.

Only dragon-bloods could be Akademy students. But Ardis had said Kaelan could be a student. Which meant she was saying that Kaelan was somehow, impossibly, a dragon-blood. And she knew for a fact that her mother didn't have any dragon lineage.

Which meant her father, who she'd always believed to be a soldier and dead, was actually…

"Mordon," Ardis said.

And Kaelan's world fell apart.

She ran.

The packed dirt of the goat path stretched up the mountainside, its pebbles skittering beneath her steps. Her breath ached with each inhale. That was all she could hear, all she could see, all she would allow herself to think about.

"He was charming," Ardis had said after her confession, her smile turning sad. *"He was handsome. I loved him. I'm not sure if he ever felt the same about me, but I wanted him to."*

Kaelan's father had been a dragon. But not just any dragon. He'd been Mordon. The most infamous and villainous rogue dragon to ever exist, who'd disappeared decades ago. Except that he hadn't disappeared, had he? He'd been with Ardis, at least for long enough to give life to Kaelan.

The roar in the market. The dragon skull the village boys had mocked her with. *Better watch out. It could be the great Mordon come back to destroy the land.*

She stumbled to the top of a rocky cliff. She slowed to a stop there, gasping for air, her hands on her knees. Her thinking had become disjointed. She tried to lay it flat, stretch it out, but her mind refused to be still.

"I never saw him as a dragon," Ardis had said back in the cabin as Kaelan had stood frozen, stunned. *"I didn't know*

what he was till after he was gone. He left a letter. This letter. To get you into the Akademy, should we ever wish it."

And she'd never told Kaelan. Never so much as hinted that her father had been anything but a soldier killed in battle. Kaelan's whole life, sixteen long years, and not one shred of truth in any of them.

The tattered book on the shelf, the one with the worn cover and crinkled pages. The one she'd read so many times without having any idea how it applied to her. What had it said about dragon-bloods? *When in human form, dragons may take a human lover, and if there is a child, it will be born in human form. Such children may or may not be able to shift into dragon form—if they do have the capability, it will show itself before a child turns fifteen. Otherwise, the non-dragon children of such unions are often put to excellent use as tamers.*

A tamer. That was what her mother wanted her to become. Kaelan was a year past the fifteen-year-old deadline for revealing a dragon form, which meant that her role at the Akademy could only be to team up with a dragon. With one of those majestic, deadly creatures, the ones that she now knew were a part of her. Flesh and blood and bone and soul—if dragons had those—she was one of them.

And, ironically enough, that was something she might have been cautiously excited about—if her father hadn't been Mordon. The fairytale villain. One of the most powerful dragons in the land, gone evil. She was a little bit afraid of regular dragons, but her fascination with them outweighed her fear. With Mordon, though—how could she ever be anything but terrified of him? How could she be anything but terrified of *herself*, now that she knew he was a part of her?

And also—the only other people she knew who had dragon blood were the nobles. What did that make her? And how could she ever be anything but a penniless peasant?

She flung herself forward blindly, needing to expend her restless energy, but skidded to a stop when she realized she was at the cliff's edge. She peered down at the hazy treetops far below her, dim in the dusk. A brisk wind tugged at her hair and curled around her fingers, beckoning her forward.

She hugged herself, trying to still her tremors, and backed away from the edge.

She didn't know what she was. She didn't know *who* she was.

And she had never been more afraid in her life.

It was a long, cold walk home. She dawdled as much as she could, and by the time she stood before the cabin's door again, it was full dark out. The wolves sang at her back, signaling a hunt in the foothills. The sound was both beautiful and eerie. It echoed off the slopes surrounding her home and filled her up inside, giving her the courage to ease the creaky door open into the dark, silent warmth of the cabin.

She stepped in and closed the door behind her. The music of the wolves was cut off, replaced by the quiet creak of Haldis' rocking chair.

"Did you know?" Kaelan asked the darkness. "That Mordon was my father?"

Her grandmother sighed. "Of course," she said, her tone irritable as always.

"Then why," Kaelan began, and then checked her voice—her eyes had adjusted, and she could see now that her mother was curled up sleeping on her cot again—"didn't you *tell me?*"

"What, and get to enjoy this conversation that much sooner?" Haldis scoffed.

"I had a right to know." Kaelan seethed. It was easier than crying.

"No, you have a right to be safe. To grow up normal. Were it up to me, you still wouldn't know."

Kaelan's mind snagged on the words, and she frowned. Haldis hadn't wanted Kaelan to know the truth, and judging from the fact that Ardis had kept it a secret this long, she'd probably felt the same. But her mother had told her anyway. Why? Why now? Ardis could've just brushed off the roar, not told her it was the result of her dragon blood. Instead, she'd come clean and given her an opening to the Akademy.

The villagers. It was the only possible answer. Kaelan's roar had turned the villagers against her family, and Ardis and Haldis couldn't afford to move again—so, instead, they were sending Kaelan away. Kaelan, the source of the problem, would no longer be around to frighten the villagers. It would be a peace offering, a show of good faith… a way to reclaim their family's good reputation and the trust of the people.

For her family to survive, they had to give Kaelan to the dragons.

Tears pricked her eyes. "I have to go," she realized. "It'll be better for you if I'm gone. You'll be a part of the village and they'll accept you." She cursed herself with the realization. She shouldn't feel betrayed. This made sense. Hadn't she wished for a way to fix the catastrophe she'd brought upon her mother and grandmother? And here it was, presented to her on a silver platter. So, why did she want to curl up and weep?

"Don't be stupid," Haldis said roughly. "Ardis would sacrifice herself to those wolves out there to keep you home with her, never mind the good-for-nothing villagers. Same goes for me. Ardis thinks you need to go not because we give a rat's tail about what they think, but because your powers are finally emerging. They need to be honed. You need to be taught how to control them, so you don't do something stupid and terrify a bunch of idiot villagers into burning you at the stake or something equally ridiculous. It's for your own safety, not for the good of our healing business."

"Oh," Kaelan said weakly. What an impossibly confusing day this had been—and, suddenly, she wanted nothing more than for it to be over.

The creaking of the rocking chair stilled. "But," her grandmother said, her voice so quiet that Kaelan could barely hear her now, "just between you and me, there's another reason you ought to go."

Kaelan blinked and squinted, trying to make out her grandmother's expression. Foreboding crept up her spine. "What's that?" she asked cautiously.

"The Akademy is in Bellsor, the capital, the City of Dragons. And the only thing that can heal your mother is the energy of a dragon."

Sharp electric realization and something like joy shot through Kaelan's veins. She wheeled around, starting for her mother, thinking to heal her right now—at least one good thing could come out of today—but Haldis' hand snaked out of the darkness to grip her wrist.

"You're not trained," she explained, "not tried. If you try to access your powers, you could kill her as easy as heal her."

The realization and joy churned back into dull grief, leaden disappointment filling her. "Then, what?" she demanded, pain wrenching at her words. "What's the point of being a dragon-blood, of being *his* daughter? What's the use of any of this, if I can't even heal her?"

For one moment, she'd thought there could be an upside to what she was, something other than horror and confusion. To have that bright hope snatched back so quickly felt like being plunged into an icy river, so deep she couldn't feel the bottom.

Haldis' voice sharpened. "The point is, you need to stop feeling sorry for yourself and see that you *could* be the one to help heal her if you go to the Akademy and become a tamer—bond with a dragon so you can bring him or her back here to heal your mother."

The cabin went silent again. Kaelan turned these words over in her mind, afraid this hope would be ripped away from her, too, but Haldis stayed quiet.

Kaelan's mother could be healed. Could be well again, and could have enough energy to resume the work she loved. But again, still, always, Kaelan would have to go to the dragons. Would they accept her, a peasant among nobles? Not to mention what they might think of her once they found out who her father was.

"I'm scared," she admitted, to herself as much as the old woman.

"I know."

"I don't want to go. I don't want to be away from you, from Ma."

The creaking of the rocking chair resumed. "I know."

Kaelan looked over to her mother's bed. Ardis was so small, her bony hips making sharp angles beneath the blanket. What would her mother have given up for her, if their positions had been reversed? What would she have done to heal her only daughter?

Anything. Everything. As Kaelan would for her.

"I'll go," she told her grandmother.

CHAPTER 4

P rince Lasaro Afkarr hated arguing with his mother.

On bad days, this was because she ended arguments by turning into a creature a hundred times larger than him, with long, sharp teeth that she would never dream of threatening him with, but still kept in his line of sight all the same. Even on good days, though, the argument never ended up going his way. No one took him seriously—Queen Celede, most of all. But today he was going to change that.

He squared his shoulders, pushed open the door to the throne room, and approached his mother.

Queen Celede, dragon-blooded ruler of all of Alveria, was draped over her throne in her human form. He had no idea how she managed to turn an action so simple as sitting on a chair—albeit an intimidating chair, with long gold spikes emanating from its back—into an act of grace, but it made him feel clumsy and young by comparison. Today, she wore a simple sapphire gown decorated with golden-threaded trim. When she turned to look at him, her slender golden crown shifted atop her mass of brown-and-gray curls. She reached up to secure it with a flick of her wrist, making even that small motion look elegant.

Lasaro bowed. She ignored him.

"Linna!" she called out instead, narrowing her eyes as she peered over his head. "How many times do I have to tell you, no sword practice in the throne room? I'm about to hold court, and if you slice off another nobleman's finger, there will be hell to pay."

He glanced over his shoulder—just in time to duck as Linna, one of his older twin sisters, whirled her sword in a shining arc that would've taken his head off. Linge, the other twin, darted in to catch her sister's blade with her own. Lasaro bit back a frown, stepping well out of the way. One of these days, he'd lob his own sword at *their* heads and see how they liked it. He wasn't quite as good at combat as them—they had too much dragon blood, so that it made them warlike and hotheaded, and far more willing to chop people's heads off than he'd have preferred—but if he was swift enough, maybe he could at least get their attention.

But it wasn't their attention he was here for today.

"Mother," he tried again, moving back into her line of sight.

Finally, she looked at him. A smile warmed her features and he stood a little straighter. "Lasaro," she said. She scanned him up and down, her sharp gaze missing nothing. He reached back into his memory; he'd polished his boots, and his clothing was pressed and creased so sharply that at any second it might slice him into bits. His silver-blond hair was longer than she'd have liked, but it was neatly cut. He kept his gray-blue eyes on hers until she nodded, satisfied. He breathed a silent sigh. Normally, he didn't try quite so hard to impress her —he'd accepted the endeavor as a lost cause years ago—but today was different. Today, the stakes were higher than ever. And even if he was almost positive this would never work, that she'd pass over him as she always did, he still had to try.

"She'll pick an heir this year, I'm sure of it," he'd overheard the queen's tamer whispering this morning. *"Probably Freyr, or maybe one of the twins."*

"Mother," he said, straightening his shoulders, "I've come to talk to you about launching a preemptive strike on Unger."

A slight frown slashed across her face. "That's not something I'm willing to discuss at the moment."

He inclined his head. "Let me explain myself, at least."

She sighed, but motioned at him to go on as if she were merely indulging him. He set his teeth, but then, with an effort, relaxed. If he wanted to prove to her that he could be

48

king, that he was the only one of her children who was *capable* of being a good ruler, he had to show her that his plan was sound, and he wouldn't do that by getting frustrated.

"We all know they're planning their own attack," he said. "Any month now, they'll act, and we'll be stuck spending weeks gathering our armies and coordinating a counterattack. We have good intelligence that says—"

The clash of metal on metal interrupted, making him wince. "He's right!" Linge shouted, her eyes narrowing as she threw her sister backward and then turned toward them. "We should attack. Declare war before they can. Decimate them with a first strike; make them an example to any other countries that think they can take us."

"That would be rash," Queen Celede commented mildly, but her frown deepened.

Reining in his temper at the interruption, Lasaro turned back to his mother. "I agree. That's why I want to talk to you about a quieter preemptive strike, one surgically targeted to—"

"*Mother!*" a new voice wailed. A door slammed open and Elda, his oldest sister, stalked into the room. She was tall and beautiful, a younger mirror-image of their mother. At least as far as appearances were concerned. Her dress's sleeves had a row of buttons going up the arm that were only half done-up, and a maidservant scrambled along behind her, trying to fix them as Elda glared at her mother. "I've finally got in the new dress that I special ordered from the Southern Isles, and Freyr has already stolen the veil! Order him to give it back."

The queen raised an eyebrow, still looking serene, but Lasaro knew her well enough to understand that she was getting irritated. "You are a grown woman now. Can you not retrieve it from Freyr yourself?"

Lasaro sighed. When would Freyr ever start taking things seriously? He was Lasaro's favorite sibling, and also, according to gossip, the most likely to be named crown prince—but he would make an even worse ruler than the bloodthirsty twins or their empty-headed sister. Freyr loved being a useless prince and took every opportunity to prove it. Like now, when he poked his head of dark curls through the doorway behind Elda, the stolen veil atop his head, and did a mocking dance behind Elda's back.

Lasaro clenched his hands, his fingernails digging into his palms as he struggled for the serenity that seemed to come so easily to his mother. How was he supposed to prove his plan had merit if he kept getting interrupted? "Mother, if I could just finish my suggestion—" he tried, but Queen Celede caught sight of Freyr and her eyes narrowed to slits. She said something, but it was lost beneath the shouts of the twins who were arguing over who'd won the sparring match. Elda caught the direction of the queen's gaze and whirled around, spotting Freyr, and started shouting herself. And in the middle of all the commotion, Prince Lasaro stood with his back straight, his boots polished, and his clothes pressed, ignored by his entire family.

He swallowed hard as a memory overtook him. When he'd been eight years old, he'd walked into dinner a few minutes late, and his whole family—minus his father, who'd died when Lasaro had been a baby—had already been there. It should have been a small, inconsequential moment, or even a nice one: everyone clamoring at each other, the royal dining hall full of the noise and laughter and arguments that came with being a family. Except that Lasaro had been standing outside all of it, and no one had even noticed. Sometimes he felt like that day had never truly ended, like all the rest of them were still laughing in that hall, and he was still standing in the shadows wishing he was a part of it.

He hated feeling helpless, feeling lonely, as he did again now.

But maybe that wasn't a bad thing—maybe he could use that. He tightened his fists and closed his eyes, tracing the feelings, trying to channel his frustration to tap into his dragon blood. Transforming for the very first time right in front of all of them would surely buy him some respect, or at least a moment's silence for him to get a word in edgewise. But no matter how hard he tried, nothing happened. Just like always.

His mother, however, had no such problem.

With a flash of light, Queen Celede vanished, a massive dragon instantly taking her place. She was a beautiful orange-gold color, her scales patterned with ripples that made it look like she was on fire every time she moved. She was an Ember, able to create and control fire. It was a very common type of dragon, and she'd chosen to focus on ruling rather than expanding her powers and knowledge at the Akademy, but she was still renowned across the kingdom as one of the most beautiful dragons in Alveria. Because, of course, she would be breathtaking in dragon form as well as elegant and brilliant in human form.

Lasaro sighed and let go of his frustration. Even if he had managed to transform, he doubted his mother would have been proud given that he was already over a decade behind the point at which all of his siblings had embraced their own abilities to shift. And anyway, he was two years beyond the deadline for finding his dragon form, which meant he would likely never find it at all. He should stop trying, he supposed, but it was hard for him to just give up.

The queen glared at each of her children in turn, silencing the room before she shifted back. Human again, she dusted a bit of invisible lint off her dress and sat back down on the throne —a little heavily, though she tried to hide it. Shifting to dragon form took a lot of energy.

"Now that I've got your attention," she said briskly, "everyone out. Except you, Lasaro."

Grumbling, they shuffled away. Freyr gave him a good-natured smile and a wink, but even he forgot Lasaro as he darted out of Elda's reach.

The heavy side doors closed with a thud, and silence fell between him and his mother. She rubbed at her brow in a rare gesture of exasperation. "I'm aging," she told him.

He blinked. "People do that," he said carefully. Truth be told, Queen Celede looked great for being a hundred and twenty years old, but he knew her outer façade didn't always match her feelings. And lately she'd been waiting longer to shift into dragon form and silence her children, which meant it was getting harder for her to change. Soon, she'd be stuck as a human, and the country would start clamoring for a new dragon king or queen to keep Alveria strong.

Queen Celede tapped a finger against her lips as she gazed down at him. "Your own birthday is next month, isn't it?"

He looked away. "It was last week."

"Ah. My apologies. A seventeenth birthday is an important one. I should have scheduled a celebration. So many details have been lost lately, with all our—all of *my*—resources focused on calming Unger."

"Don't worry about it," he said graciously, trying not to notice his own lingering hurt.

Silence ticked between them for a moment longer. "Seventeen.

And yet you still cannot shift into dragon form," she observed at last.

"Not *yet*," he emphasized, even though they both knew the deadline was well past.

She leaned back in the throne. "About this plan to attack Unger, using a carefully targeted preemptive strike. It's a good idea. But we are not at war yet, and it goes against all our traditions of honor to sabotage a neighboring country without strong enough provocation. The Council of Nobles wouldn't like it."

Temper roared up in him before he could restrain it. "Forget tradition and honor!" he shouted, and the marble room rang with his words. "We have to save ourselves! Why can't they see that? All they want to do is dither about another gesture of goodwill, another useless peace talk or exchange of ambassadors. Unger is giving us nothing but pretty lies while they plot our downfall, and the council frets about *honor*?"

Queen Celede let his words settle, sinking into the stone at their feet. By the time she shifted in the throne again, Lasaro had had plenty of time to contemplate just how rashly he'd spoken. But even though he regretted shouting at her—which surely wouldn't win him any points in his efforts to be named her heir—he couldn't regret what he'd said. The council's dithering helped no one. Tradition and honor were only worth worrying about when they were of benefit. In most circumstances, he'd be more than happy to throw them out the window, and the council along with them if they disagreed.

His mother spoke at last. "I know you want to be named crown prince," she said softly. "And it's true that I need to name one of you my heir soon. But Alveria can only have a dragon ruler."

"Of course," he responded bitterly. "It's tradition."

One side of her mouth curved up in a delicate, ironic smile. "Yes. And I will not be the one to break that particular tradition."

He hesitated. "Freyr and the twins, and Elda, they're…"

"Entirely unsuited to rule," she said, her smile falling flat. "I agree. But what am I to do, Lasaro? You're unable to shift and you can't yet control your powers, if you even have any."

He tried not to wince as she listed his failures. "But I know all the histories," he protested. "I'm a great strategist. And I've had instruction from all the best swordsmen and archers in the kingdom. Will you really name Linna or Linge your heir over me? They'd expend the entire treasury on wars before five years passed."

She sighed. "I love you all more than life itself, but I have no idea which of you will rule when that life is over."

"Give me a chance," he pleaded before he could think better of it. "Let me prove I'm the best choice."

He waited, breath held, to see what she would say. He could bear another rejection, he told himself. He was used to it. He had to try anyway. Still, part of him wished he'd have said nothing and walked away rather than forced her choice now. What would he do if she said no? She wouldn't overrule herself once the decision was made. He'd be stuck as a prince forever. Never getting to prove he was worthy of following her rule. He'd always be the forgotten younger son, forever waiting in the shadows of the dining hall.

"How?" the queen asked at last.

He let out a breath, his mind scrambling for an answer. As soon as one formed, he latched onto it with both hands. "The Akademy," he said. "I'll spend a year there. They'll teach me how to tap into my powers, how to transform. I know I'd be a late bloomer, but I can find my dragon shape with the help of the masters, I swear."

His mother gazed into the distance, thinking. All of Celede's royal children had long since graduated from the Akademy. They'd found their dragon shapes much earlier than most dragon-bloods and had quickly mastered their elements, bonding with tamers or, in Freyr's case, getting approval to live without one. Lasaro, however, was two years overdue for his first transformation. But desperate times called for desperate measures, and if anyone knew how to help him find his form against all odds, the Akademy's masters would.

Of course, it meant at least a year away from the palace. That was longer than he'd ever been away. And all his prior trips had involved first-rate inns, plenty of servants catering to his every whim, and an honor guard bristling with weapons to protect the youngest prince of Alveria. If his mother agreed to this plan, he'd be on his own. The dormitories would be a downgrade to say the least, the servants would treat him like all the other students, and he almost certainly wouldn't be allowed any guards for protection. It would be frightening, unknown, and lonely. But a king had to get used to being lonely, and if this was the only way to win his mother's approval, he'd do anything the masters asked of him.

Queen Celede folded her hands. The decision was made. "I agree," she said.

He exhaled, feeling limp with relief. "Thank you," he said shakily.

She held up a hand. "These are the terms. You will spend one year at the Alverian Akademy. You will learn to shift *and* be in full control of your powers by the year's end, enough so as to be paired in an approved probationary bond with a tamer. Do this, and you will have proven yourself worthy to be named crown prince."

He bowed, victory and uncertainty and a rush of adrenaline combining to make him tremble. "Yes, Mother."

"Then go with my blessing, and may the trade be accomplished." She softened the formal wording of a sealed bargain with a smile for her youngest son, waving him out of the hall. "Be well, Lasaro," she added as he reached the doors—a rare show of affection from her.

Buoyant, he smiled back. "And you, Mother," he replied before ducking out into the palace proper.

He hurried to his rooms. The Akademy school session started in just a week, and he had some packing to do.

CHAPTER 5

Kaelan stood just inside the door of the cabin that would soon no longer be her home, grasping a bag holding all her earthly possessions, and wished she had the strength to say goodbye to her mother.

She swallowed against the tears that threatened when she looked over at the shape underneath the covers, rising and falling ever so slightly with each shallow breath. *You're the reason I'm doing this,* she told Ardis silently, and it felt like both a loving promise and an accusation—which was why, of course, Kaelan wasn't going to say it aloud.

Kaelan shifted the bag on her shoulder and straightened her spine. She would own her resentment, much as she might wish not to feel it, but that didn't mean she wanted Ardis to know about it. A hard parting would only make things worse for everybody. Better to let her mother sleep and let her think her daughter was as loving and selfless as Kaelan wished she were.

The sun was half-risen already. Time to set off.

"Bye, Grandma," she said to the old woman who stood at her side.

"Did you pack the money somewhere secure?" Haldis asked, as no-nonsense as always.

"Yes," Kaelan said. It was only half a lie. She had put the money Haldis had tried to give her somewhere secure after all: buried in the bottom of the hens' feeding trough in the back-yard. The chickens would be irate when they found coins where they expected a meal, but it was the only place Kaelan could be sure the money would stay hidden long enough for her to get away but still be found eventually. There was no way she could take funds from her family when they needed them so desperately, and anyway, Akademy students were provided with food and lodging and uniforms free of charge. In the meantime, she could forage for roots and berries, and maybe set some rabbit snares.

She thought of the envelope her mother had given her tucked away at the bottom of her pack. She hadn't gotten the nerve up to read its contents. She knew she was the daughter of Mordon, but she wasn't quite ready to see that fact in ink. What would the Akademy masters think when they read it? Ardis seemed to think the letter would guarantee her acceptance, but Mordon was a rogue dragon—what if the masters rejected her because of her connection to him?

But, no, surely they couldn't do that. Mordon might be infamous, but he was still a dragon, and Kaelan had as much right as any other dragon-blood to attend the school. Still, that didn't change the fact that the other students, and perhaps even the masters, were likely to treat her as lesser or perhaps even as a potential rogue in the making due to her parentage. Dread stirred in her gut. What if they were right?

"Well, get a move on, girl," Haldis said, breaking Kaelan's worried silence, and Kaelan smothered a laugh. She threw her arms around her grandma.

"I love you, you old bat," she said fondly.

"Yes, well, same here," Haldis said gruffly, but her eyes were wet when she pushed Kaelan away and turned her toward the door. "Be off with you. Write us when you get there. And take care of yourself, hear? We've taught you well. You're honorable; loyal. That'll serve you out in Bellsor and in the world if you let it."

Kaelan wasn't so sure of that—in a kingdom full of unrest that was surrounded by enemies like Unger, how could honor and loyalty be of any real use?—but she nodded and opened the door. The sunrise flooded in, gilding the cabin, flushing out the shadows of the night. In her bed, Ardis shifted and murmured sleepily to herself. Kaelan had to choke back the urge to run to her, tuck herself in at her side, and forget about this whole stupid plan.

She rubbed angrily at her wet cheeks. This was even worse than when her family had first started moving, back when she'd barely been of school age. That was her very first memory: standing outside a cottage, bags packed, sobbing as her mother tried to explain why she had to leave everything—including her pet rabbits—behind. They'd been standing out too much, she'd said. They needed a fresh start. But at least back then they'd all moved together. Now, Kaelan would be living with strangers.

Kaelan narrowed her eyes. She hadn't thought about that old memory, about the reasoning behind their frequent moves, in a long time. Now, she wondered whether they'd stood out because of her own dragon-blooded nature. Had there been more clues like the roar, more times when people had started to suspect what she was? All this time, had she been the reason her family kept having to uproot itself? She'd always longed for stability, for a place that would be hers forever, but what if the reason she had never had those things—and maybe never could have them—was because of what she was?

No use dwelling on it now. She had a mission; best she focus on it. She tightened her hand around the strap of her pack, kept her eyes fixed firmly forward, and took the first step of her long journey.

By the time she made it to Gladsheim, Kaelan had herself nearly convinced that everything would turn out fine. She managed to cling to that belief right up until she passed the first group of gossiping villagers.

"...heard about one a few mountains to the west," a skinny woman with a huge mole on her nose said. "A whole herd of cattle, running themselves ragged in their own pen, trying to get away from it. Half the herd stampeded themselves to death. Imagine!"

The woman across from her—a plump, motherly sort—leaned in with a scowl as she wrung out a dishrag. "Did the tamers repay the farmer, at least?"

Kaelan's steps stuttered at the mention of tamers. She ducked her head and pulled her hood up, loitering to eavesdrop without looking suspicious, which was a skill she'd had plenty of time to hone as an outsider in half a dozen villages.

The mole woman scoffed. "Of course not. I swear to Hel, goddess of the underworld, that lot should be scrubbed from the face of the earth."

"I heard a few villages were planning to throw out any dragon who tried to stay there. Can't say I blame them—they're vicious, those things are. You know what they say: never trust a dragon that's talking, and when the dragon stops talking, run." She slapped the dishrag against her hand for emphasis. "My second cousin Helda saw a dragon throw a fit once. Near burned down her house when she refused to let it lodge there, and then the soldiers had the nerve to make *her* pay a penalty!"

The mole woman clucked her tongue. "She should've followed the law. Dragons get whatever they want from anyone in the kingdom, no payment required." Her tone was sour, ironic. She leaned in. "But tamers, though. No law protecting them."

The stocky woman moved closer, as well, and lowered her voice. "Which do you think that girl is? The one who tried to demolish the market with that roar yesterday?"

Kaelan flushed ice-cold, her hands gripping the corners of her hood so hard that her knuckles went white. It was her they were talking about. They were speculating over whether she could shift into a dragon and was therefore protected by law, or if she was merely a dragon-blooded tamer who could be punished however the town pleased. And what did they mean, *demolish the market*? She hadn't damaged a thing as far as she knew, other than perhaps the vegetable vendor's potatoes. Just how wild had the rumors gotten?

The mole woman shrugged. "She's over fifteen, I think, so not a dragon. But she ought to stay up on that mountainside anyway, far as I'm concerned."

"That's probably for the best. She's friends with that Reida girl, the orphan maid at the inn, isn't she? Maybe Reida can set her straight—tell her what happens to tamers."

The mole woman's eyes widened. "What do you mean? What would Reida know about it?"

"You didn't hear? A while back, someone from Reida's family went off to become a tamer. When he came back, his own village near stoned him to death. I'd hate for any child, even a strange one like the healer's girl, to face that."

The mole woman nodded sagely. "Yes. Best for everyone she just stays away."

Their conversation turned to the ever-rising taxes. Kaelan continued walking past them, feeling numb and shaken. She'd known many of the rural villages in Alveria disliked dragons, but she hadn't realized how drastic the situation was. She could be *stoned* just for what she was? If they really hated people with dragon blood that much, and if they already suspected Kaelan fell into that category, how could she be certain Ma and Grandma would be safe even after she was gone? The villagers sounded like they had a lot of built-up resentment for Kaelan's kind. They might take that out on her family in her absence. They wouldn't even need to touch them —all they would need to do was refuse to buy their goods. With her failing vision, Haldis wouldn't be able to go to any of the neighboring villages, and without medicine and good nourishment, Ardis would succumb to her sickness even faster.

Reida. Those women had mentioned Reida, and something about her being related to a tamer. Maybe that was why she'd been so sympathetic yesterday. And if she was sympathetic to Kaelan and to tamers, maybe, just maybe, she could be depended upon to keep Kaelan's family safe while she was gone. Kaelan made a snap decision and took a sharp right turn, hurrying down an alleyway.

The inn was the tallest building in town at two stories high, its roof made of actual tiles instead of straw rushes like most of the lesser buildings, and was easy enough to get to quickly from anywhere in Gladsheim.

When Kaelan emerged from the alley, she spotted Reida toting a bag toward the front door, her red hair swinging.

"Shh," Kaelan hissed when she tugged her friend aside.

Reida yelped in surprise, then slapped a hand over her mouth when she saw who it was. "Oh! Sorry! Um, I'm going to take a break, be right back!" she called to the cook over her shoulder. The man grunted, which Reida took as permission.

"I'm leaving," Kaelan said in a low voice as soon as they found a room where they could talk privately.

"What? You're moving?"

"No. Well, yes, sort of, but just me. I'm going to… Bellsor. To the Akademy."

Reida's eyes widened as she understood. Then, before Kaelan

could register what was happening, the other girl had her wrapped in a fierce hug. "Oh, Kaelan," she whispered. Emotion made her voice tremble.

Kaelan closed her eyes, knowing what her friend's tone meant. "So, it's true."

"What?"

"About your family."

Reida released her and stepped quickly back. "I—I don't know what you heard—but I'm sure things will be different for you. You'll be fine. Of course, you will." Her tone faltered.

Kaelan steeled herself. She needed to know the truth. If she was in danger—or more danger than she'd previously thought, anyway—it would be better to be prepared than to stick her head in the sand. "What happened?"

Reida poked her head out the doorway to make sure they were alone, then shut the door and lowered her voice. "Olaf was my favorite cousin," she said, going to the window. She flicked the curtains open and stared into the street, avoiding Kaelan's gaze. "I was living with his parents, my aunt and her new husband, back then. Olaf was my aunt's son from a previous relationship. Never said who the dad was. Guess we know why now." She laughed, but it was a small, trembling thing.

Kaelan moved to her friend's side and squeezed her shoulder.

"I'm sorry, Reida," she said helplessly. "Any other time, I wouldn't ask you to tell me this, but…"

Reida shook her head. "No, you need to know. You deserve to know."

The words had sounded ominous. Kaelan hesitated, half-turning toward the door, wondering if it might be better to stick her head in the sand after all. But Reida was right—if Kaelan was going to try to become a tamer, she needed to know what sort of danger she might be putting herself in.

"Go on, then," Kaelan said at last.

Reida cleared her throat. "Well, one day Olaf got mad—dragon-bloods have a quick temper, I hear." At this, she sent Kaelan a quick ironic smile, since they both knew that description certainly applied to Kaelan, as well. "And all the grass in the field around him withered up and turned black like it'd been burnt to a crisp. His ma broke the news to him that day, told him his dad had been a dragon. No one really expected news like that—you know, usually the nobles are the only ones with dragon blood—but I guess sometimes it happens. Anyway, he went off to be trained as a tamer. Didn't have an easy time of it, from what I hear, what with all the other students being noble. But he managed, at least for a while."

She fell silent for a moment, fingers twisting in her dress, still looking out the window. Kaelan waited, forcing herself to be still.

"When he came back," Reida said at last, "his own village stoned him. People who'd watched him grow up, who'd helped raise him. They might've killed him if he hadn't fled. While he'd been off at the Akademy, a dragon had visited the town, you see. It had taken the best cattle, nearly half the herd, to feed itself while resting after an injury. It ruined the villagers. They were so *furious*. The dragon was protected by law, so they couldn't do a thing about it, but the tamers... my cousin..." She scrubbed a hand across her eyes and finally turned back to Kaelan. "You just be careful, you hear? Around the dragons *and* the common folk."

Kaelan bit her lip. The story was as bad as she'd feared. In the space of a day, she'd gone from being a tolerated outsider to having more enemies than she could count. The villagers now hated her on principle and the dragon-blooded Akademy students were unlikely to be kind to a peasant girl. And then, of course, there were the dragons themselves.

"Did you see the dragon?" she managed to ask. "The one who visited your town?"

Reida nodded, her face grim. "It was mottled brown, with eyes like stone. It looked at you and it near turned *you* to stone as well. The creature was cold and beautiful and absolutely terrifying. All of them are. And so powerful they could squash you with barely a thought. This one could cause earthquakes, I heard."

It'd been a Terra, then. Kaelan knew from the tattered book, now in her pack, that Terras were a fairly common class of dragons, with powers over the earth. Also common were Embers, the orange-gold fire-breathers. Ariels, those with power over the element of air, were much rarer. Each of the four types of dragons provided specific benefits for the kingdom, but the only kind that most commoners viewed as remotely worth the price were Aquas, who could divert floods and keep crops watered during even the worst droughts. But even they were regarded with suspicion and fear. Kaelan didn't agree with that assessment, of course, but this wasn't the time to argue.

Kaelan stepped closer to her friend. "Reida," she said, "I need you to do me a favor. Look out for Ma and Grandma while I'm gone. I'm worried people might hurt them, or even just not buy from them anymore, because of... what I am. They're in a fragile state, and they might not make it without help, without someone to look after them. I wouldn't ask you, as I know it might hurt your reputation to throw your lot in with theirs, but you're my only friend. The only one I *can* ask."

Reida lifted a hand. "Shut up, you silly goose," she said with a tearful laugh, and hugged Kaelan again. "Of course, I'll watch out for them. When it gets cold out, they can even come stay in my room to keep warm, if they like. I know Haldis gave your ma a treatment so she at least wouldn't be contagious anymore, right?"

Kaelan let out a breath, relieved. "That's right. Thank you."

She tightened her arms around Reida, thanking all the gods she had at least one good friend.

Reida pushed her away, wiping her eyes. "You'd better get a move on if you want to make Bellsor by the start of the fall term," she said, trying to sound stern, but her voice wavered. She was clearly afraid for her friend, but trying hard not to show it.

Well then. The least Kaelan could do was pretend that she wasn't scared, either. She lifted her chin and threw a determined smile in Reida's direction. "Okay then. Off I go. Be well, Reida."

"And you," Reida said, the words faint and tremulous as Kaelan marched into the hall.

Once outside, Kaelan had to make a decision: take a long detour to meet up with the main road outside the city, or take the same alleyway back and risk running into the mole woman and the lady she'd been gossiping with. After a moment's hesitation, she struck out toward the alley. If she was going to pretend she wasn't scared, she might as well go big.

Both women were still in the same spot. They recognized her this time and their eyes followed her, boring a hole into the back of her head. Kaelan did her best to ignore them at first, but couldn't shake the sick realization that this was what she would always have to deal with, from this point forward. She was no longer just an outsider. She was an enemy.

But how was that fair? She'd helped heal half the population last year when the sweating sickness had been going around. And she'd helped lay the cobbles in the main square and had pitched in to catch the pigs in the spring when their fence had broken. She may not have been born there, but she'd paid her dues to this town the same way she'd had to pay her dues to every town her family had lived in. She'd done more for the village of Gladsheim than most of the people who'd been born there had. These women had no right to her pain, no right to their own self-righteousness.

This village had been her home. She refused to slink away from it as if she'd done something wrong simply by existing.

Kaelan forced a spring into her step and a smile onto her face. She might be going to her doom. She might be sacrificing everything to save the ones she cared about. But she'd be damned if she'd let these fool-headed villagers catch her crying.

CHAPTER 6

By the second day of the journey, Kaelan regretted her decision to leave all of the money behind. By the third, she was convinced she'd never been so hungry in her life. All she could think about were the many different types of food she'd like to be eating, while her stomach grumbled so loudly it scared wildlife away.

It let out another loud complaint. She sighed as she gingerly picked shriveled berries from a thorny bush. Theoretically, she could've tried trading for food with other travelers she met along the way, but she'd decided to avoid the main roads and towns, worried that other people might see a girl traveling toward Bellsor right before the start of the Akademy's fall term and put two and two together. Plus, it was a good idea in general to stay out of sight and off the main roads if you were a girl traveling alone. Most of the Alverian countryside was relatively safe, but there were always bandits and other unsavory folk waiting to prey on those who couldn't fight back.

A thorn stabbed her finger and she cursed. These berries were already out of season and she'd been lucky to find any still on the branches at all. She doubted she'd find any more of them on this bush if she kept looking, and she'd already been pricked thrice for her trouble. With just a meager handful of purple brightberries, she trudged back to her makeshift campsite, eating as she went. Her hands were empty before she got back to her bedroll.

Hopefully, she'd come across a creek tomorrow and she'd be able to fish, or maybe use her healer's instinct to find some edible roots. She'd tried to set some rabbit snares yesterday, but even though she'd managed to catch one small hare, the thing had looked as scrawny as her and she hadn't been able to bear to kill it. She'd set it free instead, cursing herself the whole time. This wasn't a fairytale, she knew. The animal wouldn't come back and make her new shoes in the night or bring her a feast of carrots. She'd just let a full meal run off for no reason. Still, she couldn't bring herself to regret it.

She sighed as she lay down, the sun's last light dimming overhead. She would be able to fish tomorrow, she told herself firmly. She could kill a fish. And then, maybe, she would make it to Bellsor without starving.

She closed her eyes and slept.

She stood atop a cliff. Her long dress, which was a beautiful shade of green shot through with brown, billowed outward as if caught underwater. Tendrils of her hair floated around her face.

She was waiting for something. No—someone. She couldn't remember who, but she was supposed to meet... someone.

She stepped to the edge of the cliff and peered down. This was where she'd come when she'd found out she was a dragon-blood. Then, there'd been a steep fall of rocks with a hazy forest at the bottom, but now there was only a drop into unending darkness. Why would she choose this place to meet with whoever she was supposed to meet?

The earth beneath her tilted. She swayed forward, toward the edge. Gasping, she stumbled backwards, lifting her arms for balance. But her feet were caught by the impossible current, and she lifted off the ground and drifted toward the abyss.

Beneath her, a shape stirred in the darkness.

"No!" she shouted, but the word came out garbled and faint. The ground was at her back now as if it were an upturned plate and she was being scraped off of it. She reached upward for it, unable to do anything but stare up at the slab of earth as she slowly fell toward the thing that dwelt in the night beneath her.

She twisted, managing to turn herself so she could look down. The shadow moved: inky black against a canvas of darkness, nearly impossible to make out. Then it turned and looked back at her and spread its wings.

A dragon. A massive black dragon, with wings that blotted out the abyss, rising up toward her.

This was who she was here to meet. The knowledge slotted into place suddenly, like the final piece of a terrible puzzle.

Fire bloomed in the darkness. The dragon's teeth gleamed ivory against the flame. She screamed, twisting against the heat, flailing against the current...

And woke up, her blanket twisted around her, birds quietly chirping in the light of the early dawn.

She blew out a breath. A nightmare. It was just a nightmare. The edges of it still clung to her memory, leaving a lingering aftertaste of sheer panic, but she shook herself and lifted a shaky hand to her burn scar, which was aching. She frowned. The heat from the dragon's breath had been so *real,* so convincing that her brain must've linked the nightmare to the remembered pain she'd suffered when she'd nearly burned the hut down years before.

But she was awake now, and there was no reason to dwell on a simple dream—which had probably been brought on by hunger and stress—and a phantom pain. Her hair was stuck to the nape of her neck with sweat, which meant she had all the more reason to hope to find a creek today, as she probably reeked by this point. Not that the foxes and birds cared, but she preferred to cling to vestiges of civilization as much as she could.

Still shaken, she sat on a nearby log and dug through her pack before setting off. She pulled out the red dragon book and turned to the back, where a handful of pages had been left blank, likely for students to write notes in. She'd never written in the book before, feeling blasphemous for even thinking of scribbling her own paltry thoughts in one of her family's precious books, but right now she needed to rid herself of her nightmare—and writing it down felt like the best way to do that.

A nearby bird squawked and flew out of its perch as if startled by something. Kaelan paused and lifted her head, looking around warily. Her spine tingled. She'd felt this way before—in the market and around the village, whenever those jerks had been watching her and plotting their next attack. But here, she was in the middle of the woods with no other people anywhere nearby. The solitude should have made her feel calmer where instead it only made her more disconcerted. But after a long moment of quiet, the rest of the birds resumed their singing and the woods slowly started to feel normal again.

Brushing away the feeling of being watched as a remnant of her nightmare, Kaelan tugged her quill and a small inkpot out of her bag and set to work. When she was done writing out the nightmare, she felt better, and she added a few lines at the end which summed up her journey so far in as humorous a way as she could manage. She'd write home when she arrived at the Akademy, and she needed material for the letter. The more light-hearted she could make it, the better.

Finished, she pushed her things back into her pack and set off.

To her utter joy, she did manage to find a creek—freezing cold with runoff from the early mountain snows, but full of fish—and when she settled down to camp again, it was with a full belly.

Day five of her journey didn't go nearly so well, though. By noontime, she found herself in front of a narrow road, a bottle-neck that served as the only pass through the steep, mountainous terrain that would last until she arrived at Bellsor. Unless she wanted to add extra days to her journey—and risk arriving at the Akademy late for the official start of classes—she'd have to take the main road with all of the other potential travelers from here on out. Swallowing down her uncertainty, she pulled her hood up and walked quickly, hoping to remain beneath notice to whoever might appear.

No such luck. Within an hour, she heard the telltale rattle of a merchant's cart. She glanced up; sheer cliffs rose to either side of the road, a single stray mountain goat picking its way along a path only it could see. There was nowhere to hide. She'd have to pretend to fit in instead. What teenager would travel this road alone like this at this time of year, though, besides an incoming student of the Akademy? Perhaps she could be reuniting with her family in the capital after a wildfire had separated them. Or she was an orphan with a caravan of settlers but had been turned out when food stores got low. No, that was no good... she needed people to think someone was waiting for her, that someone would miss her if she didn't arrive at her destination safely. Otherwise, they might be tempted to rob her. Not that they'd get much out of it, of course—but more than money could be taken from a girl traveling alone.

She shrank into herself and moved as close as she could to the wall of the cliff, hoping the wagon would pass her by without engaging her.

Instead, it slowed. "You doin' well?" came a voice, followed by a disgusting sound that could only be phlegm-related. Something yellow and wet splattered on the rocks at her feet. Before she could stop herself, she stepped away in disgust and the merchant laughed.

She twisted to glare up at him, forgetting to hide her face—and therefore her age. "Better than you, it would seem," she bit out caustically, jerking her head at the too-thick wad of phlegm. He was obviously ailing from something for it to be that color. "Do you spit at all the travelers, or should I feel honored?"

In the silence after she spoke, her face went hot with regret. Surely, she could've held her tongue for two minutes, to just step over the phlegm and keep moving until the merchant got bored and moved on. But, no, she'd had to go and sass him. Not that he didn't more than deserve her rudeness—but she was alone and defenseless, and never more keenly aware of it than now when the man slowed his ancient donkey to a halt in front of her, blocking her path.

The merchant, his face pulled down in a frown beneath his scrubby growth of facial hair, peered at her from his seat in the cart. When he spoke again, he had an accent she couldn't quite place. "That's no concern of yours. What're you doing out here alone? You look too young to be traveling on your own."

"That's no concern of yours," she snapped back, throwing his words back at him. She moved to step around the cart.

"Just trying to watch out for my fellow traveler," the man responded, but his eyes had narrowed. "Might've been about to offer you a ride. See if you get one now with that attitude."

She edged around the front of the cart, eye-level with his feet as she passed the driver's perch. His boots looked brand new, but were much too high-quality for a simple merchant, and too big for his feet, as well. One had something brownish-red splattered across the top.

Kaelan swallowed, sweating lightly now, and forced herself to keep to a steady pace as she moved around the donkey. She raised her eyes then. The man—probably a bandit, and definitely a corpse-robber judging from those bloody boots—met her gaze. "Try some Hawthorne bark for your cough," she said, managing to keep her voice light and level.

He squinted. "What cough? I ain't coughed once since we met."

"But you have been, right? In the night when you lie down."

He turned the reins over in his hands, still suspicious. "And how would you know that?"

She shrugged. "I'm a healer. My two big brothers are meeting me at the next waystation along the pass," she added—the more fictional men traveling with her, the better. "It's only another half-hour or so from here, right?"

He regarded her another moment, and she held her breath. "Right," he said at last, and twitched the reins. The donkey trudged forward, and the cart jangled back into motion. He looked down at her as he passed. "Maybe I'll see you there," he commented, and it sounded like a threat.

She nodded and smiled until he was out of sight. Then she forced herself to move forward on the road even though she wanted to turn around, to claw her way out of this awful canyon, or even just stop and breathe for a while. She hated feeling helpless and *hated* feeling like prey.

But... she wouldn't be prey for much longer, would she? She was a dragon-blood.

If that man had tried to harm her, could she have defended

herself? Roared at him, or burnt him like Reida's cousin had burnt the grass? She wanted to flinch away from the thought, but a part of her reveled in her righteous anger and the thought of fighting back with real power. All her life, she'd been at the mercy of men like that, whether they wore blood-splattered boots or a soldier's uniform or the fine suit of a tax collector. None of them had harmed her the way that man might've, but they'd all stolen from her family in one way or another, simply because she and Ma and Grandma had been too poor and friendless to be able to defend themselves. And she might still be untrained for now, and might not be able to do much to stop them stealing from her for the moment—but it was a comfort to think that that wouldn't be the case for long if she succeeded in harnessing whatever powers she might have.

But, for the moment, it was probably best she avoid the next waystation.

She ran into a few more travelers that day, but managed to keep her hood up and her comments to herself, passing them all without much notice. By the time dusk fell, she'd discovered an abandoned hut not too far from the road. The night was freezing already, and she could hardly risk bedding down in the middle of the pass, so she barricaded the door as best she could and slept wrapped in her blanket, ready to flee at the slightest hint of bandits.

She was weightless again, but this time, she was flying.

The earth spun itself out beneath her like a tapestry on a loom, the hills rising and falling. She spread her arms and whooped out loud at the sheer, dizzying joy of it.

A shadow fell over her. It raced across the landscape beneath her like an inkblot, massive and graceful, swallowing up her much smaller shadow. She looked up. A huge blue-black dragon peered down at her. She recoiled, her flight path stuttering as she started to veer away, remembering the dragon from her last dream, the one that she'd been there to meet who had nearly eaten her. But then she caught sight of this dragon's eyes: dazzlingly green and intelligent... not the eyes of a monster, but of a thinking being. One who was... flying with her? Not attacking her? She steadied herself and waited, but it simply continued to glide above her.

She began to relax. The dragon was there to teach her. Mountains rippled beneath her now, and she wanted to get higher, away from the land she'd been bound to her whole life, up into the endless blue sky. She rose. But instead of rising with her, the dragon above dipped one wing, swept the other sharply upward, and flipped over in midair. It made the maneuver look like child's play, its green eyes smiling as it rolled to fly beneath her. It had a black spine, she noticed—right before a gust of wind from the creature's wings slammed into her, knocking her off-course.

She scrambled to climb, to straighten out, but she'd lost

control. Earth, sky, mountain, and dragon spun through her view faster than she could keep track of as she plummeted toward her death. She couldn't remember how to fly and didn't know how she'd been able to do it in the first place, so she resorted to pinwheeling her arms and screaming out for help.

The dragon. The dragon was there to teach her. It would help her. But she was falling too fast, and the dragon was still just watching, and she realized with a sick jolt that she was about to die.

Kaelan woke up half a second before she hit the ground.

She raised a shaking hand to her head, squeezing her eyes shut again and trying to piece together the meaning of the dream before she was even fully awake. The dreams were unnatural. She'd *never* had nightmares before this. So... maybe they meant something. Maybe they came from some sort of tamer magic manifesting itself already, Odin help her. If she could just figure out what the dreams meant, she wouldn't be so terrified, and maybe she wouldn't have any more of these awful nightmares.

She had to think. Dragons. Fire, falling, flying. Meeting someone. Someone teaching her.

Okay. Dreams were all about symbolism, or at least that was what Ma always said. So, maybe these dragons were figurative, not literal. What did dragons mean to her? Danger, maybe. So, she was going to meet someone dangerous who would… teach her something? Maybe they suggested one of the masters at the Akademy. In which case the dragons would be both literal and figurative.

I will watch out for dangerous teachers, she promised her brain. *Now, please stop giving me nightmares.*

Finally, she sat up and opened her eyes. She was freezing—her blanket was missing. She spit out a litany of shaky curses. She must've thrown it away in her sleep. At least it was warm in the small space; the fire crackling in the grate had done a good job of chasing the chill of the mountain night away.

With that thought, she froze. She reached back in her memory, certain she must be forgetting something—but her memory of falling asleep was as clear as day. She'd found the hut. She'd closed the door and barricaded it with the table. She'd wrapped herself in her blanket and fallen asleep against the far wall.

She *hadn't* started a fire because she hadn't wanted to attract any bandits.

"Well," said a voice in the darkness, "it's nice to meet you, Kaelan Younger."

CHAPTER 7

K aelan scrambled to her feet, snatching up the closest heavy thing she could find—a pot from her pack—and putting her back up against the wall. Ma and Grandma hadn't been able to give her many self-defense lessons, but she at least knew enough to do that much. She squinted. The cabin was lit dimly by the low-burning fire, but shadows grew long in the corners of the room, and she could barely make out the vague silhouette of a man by the door. "Stay back," she warned, eyeing the distance to the nearest window in case she needed an escape route.

A resonant chuckle wound through the darkness. "No need for that. I'd hate for you to lose your only pot, and I'll admit a reluctance to have it thrown at my head."

She held the pot out like a sword. "Show yourself!" she

demanded, hating how shaky her voice was. "How did you know my name? How did you get in here?"

A shape stirred in the darkness, inky black against the shadows, unsettling her with the memory of that first dream-dragon. But then a man stepped out: tall, middle-aged, broad and muscular with olive skin, his hands held up in surrender as he moved into the circle of firelight. A scar stretched across his right cheek.

"I hate to say it, but your door-barricading skills need work," the man said.

The pot in her hand wavered. She glanced at the hearth. Whoever he was, he'd built a fire when he could easily have attacked her while she slept. "Why are you here? Who are you?" she demanded.

He elected to answer only the first question. "I wanted to warn you."

Her heartbeat jumped, and she firmed her grip on the pot. "About what? It seems to me you're the only one here worth being warned about."

"Nah," he said, casually motioning over his shoulder in the direction of the door. "If I were you, I'd worry much more about them."

"Who?" Kaelan asked—right as the door burst off its hinges.

Three strangers shoved their way into the hut, stomping over the battered door. Kaelan leapt backwards, pressing herself against the far wall and hoping she might blend into the shadows in the corners the way the first man had earlier. The new strangers paused to survey the room. Kaelan's breath stopped when she recognized the so-called merchant from the pass, the one who'd spit at her. The firelight flickered across the dried blood on his boots when he stepped further into the room, his eyes landing on her.

Her body stayed motionless, but her mind sprinted forward, analyzing escape routes, spurred by her panic. The window. It was her only chance. She had to get out the window. She took two steps toward it—right as the scarred man moved.

She'd seen fights before. Even been in a few minor ones herself. But none of the men and women she'd seen had ever fought like this. He moved easily, casually, like it meant nothing when he took the dagger from one bandit, and as if it was an afterthought when he plunged it into the merchant's phlegmy chest. The third bandit, a woman, stepped behind him with her own sword held high. He pivoted in close, caught her off-balance, and elbowed her hard in the chest. While she was bent double trying to get her breath back, he pulled the dagger from her friend's chest and stalked toward her.

The man he'd stabbed slid to the ground, dead. The two remaining bandits paused for the space of a single heartbeat while they assessed their new circumstances—then, as one, they turned and fled out the open door. And just like that, the conflict was over scant seconds after it had begun.

The night wind whistled as the scarred man watched his opponents run away. He shrugged, cleaned the dagger with two quick swipes against the dead man's pants, and turned toward Kaelan.

She dropped the pot, its metal ringing out loudly as it clattered to the floor. It wouldn't be of any use if this soldier attacked her—for he could only be a soldier, or some kind of mercenary, or even an assassin.

"Pitiful, the state of criminals nowadays," the man commented idly, and with that he flipped the dagger around. He held it out to her, hilt-first.

She eyed the man in front of her for a long moment. He had his back to the door like he wasn't even worried about the two bandits coming back. His stance was casual, and what kind of person could be casual after murdering someone? Although it hadn't exactly been murder, and technically, he *had* saved her life. And started a fire to keep her warm while she'd slept and warned her about the imminent attack. But, on the other hand, his fire had probably advertised her presence to the bandits in the first place, so if he hadn't snuck in and started it, they might not have found her at all.

She stepped away from the wall and accepted the dagger. It wouldn't be of much more use in her hands than the pot, but it would be nice to have something sharp to protect herself with if those bandits came back. Or if this mystery soldier/mercenary/assassin turned out to have darker motives than he claimed.

"Just a traveler looking for a bit of shelter in the night," he said, seeing the question in her eyes.

"A traveler who knows my name," she countered warily.

He only shrugged.

She hesitated, then nodded. He'd defended her from bandits who might've killed her; she supposed he'd earned his reticence, at least for now. Plus, it wasn't like she could *make* him tell her anything.

He saw her decision and smiled again. "Good girl." He retreated to the dead body and searched it, patting it down until he found a sack of coins and another dagger. He pocketed both—though he didn't touch the fancy, bloodstained boots, Kaelan noticed—and then hauled the body out the door and into the night. He dusted his hands together upon returning. "That'll be found in the morning, by his friends or wolves or both," he said. "Best we be on our way before then?"

Kaelan moved to the window and craned her neck to look at the horizon. It was nearly dawn. She'd have liked to sleep just a little longer, but there was certainly no chance of that now. "Yeah," she agreed, and gathered up her things. She kept one eye on the man the whole time, but he only leaned against the wall and waited for her.

"I'll keep you company for today, if it's alright with you," he said when he saw her watching him. "For safety."

For *her* safety, he meant. Odin knew, she couldn't provide him any protection. Still, it was a generous offer and one she couldn't afford to turn down, no matter how wary she was of him.

"Thank you," she said honestly, hoping he understood her meaning extended beyond just his offer. He had saved her life, after all, and Ma hadn't raised her to be rude.

He nodded graciously. "It was no problem."

"It really wasn't," she agreed, raising an eyebrow at him as she rolled up her blanket and stuffed it into her pack. "Where did you learn to fight like that?"

"Here and there."

"Uh-huh." She waited for him to explain further, but he just kept leaning against the wall, hands in his pockets.

He wasn't any more forthcoming when they were out on the road. "How did you know those bandits were coming?" she prodded after they'd been walking for a short while.

He shrugged. "There are quite a few bandits about these days. Many aren't even really bandits—they're from Unger, sent to test the throne, see whether it can protect its people. I'd like to think it can, but nobles are hard ones to trust."

"That's not an answer," Kaelan observed.

"Is it not?" He gave her an enigmatic smile.

She rolled her eyes. "How did you know my name, then?" she tried.

"I'm sure you must've introduced yourself."

"In my sleep?"

He shrugged again. She stopped and crossed her arms. She wasn't taking one more step at this man's side until she found out *something* about him. "If you keep giving me non-answers, I'll invent a history for you myself," she warned him.

He stopped, too, but stayed silent, one eyebrow raised.

"You're a turnip farmer," she determined. "You got all your muscles from heaving a hoe. You try to act tough, but you secretly have a whole herd of cats waiting for you back home, all of which you've spoiled terribly."

"Who would feed the cats while I'm gone?"

"Your elderly mother. You live with her. She's very sweet. And ashamed of her very rude son, who despite all her attempts at education, is unable to answer simple questions properly."

He snorted. "Animals don't care for me. And my mother is long dead."

Ma's voice rose in the back of Kaelan's head, urging her to apologize for her insensitivity, but she resisted. "How did you know my name?" she asked again.

He gazed at her, something like approval in his eyes. "Stubborn one, aren't you?"

She waited. After a moment, he gave in with a half-laugh, and pulled something out of a pocket. He held it out to her: her tattered red dragon book, which had her name scrawled across its title page.

And which also contained the details of her dream and the start of a letter to her family.

She snatched it back. "That's private," she said, fuming.

"Interesting dream you had," he said, not even trying to pretend he hadn't read it. "Do you have those often?"

She started to snap at him, but then paused. "I'll trade you an answer for an answer," she offered instead.

He considered it for a moment. "Deal. But I get to pick which question I'll answer."

"That's hardly fair."

He waited.

She sighed, defeated. "No," she said. "That was not the first dream I've had like that. I had another one last night as well, though that was the first. I'm hoping I don't make a habit of it. They're… unsettling."

She paused. Earlier, she'd thought the nightmares might actually be trying to tell her something—that she would meet someone, a teacher, and that he would be dangerous. And then she'd met this man who was most certainly dangerous. He hadn't tried to teach her anything yet, but what if her dream had been trying to warn her about him?

He nodded, his gaze far away. "Interesting," was all he said.

"Your turn."

"Hmmm." He turned to begin walking again while he considered which question of hers to answer. She followed a few steps behind. "I first learned to fight from an old monk named Solveig," he said. "I've had many instructors since then, but none quite so inspiring. He used to make me carry water from the sacred springs for him to make his afternoon tea, one leaf-full at a time."

"That sounds unnecessary."

"Oh, it was. The true lesson was meant to teach me to stand up for myself. I carried leaves full of water for that old man for six months before I finally snapped and told him I wouldn't do it anymore."

"Couldn't he have just told you to stand up for yourself and moved on to the next lesson?"

He gave her a sideways glance. "True learning comes from doing, not from being handed the answers. I'm sure you'll learn that at the Akademy. That's where you're headed, right?"

She hadn't put that detail in the book, but she guessed it was no surprise he'd pieced together the clues—particularly since he already knew her name. "Yes," she said reluctantly. "I'm going to be a tamer."

He laughed.

She bristled. "I have a promise to keep," she said defensively. "I don't care if everyone else there is a noble, or if everyone in the whole countryside wants to stone me for what I am now. I keep my promises."

"That's honorable, I suppose. But wouldn't you rather look to yourself than a promise? What is it that *you* want, Kaelan?"

She snapped her mouth shut, caught off guard. Her grandmother had said something similar. *What's more important? Loyalty to yourself or honoring promises to others?* Of course, she got the feeling her grandmother and the man in front of her had different ideas about which goal was most important.

"What, no quick answer for that?" The man appeared amused.

And at her expense. Well, she knew *exactly* where he could stuff his amusement.

She narrowed her eyes. "I don't take life advice from people whose names I don't know, thank you very much."

"Well then, no harm in giving you a bit more advice in that case. You should at least know if you want more than what you have. You'll have to discover that answer for yourself, though. One can only hope you won't have to carry leaves full of water for six months before you do it."

Stung by his condescension, she replied quickly. "Keeping promises is more important than whatever I might want for myself. No amount of leaves will change my mind. Although I doubt water-carrying is a course at the Akademy, anyway."

He tilted his head. "How can you keep a promise if you have no real idea who you are, or your strengths and weaknesses? Don't you want to be open to learning whatever you might discover about yourself? If your mind is set only on the goal you came with, you may miss out on the true purpose of learning."

"And what would that be?"

He smiled vaguely and fell silent.

She threw her hands up and marched past him, taking the lead. His words had unsettled her, and she didn't want him to see it.

Although he'd probably guess it anyway. He'd shown an unnerving ability to read her thoughts thus far.

She was going to become a tamer and bring whatever dragon she bonded with back to heal her mother. That was the promise she'd made, and it was a promise she'd keep, no matter what she discovered about herself during the school term. Why would the stranger care, anyway? It was none of his business.

Now mad enough to confront him again, she whirled around. "What is it *you* want?" she demanded, hoping her words pricked him the way his had pricked her. "You're obviously well educated, but you have no money or you wouldn't have bothered to take that bandit's coin. So, that means you have no job. And you made sure we got away from the hut before we ran into any other travelers, even though we wouldn't have gotten into any trouble for defending ourselves from bandits, which means you don't want any lawmen to find you. You're on the run from something, aren't you? You're one to talk about going after what you want, when I'm guessing that's what got you into whatever mess you're in right now."

His face didn't change, but his steps paused for the space of a single heartbeat, long enough for Kaelan to see that she'd been right—or at least hit too close for his comfort. She had a moment of unease, remembering what this man was capable of. *Stupid mouth, always moving faster than my brain.* When would it ever stop getting her into trouble?

The man's steps carried him nearer, and he looked down at Kaelan. "So, you're smart as well as stubborn," he said mildly, and she let out a breath in relief that he wasn't angry. "That's not an admission, mind you," he added—but Kaelan hardly heard this comment, because the dawn had broken in full now and she could finally see his face well enough to make out the color of his eyes, which were exactly the same dazzling green-shot-through-with-brown as the dragon's in her last dream.

"Something on my face?" the man asked, and Kaelan realized she was staring. And also not breathing. She sucked in air and jolted back into motion, tearing her gaze away from his, her mind racing. Did this mean he really was the person the dream had been warning her about? And now that she thought about it, hadn't her dress in the first dream been that same shade of green-brown?

It couldn't be a coincidence. The dreams, both of them, had involved him somehow. The only question was, what exactly was she supposed to do about it? The dragon, the fire, the gust of wind that had knocked her off-course, were they some kind of metaphor telling her not to trust him? Or did her powers simply show her vague snatches of the future that were buried in otherwise meaningless images? Which seemed a bit useless, if she was being honest, but right now she'd vastly prefer the meaningless option to the one that meant this man was a danger to her.

"Uh, no. Just—something about you looked… familiar, for a second," she said at last.

The man smiled, apparently oblivious to her racing thoughts. "Ah, I see. I have one of those faces, I suppose."

"Right." She fell silent, uncomfortable, and they traveled the rest of the day in relative silence.

It was only when they reached the end of the mountain pass road that she broke out of her thoughts enough to speak again. "Wow," was all she could manage to say, though, looking down across the last few foothills that lay between them and the city of Bellsor.

Alveria's capital city was beautiful. It sprawled across the hills, rippling over the landscape like a living thing. It was more colorful than she'd expected, especially at the outskirts where the shanties perched above narrow dirt streets. The bright colors of the housing disguised their poor construction, she supposed, and perhaps brightened the lives of the folk who weren't rich enough to live deeper in the city. Those buildings were much more graceful, the lines of their construction swooping and rising into elegant gables and noble columns. The most ostentatious—like the palace, whose spiraling towers reached toward the sky from the middle of the city— were made of polished, marbled, blue-and-white stone. But none of that was what held her attention—because above all of it towered the Alverian Akademy.

She recognized its outline immediately from her book. Built of no-nonsense gray stone, it looked as much like a fortress as a school. Although there were echoes of palatial inspiration as well, tucked away in the looming spires and the massive, elaborately carved front door. It had a drawbridge, too, made necessary by the river that tumbled past its entrance, foaming with whitewater. The whole building, if such a magnificent and massive thing could be called such, was built into the side of a mountain on the far end of the city. The path to reach the Akademy looked skinny and terrifying, laden with switchbacks and sheer cliffs. The place might as well be a military base. It would be impossible for an enemy to storm, except perhaps from the air.

With that thought, her breath caught in her throat and she craned her neck, searching the skies, her heart thudding in her chest as she strained to catch sight of a dragon. That feeling was back, that trembling, addictive mix of awe and uncertainty that she'd felt all her life when she'd thought of the creatures. Overwhelmed as she was to be attending a school like this, it would also mean she'd get to see many more dragons, and far closer-up than she ever had before. Was she thrilled by that, or nervous?

She wouldn't have to figure it out today, it appeared. No dragons showed themselves, and after a moment, the man turned to her. "It'll be dark out soon, and you've still got a bit of a ways to go," he said. "Shall we bed down here for tonight?"

She gave him a sideways glance. The dagger he'd given her was heavy at her belt, but it would be of little use if her dreams truly had been warning her about him. And yet, he was right about still having a good half-day's trip left to get to the Akademy, and he'd so far been perfectly polite—if frustratingly unforthcoming. And even this close to the city, there was still the risk of bandits.

She sighed. She would argue herself in circles if she tried to think it through any further, so she simply dropped her pack and nodded her agreement. She supposed she'd have to take the known risk of keeping her traveling companion close over the unknown risk of being on her own for the night.

Despite her worries and the uncertainty of what tomorrow would bring, Kaelan slept deeply. Or at least well enough that she didn't hear the stranger skulk off sometime during the night. When she awoke, he was gone, having left her only three gold coins as a sign he'd ever been present at all.

She rolled to her side and picked them up, turning them in her hands. They had to be some of the coins he'd taken from the bandit. Gold quarter-weights. They were stamped with the official seal of Alveria on one side, and the profile of a boy on the other. She rubbed at the gold, squinting as she tried to make out the words beneath the portrait. *Prince Lasaro of Alveria,* they proclaimed. So, this was the queen's youngest son. She'd never seen his likeness before, mostly because she'd never held a coin this valuable in her life. He looked nice enough, she supposed, and perhaps even handsome, though it was hard to tell from a coin. She tucked all three of the coins in her purse, then stood and tucked her purse beneath her cloak where it would be safe from pickpockets. Thanks to the gods, now she had plenty of money to buy a good breakfast. No more fish and berries for her. She could have a cinnamon pasty, or even some smoked ham, and still have more than enough left over to squirrel away for any unexpected expenses at the Akademy. Maybe she'd better pay for a bath, too, and a change of clothes. She was already going to stand out enough among all the noble students—at least she wouldn't need to fulfill the peasant stereotype of being smelly and clothed in rags. She mentally thanked her traveling companion, whoever he'd been, and picked up her pack to make ready.

Something crinkled beneath her hands. She frowned and opened the pack, finding an old piece of thick parchment lying on top of her belongings. It was a map of some sort although she had no idea what it was supposed to be for. She turned it this way and that, but none of it made any sense, and the words were so tiny she could barely make them out. A library? And something called the Emerald Lake? Why would the stranger have left her this?

He'd known too much about her and what she needed, and she felt discomfited by her certainty that this map, whatever it was, would somehow come in handy eventually. Uneasy all over again, she stuffed the map back into her pack. She could figure out the meaning of his gifts later. Right now, she had breakfast to worry about. And, after that, her first day as a student at the Alverian Akademy.

She took a deep breath, squared her shoulders, and started down the road toward her destiny.

CHAPTER 8

Her belly full and her body clean, Kaelan hurried through the winding streets of Bellsor a few hours later. The fabric of her new clothing was inexpensive but durable and felt soft against her skin as she moved. She'd chosen something that was nice for peasant wear but would never be mistaken for the garb of a noble—there was no point pretending she was something she wasn't, and anyway, she needed to save her money for something she needed more than pretty clothes. The Akademy would provide uniforms once she was officially accepted as a student, in any case.

She shook her mind away from thoughts of clothing. Her brain was all over the place this morning, mostly because she was trying hard not to think about how the woman she'd just nearly bumped into could be a dragon, or how the hassled-looking boy at the meat-seller's stall could be a fellow student.

Anyone here could transform and swallow her up, or, alternatively, become *her* dragon. It was all too much, and it was no wonder her mind preferred to wander rather than dwell on such things.

On top of the dragon issue, she was overwhelmed by the city itself. It was impossibly loud. Having lived in small villages all her life, she'd had no idea what a big capital city would be like—bigger than the villages, she'd known, and most definitely wealthier, but she'd forgotten to account for the noise. Thousands of people all crammed together, some of them piled up in multi-storied buildings that were like houses stacked atop each other; all of them scrambling to be somewhere, to do something. No matter which of the winding streets she turned down, she was surrounded by a yelling, chiding, complaining, bickering mass of humanity.

But there was an even stranger sound, too, one that followed her wherever she went: the sound of coins jingling in her pocket. Even after her purchases, she still had the two heavy gold quarter-weights and a handful of smaller gold pennies, and the foreign sensation of having money to spare. It made her extra wary of pickpockets, a caution which had served her well since two small boys had already tried to steal from her.

She paused at an intersection. The city streets were lovely, cobbled with red and black, but they were impossible to traverse. They appeared to curve one way, but then doubled back on themselves like twisting snakes, taking her to parts of the city she'd never meant to visit, making her more than an hour later than she'd wanted to be already. And this time, somehow, she'd ended up pretty much right back where she'd started. She crossed her arms and glared at the cobbles. She'd never get there at this rate. She had to ask for directions.

She ducked into a nearby shop. "Excuse me," she said to the smiling old man at the front. "Can you give me directions to the Akademy?"

The man instantly dropped his smile, screwed up his face, and squinted at her. "What kinda fool-headed question is that? I'll give you the direction to the Akademy: up. Are you blind that you can't make out the enormous mountain with the huge fortress of a school looming over the whole city?"

She should probably have been offended at his tone, but he reminded her a bit of Haldis with that attitude. She smothered a fond smile, and a surge of unexpected homesickness nearly bowled her over.

"Girl?" the man prodded, frowning even more deeply. "You look ill. If you've the plague, I warn you, I'll not have you in my shop. Damn flea-bitten, lice-eaten peasants."

Well. He officially no longer reminded her of Grandma. The homesickness faded, allowing her to breathe again. She scowled at him. "I'm fine, thank you for your concern. The Akademy, though—how do I get there exactly?"

He crossed his arms. "You climb. How else would you get up

Mount Firewyrm?" He pronounced the last word as fire-weerm. "Worm" was often used as an insult aimed at the dragons, but apparently "wyrm," the more ancient form of the word, was different. "Firewyrm" likely referred to Embers, the fire-breathing kind of dragons.

But Kaelan was more concerned about the old man's stubborn refusal to give her directions. There was no way he could truly be misunderstanding her, which had to mean he was being purposely combative for some reason. She went back over the conversation in her head. He hadn't gotten irritable until after she'd asked for directions to the Akademy, which had implied she was a student. Maybe he had something against dragon-bloods? She frowned. She knew anti-dragon sentiment was festering in some of Alveria's rural towns, but this was Bell-sor, home to the palace as well as the Akademy. Surely, the people *here* couldn't be anti-dragon.

She crossed her arms, too, matching his pose, and stared him down. "What streets, exactly, would I need to take to get to Mount Firewyrm?"

The man rolled his eyes and mumbled something under his breath. "Fine," he said more loudly, and snatched a piece of paper from a shelf. He scribbled on it for a moment and then shoved it at her. "Be off with you, then."

Kaelan glanced down at the writing—street names. They were barely legible, but they'd do. She started to thank the old man, but he'd already turned his back and began rearranging bolts of cloth on the counter. Which was fine with her. She didn't want to talk to him anymore, either.

She stepped out of the shop and glanced at the paper in her hand. Hopefully, the irate shopkeeper had given her correct directions. Only one way to find out.

Half an hour later, Kaelan found herself in the shadow of Mount Firewyrm, with Bellsor at her back. She had maybe another hour's journey before she reached the start of the switchbacks, and then it was a long, hard climb from there. The crabby old man had aimed her true after all, but she was still running hours behind and she hadn't even had lunch yet. She'd been so concerned about getting through Bellsor that she hadn't stopped to grab a meal, and she definitely wasn't going back in there now.

She tilted her head, listening. Beneath the now-distant clamor of the city, she could faintly hear the rushing of a nearby river. If she followed the noise, she might be able to fish and maybe get in a quick rest before attempting what looked to be a daunting climb. Decision made, she hiked up her pack and strode toward the sound of water.

She found the river easily and tramped through the reeds close to the bank in search of a good fishing spot. As she walked, she luxuriated in the relative peace and quiet. If she listened hard, she could even hear birdsong. Another pang of home-sickness trickled through her as she thought about her austere mountaintop and all the other peaceful valleys and lakeside meadows that had been her homes. She missed the sharp beauty of the wind whistling through the peaks, the call of one wolf to another. It would be a long time before she heard those sounds again.

She tried to enjoy the quiet while it lasted rather than focus on how much she missed home. After all, who knew how many free days she might get as a student, or when she'd be able to just go somewhere peaceful for a while again?

She found a rocky outcropping over the river in a little reed-free area and settled down to fish. A small cliff at her back blocked out the noise from Bellsor and provided shade, making the spot perfect. Forty minutes later, she'd caught two decent-sized trout and roasted them over the fire with the last of her stores of salt. They were delicious, made even more so by the calming environment. She lay on her back afterward, planning to rest for a moment before starting what would probably be the most physically demanding leg of her journey, and watched the clouds drift past the cliff overhead.

She woke up to the sounds of dragons fighting.

Disoriented, she shot bolt upright, scrambling backwards until she nearly tumbled into the river below. The noises that had woken her were horrible—bellowing shrieks and rabid snarls, and the hard thumping of heavy bodies against the earth as well as massive splashes. The sounds were coming from below her, a little way down the river, but didn't seem to be coming any closer.

Once her heart re-started, she lay down flat on her outcropping and peered downriver. The reeds in that direction were taller than her and obscured most of what was happening, but she could just make out the flash of sunlight against scales and the gleam of bared teeth about a field's length away, moving too quickly for her to judge what was going on.

She hesitated. She should go. She should stuff everything back in her pack and sprint upriver, leaving the fighting dragons to themselves. Moving closer to get a better view was a *terrible* idea, and it could only put her in danger.

But… they were *right there*. So close, closer than any dragon she'd seen her whole life. If she was very quiet and very careful, she might actually be able to see a whole dragon right here and now, at long last.

It was foolish. She should run.

She crept off the outcropping, leaving her pack behind, and moved stealthily through the reeds toward the dragons.

A bellow rent the air. *BOOM.* Something huge slammed into the earth a dozen yards ahead of her, spraying water and river pebbles above the reeds. She ducked and covered her head as the rocks pelted her. After a moment, she rose again, moving carefully sideways so she could get a view of whatever was happening that was unobscured by the reeds.

THUD. A dragon crashed barely a few yards in front of her. She froze, drinking in the sight, paralyzed by the adrenaline rushing through her veins with every thundering heartbeat. The dragon was smaller than she'd thought one would be, but still as big as her family's little one-room cabin. Its scales— wet with river water that beaded into shimmering droplets— gleamed light brown with green undertones. Its head was crowned with two short horns that curved up into deadly points above ears that looked floppy and, incongruously, kind of sweet. She was reminded of the floppy-eared rabbits she'd kept before her family's first move. None of them had had teeth as sharp as this, though. When the small dragon rolled over and righted himself with one quick upward thrust, it snarled at the sky above Kaelan, baring teeth the size of daggers.

A shadow fell over Kaelan. Jolted out of her reverie, she jerked backward and looked up. Another dragon, the same size but blue in color, swooped out of the sky toward the other before it veered sharply sideways. It was carrying something, and when it got over the river, it released its burden to fall into the current. A cow carcass, its head flopping lifelessly as it sank.

The brown dragon roared angrily and swept its own wings wide, launching itself into the air as the blue one flew over- head. The two collided in midair with a *whump* Kaelan could feel deep in her chest, and they fell together to the earth, tearing at each other. They separated quickly, though, and with no visible harm done to either party—which, combined with their small size, made Kaelan suddenly think they might be young and perhaps not fighting seriously, but only squabbling over their dinner. They roared and snarled again as they circled each other now, reminding her of clumsy, unruly kids.

Gigantic, dangerous, potentially people-eating, unruly kids.

Kaelan swallowed and started to back away. She'd seen her dragons, and now it was time to go. But before she could take more than a step, both dragons paused, sniffed the air, and turned toward her.

Oh, Hel, Thor, and Odin, she was as good as dead.

Her mind raced through everything she knew of predators. She'd come across a black bear once last winter, and she'd managed to get out of that situation by speaking calmly and backing slowly away. She at least knew enough not to run. Run, and you're prey.

"Easy now," she said, holding out her hands. "I'm just passing through, okay? No reason to get upset."

The blue one shook out its wings and roared, but the brown one cocked its head like it was listening.

Okay. She could do this. She was going to be a tamer after all. She wasn't sure exactly what they did or how they did it, but she knew a big part of their job was to tame dragon tempers. Plus, she had an advantage: she was a healer. She might not have ever shown the particular healer ability of calming people, but maybe it would emerge in her moment of need.

She took a deep breath to steady herself. "Just... let's just be calm, okay? There's no need to—"

The blue dragon snarled, opening its mouth wide and showing its teeth, and she skittered backwards several steps before she could stop herself. Damn. She'd shown weakness, uncertainty, and that would engage a predator's instincts to chase her—but she had to keep trying. If she could just—

The brown one reared up on its hind legs, its heavy tail lashing behind it. The end was barbed with foot-long spikes. She scrambled backwards a few more steps, unable to help herself as her fear and excitement churned into pure terror. She was going to be eaten. Could the dragons even understand her in this form? Did they know what they were doing, or were they running on sheer instinct? Would they regret eating her after they were done?

Dragons get whatever they want from anyone in the kingdom, that woman back in Gladsheim had said. What if what they wanted was her?

She edged another step away, trying to judge the distance back to the outcropping. The space beneath it was small. Perhaps she could wedge herself into it, deep enough to keep the dragons from being able to snap her up. But while she'd been looking away, both dragons had advanced on her, their heads lowered, reminding her of the way the wolves back home had stalked a lone fawn.

She stopped, her terror flashing into anger. Who were they, to try to frighten her like this? She had dragon blood, too. And even if she was fully human, they still had no right to treat *anyone* like prey.

The anger flowed up from her feet, into her torso, through her throat and out of her mouth. "STOP!" she screamed, and it came out as a roar. It vibrated from her just like last time, a wall of sound and fury and command, a near-visible force that knocked the reeds flat around her in a wide circle. But unlike last time, she was prepared for it, and when the two dragons flinched backward, she took advantage of their distraction and turned to run for the outcropping.

Twenty more steps. Ten. Five. Behind her, the dragons had recovered, and their snarls sounded furious as they pounded through the reeds after her. She skidded beneath the outcropping—and nearly wailed in despair. There was no hollow spot for her to wedge herself in as she'd thought to do. The space was plenty big enough for the dragons to shove a head or a claw in and drag her out. She was doomed. She was dead.

She darted out the other side. The cliff behind her blocked off any escape to the west, but maybe she could get into the trees, and maybe these dragons were too big to follow her through the forest. But she'd forgotten the dragons' biggest advantage: wings.

The blue one wheeled overhead, skidding to a rough landing in front of her. She reversed course, scrambling backwards, but the brown one was already behind her. She put her hands on her knees, wheezing for breath as she frantically tried to think of any way out of this—but there was nothing left, no tricks up her sleeve, and nowhere to run.

She would never heal her mother. She would never even reach the Akademy. She would die here, with no witnesses, and maybe even no corpse left behind to be buried. The only thing left to her was to die bravely.

She stood up straight, stared the blue dragon in the eye, and waited to be eaten.

CHAPTER 9

L asaro had nearly reached Mount Firewyrm when he heard the roar.

He reined his stallion in, the dappled gray dancing sideways and snorting in protest. Allfather had been bred in Bellsor and was relatively comfortable in the presence of dragon-bloods, but still, being this close to the Akademy had him more on edge than usual. Or maybe it had been that roar. If so, Lasaro couldn't blame the stallion—he'd never heard anything quite so unsettling. It was hard to tell if it had been a dragon or perhaps a dragon-blooded human who'd made the sound, but whoever it was, they were in trouble.

Several snarls rent the air next, these definitely coming from fully transformed dragons. From a lifetime lived in close proximity to creatures like these—his twin sisters in particular tended to spend more time as dragons than girls—he recognized the sound of a hunting dragon who'd been wholly over-taken by sheer animal instinct. Alarmed, Lasaro dug his knees into the side of his horse, but Allfather didn't move. The stallion was a trained warhorse, but it seemed even he wasn't keen on diving into the middle of what sounded like a dragon fight. Lasaro cursed. Trying to intervene in whatever this was on foot could be suicidal, but this damn stallion refused to budge.

Lasaro hesitated, glancing back at the palace, its white spires climbing toward the sky above Bellsor. If he was careless with his safety, it would anger the queen, and winning her approval was the whole point of going to the Akademy. His future, and the future of the entire kingdom, depended on it. Could he really risk that?

A desperate scream sounded out—this one undoubtedly human. With another curse, Lasaro threw himself out of his saddle, grabbed his sword, and hurried away from the road.

He shoved his way through the brush, following his ears toward the sound of the fight. The weeds and bushes here were wildly overgrown and taller than him, obscuring his vision, so when he nearly stepped into the empty air above a sharply angled embankment—which would have ended with him impaled by the jagged rocks below—it came as a complete surprise. He teetered on the edge for a breathless moment before he managed to throw himself backwards to safety. He blew out a shaky breath. That was what he got for rushing headlong into danger without watching where he was going, he supposed.

He jumped to his feet and scanned the riverbank below him for the source of the screams. There—a girl, standing between two young dragons, both of them stalking toward her with no trace of humanity in their movements. The scene held him enthralled for a split second: the reeds rippling all around them, the sunlight shimmering in tiny iridescent rainbows off the dragons' wet scales, the tangle of the girl's dark braid tumbling down her back. The way she stood with her back straight as a soldier's and her hands clenched at her sides as she faced her death.

He tore himself away from his trance and glanced down, quickly judging the distance between him and them. They were too far, the cliff between them too steep. By the time he found a path down, she would long since have been eaten. His pulse jumped a few notches. This couldn't happen, not in his city, not right in front of him. He cupped his free hand around his mouth. "Hey!" he bellowed as loudly as he could, channeling the captains he always saw shouting at new recruits in the palace's training yard. His anger and fear lent his voice more power. "HEY!"

None of them looked up. He was too far away, and the wind too loud, and they were all too focused on each other. The girl would die right there before his very eyes while he stood helpless. The scene blinked through his mind: the white of broken bone, the red blood smeared against scales, the shame and horror in the dragons' eyes when they returned to their human forms and realized what they'd done. The terror the girl would feel as she was attacked as the claws and teeth broke her apart.

"WAKE UP! STOP IT!" he shouted at the dragons, dropping his sword now to cup both hands around his mouth, but they ignored him. A savage laugh tore out of him—he'd been ignored his whole life, so why would he expect this to be any different? He was as helpless here as he was in his own court, as irrelevant to them as he was to his own family, as powerless to change this girl's fate as he was to change his kingdom's.

A white, blinding fury swept him up. He *was not* irrelevant, *would not* be helpless, and *refused* to stand by and just watch this happen. The emotions fizzed through his blood, rising, raging, and tightening to a point so sharp that it was almost painful. *Yes,* he thought exultantly, grabbing onto the feeling with both hands. He could use this. He could transform, right now, for the first time ever. As a dragon, he could fly over the river in seconds, stopping the murder that was about to happen. He could save the girl. He could quell the dragons, victims to their own unthinking instinct. *Come on*, he thought, urging on the change.

But the fury, as quickly as it had risen up, began to fade. "No!" he shouted aloud, the word torn from him. He'd failed to change yet again. And, this time, the consequences would be unbearable.

He looked up. The Aqua was nearly upon the girl now, stalking forward with panther-soft and oddly graceful steps, his slit-eyed gaze wholly inhuman. But still the girl stood there, refusing to budge, refusing to look away. Her courage emanated from her like gravity as if she were a star and the dragons merely bits of debris that happened to be in orbit around her.

And suddenly, like magic, the sight of her bravery slotted into place inside of him like a missing puzzle piece, and he transformed.

The change was instant. One moment, he was human, standing on the far bank, helpless, impotent—and the next he had scales, teeth sharp as daggers, and wings... glorious, massive wings like sails, which he snapped wide as soon as he thought of them. They caught the wind and, running on instinct, he swept them downward and lifted into the air. The wind was magnificent. The sun, dazzling. The sky—oh, the *sky*. It stretched on forever, blue and brilliant, and he wanted to launch himself into it and fly until he faded to nothing, just a speck against its vastness.

Snarls tore through the air. His gaze jerked down from the sky to land on the scene below him. With a jolt, he came back to himself and dove.

He caught sight of a strange lump in the shallows of the river and wheeled above it for a moment to assess. It was a cow carcass, probably what had started the dragons fighting in the first place. He swooped down—oh, how amazing flying felt, he wanted to do it forever—speared it with the claws on his front feet and lifted it into the air without a struggle. He was so strong in this form, his sinuous muscles barely strained to carry his burden.

He circled above the fight, opened his mouth, and roared. The sound flattened the reeds in a massive circle beneath him. The girl ducked, covering her head, but the two dragons looked up. He waggled the carcass at them and they, easily distracted like the younglings they were, took the bait.

Both of them launched themselves off the ground, snarling as they tore after him. He flapped his wings twice, easily staying ahead of them. When they started to get discouraged, he slowed, tossing the carcass from foot to foot to taunt them. They growled and caught up. Once they were far enough into the forest to no longer be a threat to the girl, he dropped the cow and they spun down to fight over it where it landed.

He looked up at the sky. His blood sang as he rose higher into it, but he cut off the urge to fly further and instead raced back toward the river to make sure the girl was alright. She was still in the same spot, standing again and staring wordlessly at him as he landed—rather less gracefully than he'd have preferred, but in his defense, he'd had absolutely no practice. He skidded to a stop, folded his wings in, and, after a moment's hesitation —none of his diplomatic training had taught him the proper greeting for this situation—said, "*Uh, hi.*"

The girl gasped and stumbled backwards, clapping her hands over her ears. Too late, he remembered that in dragon form he could only communicate telepathically, which she must not have ever experienced before judging from her shocked reaction. He guessed that she'd not been around many dragons—and the ones she'd just met, possibly the first ones she'd *ever* met, had nearly eaten her. He couldn't blame her for being scared of him as well.

Only one thing for it, then. After one last regretful look at the sky, he bowed his head, closed his eyes, and shifted back into human form.

He opened his eyes. The girl was gaping at him. He looked down and realized why: he was completely, horrifyingly nude.

"Um. Hi," he tried again. "I'm Prince Lasaro. I don't suppose you have any extra clothes?"

The girl was skilled at building a fire, which was fortunate indeed, because Lasaro was certain he would otherwise have frozen to death. Or perhaps died of shock or hunger. She'd already fished for him, landing the four trout that were now cooking on a makeshift spit over the fire. He'd been eyeing them for the last ten minutes, weighing the embarrassment of pouncing on them and eating them raw against the threat of imminent death from starvation. His brother and sisters had mentioned that their first transformations had had enormous energy requirements, but experiencing the drain was something entirely different from hearing about it. He'd been shivering ever since he'd returned to this form, too, even though he was wrapped in a blanket the girl had produced, and he desperately hoped those other two dragons didn't return—because the most he'd be able to contribute to any fight right now would be to fall flat on his face and hope that move served as a distraction.

The girl rose from her spot across the fire to check the trout. After a moment's hesitation—she hadn't met his eyes since he'd appeared in front of her naked and announced he was the prince—she glanced up. "Are you well?" she asked carefully, and then as an afterthought, tacked on, "Sire? Or... my liege? Your majesty?"

The formalities sounded awkward and clunky, and the half-baffled, half-defensive look on her face was kind of adorable. The corners of his mouth curved slightly upward, offering all the smile he had energy for. "Just Lasaro is fine. You have seen me naked after all."

She blushed, a furious red creeping along beneath her olive skin. He watched in fascination. So incredibly brave when facing down two dragons that could swallow her whole and yet rendered speechless by the sight of a single naked prince. She was a puzzle, an anomaly. He liked her already.

His smile fell and he looked away. He shouldn't be bantering with her. He shouldn't have told her to call him by his name, either. He was trying to be a king, and when he earned that title, he would have subjects, not friends. And before that, he'd need to stay focused on earning his mother's approval. Being too friendly with this girl could only end up hurting the both of them, and she didn't deserve that. And of course, there could be nothing beyond friendship for them in any case. Dragons—as he irrefutably was now—were forbidden to be in romantic relationships with anyone who wasn't also a dragon. And, judging by today, this girl was clearly no dragon.

"I'm fine," he said curtly, answering her question. He'd meant to leave it at that, but the look on her face—surprised and a little bit hurt by his sudden rudeness—forced him to elaborate a bit more gently. "It takes a lot of energy to shift into a dragon. I'm... very drained."

There was a long silence. She cleared her throat. "You know, I saw you for the first time earlier this morning," she said, turning the spit with jerky movements. "On a coin."

Despite himself, he asked, "Was I handsome?"

She snorted. "You weren't a dragon, that's for sure."

"I notice you didn't answer the question."

She blushed harder, pulled the spit off the fire, and tossed it at him. He caught it right before it would've speared into his chest, and he tossed it from hand to hand, grinning now. Then the smell of cooked fish struck him and all thoughts of banter went straight out of his head as he yanked all four of the trout off and began devouring them one after another, barely thinking enough to eat around the bones.

She sat back down on her side of the fire and watched, apparently half wary and half amused. "Thank you," she said after a moment. "For saving me from those dragons."

He swallowed and wiped his mouth, still too starved to be embarrassed by his bad manners in taking all the fish. And also stuffing them in his face as fast as he could manage. His tutor would have been nothing less than dismayed. Although, from what he could tell, this girl wasn't nobility, so she hopefully wasn't as horrified as some of the members of his court would've been. From the looks of her, she probably understood hunger pretty well herself, too. She had a slight build, and the broad shoulders and lean, ropy muscles that spoke of a lifetime of hard work.

"I apologize on their behalf," he replied. "They'll be horrified when they come back to themselves and realize what they almost did."

"So, dragons *aren't* allowed to eat people?"

He stopped and stared at her, a piece of the second-to-last trout halfway to his mouth. "What? No, of course not. I mean, it's happened before, unfortunately, but the punishment for doing it is pretty steep. Those two younglings better get a stronger hold of their instincts if they want to avoid being marked as rogue dragons by my mother."

She sat forward, interested. "I've heard of those before, but I didn't realize the queen was the one who marked dragons as rogues, or that it was an official punishment."

"It's not necessarily a popular one," he admitted. "Being marked as a rogue usually means you're fully animalistic, fair game for any dragon hunter. It's basically a death sentence. Many dragons —full dragons, I mean, the handful of them that are left—ignore the label, and kill any dragon hunter they find on sight."

"What makes dragons go rogue, exactly?"

He gulped down another piece of fish before he answered. "It varies. Most of the time, you're more likely to go rogue if you don't have a tamer which is why the Akademy was first established. But there are plenty of dragon-bloods who do okay without one, like my brother Freyr. Really, it depends—it just happens when you give in to your instincts too much, becoming more animal than person."

With a sick jolt, he remembered the way he'd felt when he'd looked at the sky, the way his instinct had taken over. What if he'd been overtaken by those instincts the same way the younglings had? What if he'd gotten drawn into the fight and ended up attacking the girl, too? He'd loved being a dragon, but from now on, he needed to be more careful. More focused.

He didn't ever want to find out if his mother might be willing to mark her own son as a rogue.

Suddenly no longer hungry, he tossed the last fish over the fire to the girl. "You still haven't told me your name," he said against his better judgment. He didn't need to know her name. He needed to be gracious and distant and send her on her way as soon as possible. He had somewhere else to be, important things to do, and he couldn't afford to be distracted by a girl, even a girl as fascinating as her. But still, he waited for her reply.

"Kaelan Younger," she answered, peeling apart the fish and popping a bite in her mouth with as little manners as he'd had. "I'm on my way to the Akademy to be a tamer."

He jolted upright. "No! Really?" He hadn't expected that answer at all, but of course—it made perfect sense. Hadn't he been looking at her, *connecting* with her, right before he'd transformed for the first time? This was why. She was supposed to be a tamer.

She could be *his* tamer, for that matter.

He refocused on her and realized she was glaring at him. Momentarily confused, he traced back over the conversation in his mind, but couldn't figure out why she would be angry. "What?" he asked, puzzled.

"I may be a peasant," she bit out, "but I still have as much right to attend the Akademy as any hoity-toity dragon-blooded noble."

He blinked. "Oh! No! That wasn't what I—wait, did you just say *hoity-toity?*"

Her lips twitched and she blushed again. "You are getting off topic," she informed him frostily. "Let's go back to the part where you were apologizing for calling me a dirty peasant."

He pressed his lips together to avoid smiling. "I did *not* call you a dirty peasant."

"You were thinking it."

"Oh, so your powers include mind reading now?"

She looked down her nose at him and stuffed another bit of fish in her mouth, not deigning to answer. She was adorable when she was in a huff—not that he was about to tell her that —and smart, and funny, and brave as Thor himself. Oh, gods help him, he might be in love with this girl.

He was in so much trouble.

Well, he might as well dig the hole a little deeper. "Be my tamer," he said impulsively.

Kaelan froze. "What?" she asked through a mouthful of fish.

"Be my tamer," he repeated. "I've tried to change hundreds of times, and I've never been successful until now. You're the difference. *You* are what made this change successful. I was able to transform because I... I don't know, connected with you somehow while you were down there. It was like you were the center of the world, the only thing in the universe. Like you were calling to me and I couldn't ignore it. So, I changed. Because of you."

She blinked at him. "You... I can't..." She shook herself, clearly caught off guard, and then looked to the south—to the mountains, or more likely to something beyond them. Her mind seemed far away for a moment, and then she looked back at him. "Are you even allowed to pick your own tamer? I assumed the Akademy was supposed to pair us up, you know, after we finished training."

"Technically, yes, they are supposed to pair up trainee dragons and tamers in probationary bonds during the first few months of classes, but they'll have to see we're right for each other. And even if they don't, I'm the prince. I'll *make* them see. You can help me transform again; help me control my powers, I know it." Hearing himself, he realized how one-sided his offer sounded and scrambled to sweeten it. "And I'll help you, too. Whatever you want. Name it, and once our probationary bond is approved by the masters, I'll do it." That sounded like a bit *too* much, though. He was supposed to be her future king even if he was also going to be her dragon. If he gave her too much leeway, she might take advantage of him, or take him for granted the way he'd been taken for granted his whole life. He needed to start thinking like a king, especially in cases like this when he didn't really want to. He needed to put distance between them. "If you'll swear loyalty to me," he tacked on.

She regarded him for a long moment, and he held his breath. He needed this and needed *her*. She couldn't know how much power she held over him, though. The silence stretched out and he started to panic. What else could he say to make her agree?

"I did save your life," he reminded her. "Doesn't tradition say you owe me a debt now?" He winced as he said it—it was so low, demanding a favor in return for something that common decency would've made him do no matter what… but he was desperate. And if they were going to do this, they needed clear boundaries. Prince and pledged, dragon and tamer. Not friend and friend, much as he might wish otherwise.

She narrowed her eyes and stood. Uncertain, he did the same.

"I am your subject and loyal to you already," she said stiffly, "as is everyone in Alveria. But it just so happens that I *would* like to be your tamer, and that I *am* an honorable person, and far be it from me to deny tradition. So, Prince Lasaro, youngest son of Alveria, in exchange for saving my life, I give you my solemn oath of loyalty, and pledge to serve you—" Here she held up a hand, "—but only if you don't ask me to do anything immoral or weird, in which case I reserve the right to refuse. And, at my discretion, to yell at you until you see sense and retract your order. Also, don't order me around. And, also, I still get that favor once we're officially paired."

He laughed out loud. "You, Kaelan Younger, are delightful," he proclaimed. The official sealing of a pledge would require her to bow and kiss his royal ring, but his royal ring had fallen off when he'd transformed and still hadn't been retrieved. Plus, he suddenly had no desire to see her bow to him. Instead, he held out his hand for a handshake. The blanket, which he'd momentarily forgotten about, fluttered loose around his knees for a second before he snatched it back closed with his free hand. Probably, most royals were better clothed when they received their subjects' oaths, but it wasn't like she hadn't already seen him naked, he thought with resignation.

Smothering a smirk behind one hand, Kaelan extended her other to shake his.

And just like that, Prince Lasaro of Alveria had a tamer.

CHAPTER 10

Her arms full of clothing, Kaelan ducked through the brush and headed toward the prince she'd just met. The prince who'd saved her life and who'd become her dragon. The currently very, very naked prince.

She sternly ordered herself not to blush again. She had no idea what had driven her to act the way she had around him. Maybe it had been the shock of almost dying that had driven her to be so disrespectful. That had to be understandable, right?

The brush ended abruptly and she nearly fell face-first down the steep, rocky embankment next to the river. She caught her balance, but almost dropped the entire armload of new clothing she'd found in the saddlebags of the very handsome, if irate, horse that Lasaro had left standing in the middle of the road above. Something clinked below her as it fell down the embankment, metal hitting stone. She swore under her breath. What had she dropped, and how was she supposed to retrieve it if it got hung up halfway down this small cliff? She shifted her load and looked around it, down the embankment. Something tiny and golden gleamed at the bottom: a ring. A sudden suspicion rose in her, that it hadn't fallen from the load she was carrying at all. Ignoring it for now, she kicked through the brush behind her and found the clothing Lasaro had been wearing before he'd shifted. They were useless now, torn to rags. Dragon-bloods must go through an awful big wardrobe if they ruined every outfit they had on when shifting. Or was there some sort of magical clothing the Akademy handed out that stayed intact?

She peered down the embankment again, searching for the path up its shallow side that she'd climbed to get to the road a few minutes before—and then, struck by a sudden realization, she stopped and lifted her head to look out over the river. The clothing, the ring... they meant that this spot was where Lasaro had been standing when he'd seen her. *Connected* with her, according to him. There was the outcropping, and there was the spot where her roar had flattened the reeds. Her mind superimposed the image over her vision: a lone girl surrounded by monsters, too far away to help. How had he felt when he'd thought he couldn't save her? How would *she* have felt, in his position?

She knew what she would've felt: fury, rage, familiar flames licking at her insides. That was the anger that had made her roar twice now, displaying her dragon-blood powers. It must've been something similar that had made Lasaro shift for the first time. How strange, to think that someone—a boy, unlike any other boy she'd ever met—would feel that way upon seeing a girl he'd never met in trouble. It spoke to his character; not that he would try to help her, which in her opinion any decent person should've done, but that his inability to help would've spurred such deep emotion on his part.

Slowly, she picked out the path on the embankment, skidded down it, and retrieved the ring.

"Here you go," she told Lasaro, pushing the clothing and the ring at him when she found him again. He almost let go of his blanket to grab everything, and she turned quickly away. She'd seen semi-naked guys in the past—peasant boys weren't exactly shy—but it had never inspired feelings like this before. She was… *interested*. In the body of the prince who had saved her life and was now her dragon, and to whom she'd sworn her loyalty.

She cursed under her breath again.

"What was that?" Lasaro asked.

"Just… your horse is pretty," she blurted, keeping her eyes on the sky above them as she said the first thing that came to mind.

He laughed quietly. And even his laugh was pretty. Just like the rest of him: blue-gray eyes, pale skin, lean muscles, silver-blond hair that was just a little unrulier than she'd have expected of a prince. A cute, tiny gap between his front teeth. Big ears. And a laugh that felt like warm apple cider on a snowy winter day.

"The stable master keeps a few horses set aside for my own personal use, but Allfather has always been my favorite," Lasaro replied.

Forgetting herself, she turned around with a smirk. "Were you the one who named him *Allfather*?"

Luckily, he was just pulling on his tunic, his trousers already secured around his waist.

"I guess that was a bit arrogant of me, hearing it aloud now," he admitted, his voice muffled by the fabric. "But in my defense, when I named him, I was nine and more than a little obsessed with the old epics of the gods."

With a jolt, she came back to herself, and the smirk fell from her face. He had *a few* personal horses—and a *stable master*—when no one in the entire village of Gladsheim could afford more than one horse, and most peasants couldn't even afford that. He'd been given one of those horses at nine years of age. When *she'd* been nine, she'd had to survive an entire winter on rabbits and dried berries because her family had just moved, and they hadn't built up enough reputation yet to get a steady flow of customers.

She and Lasaro were from completely different worlds. She didn't belong with him, she realized suddenly. She couldn't possibly live up to his expectations, whatever those were.

But what could he expect of her after all? Had he not made her swear fealty? Didn't that mean he saw her as a servant, a particularly useful subject of his? And if those were his expectations, was she sure she wanted to fulfill them?

She looked to the south, to the mountains she'd hiked through over the last week. Somewhere beyond them was her home. Somewhere out there was her mother, lying sick in bed, relying on her to find a dragon to heal her. And Kaelan had found one. She'd had to swear to serve him and be his tamer, which if she wasn't mistaken meant a lifetime commitment, something she hadn't quite had time to process yet—but when they were officially paired, he would grant her a favor, and she would see her mother well again.

"Kaelan? Are you okay?" Lasaro asked from behind her. Gods, she liked the way her name sounded in his mouth.

She shook such thoughts away. "I'm fine," she said curtly, and then thought to amend her statement, holding up her arm. It had a curving line of red indents right above her elbow. "No, actually, I'm not fine. Allfather bit me."

Lasaro made a sympathetic sound, sliding his shoes on now.

"He does that, I'm afraid. If it's any condolence, that usually means he likes you."

"Strangely, I am not condoled," she answered dryly, dropping her arm and wincing at the pain in her muscle.

Lasaro smiled and then glanced up at the sun to check the time. His smile faded at the sight of it, going distant and formal. He'd done that a few times now—gone from being annoyingly charming and witty to acting... well, like she'd *expect* a noble to act. She didn't like it, and she rather wanted to call him on it. But who was she to question a prince?

Then again, this new partnership of theirs wasn't going to last long if she had to constantly wonder what was going on in his head.

"What's wrong?" she demanded. "Why do you keep doing that? Going all stiff and princely."

He blinked in surprise and stood up straight, finished with his shoes. "Princely? I'm always a prince. I fail to see how I could be *un*-princely."

She waved a hand, impatient. "No, I mean, you go all distant and formal. I'm fine with serving you, and I know my place —" He snorted at that. She ignored him. "—but if we're going to be spending a lot of time together, I need to know where we stand."

He hesitated, still a bit distant, and then something shifted in his eyes and he stepped closer. "You're right, I guess. You deserve to know the truth," he answered in a low voice, even though there was nobody nearby. "We're about to be attacked by Unger."

She straightened, alarmed. "What, like right now? Is their army on the move?"

"The attack is not imminent, and outwardly their actions all seem like simple posturing and sword-rattling without any real threat behind them—but we've had intel that shows they're planning a real attack, and soon. We've even found spies in the villages right outside Bellsor. Our country is vulnerable, and... and there are other worries on the horizon, too, beyond the immediate threat." He looked away. "One of which is the fact that my mother has ruled long and well, but she's growing old and needs to name an heir."

Kaelan nodded. That much, she'd known.

"I want it to be me," Lasaro declared, and his stance was rigid, like he expected her to laugh in his face.

She frowned. "Oh," she said. The puzzle pieces that made up the boy who was Lasaro shifted a bit in her mind: he was ambitious. But other people likely didn't believe he'd be able to fulfill that ambition, judging from his automatic defensiveness. "You want to be the next king, but your mother and the nobles aren't convinced it should be you," she said slowly.

From the set of his shoulders after she said it, she knew she was right.

He swept a hand at Mount Firewyrm. "This is how I'm supposed to prove myself. I have to publicly show that I'd be a strong leader, a *traditional* leader." He made a face. Apparently, he wasn't a big believer in tradition. "To do that, I have to show that I can shift into my dragon form and harness and control my powers. If I can do those things well enough to be officially paired with a tamer—you, by the end of the term—I'll be named heir. But, if not, then my mother will have no choice but to name one of my siblings."

"Who aren't the best fit for being our future leader?" Kaelan hazarded, raising an eyebrow. She didn't know enough about the royal children to judge whether or not that was actually true or if any of his siblings might have said the same thing.

A rueful smile from Lasaro showed he knew what she was thinking. "I love my brother and sisters—well, most of the time —but every one of them would bring disaster on Alveria in one way or another. And if Mother delays naming an heir any longer, Unger would see it as weakness and use it as an opening to attack. If I'm to save Alveria, I have to do well at the Akademy." He looked down, rolling something around in his hands: the ring Kaelan had saved. "But to do well at the Akademy, to control my powers, I'll need help. And I'll likely need help there for other things, as well—things I can't trust the other students for."

"Like laundering your shirts? Because I'm *not* doing that."

The ghost of a smile crossed his face. "What, laundry falls into the category of 'immoral or weird'?"

"Yes," she said firmly.

"No worries. I can wash my own shirts. I may have asked you to swear fealty to me, but I don't intend to treat you like a servant. No, what I could really use is…"

A friend, Kaelan willed silently. *Say you could use a friend.*

"An ally," he finished, and she swallowed the disappointment she shouldn't be feeling. An ally was basically the same thing as a friend, anyway. Only more formal. And professional. And distant.

Before he could sense her emotion, she deflected. "And you can't trust the other noble students to be that for you?"

His mouth twisted. "No," he said shortly.

She frowned, taken aback. "You don't anticipate having any friends among the Akademy students?"

"I know better than anyone that the nobles, by and large, only seek friendship where it is of benefit to them. I've never in my life had a single 'friend' who would still be my friend if I weren't a prince. Nor even any reliable allies, either."

"Well. That's depressing."

His quick laugh rewarded her, and a cozy feeling that she should also not be feeling shot through her chest. "It is, I suppose," he admitted.

Kaelan thought through what he'd told her. Today had been a lot to take in, and it would be a while till she could sort through all of the new information, feelings, and experiences, but it sounded like she might've just tied her fate to that of the future King of Alveria. Which was... good? Strange? Risky? All three, likely.

"Can I ask you a question?" he asked suddenly, pulling her from her thoughts.

She spread her hands. "You can ask; I might answer."

He raised an eyebrow, but something was obviously heavy on his mind, because he didn't smile at her boldness like he'd been doing. "What color was I?" he asked.

She tilted her head. "What?"

He cleared his throat, looking away. "It all happened so fast, and I was so focused on the fight and on flying, I didn't even think to look at myself in my dragon form. And this was my first time changing. And I'm not sure how long it'll be before I can control it enough to change again. I just... wondered what I was like."

"Terrifying," she answered without thought, but when his face fell, she winced and dug quickly back into her memory to the moment when he'd landed in front of her. He'd been terrifying, yes, but mainly because she hadn't been sure at the time if he was going to eat her or save her. But even then, he'd been beautiful. Larger than the other two dragons and silver-gray, like the autumn mist in the mountains of her home. His scales had had an almost pearlescent shimmer. His eyes had been just the same in dragon form as they were in his human form, except, of course, in that his pupils had been slits when he'd been a dragon. She relayed the description and he listened, his face softening with something like wonder.

"So, I'm an Ariel, then," he said at last. It was the rarest form of dragon, Kaelan remembered—the ones who were colored pale or gray, and able to control the air when their powers were developed. "Thank you, Kaelan."

"Sure," she said awkwardly. She was torn between wanting to see him as a dragon again—he really had been magnificent—and worrying that she'd still be scared of dragon-Lasaro. A lifetime of being simultaneously afraid of and thrilled by dragons was hard to get over quickly.

Lasaro slipped his ring back on his finger and flexed his hand. The softness fell away from his features and he lifted his eyes back toward the Akademy. "We should be going if we want to make it before nightfall," he said abruptly, and with that he started toward the road where Allfather waited.

She sighed. A few moments ago, she'd asked where she stood with him, and he'd told her a long story that had ended with him asking her to be his ally, and yet it appeared that she was still stuck with a prince who was constantly going to run hot and cold. "Yes, my liege," she muttered, picking up the blanket he'd dropped and hurrying to catch up to her new dragon, who was also a prince, and who she wished also wanted to be her friend.

Because, where they were headed, she was going to need one.

CHAPTER 11

"Holy Hel," Kaelan breathed out two hours later when they finally stood before the entrance of the Akademy.

"That's one way to put it," Lasaro murmured.

"It's an *accurate* way to put it."

Lasaro smiled faintly, but his expression lacked the awe that she could feel trembling just under her own skin. This place was the most intimidating, incredible, terrifyingly *massive* thing she'd ever seen in her life, and she took her time marveling at it. The front doors were large enough for an entire herd of horses to enter by—or, she supposed, large enough for a dragon. The entire place was built to be big enough for dragons, in fact. The huge slab of a drawbridge, the tiled courtyard, the wide towers that jutted out of the mountainside. Even the stones the Akademy was made from were gigantic, bigger than any wagon could carry. They could only have been lifted up Mount Firewyrm with the help of a Terra. Or maybe the whole place had been carved out of the mountainside with magic.

It had to have been magic, she decided. The whole place tingled with it, raising the fine hairs on her arms, gliding through the air like the smell of ozone before a storm. It was tantalizing. Thrilling. Fearsome. The same addictive mixture she'd been feeling her whole life, now concentrated and boiled down to its essence.

And she was going to *live* here.

The massive doors creaked open far enough to let two men and a woman through into the courtyard where Kaelan and Lasaro stood. The woman and one of the men wore robes so white that they hurt Kaelan's eyes, and the other man wore what looked to be a guard's uniform.

"Welcome!" boomed the robed man. His white robes were trimmed with red the color of hot coals around the collar and sleeves, and he had a yellow belt that seemed to shimmer like candlelight. "Prince Lasaro, we've been—" He cut himself off a few steps away from them, staring down at Kaelan. With his portly stature, huge beard, and twinkling eyes, he looked downright friendly—or at least, he had until he'd spotted her. "Who are you?" he asked abruptly.

She fought against the instinct to snap back at him, her tension heightening her normally sharp temper further. She'd known she'd get this sort of reception and she'd planned for it. She *belonged* here, as much as anyone, but it wouldn't do any good to anger someone who seemed to be a master on her first day.

She set her bag down and dug through it, pulling the envelope her mother had given her from the bottom of the pack. Her heart thumped as she handed it to the man. She never had gotten the nerve up to read it; she'd have to trust her mother. And, she supposed, trust Mordon, who had originally written the letter. Her stomach clenched at the thought.

"I'm Kaelan Younger," she said. "I've come to be a tamer."

The man snatched the parchment from her hand, his eyes narrowed. "Not likely," he muttered, tearing the envelope open.

Lasaro stepped forward. "She's qualified. I'll vouch for that," he said firmly.

Kaelan's lips tightened with her warring emotions. On the one hand, she couldn't help feeling a little thrill at the fact that the prince had stood up for her; on the other hand, he shouldn't have *had* to stand up for her. The master, or whoever he was, shouldn't have been so immediately prejudiced against her just because she was a peasant. If Lasaro became king and their bond stuck, she hoped she could influence him to do away with the sharp divide between nobles and peasants that was currently dealing his country so much internal damage.

She shook herself away from the thought as the man before her read Mordon's letter. She was thinking too far into the future, taking too many things for granted. Lasaro might or might not become king, and even if he did, she might not have any influence over him in any case. They weren't *friends* after all.

The man finished reading the single piece of parchment, then raised his eyes to Kaelan. Her heart thumped hard again— she'd almost managed to forget her fears about whether her father's identity might do her more harm than good here—but the man just shook his head. "This doesn't say who your father is, only that he's a dragon." His tone was accusatory, but Kaelan went limp with relief. Surely, they'd need to know who her father was at some point, but at least that point wasn't right this very second.

The woman pursed her lips. She was tall and whip-thin, with a jutting jaw and a severe sort of beauty. Her robes were trimmed in shades of sapphire. "Does it provide any proof of her dragon blood?"

Reluctantly, the man handed her the paper. "It provides knowledge that only a full dragon would have, which I suppose supports her claim," he said. Which made Kaelan wonder if she might actually be face to face with a full dragon at this very moment.

The woman nodded. "Then she stays."

"But there's no name for the father. We need to question her, determine who he was. It's highly irregular—" the man started to protest, but the woman held up a hand.

"She probably doesn't even know who her father is, anyway. Few of the other peasant trainees we've accepted in the past have, and there's nothing in the school's charter that demands the parents' names. Noble or not, she stays."

The man huffed and turned sharply, waving at Lasaro. "Fine. Come with me, your majesty, and I'll get you settled. My assistant here will return your horse to the palace."

Kaelan froze, staring at Lasaro. She hadn't thought they'd be separated so quickly, but of course they would be. He was going to train as a dragon, and she as a tamer; plus, the male and female students must be housed separately. But he was the only person she knew here, and he was her best shot at healing her ma—she couldn't let him go.

She reached out and snagged his sleeve. "Lasaro," she said, hating how desperate her voice sounded.

He covered her hand with his own. His fingers were slender, warm, reassuring. She calmed a bit. "Don't worry," he said quietly, "I'll find you later. Remember what we talked about."

He didn't trust the other students. He needed her. She was his ally. She repeated the words in her mind, trying to steady her belief in them.

"Right," she said.

He took his hand away, leaving behind a sudden absence of warmth that made her fingers ache. Then he gave Allfather's reins to the assistant, unhitched his saddlebags, and threw them over his shoulder as he followed the portly teacher into the Akademy.

Kaelan was left alone with the woman, who peered down her hawk-like nose at her. "Miss Younger," she said at last. "I am Master Olga. I and Master Lars, who you just had the misfortune to meet, run the Akademy along with the rest of the Council of Masters." Her expression remained severe, but her words had a faint undercurrent of humor. Kaelan warily decided she might like the woman. Or... lady dragon? She wasn't sure of the terminology.

Best to go with a safe reply then. "You and Master Lars are so gracious to allow me into your school. It's beautiful," she said, trying to sound humble and grateful.

Master Olga raised an eyebrow. Kaelan's humility and gratitude had always been about on par with her charm, which was to say the traits were basically nonexistent.

Kaelan decided to come clean. "That is to say, I think your school is slightly terrifying, and Master Lars is about as gracious as the south end of a northbound mule, but I want

—*need*—to become a tamer, and I appreciate you giving me the chance to do that." She held her breath.

Master Olga's eyebrow lowered and she nodded. She didn't smile, but her face looked like it might be thinking about the possibility of smiling, someday. "Better," she declared. "Always be honest with me, Pupil Younger."

She turned and strode into the Akademy, disappearing through the relatively tiny crack in the massive front doors. After a brief hesitation, Kaelan took a deep breath and followed, feeling like she was walking into the jaws of a monster.

Ten minutes later, Kaelan was left alone in the Great Hall.

The room was, of course, massive. Long stone benches and tables were shoved up against the walls and piled on top of each other although she guessed they would be pulled to the middle of the room for eating. There were also balconies everywhere, and long beams crisscrossing over her head at various heights—perches for dragons, maybe?—all the way up to the ceiling which was so distant she could barely make it out. Instead of windows, the room had fireplaces, six of them, each big enough to roast a cow whole. Huge, open arches led out to hallways at her left and right, and smaller arches ringed the room. She counted them to distract herself while she waited for Master Olga to return with her room assignment.

She finished counting. Master Olga still hadn't returned, so Kaelan resorted to pacing behind the dais at the far end of the room. She'd made three circuits when the wall behind her finally caught her eye.

It was carved with what looked like words. She ventured closer to read them. *Valencia. Gala. Elin. Ingmar...*

Ingmar. That rang a bell. She dug through her pack and pulled out the tattered red book, flipping to the middle. There! Ingmar had been a dragon, one of the founders of Alveria. And there was Valencia as well—she'd been his daughter.

She kept her thumb in the book to mark her spot and looked back up at the wall. Were these all dragons' names, then? Curious, she followed the wall further down, reaching out a hand to trace the carved stone. It felt strangely warm to her touch, almost alive. Friendly, even.

Until she got to Mordon's name.

She snatched her hand away, and then, slowly, grazed just her fingertips across the jagged surface of his name. It was jagged because it had been slashed through, crossed out with much more crude and savage lines than the graceful marks that had carved out the letters. And the stone beneath it felt cold— unfriendly and deadened.

She pulled her fingers back. A chill snaked down her spine. Her father's name was scratched out from the wall of the Great Hall of the Akademy. Because he was a rogue? Or because of whatever he'd done that had resulted in him being named a rogue?

And, more importantly—if the dragons here thought so poorly of Mordon that they'd cross out his name like this, would the masters let her stay if they found out he was her father?

"I see you've found the Wall of Names." The hurricane of a voice tore through her head, and she dropped her book to cover her ears as she wheeled around. There was a dragon behind her. A colossal Ember, all red and glittering yellow, looming above her like a storm about to break.

A droll, slightly irritated female voice cut in over the voice that had echoed through her mind, this one speaking aloud. "It was rather uncreatively named, but alas, pedantry is the curse of so many of my kind." Master Olga stepped out from behind the dragon.

Kaelan glanced back up at the dragon, and then at Olga, who had that one eyebrow raised again like this was a test and she hoped Kaelan would pass. Kaelan narrowed her eyes and examined the dragon more closely. It held its head high, with an arrogant tilt. It stood squarely as if it were trying to make itself look larger, and the way it had snuck up behind her and the way it held itself now said the creature had intended to shock her, to make her feel small and threatened. And its size —about half again as big as dragon-Lasaro—meant it was older. A master, perhaps.

Kaelan dropped her hands and, by some miracle, kept her simmering dislike out of her voice. "Master Lars," she identified the dragon.

Master Lars made no reply, but his tail twitched in irritation, which she took as confirmation. And, probably, disappointment that her fright hadn't lasted longer.

"We'll take you to your room," Master Olga said, and without another word, both of them moved off toward one of the bigger hallways. Kaelan hurried along behind them, trying to keep close enough to hear Olga's instructions but also far enough to stay out of range of Lars' tail. He was a strange color, different from Lasaro and the other two dragons—his scales seemed red and yellow at a glance, like a typical Ember's, but as he moved, they seemed to shimmer. She caught a gleam of blue, a sheen of brown, and a hint of gray. Her book said that the older, more powerful dragons sometimes took on new colors like that when they mastered more than one element. So, apparently, Lars' 'master' title was literal.

"Is everything always so big here?" Kaelan ventured as they walked. Her voice echoed off the walls.

"Everywhere except the cloisters," Master Olga replied crisply over her shoulder. "That's where the humans live." She waved a hand at a sconce as they passed—it was made of silver edged in gold. "A tip for how to find that area if you're ever lost: as you get closer to the human areas of the Akademy, the metal turns to copper and brass. Where the Akademy is dedicated to dragons, everything metal is gold and silver."

So, the myths about dragons liking valuable metals were true. Kaelan absorbed the information hungrily, her eagerness for knowledge slowly reasserting itself. After all, hadn't she always yearned to attend a real school, to learn new things? Here was her chance. Yes, this place felt completely alien, and she'd already gained a potential enemy in Master Lars, but at least she could finally be a student.

"So... how exactly does the school work?" she hazarded. "How long does training here last?"

Master Olga glanced back. "Once the council officially accepts you as a student, you'll be named a trainee. You'll attend tamer classes where your skills will be assessed, sharpened, and tested. You'll pair with a dragon in a tentative probationary bond, and once that bond is judged strong enough to be officially approved, you'll move up to the next level of classes and become an initiate. The two of you will then train together in battle maneuvering, magic manipulation —if you have any control of an element, but most tamers don't —and other areas until the Council of Masters believes you and your dragon are fully trained. Then you become a graduate at which point your bond becomes permanent."

They turned down another hallway, and then another, each smaller than the last until Lars finally had to shift back into a human. His clothing, a sleek black suit that looked almost like leather, transformed with him so that he wasn't naked as a human—a fact for which Kaelan was unendingly grateful. Apparently, her guess about the Akademy having special clothes that could survive transformation had been correct.

They stopped at a hall of regular, human-sized doors, and the relief of seeing entries that weren't tall enough to admit a dragon nearly knocked Kaelan over. She could feel safe in a place like this. The stone had an almost living warmth again, and the copper sconces looked worn and beaten like something she might have seen at home. She knew that, technically, this place was just as open to dragons as the rest of the Akademy, as the presence of Master Lars proved, but at least they'd have to take human form. Not that that made them any less dangerous, of course.

She flashed back to the river, to the dragons before and behind her, to the slitted eyes of a predator as it stalked her. Shuddering, she forced herself to the present. Dragons weren't allowed to eat humans, she reminded herself. Then, belatedly, she wondered if the dragons who'd attacked her were students here. Would she meet them? Would they remember her? She hoped not.

Master Olga swung open the door to her room, breaking Kaelan out of her thoughts as she peered apprehensively into her new home. It was small but cozy, with a stone-lined window that peered into a courtyard and rustic, simple furnishings that put her at ease.

Only one problem. There were two beds.

She wheeled around to Master Olga. "I have a roommate?" she asked, trying not to sound as panicked as she felt.

"You'll be assigned one soon," the woman answered.

Great. There was exactly zero chance she'd be paired with Lasaro, and everyone else would almost certainly be a noble who would automatically either disdain or pity her. Kaelan had been prepared to face the other students during classes and meal times, but realizing she'd *never* have a moment free of them was a blow she'd been unprepared for.

"I'll be going now, but Master Lars will show you the kitchens," Olga said, and then she whooshed off down the hallway without another word, her white robes flaring majestically around her.

"Kitchens?" Kaelan asked Lars when they were alone. She was starving, it was true, but there'd been a strange undertone in Olga's words, as if there was some other reason she'd be shown the kitchens. By this point, she was pretty sure they didn't mean to cook and eat her, but a little reasonable suspicion never hurt.

"First, there is the matter of your... knife," Lars said, his mouth twisting around the last word, like he'd eaten something bitter. He held out his hand.

She hesitated. She had no idea how to use the knife that her mysterious traveling companion had given her, but it had afforded her a sense of safety. Unfortunately, it looked like she had no choice but to give it up. Reluctant as she was, she nevertheless pulled it out of her belt and handed it over.

Master Lars held it with two fingers, far away from his body, as if it were a dead mouse. "Iron is *never* used at the Akademy," he said, motioning with his free hand at the blade. "Dragons dislike it. If you're caught with any more of it, you'll be punished." Then he turned on his heel and marched down the hall, apparently expecting her to follow.

She tried to memorize the turns they took, but the school was like a maze. There were few students—they were probably all in classes at the moment—but members of the staff bustled everywhere. She was so distracted with watching them all that she didn't realize they had found the library until her surroundings suddenly went quiet.

She looked up. A massive, dimly lit labyrinth of bookshelves stretched out before her. The shelves were mismatched—some towering precariously high while others that looked more suited for children were scattered in the middle of aisles at random. Bright alcoves were tucked against the walls every so often, the windows above them allowing sunshine to warm the comfy-looking chairs beneath. The room went back so deep that Kaelan couldn't even see the far wall, only the endless books. She squinted to make out the handwritten signs on the ends of the shelves nearest her: history, magic, architecture, military strategy, dragons, geography, ancient lore…

She now lived down the hall from a wealth of knowledge. And, even better, she could easily get lost in here—she could find a quiet alcove, curl up with a book, and get a bit of time to be herself away from the other students. Tears pricked at her eyes, the relief of it near to overwhelming, and she blinked them back before Lars could see. Instinct told her not to show any vulnerability in front of him.

He led her along the front wall, past several archways that opened into other areas of the library—she tried to peer in to see what they held, but didn't dare lag enough to allow Lars to see her interest—and several huge aisles that housed dragon-sized tomes, each of them bigger than she was. Some were crisscrossed with silver or gold chains, locked to the shelves. As they neared the west wall, she spotted a lone student at a table with his head bent over a blank book, staring intently at it like he was reading.

Lars noticed her curiosity. "Some of the books here are locked by spells," he said shortly. "The pages look blank until the right words are spoken, or until the right type of blood is spilled on the cover."

She swallowed. "How… archaic."

He smiled faintly at that. The expression looked predatory.

He led her out into what looked like a main hallway, and the reverently mysterious atmosphere of the library faded behind her. She brushed a hand against the archway as she left, promising herself she'd return soon.

Lars rounded two corners, marched down another long hallway, and stopped in front of a wide entry. "Ragnhild!" he called. "I've got your new lackey."

Kaelan took a step back before she could stop herself, and Lars smiled unpleasantly. She shut her expression down before it could reveal more of what she was feeling, but on the inside, she seethed. *Lackey?* So they meant to make her a kitchen aide, to circumvent the requirement that all dragon-bloods be allowed to attend the Akademy with a technicality. She would live here, all right. Just not as a student.

No. She *had* to be a tamer. Had to be Lasaro's tamer. He'd promised her a favor, and she'd promised Haldis she'd bring back a dragon to heal her mother. Master Olga had called her a *pupil* earlier, right? That had to mean there was still hope, that they didn't intend to stick her in the kitchens and forget about her. Panic churned in her veins as she frantically tried to figure out what she could do to convince them to allow her to attend tamer classes.

A woman with frizzy red hair popped out of the kitchens. "What?" she demanded.

Lars motioned at Kaelan. "You've a new helper."

"I'm a *student*," Kaelan said woodenly. Maybe if she told

them her father was the great Mordon, one of the most powerful dragons to ever teach there, they'd stop this nonsense. Or perhaps they'd cast her out right away, judging from the anger that had evidently gone into scarring his name on the wall. No, she couldn't chance it.

Both of them ignored her. The woman, Ragnhild, gave her a doubtful glance. "She doesn't look like she'd be of any use."

"She doesn't, does she?" Lars asked speculatively, with a pleased undertone that instantly got Kaelan's hackles up in warning.

She stiffened. If she didn't prove herself useful, Lars would have reason enough to kick her out, and then she wouldn't even have the chance to prove she should attend classes rather than stir stew vats. "I know herbs," she said quickly. "I'm a healer."

Ragnhild's look turned thoughtful. "That could be handy," she admitted. "Okay, I'll take you. Come, I'll show you around." She leaned a little closer and lowered her voice. "And just as a tip, I'd stay away from the other cooks if I were you. Most people who work in here are failed tamers who didn't want to leave."

Great. More nobles who'd resent her on sight.

Lars shrugged, smirked, and turned to go. "Master Lars!" Kaelan called out before he could take more than a step.

He turned back. "Yes?"

She steeled herself, trying to project the easy confidence that her mysterious traveling companion had had. "I look forward to learning from you. In the tamer classes."

He pursed his lips. "We'll see about that." And then he was gone.

Well. That wasn't promising, but it wasn't a complete denial, either. It meant she still had a chance.

She just had to figure out what to do with it.

CHAPTER 12

L asaro leaned over the edge of the parapet, trying to look bored rather than utterly terrified. Which was particularly difficult when one was standing on the edge of a tower and being ordered to either fly as a dragon or fall to your death.

The wind tugged at his uniform—a form-fitting, leather-like suit covered by the black robes of a trainee whose dragon form had not yet been verified by the Akademy—and it swirled the strands of his hair that had come loose. Lasaro craned his neck to look at the handful of students lined up at his side. Maybe if he kept his eyes on them rather than the ground, he could manage this. He was royalty, for crying out loud. If he could suffer through one of his eldest sister's balls, he could pass this class. But he had spent a week at the Akademy already and he—unlike all the other dragon students—hadn't yet managed so much as a single successful transformation. If that trend continued, in a matter of minutes he would be a tiny red splatter on the courtyard below. Far, far below.

"No problem, right, Las?" came a voice from his right. He gritted his teeth at the nickname which he'd neither invited nor liked, and looked up at his roommate. Stav was just like every other *friend* he'd had his entire life: a social climber, far too friendly with Lasaro, and agreeable to the point of annoyance. In fact, not a single one of the noble students here had yet dared to disagree with Lasaro on anything.

Kaelan was the only one who did that.

He sighed at the thought of her. He'd been looking for her every time he'd gotten a spare moment, which hadn't been often with all the training and testing he was required to undergo, but he hadn't been able to find her yet. Apparently, dragons and tamers shared few classes until they'd been officially paired up, and they were housed on opposite ends of the cloister. With every day that passed, as the other students— especially the tamer trainees—kept trying to win his favor, he only wished to see her more. He wanted to talk with her, vent to her, and hear her sarcastic comebacks. She was the only one he could count on in this whole place to be straight with him. She made him stronger, steadier, and he desperately needed that right now.

He could ask one of the other students to track her down for him. They were all trying to curry his favor—why not put that to good use? But he feared that making his relationship with her known before it was official might paint a target on her back for the noble tamer students, who would likely have few qualms about taking out their competition once they realized she was a peasant.

"Right," he answered Stav, forcing a quick smile. He might not like the boy—especially since Stav, like most of the new trainees, was a year or two younger than him but already had more experience as a dragon—but Stav was his roommate and the son of a duke, and Lasaro couldn't afford to offend him. When he was named crown prince, he'd need all the support he could get.

The teacher, Master Henra, stopped behind Lasaro. "Discussing tactics, are we, boys?" she asked in her quiet, cold voice. She was very old, even for a dragon, and her dragon's temper came out as icy ruthlessness rather than it harboring the red-hot rage that most bent toward. Although her white robe was trimmed in the shimmering grays of an Ariel dragon, it was rumored that she herself hadn't transformed in decades, being one of the few who'd chosen to live as a human without shifting. How ironic, then, that she was the teacher for the trainees' first transformation classes. In which the first test was to jump off a tower and transform instantly into a dragon—or, alternatively, die.

Lasaro blew out a breath, keeping his eyes on the massive training court below their tower.

"Good," Henra said smoothly, her voice like snake scales gliding over him. She raised her voice to be heard by the rest of the students lined up across the edge of the parapet. "When a dragon takes on human form, they're shifting their mass to energy. That means they suddenly have quite a lot of extra magic once they're human, which gives them a bit of a glow —the longer they've spent in dragon form, the more leftover magic there is, and the brighter the glow. A good amount of this magic must be expended quickly or it will find its own way out, which typically results in... unpleasant incidents."

"Is that how the South Tower nearly burned down last year? I heard Master Lars spent too long as a dragon and nearly went rogue before he managed to shift back," Stav piped up, smirking.

Master Henra, who had been slowly pacing at their backs, stopped behind him. "That's correct," she said, and then she shoved him off the edge of the parapet.

Lasaro's heart stopped. He leaned as far out as he dared. Stav let out one short shriek and then, before he'd gotten halfway to the ground, wings and scales exploded from him as he shifted into a brown Terra dragon. He circled once, doing a wobbly celebratory barrel roll, and then drifted awkwardly to the courtyard below.

The students still on the parapet clapped nervously. Master Henra's methods—which might have ended in a student's death had Stav been unable to transform—would likely be viewed as barbaric anywhere else, but for dragons, swim-or-sink teaching had always been the norm. Lasaro wouldn't receive any special treatment, either. Alveria needed strong royals, not coddled ones, which meant he would face the risks of training just the same as any other student.

Master Henra continued pacing. "When you shift back into dragon form, you're transforming your energy into mass, which means you'll need food and rest—in that order—to recover."

"I hear that's why newly transformed dragons are extra cranky," whispered one girl who looked about thirteen, causing titters to erupt near her. Until Henra strode over and pushed her off, too. She only fell for a second before she erupted into a crimson Ember dragon and floated jerkily toward the ground.

The rest of the class fell utterly silent, fearing opening their mouths and attracting Henra's attention next.

"Also correct," Master Henra went on as if nothing had happened.

Everyone shifted nervously, trying not to look down.

Henra began to pace again. Lasaro tensed up whenever she was behind him, and only breathed when she reappeared in his peripheral vision. "Spend too long in either form and you risk getting stuck," she said. "Stay in human form and your magic will wane until you have none left. At that point, you'll have to acquire energy from a magical source to shift—and if you don't, you'll no longer be a dragon at all, which would be a tragedy since there are less than two hundred of us left in the world now. Most of which reside here in Alveria."

She stopped at the end of the parapet and reached out her hand to push the freckled, brown-skinned student standing there— Hava was her name, Lasaro recalled. Hava, having seen it coming, jumped before Henra's hand landed. The teacher's lips curved in a rare smile of approval as the girl transformed into another Ember dragon, an orange-gold one this time, and then Henra pivoted to continue pacing.

"Stay in dragon form—especially without a tamer—for too long, and you also risk becoming territorial, animalistic, a danger to everyone around you if you live too near to people. It is this, or sometimes a specific act of antagonism or illegal activity, that will get you marked as a rogue and hunted by dragon hunters."

Though Henra's voice stayed smooth and cool, her eyes tightened at the mention of hunters. The temperature dropped by several degrees, as well, and an icy wind wailed up the side of the tower, causing the student next to Lasaro to lose his balance and tumble down, falling almost all the way to the ground before he shifted into a small blue dragon that looked vaguely familiar.

Henra's lips pulled down and she shook her head. That student's future wasn't looking very bright, apparently. Lasaro hoped he'd improve soon, although it wouldn't do Lasaro much good to worry about his classmates when he himself might fail his own class at any moment. And also potentially die.

And fail his mother. And his country. And himself.

He leaned out over the edge again and tried to convince himself to jump. It would be more honorable than waiting until the master pushed him. He could transform into a dragon, he *knew* it, but he wasn't quite certain enough to take the leap. Ashamed, he took a half-step back.

"No one knows who the first dragon to shift into human form was," continued Henra. She stopped in front of the second-to-last student. The boy caught sight of her hand reaching toward him and took a running jump off the parapet before she could touch him, instantly transforming into another Ember dragon.

Master Henra and Lasaro were now the only ones left. He prayed silently to Odin, hoping the god might give him some tip that would help him figure out how to force a transformation before Henra simply shoved him to his death. He tried to call up his dragon blood, too, attempting to remember the way he'd felt when he'd looked at Kaelan, but the shift refused to happen.

"Unlike tamers, who have limited abilities—they can speak telepathically to their bonded dragon but no one else, and the experienced ones can sometimes control a very small amount of their elemental magic—dragons can communicate telepathically with anyone. As for magic, all dragons start out controlling a single element: fire, earth, air, or water. Almost all remain that way their entire life," Henra said, pacing again. He knew that the wind—which he had no doubt she controlled, being an Ariel dragon herself—magically carried her voice to the students gathered in the courtyard below, who stared up raptly while they waited for the prince's turn. The pressure of their expectations was an almost physical force, and he struggled to breathe beneath its weight.

"Embers can breathe fire. Terras can cause earthquakes and sometimes levitate rocks as well as help grow and work with certain types of vegetation. Aquas can shoot streams of water, and the strongest among them can also bring rain, divert floods, and assist with irrigation efforts. Ariels, the rarest kind of dragon, can summon winds, change the temperature of the air, and cause tornadoes, if rarely. Older, exceptionally powerful dragons can learn to control more than one element. These are called masters. If lucky, one in a hundred students will become a master. I doubt any of you will ever be among them."

She stopped behind Lasaro. He clenched his hands to hide their trembling. He could do this. Right now. *Come on. Transform.*

Nothing happened.

Master Henra reached out, placed a single hand between his shoulder blades, and pushed.

And, just like that, he was falling.

The wind screamed in his ears, streaked tears across his cheeks, and battered and blinded him. The ground filled the whole of his vision. He was going to die. He was going to fail. He would never be king. Would never make his mother proud. Would never prove that little voice in the back of his head wrong—the one that said he'd been useless and ignored for his whole life and would never be anything other.

No. He wouldn't die, not like this. Iron-willed, he reached deep inside himself and wrapped his hands around the thing that was a dragon, and he *yanked* it up and out.

The transformation crashed over him like a wave. He snapped his wings wide just in time for his back feet to scrape the cobblestones before he pulled up. The dragons beneath him roared in applause as one of them—Hava?—blew out a stuttering stream of celebratory fire.

Lasaro barely noticed them. All he could see was the sky. It was glowing with blue, rolled out from horizon to horizon, waiting for him. He spiraled up into it. He would fly forever. His wings would carry him, cutting through the blue, absorbing it. He flew up, past the tower, past the peak of Mount Firewyrm. Climbed higher. Higher. Turned south and gazed over the jewel-bright green landscape. Beautiful as it was, it could never match the sky.

He turned himself toward the horizon and flew into it.

One week later, Lasaro still couldn't get that day on the parapets out of his head. He'd taken to hiding in the library in an attempt to get out of his never-ending classes. If the masters couldn't find him, they couldn't make him change again. Not until he'd had a chance to ensure that he wasn't going rogue.

His hands tightened on the book he'd been reading in his research. He remembered so clearly how he'd felt when he'd looked at the sky that day: like it was all that mattered, the only thing he needed to concern himself with for the rest of his life. Not being named crown prince, not earning his mother's approval. Not even staying human.

He'd only flown for five minutes before coming back to himself and realizing he needed to return to the courtyard, but it had been five minutes too long.

Footsteps sounded a few aisles away. Lasaro leaned out of his chair—he was secreted away in one of the library's more shadowy alcoves, tucked against the farthest wall of the library where few students had time to venture—to check if the footsteps might belong to Kaelan. That was another reason he'd chosen this place as his hideout. He'd only spent half a day with her when they'd first met, but he'd quickly gotten the sense that she was educated, for a peasant anyway, and curious. Sooner or later, he had no doubt that her sense of curiosity would lead her here. And if he had his way, he'd be here when she appeared.

He peered through the gaps between the books. The student wasn't Kaelan, but Def, an Aqua "friend" of Lasaro's.

Lasaro pulled up his feet, sank back into his chair, and grabbed a new book to hold in front of his face like a shield. The words blurred before his eyes. He frowned, holding the tome a little further away, but he still couldn't read it. He glanced at the nearest shelf, finding a sign and trying to read it so that he could see if his eyesight was the problem, but it looked completely normal.

It had to be the book. It didn't want to be read. He'd heard the library was semi-sentient, even more so than the rest of the Akademy, and took it upon itself to dictate which books certain students should read. His mouth twisted. Just what he needed: an enormous, inhuman nanny. Yet another being who didn't take him seriously enough to allow him to do what he needed to.

He slammed the book shut—it had been a treatise on rogues, and he'd hoped to find more specific instructions on how to stay focused as a dragon who didn't yet have a tamer. Near as soon as he'd closed it, another book appeared on the arm of his chair. It was open. He put his finger on the page to save the spot and flipped it closed to look at the cover. *Sayings of Kanto the Wise,* it proclaimed. A book of proverbs? Why would the library think *that* would be of any use to him? He flipped back to the page it had been opened to and peered at the only proverb there.

He who hides from his troubles only invents more.

He made a disgusted sound and slammed this book shut, too, dropping it next to the blurred tome. So, the library wanted him to go and face his fears, did it? Well, *it* wasn't the one with the pressure of an entire kingdom's fate on its shoulders. *It* wasn't the one who would be declared a rogue by its own mother if it failed—or, if it didn't become a rogue but instead was simply unable to transform except in the direst of circumstances, the one who the entire kingdom would continue to deem useless.

"Lasaro!" boomed a voice. Def had found him. Damn.

Lasaro glanced up at the other boy, whose brown hair was artfully tousled, and who stood with one arm possessively slung around a small, slender girl. It was very early in the term, but already the masters had paired a handful of the newest dragons with trainee tamers. Over the last three days since these two had established their tentatively successful bond—a process Lasaro still didn't completely understand— Def had been showing off his new tamer to any dragon who so much as glanced his way. It was insufferable.

"Hi, Def," Lasaro said, trying hard to sound polite and not like he wanted to strangle the boy. Crown princes didn't strangle their subjects, no matter how insincere and arrogant they were. Lasaro's current state of exhaustion made that more difficult than usual, though. He'd barely had enough time to sleep during the last week, which was yet another reason he'd chosen the library to hide out in—this alcove was great for napping.

"Lasaro," Def repeated, unsubtly showing off his first-name basis with the prince to his tamer. Like about half of the trainee class, Def was the same age as Lasaro even though he'd found his dragon form several years ago. It was popular among some of the nobles to train their children privately for a few years before sending them to the Akademy, to give them an edge over the other students. "I overheard Master Lars earlier. You've missed five of your classes this week, and if you miss anymore they're threatening to suspend you. Thought I ought to come warn you."

With a deep sigh, Lasaro peeled himself out of his seat. He couldn't risk suspension. "Thank you," he replied.

Def nodded benevolently as if he'd done Lasaro some great favor and now the prince owed him. "Love the new robes, by the way," he added.

After Lasaro had been confirmed as an Ariel dragon, he'd traded in his black robes for beautiful mist-gray ones. They weren't trimmed in any other color like the masters' were, but he rather enjoyed the simplicity of the new uniform—plus, the gray was calming. "Thank you," he told Def again.

"Oh, one more thing," Def said, as if he'd just thought of it. "I wanted to apologize for attacking your little friend the other day."

Lasaro stiffened. So *that* was why Def's dragon form had looked familiar last week, out on the parapets. He'd been the blue dragon at the river—the one who'd nearly eaten Kaelan. "That was you?" he asked, more sharply than intended.

Def's expression remained congenial, but went somewhat wooden, as if he was holding it in place by force of will. "I don't remember a lot, but yes. Anyway, no worries. I've got a tamer now, so that's taken care of. Won't happen again and all that."

Anger burnt low in Lasaro's stomach. He took a step forward, into the other boy's space. The tamer shifted uncomfortably, but Lasaro kept his eyes on Def. "No worries?" he asked, incredulous. "You almost *ate* someone."

Def shrugged. "But I didn't. And she's just a peasant, anyway."

The fire burned hotter. "Her status has nothing to do with her worth," Lasaro said in a low voice, trying to control his tone.

Def blinked as if he'd never considered that. "Right, of course."

Was this what all the students thought of peasants, and by extension of Kaelan? His need to find her intensified—he hoped she hadn't gotten into any kind of trouble with the other nobles. "Have you seen her? Since then, I mean," he demanded. "She's in training to be a tamer."

Def shrugged. "Nah. Sorry."

Lasaro took a deep breath to calm himself. He couldn't risk getting angry and shifting into a dragon right here in the library. No one else would care—the space had been built with dragons in mind, after all—but he wasn't ready to take the library's advice and "face his fears" without Kaelan at his side to keep him focused.

"Fine. Thanks for telling me about Master Lars. I'd better be off to class," he said at last, his voice tight, and with that he brushed past the other two. He tried not to think about whether today's classes might require him to become a dragon again, and what the consequences might be if he refused.

He *had* to find his tamer.

CHAPTER 13

Kaelan leaned over the bubbling vat of soup and breathed in deeply. The smell of Ma's favorite chicken-vegetable soup washed over her, along with a nearly unbearable wave of homesickness. The last time she'd smelled this, she'd had a cold, and Ma had forced herself out of bed to make this soup for her even over her daughter's protests. If Kaelan closed her eyes now, she could almost sense her mother hovering over the soup, her grandma grumbling from her rocking chair while secretly adding a few of her own favorite herbs to the pot; Kaelan wouldn't have to do anything except eat it and be loved.

Tears stung her eyes and she wiped at them angrily. Ugh, when had she become a crier? She stirred the pot vengefully with a long wooden spoon, peering around her, but no one had seen her tears. That wasn't surprising. Everyone in the kitchens was constantly busy, with no time to babysit the girl who kept claiming she was a student but had been banished to the kitchens.

She snatched a bowl off the shelf and dumped a ladle-full of soup into it, splashing the broth across her tunic in her anger. Since she wasn't a student, she'd been forced to continue wearing the clothes she'd bought in Bellsor. She'd managed to sneak into three tamer classes over the last two weeks, at least. She'd even slipped into the back of a dragon class, her heart thundering like a stampede of wild horses the whole time as she searched in vain for Lasaro, but Master Henra had caught her and threatened her with full expulsion if she did it again. Now she had no choice but to attend to the kitchens, fetch snacks for any dragons and tamer students who felt like torturing her—which was most of them—and try to figure out a new plan.

For now, she'd settled on trying to befriend a dragon. Any dragon. She wished she could just walk out of the kitchens right now and track down Master Olga, come clean and beg for help, but she doubted even Olga would be willing to go out of her way to heal a peasant. Plus, Kaelan risked getting thrown out entirely if she revealed she was only here to get Ma healed. And anyway, she felt sick at the thought of giving up on Lasaro. She'd spent almost all of her precious free time looking for him—admittedly, though, that wasn't much time, as the kitchen staff worked her to the bone—and she'd only spotted him a handful of times at a distance. He was always absorbed in his classes, staring so intently at his books or the sky or the master in front of him that he scarcely noticed anything else. She wasn't sure if he was so focused because of his need to do well so he could win the title of heir to the kingdom, or if his rigid attention meant he was worried. About what, she wasn't sure. What did a prince have to be afraid of?

Not needy dragons calling for soup at all hours of the day and night, that was for sure.

Kaelan plopped a spoon into the bowl she held and carried it to the long counter where she set it in front of an immaculately beautiful dragon student. "Your soup," Kaelan said, trying to sound gracious. She needed to make one dragon friend. Just *one* who would give her the time of day for just long enough to fly back to Gladsheim and heal her mother.

The student leaned over to sniff the soup and curled her lip, shoving it back toward Kaelan. "What is this? Peasant fare? Disgusting. I've changed my mind—I don't want soup. I want something sweet. A cinnamon pasty. Make one, now."

Kaelan gritted her teeth. Dumping the whole bowl in the girl's lap wouldn't win her any favors.

A new girl slithered up to the counter—a heavyset, porcelain-skinned tamer student, one of the most popular girls. Kaelan thought her name was Inga. And if rumor served, she'd already landed her dragon last week, though none of the newly formed bonds were official until they'd been tested by the masters.

Inga raised an eyebrow, her cool gaze sliding over Kaelan's messy hair and ruddy features. "Oh, dear," she said, faking sympathy. "Is the peasant feeling sad today?"

Damn it. Kaelan swiped at her face again, feeling a wetness on her cheeks that meant she'd missed a tear earlier. Crying in front of these girls was as good as social suicide. Not that they'd have had any respect for her in any case.

"Why don't you go home and cry to your mama? You don't belong here anyway," Inga taunted in her delicate voice.

That was it. Kaelan wasn't taking any more of this ridiculous, petty bullying. Making a split-second decision, she picked up the bowl of soup and flung it at Inga. The satisfaction was instant.

The dragon student screeched, caught in the crossfire, and retreated. Inga sat still as a stone and pulled a carrot from her dripping blonde hair. "You'll regret that," she said coolly.

Kaelan's smile widened. "Not today," she said, and marched away.

Ragnhild noticed her. "What are you so happy about?" she shouted over the din. She stood before a fireplace where a pie was being prepped for one of the masters. A tiny tornado of fire whipped and toasted it, turning it into a magically perfect dish as she watched.

"You'll find out soon, I'm sure," Kaelan replied under her breath as she tore off her apron and ducked out into the hall.

"Hey, your shift isn't over yet!" Ragnhild called from behind her, but Kaelan ignored her. She'd earned a break. The time away wouldn't discourage Inga any—if anything, it would only give her time to plan her vengeance—but Kaelan was going to suffocate if she had to spend another second in the windowless kitchen with all that noise and the smell of her Ma's special soup being so out of place.

Thinking twice, she turned around and fetched a bowlful of it before leaving.

She avoided everyone on her way back to her room. She was well-practiced at that by this point, and there were plenty of hidden alcoves and secret staircases that seemed to appear just when she needed an out-of-the-way spot to duck into. She found her room easily and held her breath as she opened the door, hoping her roommate—an aloof, if not completely unkind, tamer student named Frigg—was still in class. It was late in the evening by this point, but Akademy classes happened at all hours, and there was always the library, as well. It was a popular place for students to study and hang out. Not that Kaelan would know from experience. She'd spent so much of her meager free time searching for Lasaro that she hadn't had the chance to visit the library yet.

Kaelan pushed the door to her room open. Frigg was still gone. Kaelan let out a breath of relief—which turned into a strangled yelp when the door opened wider to show Master Olga standing by the window.

Kaelan stepped back in shock, dropping the bowl of soup. Before it could hit the ground, Master Olga twirled a finger and a tiny stream of wind flipped the bowl back upright before any soup could spill. The wind carried it to Kaelan's nightstand. "Hello, Pupil Younger," Olga said calmly.

The phrase shook Kaelan out of her shock. She closed the door and crossed her arms. "That's twice you've called me *pupil*, and yet I'm stuck in the kitchens, not allowed to actually learn anything," she dared to say.

An expression crossed Master Olga's face: the slightest tightening of her lips, a tiny narrowing of the eyes. If Kaelan had had to guess, she'd have said Olga was displeased. Hopefully not at Kaelan.

"I am aware," Olga said. "Lars overruled me with the support of the other masters, I'm afraid, to have you closeted in the kitchens without even trying your skills and talents."

Kaelan's heart leapt. "Can you change my assignment then?" she asked eagerly. "Let me be a student?"

And let me find Lasaro?

If he even still remembered their deal, that was. If he still wanted her. She'd looked for him so much she'd even started dreaming about him—or, rather, dreaming of flying with the beautiful gray dragon-Lasaro, who sometimes randomly turned into the vast black dragon from her earlier dreams—but the boy she'd sworn herself to had shown no sign that he was looking for her in return.

But Olga shook her head. "I can't overturn their decision. Not without more dragons from the Council of Masters on my side."

Everything within Kaelan spiraled downward. Unable to hold herself upright, she sagged down on her bed. Her lip trembled. She refused to embarrass herself further by crying again, but her watering eyes didn't seem to get the message.

"Something is wrong," Olga observed. Everything about her seemed to sharpen, her white robes suddenly seeming too bright to be contained in the room, like she was a streak of lightning caught in a jar.

"No," Kaelan said, too used to hiding her feelings from others. "I'm fine."

Olga raised that one eyebrow again. "I thought I told you to always be honest with me."

Kaelan hesitated, picking at a thread on her tunic, which still smelled like the kitchens and Ma's soup. How was Ma doing right at this very second? Had she gotten sicker as the cool of autumn had advanced in the mountains? Kaelan had received her first letter from her grandma just a few days before, and according to her they were doing well, but Kaelan wasn't reassured. The coma stage of the illness could start any day now, and there wouldn't be much Haldis could do for Ma at that point.

The lump in Kaelan's throat grew heavier. She couldn't keep her worries to herself any longer. They would suffocate her—and Master Olga seemed like the only person here who might be sympathetic enough to help. "It's my mother," she said at last, hating the helpless tone of her voice.

Olga softened, fading back into normalcy. "Go on."

"She's very sick. With a wasting illness. She's a healer, and the people in our village were ill, and she couldn't afford to turn them away—she caught their sickness." Kaelan pursed her lips. "She wouldn't have turned them away even if they hadn't had a copper bit between the lot of them, though. She's too kind for her own good."

Olga stayed still, listening.

Encouraged, Kaelan went on. "That's why I'm at the Akademy," she added, twisting the hem of her tunic between her nervous fingers. "That's why I agreed to come even though I knew I wouldn't fit in here. I have to find a dragon and do whatever I have to do—including becoming a tamer—to get it to come back and heal my mother."

She held her breath. Olga stayed quiet for a moment, thinking. "Do you hate it here?" she asked finally.

Kaelan flushed. "I... I'm sure it's not..."

Olga did her almost-smiling thing. "I don't expect you to enjoy being stuck somewhere that must be very unlike your home, endlessly teased by those who think they're better than you. I only meant—you may not always feel that way. Give it time. Give *yourself* time. The Akademy already likes you. You may grow to feel the same about it."

Kaelan frowned. "You talk like the Akademy is alive."

Olga lifted one slender shoulder. "A bit of the essence of the masters who've lived, taught, and died here lives on in the stone and mortar. The Akademy is more than a building, you know."

"Oh," Kaelan said, at a loss for words. The Akademy was alive. Sort of. And it *liked* her. Which was both weird and comforting.

"You say you're here because you'll do anything to save your mother. *Even* becoming a tamer. Do you intend to sneak away from your duties as soon as she's healed, then, and leave your dragon alone?" Olga asked calmly.

Kaelan gaped at her. "No!" she said, too loudly. "Of course not! I would never walk out on such an obligation. I just meant to say… even if I have to dedicate my life to a cause I wouldn't otherwise, I'll do it for her. Although—I mean, I would rather just find a dragon who can help me right now, and then I can go home and everyone would end up happy since I'm not even wanted here. That would be the best-case scenario."

She waited, heart in her mouth, hoping Olga might volunteer to help. She wasn't sure if she could really abandon Lasaro and go back on her promise to him, but maybe she could speak to him before she went and see if there might be a way she could help his cause and fulfill her vow of fealty without being his tamer. Ma needed her, and time was short.

But Olga just tilted her head. "I'm afraid that's not possible. Even the masters don't have limitless power, which is why it's the dragons' policy to only use our magic to help either the kingdom in general—like when Aquas irrigate crops—or people who have committed themselves to us personally. If we made cross-country trips willy-nilly to help one peasant simply because you asked, we would have to help *all* of the peasants who ever came to us asking for assistance, and we simply do not have the resources for that. It's a strict policy, but alas, it's a necessary one, and it applies to all dragons in the kingdom. Breaking it would only foment even more anti-dragon sentiment than already plagues Alveria."

Kaelan hunched her shoulders. She wanted to rail against the master and call her heartless, or maybe just curl up and cry. "So, what should I do, then?" she asked, her voice wavering.

"You're the honorable sort, Pupil Younger. But soon now, I fear you must decide where your loyalties lie." She stepped toward the door and reached for the handle and then paused. "You can stay loyal to your promise—and to yourself, as I'm beginning to believe you were meant to end up here—and remain at the Akademy. You might yet find a way to convince the other masters that you should become a tamer. I know you long for stability, for a permanent home. This could be that for you if you want. Or you can bow to the opinions of Master Lars and those who tease you and return to your cabin."

"I'm not going to give up," Kaelan said hotly.

"I did not necessarily mean giving up on your mother. I don't doubt you would do whatever it takes to save her. But what about giving up on yourself? On what you could be if you allowed it?"

Kaelan hesitated. Before she could reply, however, Olga offered a small smile and swept out the door, leaving Kaelan to wonder what she'd meant—and whether she might be right.

CHAPTER 14

Master Olga's words lingered in Kaelan's mind long after the master had left. Kaelan ate her now-cold soup, stared out her tiny window as the sun dipped below the courtyard's walls, and thought about what she wanted for herself.

Over the last two weeks, she'd tried to forget who her father was. But the truth was, he was everywhere here: in a name on the wall, as vague cautionary tales about rogues in one of the classes she'd snuck into. In her. He was there, too. And that, more than anything, terrified her. But... she was also enthralled by dragons in general. More so than ever now. She was fascinated by their history and entranced by the magic that seemed to inundate even the simplest parts of their lives. Maybe what Kaelan needed was to finally decide which part of her feelings was stronger. Which part of *her* was stronger. She couldn't be torn between fear and fascination forever.

If she chose fascination, she would have to work harder than she ever had, at the risk of getting nothing in return. She'd have to face her fears. Head-first, dead-on, not willing to try and then run away if she failed... the way she had when she'd attempted to tame the dragons at the river. She'd have to work harder than any tamer student, and be better than all of those petty nobles, just to prove to the Council of Masters that she deserved her place.

But meanwhile, Ma would still be wasting away, at least until the masters officiated her bond with Lasaro. Ma hadn't gotten to the coma stage of the sickness yet—there was still at least a little bit of time. She hoped. By then, if the prince ever showed up and fulfilled his end of the bargain, he'd owe her that favor. And then, after her ma was well, Kaelan would have... what? A job? A role? A purpose?

In truth, even though she'd only been at the Akademy for two weeks and had spent most of that time homesick for her austere mountain, it was already hard to imagine going back to her old life. The hens pecking out back, the regular human-sized cabin with its measly single shelf of books. The suspicious villagers. All of it would feel too small now—like shoes that no longer fit right. The thought made her uncomfortable and lonelier than ever, and more than a little resentful, though she wasn't sure of whom.

She paused. Now that she thought about it, maybe that was how the other kitchen workers felt, too. Ragnhild had said they were mostly failed tamers—perhaps the thought of going back to their old, comparatively empty lives as nobles was what made them want to stay at the Akademy, even if it meant doing peasants' work in the kitchen. It also might explain why they were extra resentful of Kaelan, who was not only an *actual* peasant, but who might still have a shot at becoming something they'd already failed to achieve.

She dropped her empty bowl to the nightstand with a clank and lay down on her bed, her head propped up on the pack that she still used as a pillow out of habit. The too-soft feather pillow that the Akademy had provided was so fluffy it felt suffocating. The familiar lumpiness of her pack was much more soothing. She'd curled on her side, still pondering her predicament and the choice she needed to make, when something crinkled beneath her cheek.

She sat up, frowning, and pulled a folded piece of parchment out of the pack's front pocket. The paper that her traveling companion had given her—she'd forgotten about it. She unfolded it and smoothed out the creases to examine it again, a tingle of suspicion shooting through her as she remembered how much the man had guessed about her, and so easily, so that she recalled her earlier certainty that, whatever this paper was, it would likely come in handy at some point.

She squinted down at the fine strokes, the interlocking squares and rectangles like a puzzle box, the scribbled words so small that she could barely make them out. She was trying to make out something that started with a K when suddenly the map zoomed in to the spot: a large rectangle marked with entrances, exits, and fireplaces that was marked "kitchens."

Fingers suddenly numb, Kaelan dropped the parchment. It was magic. A magical map. And she'd been *sleeping* on it.

The map lay on the floor, innocuous, and after waiting a long moment to make sure it wasn't going to explode or require a blood sacrifice or anything else, she slowly ducked down to retrieve it. This time, the map zoomed out, but only a little—and much more slowly than before. She traced the familiar wide hallway out of the kitchens and across to a smaller series of hallways where one square was marked "Kaelan's room."

The stranger had given her a map of the Akademy.

A grin spread over her face. Oh yes, she could put this to *excellent* use.

After poking her head into the hallway to make sure Frigg wasn't on her way—the corridors were quiet, the lamps lit for evening—Kaelan quickly pulled her messy hair up, washed her face, and changed into the spare set of black tamer trainee robes in the closet. They were too big for her, of course. If she'd been accepted as an official student, they'd have been altered to fit her, but as things stood, they were at least black and would help her blend in as she crept through the sleeping

Akademy to explore. Because she was in the middle of a massive, mysterious dragon school with a magical map to unlock all its secrets, and *of course* she was going to go exploring. Maybe she could finally find Lasaro's room. It was better than trying to sleep now that Olga had her all worked up, anyway. Plus, if she really did want to stay here, it would be good to learn more about this place.

She paused in the act of pulling her hood up. Had she just made her decision? She was sneaking out to learn more about the Akademy—that didn't feel like the choice of someone who wanted to give up and go home.

Slowly, she finished pulling her hood up, and the decision settled around her with the fabric. Yes. This was what she would do. She was going to bet on herself—bet that she could do this, face her fears about her father, face the masters and the arrogant noble students, and become a tamer. And not just because she was honor-bound to fulfill her promise to her mother even if it meant a lifetime commitment on Kaelan's part. She might not have asked to be put in this situation, but she was here now, and she suddenly found she wanted to make something of it.

She slipped into the hall and found a deserted stairway where she could wait for nightfall. There was a strict curfew for the Akademy's underage residents and it was a risk to do her exploring after hours, but otherwise she risked running into Inga or one of her many minions, who were almost certainly out for Kaelan's blood now. Plus, if she was going to try to sneak into the dragon trainee quarters to find Lasaro, she would need the cover of nightfall to do it. Non-students like herself weren't allowed in the classroom areas she'd have to cross to get there.

She dozed off a few times. When she woke, the lamps in the hall had been turned nearly all the way down, leaving the corridor simmering in shadows. She blended into them and pulled out the map. Responding to her thoughts, the map pulled out to show a wider view of her surroundings. There— the dragon side of the cloister. She started toward it.

A pair of voices floated down the hallway and her heartbeat tripled as she quickly ducked into a wide staircase, skittering downward as the voices passed. If she got caught out past curfew by a master, she risked getting expelled and losing her shot at fulfilling her newfound goals. Best to avoid the areas that were likely to have lots of people or dragons moving about.

Sensing her request, the map zoomed out again and scrolled westward. She carefully finished descending the long staircase and followed the parchment's guidance. Then she caught the edge of a word on the map ahead of her—"dungeons"—and took a sharp right to avoid it. *That* wasn't anywhere she wanted to go, thank you very much.

Her next footstep echoed much more loudly than she'd expected. Startled, she glanced up to find herself in a massive, cave-like open room. Steam hissed up from porous floors that looked volcanic, and stalactites that stabbed down from the ceiling slowly dripped moisture back to the rock below. Veins of some sort of greenish ore let off a faint glow throughout the cavern. As her eyes adjusted, she realized it went back further than she could see, into the heart of the mountain. She peered back at the map. *Clutch Room*, it told her.

She jerked her head up. Clutch? As in eggs? Dragon eggs? Excitement lit her steps as she hurried deeper into the cavern, curiosity burning through her. She knew from her book and the scant amount of time she'd been able to spend in the library that if a dragon or dragon-blood got pregnant in dragon form, they'd have to stay that way throughout the pregnancy and would eventually lay an egg rather than give birth to a live human baby the way they would have if they'd been in human form when they got pregnant. So, any eggs in here would hatch out baby dragons, which would eventually learn how to shift into human form when they were old enough. She'd never seen a dragon egg, let alone a baby dragon, and the prospect of seeing either now drove her so deep into the room that she could no longer make out the door in the cavern's greenish glow.

She frowned, stopping. There were no eggs here.

Then something round and smooth caught her eye from behind a stalactite. She darted toward it and skidded to a stop in front of the nest—for it could only be a nest, tucked into a pile of smooth black-glass pebbles. She reached out a hand to touch one of the pebbles and smothered a yelp, yanking it back. They were burning hot. After sucking on her finger for a moment, she reached out to touch the nest's single egg, uncertain whether it was proper but unable to resist. It felt rough and hard, but had a bit of a give to it, like leather. She ran her whole hand over it gently.

Her healer's instinct tingled, and then, suddenly, expanded. She jerked in surprise as new information flooded her. Inside the egg, a tiny scaled creature stretched, little wings moving sluggishly through the liquid around it and then curled back up and slept. It was healthy, and it would be a Terra, Kaelan knew. But also… it had been inside the egg a *long* time. And it had barely grown at all.

She drew her hand back and stared at her palm. She had no idea how she knew all that. Her healer's instincts had never done anything like this before. Maybe her powers were growing, responding to the concentration of magic at the Akademy? But a healer's instinct wasn't magic-based, it was natural. Or at least that was what she'd always been taught.

Frowning, she got up and wandered deeper into the cavern and found another nest. This one had a pebbled surface, and the baby inside was… an Ember? And there was a strange sense of lethargy coming from it, a sort of staleness. It had been in its egg even longer than the Terra, she thought, although she couldn't get a specific sense of time from the baby. She found two dozen more eggs at the back of the vast cavern and all of them felt old. She stood back when she'd examined them all, and her brow crinkled. She was still puzzled by the sudden growth of her healer's abilities, but also by the strangeness of the eggs here. How many eggs did dragons normally lay, and how often? Maybe it was typical for dragons to spend such a long time growing inside of their eggs before hatching, but if that was so, why the sense of sluggishness and wrongness she'd gotten from the babies?

Maybe the library might have more information on the topic. If she remembered the map correctly, the route to the dragon trainees' side of the cloister ran through there anyway. She could nab a few books and take them back to her room to read later. A thrill of excitement ran through her—she'd been longing to visit the library again ever since she'd arrived.

She unfolded her map and followed its guidance out of the cavern, up a staircase, through a tower, and into the library. Last time she'd been here, Master Lars had taken her straight through to the kitchens and there'd hardly been time to take anything in. Now, she was on the opposite side of the vast area from where she'd been before, surrounded by unfamiliar shelves and small hallways that seemed to lead into side rooms.

Late as it was, she could hear a few students speaking in hushed whispers and giggles down a few aisles, so she snuck around them and veered into one of the library's offshoots.

The huge hall ended and the dim light from the lamps in the main library faded into the darkness of a room that felt big, but also strangely muffled. Kaelan took a step forward, straining her eyes. There was a skylight far above her, laid into a beautifully wrought glass ceiling that let some moonlight filter through, but it was cloudy tonight and she could barely see a thing.

Light flared into existence. She clapped a hand over her mouth to muffle a shriek, staring wildly around, afraid she'd been caught—but no one was in the room. Apparently, the golden-and-silver sconces had magically lit themselves as soon as she'd entered. She'd never seen them do that anywhere else in the Akademy, and wondered if this was another sign of the school's sort-of sentience, and if it was, what it meant that it would light the way for her.

She glanced around to see what the room held. She'd been expecting more books, or maybe a special collection of museum pieces, but instead the walls were covered with tapestries. She frowned, walking over to one. It was masterfully woven from what looked like plant fibers and maybe horse hair. It was huge as well, about as tall as a full-grown man. She lifted a corner of it. There was another tapestry behind it, and another behind that, all of them set up on rings and rods embedded high on the walls. She had no idea how anyone was supposed to turn them over to see the tapestries further beneath them, though. Unless, she supposed, you were a dragon.

She started to drop the tapestry she'd lifted and then paused. The tapestry underneath showed a claw and the corner of a black dragon tail. The same color as the dragon in her dream. An eerie feeling stirred in her and she peered around, half-expecting someone to jump out at her. She glanced back down at her map to see if there were any secret exits she should know about, but there were none. She squinted at the room's name. *Tapestry Room,* the map declared.

Kaelan snorted. Master Olga hadn't been kidding about the literalism of dragons.

She stuffed the map into her robe's pocket and returned her attention to the tapestry. She peeled the top one slowly upward as much as she could to reveal a blue-and-white patterned sky background with the lower leg and tail of a black dragon stretching across the corner she could see. She huffed with strain; the top tapestry was heavy, and she couldn't think of any way to get the whole thing out of the way so she could see the full black dragon. She reached out a hand to run her fingertips over the beautifully wrought tail.

And then the room exploded around her. She grew, or shrank, or spun, or maybe all three. And suddenly she was standing in a blue-and-white sky, a vast woven black dragon flapping its wings in slow motion before her.

She screamed and reeled backward—and came back to herself, standing in front of an inanimate tapestry.

She stood stock-still and allowed herself three deep breaths, and waited to see if anyone had heard her scream and would come to help, or perhaps expel her, but no one showed up. Her heart thumping hard, she lifted the top tapestry and lay down her whole hand on the black dragon again.

She was in the sky again. She lifted a hand and brushed it over the fabric of a nearby cloud. It was flat, and woven of gray willow fibers and, she thought, white rabbit fur. The black dragon hovered before her again, three-dimensional and massive, woven from shimmering black undertones with red, blue, gray, and green highlights.

She was inside the tapestry.

She looked down at herself, curious if she'd appear to have been woven into existence as well, but she looked normal.

The rise of Mordon, boomed a telepathic voice, and she jerked her head up and nearly shrieked again. The scene had changed. The black dragon was perched atop Mount Firewyrm, gazing down at the Akademy below while Kaelan seemed to hover in midair before them. *Mordon was the youngest dragon to ever achieve mastery of all four elements,* the voice went on. She cocked her head, beginning to understand. So this was why the tapestries were kept in the library; it was another way to save knowledge, to tell a story.

Then her mind processed the words the tapestry had spoken. Mordon. The black dragon on the tapestry who looked so much like the one in her dream, was Mordon. Her father. The most powerful master to ever teach at the Akademy, who had later gone rogue and disappeared.

Breath caught in her throat, and she stared at him. He looked benevolent and wise here, gazing down at the students below him, but a chill snaked through her, anyway.

He had great healing skill, highly unusual for a dragon, the voice went on. The scene shifted to show Mordon, still in dragon form, with both his wings raised protectively over a fallen yellow dragon. Energy streamed out of him in shining golden streaks, landing on the smaller dragon who rose up healed after a moment and shook out its wings.

Kaelan reached out as if to trace the glowing lines of healing power. So, he was a healer, like Ardis. Was that part of what had brought them together? Would that bring them together just one more time? With that much healing ability—the ability to actually physically fix those who were ailing, not just find herbs and make stronger potions like human healers —Mordon could easily heal Ardis. Did he even know she was sick? Would he care?

He rose to be the headmaster of the Akademy, until—

A hand landed on her shoulder, yanking her out of the tapestry and back into the library room. She gasped, whirling around, dreading the idea of who might've caught her: a master, a dragon student, Inga. But it was none of them who stood in front of her, hand still on her shoulder.

"My roommate Stav is learning how to make these," said the boy before her. "Apparently, Terras weave them magically from plant and animal fibers. Stav's all thumbs at it, though."

Kaelan gaped at him. Then, without thinking, she launched herself at him and wrapped him in a fierce hug.

Lasaro had found her.

CHAPTER 15

L asaro froze, Kaelan's arms so tight around him that he thought a rib might break. It wasn't the strength of the gesture that caught him off guard, though—it was how suddenly *female* Kaelan felt pressed up against him. The hug was warm, offering a strange, wonderfully unique combination of soft curves and lean muscle and sharp edges that was all Kaelan.

He had no idea what he was supposed to do about it.

Hug her back? Surely, that would be improper. Push her away? That might hurt her feelings, and he'd worked so hard to find her—and needed her so badly—that he didn't want to ruin their reunion like that. So he just stood there, stiff as a board with his face flushed hot from the confused happiness of the moment, until she recovered herself enough to drop her arms and step back.

The room felt suddenly colder. He shrugged it off.

"You found me!" she said, her gleeful voice bouncing off the skylight and fading into the thick tapestries. Then she tucked a strand of black hair behind one ear and her smile vanished as she took in Lasaro's stiff expression. "You... were looking for me, right?"

"Yes!" he said. He hated to think she might've believed he'd forgotten about her. But then he cleared his throat and looked away. He didn't want her to know the power she held over him, either, and he needed to remember to keep a professional prince-subject distance between them. That was what a good king would do, right? He didn't want to lead her on, after all, or imply promises—such as friendship, rather than the clear-cut allyship they'd negotiated—that he would be unable to fulfill. "I mean, I have been keeping an eye out for you, yes. But... that wasn't why I was here."

"Oh." She folded her hands and took another step back, looking confused and a little deflated. "Right. Of course. No reason you'd look for me here, after all, and so late in the night." She paused, looking embarrassed, and then her expression crinkled—adorably—and she tilted her head. "Why *were* you here, then?"

He looked away, hemming and hawing while he took a moment to think up a good story. The truth was, he'd finally given in and risked bribing a tamer student to tell him the location of Kaelan's room. He'd gone there a few minutes ago, unwilling to wait another moment to track her down, but had found only her roommate Frigg. Worried that Kaelan may have gotten into trouble, he'd checked the kitchens—after Frigg had told him that's where Kaelan had been—and when that had turned up nothing, he'd once again gone to the only place he could hope she might eventually turn up: the library. And, finally, it had paid off.

"I was…" he started, uncertain of what to say. He didn't want her to know how desperate he'd been to find her, so much so that he'd even been willing to break curfew tonight to do it. Then a grin crept over his face as an idea presented itself to him. "The library was just part of a shortcut I was taking. Here, come with me. I'll show you where I was going." He reached for her hand and she let him take it, and warmth stole back over him.

He'd found Kaelan. He'd finally found his tamer. He felt calmer already, more capable, less frightened of becoming a rogue. The relief was so great that the sudden absence of worry felt almost alien—he hadn't realized how much stress he'd been walking around with.

They wound through the hallways and staircases, heading to the very back of the Akademy. "By the way, be careful next time you're in the Tapestry Room," he said over his shoulder. "I've heard that if you spend too long in a tapestry, your mind can get stuck in there forever."

Kaelan shuddered. "Noted. Now, where exactly are you taking me?"

He leaned against a set of double doors, listening closely. When he didn't hear anything from inside, he pushed them open with a flourish. Cold, bright starlight swirled through the air around them, leading their eyes up to a massive, rounded glass ceiling set into the mountain's peak. "The Observatory," he said proudly. He'd only been here once or twice, but he'd known the first time he saw it last week that it would be a great way to impress girls. Not that he was trying to impress Kaelan. Just distract her.

Right?

"Wow," she breathed out, striding to the middle of the floor and twirling. The starlight seemed to catch in her hair like a diadem, smoothing and shadowing her features like they were the highest form of art. Her robes flared around her ankles as she spun, and she suddenly looked invincible and vulnerable and beautiful and impossible all at once. It was the same way he'd felt when he'd seen her at the river, and a potential shift tingled just beneath the surface of his skin in response. It wasn't anger that spurred it, though. It was *her.* Whatever she was to him, he'd never felt the likes of it before.

Then she flopped down on the ground, spread out her arms and legs like a starfish, and goggled at the stars. Lasaro smothered a grin. Such a wonderfully strange, incredibly unaware girl she was—or perhaps uncaring, which felt downright heroic to a prince who'd always had to care what everyone around him thought.

He took a moment to let the shift fade and then closed the doors. The masters didn't set patrols to enforce curfew, and even though many of them were up at all hours of the night, usually they didn't come here except on the solstices or for special classes. Which meant that Lasaro and Kaelan were probably safe to stay for at least a few minutes without getting caught.

He lay down at her side, the six inches between them feeling like no space at all. "This is where the masters come to research the prophecies made by the old dragon seers, and sometimes to make new prophecies based on celestial sightings," he told her. "They watch how the stars align, keep an eye out for unusual comets, signs from the gods, that sort of thing."

"Do you believe in the gods?"

He shifted, turning his head to look at her. He was tempted to answer with a quick "of course" the way he would to anyone else who asked—but she wasn't anyone, and she deserved his honesty. After a brief hesitation, he said, "I'm not sure. Sometimes I wish I could believe better than I do. It must be such a comfort to those who hold to those old traditions. Never a doubt, never a question." His lack of belief was yet another of his failings. How could a king who couldn't sustain faith in his country's gods rule a people who worshipped them? He'd tried to *force* himself to believe, tried to ignore the questions that kept popping up in his head when he visited the temples, but his doubts were like hydras. For each one he tried to shove away, ten more rose up in the banished one's place.

Kaelan was watching him, her green eyes like emeralds in the starlight. "Faith isn't about not questioning," she said. "Sometimes I think the most faithful believers are those who embrace their doubts and questions, and don't deny themselves a search for answers, and choose to believe even while knowing they may never find them."

That wasn't what he'd expected. He liked it, though—liked the hope it offered, the honesty of it. "I suppose you're a believer, then?"

She shrugged one shoulder and turned her head to look back up at the stars. "I suppose so. I've always been a bit traditional, I guess."

"Not me," he said, certainty deepening his voice. "My country is on the cusp of a great change and clinging to tradition will only get everyone drowned when the tide turns."

"You mean Unger," she said quietly.

"Yes. Their king might be lazy, but their general isn't, and they've made a hobby of overthrowing most of their neighboring kingdoms. Sooner or later, they'll spot their opening to do the same to Alveria. We need to do whatever it takes to be ready for it." He shifted. "And also—there are other things I want to change, traditions I want to eradicate once I'm king. Like how nobles treat peasants, and what rights peasants have."

"Good," she said firmly.

He raised an eyebrow. "That's one tradition you'd like to see change, I take it?"

"That's not tradition. That's common pettiness. Tradition, faith —they raise people *above* stuff like that."

He scoffed, unable to stop himself. "It's foolish tradition that even requires me to be here in the first place. I have to jump through all these hoops, go much farther than any of my siblings ever have just to prove myself simply because the throne has always gone to a dragon and, therefore, according to *tradition*, must always go to a dragon—and not just someone who can transform, but someone who's proven themselves able to shift at the drop of a hat, who's been trained until they can perform for the nobles like a show pony and win their approval. It's ridiculous and unnecessary. That's another thing I'll change when I'm king."

"I don't know. I think there's a reason for it."

"What reason could there possibly be? In what way does a dragon automatically make a better ruler than a dragon-blood who can't shift? In fact, it could be argued that being a dragon makes a ruler *less* likely to rule well—they're well-known to be hotheaded, less kind, more warlike. Like my twin sisters, for example."

"That's true," Kaelan allowed, "but proving that you can shift and control your powers also proves that you can control *yourself*. And self-control can only help you once you gain the throne. Maybe your mom isn't trying to force you into pointless formalities. Maybe what she really wants is for you to fulfill your potential—to use your self-control to help you decide when to respect tradition and when to overturn it."

Lasaro frowned, thinking that through. "I suppose you might be right," he said at last.

"I'm always right," Kaelan said smugly, and he gave a very unprincely snort.

"So," he said after a moment, "are you going to tell me why Frigg said I should look for you in the kitchens tonight?"

She stiffened. "I've been banned from classes and made to work in the kitchens. I'm going to fight it, though, I promise. Master Olga said I still have a shot at convincing the Council of Masters to make me an official trainee. We can still make them approve our bond. And then—and then I'll get that favor you promised, right?"

He glanced over at her. She sounded almost panicked as if she thought he would abandon her. "Of course," he soothed her. "I'll help you convince the masters. We'll figure something out."

She blew out a breath. "That's good to know," she murmured.

They were silent for a moment. His eyes fell on a cluster of stars near the southern horizon. "Those are Mordon's stars," he said idly, pointing at them.

At his side, Kaelan's whole body stiffened. "What?" Her voice cut through the sense of ease that had grown between them as sharply as a knife. The starlight felt hard and cold again.

Confused, he tried to explain. "Mordon's stars," he said again. "I've heard those stars are the ones the dragon seers used to foretell his destiny. Before he disappeared, I mean."

Lasaro had often wished he himself had a prophecy to guide him. He had no idea what Mordon's had been—probably something about his quest to overthrow the throne of Alveria, which was why he'd been named rogue—but surely it must ease one's mind to know their future. This was an area in which he had plenty of faith; dragon prophecies always came true, though they often took centuries to do so.

Kaelan stood up, robes swinging as she brushed herself off. "I'm sorry. I've got to be going," she told him, somewhat brusquely.

He climbed to his feet also, trying to tamp down his alarm. Had he said something to offend her? He still needed her. And —he missed the way she'd felt, lying at his side. "Okay. Could you come watch my training tomorrow, though? We'll be in the main courtyard after lunch."

She gave him a rueful smile. "I'll try, but I doubt I'll make it. Ragnhild keeps a close eye on me when I'm on shift, which is pretty much all day."

He hesitated. "Master Olga keeps pushing tamers at me," he admitted, "but none of them are helping. And they're starting to get wary of me."

She snorted. "Why? Did you bite one?"

He made a mocking face. "Never. Nobility tastes disgusting."

She laughed, and he wanted to tuck the sound away in his pocket.

"They're wary because tamers who fail to bond are thrown out," he told her. "If they risk trying to bond with me and it doesn't hold, it's a mark against them, and meanwhile they've lost time they could've used trying to bond a dragon who would be a better match."

She sobered. "Right. I should've guessed that. There are plenty of ex-tamers working in the kitchens. All of whom hate me, by the way."

His lips tightened into a thin line. "We'll get you out of there soon. Once we prove to the masters that you and I are meant to be together, they'll have no choice but to induct you as a full student. And you'll get proper robes, too, gray like mine, after our probationary bond is approved."

"How exactly are we going to convince them to approve us?"

"I'll talk to them," he said firmly. "We'll figure something out."

She bit her lip, unconvinced. He couldn't blame her. He wished he had a more solid plan, too, but he'd only just now discovered the truth of her situation.

She pushed herself up onto one elbow. "I've been wondering —what exactly is it that tamers do, anyway? I've tried to sneak into some classes to find out more, but I haven't learned much. Maybe if we could find a way to prove I'm a good tamer already, that would show the masters I belong here."

"Tamers ground the dragon nature," he explained. "They're special because they're part dragon, but usually with more human blood than those who actually shift into dragon form. Tamers are dragon enough to understand us, and human enough to ground us—make us smarter, kinder, stronger." She tilted her head, inviting more information, and he obliged. "They live longer than most humans and have some telepathic ability—that's how you could hear me in dragon form—and sometimes the more experienced ones have limited control over an element."

"And the bond?"

"It just happens, when the right people are paired up. It's not like fate, since a dragon can have more than one match for a tamer, but different pairings have varying levels of compatibility and effectiveness. Plus, the bond grows stronger over time, as the dragon and tamer become more attuned to each other."

One side of her mouth turned up. "You know, if you aren't named king, you could always make a living as a teacher."

"Don't even say such a thing," he said, feigning horror.

She hesitated, then pulled something out of her pocket. "By the way. This is what I was doing tonight, when you found me," she said, holding up some parchment. "It's a magical map of the Akademy. Want to go exploring with me tomorrow night? Since apparently that's the only way we're going to steal any time to talk and, you know, plot how to overthrow the masters."

He smiled, a sense of rightness settling over him as he looked at her. "I'd like nothing better."

Three nights later, he flopped down on a balcony next to Kaelan. "This is impossible," he moaned.

She turned to him with a grim smile and tossed him something. He caught it: a steaming bun, fresh from the kitchens. Where she was still practically enslaved by that horror of a head cook who had barred him from visiting for fear that he'd try to extract her again. Which he'd only done twice. Yesterday.

He sighed and took a bite. "Thanks."

"Who did Master Olga try to team you up with today?" Kaelan asked.

"Inga." He shuddered, and the dislike on Kaelan's face matched his own. The noble tamer was saccharine-sweet with Lasaro and coyly cutting with everyone else when she didn't think he was watching. He hadn't felt a shred of response to her attempts to bond with him. Luckily, Master Olga had seen the way the wind was blowing and had called the attempt off.

He had managed to shift a handful of times over the last few days, at least. Only for a few minutes at a time only when he'd spotted Kaelan hidden somewhere and watching him. She'd come every chance she'd gotten, he knew, sneaking away from the kitchens to find his class and encourage him from a distance. Once or twice, he could've sworn he'd gotten a faint sense of emotion from her: a fizzing happiness mixed with grumpy displeasure, all of it overshadowed by a stony, grim determination that felt as vast as the mountain they stood on. Such a heady mixture of contradictions, his tamer was.

He finished the bun and stood, looking out at the rolling hills below. They were on a parapet overlooking the back side of the mountain and the wilderness beyond. "Why do we meet here?" he asked, brushing his hands together. "The towers on the other side have a much better view. I could show you the palace—it's all lit up at night, like a beacon."

She was quiet for a moment. "This reminds me of home," she said at last.

"Your home is like this?" He looked out over the emptiness below him. He didn't know if he could have stood it if *his* home had been like this—empty, silent.

"My latest home, anyway. Not that any of them last very long. Listen," she ordered him.

He sighed and obeyed. For a minute, he itched to say something, but after a while he started to make out more detail. The wind sang an eerie tune as it wound up the mountain, through the rock formations, over the barren field below. Off in the hills, a wolf howled, and another joined in. An owl called to its mate.

"It's lovely in a way," he admitted at last.

She smirked, turning to him. "But you still prefer your hustle and bustle."

He spread his hands helplessly.

"Heathen," she accused, and then she turned and marched toward the door to the Akademy.

"Where are we going tonight?" he asked, following.

"The Tapestry Room," she said immediately, and he groaned. "What?" she asked defensively.

"Again?" But his reluctance was good-natured; her passion for learning was so strong it couldn't help but draw him in, like a planet falling toward the gravity of its star. Which was why they'd ended each of the last three nights of exploration in the Tapestry Room.

"Again," she said firmly. "Tonight, I want to look at the founding of the Akademy, and maybe the legends of the first dragons. Did you know that dragons and sometimes tamers are basically the historians of the kingdom? They've lived so long, and their memories are so great, they're naturals for the job."

"Yes, I did know that. Because you've told me four times already."

She punched him lightly in the arm with that. He rolled his eyes and rubbed at the spot, but smiled when she turned away.

"Last night, I stayed in the Tapestry Room for a while after you left," she said in a low voice as she led him through the silent halls.

"How long did you stay? You need your sleep, Kaelan."

"You sound just like Ragnhild," she muttered.

"No need for insults."

"I only stayed an hour. Or so." Before he could respond, she hurried on. "Anyway, I found out some really interesting things about the Akademy's past."

"About Mordon, you mean." He waited for her response. He knew she'd been researching the rogue dragon, though he didn't know why. Mordon was an enemy to the throne and to the whole of Alveria since he'd proclaimed he'd take over the kingdom. Perhaps the mention of his stars in the observatory had interested her. Still, Kaelan's level of obsession seemed borderline unhealthy.

She fell silent.

"I know you've been researching him. Are you just curious, or are you trying to research something specific? Can I help?"

"I'm not—" she started, and then both of them froze when a white form materialized out of the darkness in front of them.

"Students," said Master Henra in that cold voice that seemed to slither across the floor toward them. "What are you doing out of bed at this hour?"

Lasaro shifted his weight to cover for Kaelan as she slipped the map into her pocket. His mind raced, searching for an excuse. He didn't think Henra would do more than reprimand him, since he was the prince and a dragon, but the masters were all looking for any excuse to throw Kaelan out on her ear.

Damn it. This was the risk of meeting after curfew—but it was the only time they could ever talk. They'd made a bit of progress in planning how to prove Kaelan's worth to the masters, but if she got kicked out now, none of that would do any good.

"I found Kaelan at dinner earlier," he said, thinking quickly, "and we wanted to take a walk, and we got lost."

"Lost," Henra repeated flatly.

Lasaro couldn't see Kaelan from his spot in front of her, but he could feel waves of fear and dislike emanating from her like heat off a fire.

"Yes," he said defiantly.

Henra's voice went smoother, almost conciliatory, which felt so wrong that Lasaro took an involuntary half-step backwards. "Students have been expelled for getting 'lost' in the wrong area of the Akademy, you know," she said.

"We were just on the balconies," Kaelan said quickly, the anger and fear he'd felt from her earlier underpinning her tone.

"And why, Miss Younger, are you wearing a trainee's robe?"

"Uh," Kaelan started, looking down at herself, caught off guard. He knew she could hardly admit she wore the robes because they were black and helped her blend in with the shadows while she snuck around the Akademy at night.

Lasaro spoke up quickly. "She spilled soup over her normal clothes."

Henra raised one perfect eyebrow. "And she did not change into one of her other sets of clothing?"

Kaelan glared, recovering herself. "I'm a peasant, remember?" she asked sharply. "I can only afford one set of clothing. Unless you expect me to stir vats of broth in my nightgown."

Henra lifted her chin and stared at them a moment longer, waiting for them to break. Lasaro's hands curled into fists with the effort of staying silent. But he'd learned from his brother that, when one got into trouble, the simplest lies were better than any complicated excuse made to get out of it.

"Back to your rooms," Master Henra said at last, and Lasaro let out a quiet breath. She held out a hand. "Miss Younger, I'll escort you back to your quarters."

Lasaro turned, his eyes locking with Kaelan's. She gave him a helpless look and then swallowed and obeyed Henra. He wanted to snarl as the master's claw-like fingers sank into Kaelan's shoulder, but he held himself back, not wanting to get her into trouble or give Henra any reason to suspect the two of them further.

As Kaelan and Henra turned the corner, Lasaro tensed up all over again. There was no way Henra wouldn't take Kaelan's robes away. And when she did, she would find the map. Would it be enough to get Kaelan kicked out? It was clearly a magical artifact, and Henra might assume she'd stolen it.

His nails were digging into his palms. With conscious effort, he relaxed his hands, dropping them into his pocket.

Paper crinkled beneath his fingers.

He breathed out a laugh, pulling out the map that Kaelan had —of course—stuffed into his pocket when he and Henra had been distracted. He was lucky she was such a quick thinker.

Satisfied that Kaelan could handle anything Henra could throw at her, Lasaro retreated to his room to plan out the next night's meeting spot. No way were they going to the Tapestry Room again.

He had something much better in mind.

CHAPTER 16

After the night with Lasaro and an unending day of kitchen work, Kaelan tried to drag herself to the Solarium late the next afternoon to read one of the books she'd brought from the library about dragon eggs. But instead of reading, she fell asleep. She woke to a vast, empty room drenched in the colors of sunset, which leached down from the many skylights peppered over the dragon perches that spanned the walls above. Yawning, she cursed herself. Weren't dragon-bloods and tamers supposed to be able to get by on less sleep? She was positive she'd read that somewhere. She wished *that* trait was the one that had manifested in her. It would be much more useful than roaring.

She glanced around. Henra had been teaching a class here earlier—which was part of the reason why Kaelan had chosen this spot to read, since technically the Solarium was open to everyone and they couldn't kick her out for "spying" on the class being held here. Still, Kaelan had figured it was better to not be seen at all, so she'd tucked herself under a blanket on this corner couch. Which was probably why she'd fallen asleep so easily. But she couldn't risk giving Henra any more reasons to kick her out. Last night had gone better than it might've—Henra had confiscated her robes, and given a faintly disappointed frown when her search of its pockets had turned up nothing—but Kaelan knew most of the masters would love to dump her peasant tush in Bellsor if she gave them a good enough excuse. And if that happened, any hope for healing Ma would be lost.

Kaelan bit her lip. She'd tried to tell Lasaro about Ma so many times over the last few nights. He'd been acting so warmly toward her—surely, he would've understood and been receptive. Maybe they could figure out a solution together. But every time she'd come close to telling him the truth, she'd remembered Olga telling her about the dragons' policy. Lasaro wouldn't be allowed to help her, not until their bond was official—even if he was sympathetic, he couldn't put his own future at risk by breaking the law. Plus, he hadn't harnessed his powers yet, and Haldis had said an untrained dragon-blood was as likely to kill Ma as heal her.

And also, if Kaelan was honest with herself, she simply didn't *want* to tell Lasaro the truth. She'd been enjoying their time together—it had become a refuge, a few stolen hours each night that belonged to just them. If she told him about Ma, those hours would be burdened by reality, and she didn't want that. Not yet, not when it wouldn't make a difference, anyway.

She pushed the thoughts out of her head and sat up on the couch. Earlier, the Solarium had been home to Henra's class of tamers—which was much larger than the class of new dragons, itself probably a factor behind the fierce competitiveness of the tamer students—but now it echoed with a vast, lazy silence. The quality of the quiet felt like that of a house cat curled up in a sunbeam on a late afternoon, only moving when its little slice of the sun traveled across the floor.

Smiling, Kaelan put a hand on the stone wall nearest her. It was, as she'd suspected, warm and cozy-feeling.

A tingle of affection trembled up from the stone and into her arm.

She jumped, shocked. She glanced around, but no one else was in the room, and there was nothing to suggest that anything out of the ordinary had happened. But something *had.* The Akademy had just... what, greeted her? Spoken to her, in a way? She smiled in wonder.

"I like you, too," she dared to whisper. She couldn't wait to explore this strange, magnificent place more tonight. With Lasaro. And hopefully, they might finally come up with a concrete plan to get her accepted as a trainee.

Her smile grew as she remembered that night in the Observatory, and the heady mix of pride and uncertainty and happiness she'd seen on Lasaro's face when he'd opened the doors with that little flourish, like he was giving her a gift he hoped she'd like. Lasaro was a fascinating boy... one who acted more every night like her friend rather than a distant prince. He talked to her like she mattered. He gave her opinions weight— more weight, she thought, than he gave to the masters' teachings, and certainly more than he gave to the needy noble students. Then, he held at arm's length, acting unfailingly polite and reserved. But Kaelan, he'd laid down next to on a starlight-dusted floor and talked to about faith and tradition and his country's future.

"Talking to inanimate objects is usually not a good sign," said a mild voice from just a few feet away.

Kaelan jumped and yelped.

The girl who'd spoken stared back at her, her eyebrows raised. She was twisted around, peering at Kaelan over the back of a tall chair which must have hidden her from view earlier. She was small and slender with freckles speckled across her nose, and short auburn hair that spiked upward like a flame. A tamer student. The one who'd recently paired up with a dragon named Def, if Kaelan had correctly overheard the rumors that'd swirled through the kitchens.

Embarrassed at her reaction—and by the fact that she hadn't noticed her sooner—but still on guard, Kaelan frowned. "I wasn't talking to an inanimate object," she said defensively. "I was talking to the Akademy." She held herself rigid, ready for the inevitable teasing.

But the girl only nodded as understanding dawned across her features. "Oh, right. So you think it's sentient, too, then?"

Kaelan squinted, trying to sense the trap in the question. "Master Olga told me," she said at last.

The other girl pursed her lips, looking suddenly deflated. "You must be one of her favorites, then. She hardly tells anyone anything. Always wants us to work it out ourselves."

Kaelan huffed. "I don't get much chance to work things out myself, being banned from classes, now do I?"

The girl squinted at her, puzzled, and then her mouth formed an O. "You're the peasant student, aren't you?"

"Yes, I am," Kaelan answered defiantly.

The other girl held out her hand. "I'm Drya," she said. "Nice to meet you."

Frowning uncertainly, Kaelan shook her hand. Could it be possible she'd met the only kind noble student in the whole Akademy? "Kaelan," she replied cautiously.

"Well, Kaelan, you're not the only one having a tough time figuring things out for yourself," Drya said, her tone mournful.

"You're not doing well in your classes?"

"Nope. I mean, I've got the book knowledge part down pat; the library is my favorite place—isn't it amazing? But, I'm having a really tough time working on my bond with Def. I'm worried that if I don't get better at sensing his emotions and helping him calm down, the masters will flunk us when our bond is tested before we move to initiate status. And then I'll wind up stuck in the kitchens instead of out doing tamer work." She snapped upright, suddenly realizing what she'd said. "Oh, I didn't mean—I don't want to imply that the kitchens—"

"Are terrible?" Kaelan chuckled, relaxing fully. "They are. You definitely don't want to get stuck there."

"Right," Drya said, apparently relieved.

Kaelan hesitated, checking the sun. She really needed to get back to work before Ragnhild saddled her with pot-scrubbing duty again, the way she had after the incident with Inga and the soup. But Kaelan could really use a few more friends in this place. Five minutes, she decided, and then she would go. "Would you like some help?" she asked Drya. "I don't have any official training, but… I've kind of maybe bonded with a dragon already, too, and it seems to be going well."

"You did? Who?" Drya leaned forward, her eyes bright. "I swear on Odin's eye I won't tell if it's a secret."

Kaelan looked away. She shouldn't tell. If this girl turned out to not be as genuine as she seemed, and if she told the masters, it could be used against Kaelan. But she was tired of not trusting anyone, and tired of having only Lasaro to talk to. He was great, but he was still a guy, and a prince. Plus… if she won over Drya, it might give her an in with the other noble students, too. And if she could win over enough of them, it would mean one less obstacle to Kaelan staying here.

"Lasaro," she whispered at last.

Drya's mouth dropped open. "You bonded with the *prince?* That's *amazing,* Kaelan. I'm so happy for you!"

Kaelan nodded, relieved. "I know, right?"

"And, oh! It makes sense now, what Lasaro said to Def about you the other day."

Kaelan stared at Drya. Lasaro had talked to another dragon student about her? Nerves fluttered in her stomach, and she put a hand over the spot. "What did he say, exactly?"

"Def was apologizing for attacking you—I don't know when? —but being kind of an ass about it, and Lasaro confronted him about it; he stood up for you."

"Oh," Kaelan said faintly. Lasaro had stood up for her. To a noble student. To one of the dragons who'd attacked her by the riverside—who, apparently, Drya was bonded to. Kaelan had no idea how to feel about this wealth of new information.

"I'd love your help," Drya said decisively, returning to the original topic of conversation. "Everyone and their brother has tried to bond with the prince, and there hasn't been a whiff of compatibility. If you managed it, then I want to know all your secrets."

Kaelan swallowed. She definitely didn't want anyone knowing all her secrets. She waved a hand, trying to side-step the question. "Well, I mean, we haven't done a lot yet. I unknowingly helped him transform for the first time ever on his way here, and then in the last few days helped him focus enough to do it a few times more. But I think the biggest help hasn't really had to do with some mystical bond at all, anyway. It's just—I don't know, being there for him. And knowing that he's there for me."

Drya frowned. "So, you guys are friends?"

Kaelan shifted, tilting her head. "It… kind of sounds like we are, doesn't it?" she admitted after a moment, wondering at the sudden realization. Lasaro had made it clear from day one that their relationship was all business, but his attitude and actions over the last few nights hadn't felt businesslike at all. They'd felt like the way one friend would treat another. A slow smile spread over her face.

"That might be what's missing between Def and me," Drya went on, oblivious. "He's kind enough, and definitely generous—he's given me a ton of gifts already—but sometimes he treats me more like I'm a prized pet than a friend, or even a person."

Kaelan tried to refocus. "Sounds like dragon nature to me. Wanting to hoard all the pretty possessions and all that."

Drya looked surprised, then thoughtful. "I hadn't thought of it like that, but you're right. He does do that. I knew he loved his pretty things, but I didn't realize he thought of me as one of them."

"Maybe he's not as receptive to bonding with you because he doesn't quite see you as a person yet," Kaelan offered.

"Yeah," Drya agreed, nodding enthusiastically. "It's like I'm a tool to him, I think. What does it feel like between you and Lasaro?"

Kaelan hesitated, then answered slowly, "Have you ever known someone for so long that you can guess what they're going to do and say next? And if it's something bad, you know exactly what small gesture will head things off? It's like that. It's like... well, a sort of telepathy, I guess, only it's more than the magical kind. It's like we've grown up together, like sometimes, for a split second, we're almost the same person."

"I wish I had that."

"It sounds like you need to put your foot down with Def," Kaelan advised. "Show him that he needs to treat you as more than a tool. If he's not willing to respect you, you don't need to be in any kind of relationship with him."

Drya frowned. "I don't know," she hedged. "I'm just terrified

I'm going to wind up ruining what little bond we already have and flunking out if I stand up to him."

"Better to flunk out than to tie your life to a dragon, or anyone, who sees you as a possession instead of a person."

Drya took a deep breath, steeling herself, and then nodded firmly. "You're right. Okay. I'll see what I can do." A smile stole over her face. "Thanks for the advice, Kaelan. It was really great to meet you. Maybe we can hang out again sometime?"

"I'd love that," Kaelan said, happy to have found a real friend in this place at last.

Kaelan hurried to her room after her conversation with Drya. She didn't have her black robes anymore, but at least they still had the map. Well—*Lasaro* had the map. Which meant he'd had all day to examine it, which meant she probably wasn't going to get to go to the Tapestry Room again tonight. Her mouth twisted and she sighed. The Tapestry Room held so much knowledge and history, particularly about Mordon. Lasaro had been right last night; she was researching her father. She needed to know why he'd chosen her mother, why he'd left the Akademy, and why he'd been named a rogue.

And if he really was the same black dragon she'd dreamt about.

But, so far, she'd had little luck. Most of the tapestries she'd investigated—with the exception of the very first one—only mentioned Mordon as a side note to some larger story. She'd learned precious little about him, and certainly not enough to satisfy her thirst for knowledge about her father. She knew dragons were declared rogues when they became too animalistic, but apparently that wasn't the case for Mordon, since Ardis had known him as a human seventeen years ago—*after* he'd been named a rogue. So, what had he done? Or perhaps he'd been falsely accused of something? That could just be wishful thinking, though. Kaelan had been terrified for the last year that she was about to lose what little family she had—as much of a relief as it would be to gain a good father now, it was unlikely to turn out that way.

She wished she could ask Lasaro about him. It had sounded like he might at least know something about Mordon—surely, he'd have to, having grown up in the palace with the best of tutors. But she couldn't risk him guessing the real reason behind her interest in the infamous rogue dragon. She didn't know if she'd ever be ready to tell Lasaro the truth about her parentage, but she definitely wasn't ready right now.

As she strode down the hallway, puzzling through her thoughts, a strange sense slid over her. It was like she was being watched. She paused to look around, afraid a master was watching and would punish her for some imagined infraction. But there was no one in this quiet hallway.

There was a window, though.

The sense of being watched intensified. The hallway seemed too quiet like the world around her was holding its breath. The fine hairs on her arms rose. Slowly, she approached the window, peering out into the haze beyond the Akademy and even beyond Bellsor. It was ridiculous to think anyone would be watching her from out there. No one could see that far.

Except maybe a dragon. And if she squinted, she could almost make out a long, strange shadow in the hills—

"Kaelan!"

Kaelan yelped and spun around, her heartbeat clamoring in her ears. It was Frigg, her perpetually annoyed roommate. "What?" Kaelan snapped. The strange sixth sense slid away from her and the hallway felt normal again. It left her both relieved and edgy.

"There's a package come for you," Frigg said, narrowing her eyes. Then she whirled around and marched to their room a little further down the hall without waiting for a response.

Kaelan glanced back out the window. Nothing. Just mist, hills, and Bellsor. She *had* been pretty tired lately—maybe her exhausted brain had engineered the strange feeling?

Frowning, she followed her roommate. "Package?" she called out after her, but Frigg didn't answer. Kaelan wondered if Haldis might've sent her something. So far, there had only been the one letter from home, which had been slipped under her door while she'd been away, and she'd sent one to her family before that, which she'd snuck into the mail pile at the administration office. She only hoped Grandma hadn't found the coins Kaelan had left behind and sent them back to her.

She opened the door—sending a glare at Frigg who hadn't bothered to leave it open for her—to find a crow perched on her bed.

It was perhaps a foot tall, its feathers a beautiful onyx black that seemed to shimmer in the light. It perched atop a box nearly as big as it was. The creature swiveled its head to look up, having to tilt backwards to peer at Kaelan as she approached, going back so far that the feathers atop its head nearly laid flat against its back. It shook out its wings and ruffled its feathers at her.

"Aren't you pretty?" she asked, reaching out a hand to touch the creature.

Alarmed by the sound of her voice, Frigg swung around and caught sight of her almost touching the crow. "Careful, don't —" she started to warn her, but was interrupted when the crow opened its mouth and emitted an ear-shattering *CAW-CAW-CAW.*

Kaelan leapt backwards and clapped her hands over her ears. The bird closed its beak. Cautiously, she lowered her hands, staring at it.

"—touch it," Frigg finished with a sigh. "This kind of crow is magically augmented to be able to carry loads heavier than they are, but it has an unfortunate side effect of also augmenting their voice."

Down the hall, a door thudded. "A trainee's got a squawker," said a muffled voice, laughing.

Scowling, Kaelan fluttered her hand at the bird until it hopped off the package. It fluffed its feathers at her again and pecked her finger when she reached for the twine.

She put her hands on her hips and leveled a look at it. "I used to have a chicken like you," she told the crow. "She was delicious."

Disgruntled, the crow waddled to the window—swiveling its head back to give her one last beady-eyed glare—and then flew back out into the night. Frigg closed the pane behind it with a decisive thud.

While her back was turned, Kaelan quickly opened her package. It wasn't from Ardis and Haldis. It didn't have any indication of its sender, in fact. Nestled inside were a gold and silver knife, an old piece of parchment, and a small bag of coins.

She blinked at the box. Had the crow accidentally brought a package to the wrong student? Perhaps she should notify Master Olga.

Then the lettering at the top of the parchment caught her eye.

In heavy block lettering, different from the light, elaborately decorative writing on the rest of the page, was her name.

So, someone had sent this treasure trove to her specifically. Why? And who would want to give her anything as valuable as these coins, let alone the knife? She lifted the bag and looked inside. Gold pennies. Unable to resist, she dropped her hand in and sifted the coins through her fingers. It was more gold than she'd ever held in her life.

But, just a few days ago, she'd held different gold coins as well as another knife that had also been gifted to her—by her mysterious traveling companion. Could he have sent her this package, too? Why? If it truly was from him, Kaelan wasn't sure if she should be flattered, grateful, annoyed, or wary of his attention to her.

Glancing over to make sure Frigg wasn't watching, she hid the coins at the bottom of her pack, then took a closer look at the parchment in the box. She turned it this way and that, squinting to read the delicate writing until she managed to make out two words.

Emerald Lake.

That sounded familiar. She dug back through her memories until she found where she'd seen the name before, and then she grinned, rolled up the parchment, and went to work until nightfall.

Kaelan got a message from Lasaro an hour before curfew, asking her to meet him in the library instead of on the balcony. When she found him, he smiled and held up the map. She held up her own parchment and forestalled his words.

"Look what I found," she said excitedly. "Or, well, it was sent to me, I'm not sure by whom. But look!" She pointed to the words *Emerald Lake*. "I've seen this on the Akademy map before, I'm sure of it."

He squinted at the parchment and then made a rueful face.

"What?" Kaelan asked.

He rubbed the back of his neck. "That's where I was going to take you tonight," he said. "The Emerald Lake. I've heard rumors of it—apparently, all the new students try to find it, but hardly anyone ever does—and so I thought we would look for it on the map. I've been sneaking off to study it all day, and I think I found a few clues but haven't been able to pinpoint it yet. I figured you might be better at it than me. Plus... I thought the Emerald Lake might be a better place for us to meet and talk than out on the balconies. Wouldn't want the masters to catch us conspiring against them again."

She went warm all over like she was sitting next to a campfire on a winter's day. "We can study the parchment and see if it gives us any more clues," she said, suddenly a little shy.

He'd wanted to take her somewhere special, and he wanted to protect her from the masters. And he believed her to be better at something than he, a prince, was. And he wasn't upset about it the way most people were when they discovered the daughter of an outsider peasant was smarter, or more driven, or just *hungrier* for her goal than they were. It was… nice.

So, you guys are friends? Drya had asked earlier. And Kaelan had realized then that it was true. He treated her like a friend, for all that she'd sworn fealty to him. Apparently, his feelings truly had changed since their initial meeting. Sneaking off to a secret lake together certainly didn't sound like something a prince and his subject would do.

No. It sounded more like something a boy might want to do with his girlfriend.

Kaelan froze, her eyes wide. That couldn't be it, could it? Surely, if he had those sorts of feelings for her, she'd have noticed. But then, she'd only just recently figured out that he saw her as a friend, so that didn't say a lot for her ability to recognize relationship changes quickly.

Kaelan had only been in two romantic relationships before— neither of which had gone further than hiding in a broom closet to make out—so she had no way to know if her instincts were right about Lasaro's motivations. She *wanted* them to be right, though, which told her more than she was really comfortable knowing about her own motivations.

"Can I see?" Lasaro asked, holding out his hand for the parchment, and she gave it to him. They sat together at a nearby desk, chairs scooted so close together that her arm pressed against his, their heads bowed over the map and the new parchment as they searched both.

"There!" Kaelan said nearly an hour later, stabbing her finger at the map and nearly shouting. Laughing, Lasaro shushed her as he glanced at where she was pointing, and then they darted down the far wall of the library. Excitement and a thrill of illicit happiness shot through Kaelan's veins, sharpening her vision and heightening her senses. When they found the spot where the secret doorway was supposed to be hidden, she was the one who spotted the door's seam hidden behind a bookshelf. They eased it silently open and slipped into a rocky tunnel filled with steam.

Giggling, they followed its winding path downward.

"Holy Hel," Kaelan whispered when they found the Emerald Lake.

It was more like an underground sea than a lake, so far across that she could barely make out the other side. The ceiling was low and studded with gleaming gems and crystals, and lined with veins of some kind of phosphorescent green mineral—the same kind, she thought, as she'd seen in the Clutch Room. She bent down at the edge of the lake and scooped up a handful of the pebbles that made up its floor then let the smooth green stones fall through her fingers and back into the water.

"Emeralds," she said in awe. "Actual emeralds. An *actual lake* of *actual emeralds.*"

Lasaro didn't answer. She turned to see his reaction, but he was no longer standing behind her. The parchment and map that he'd been carrying were on the ground, a chunk of what looked like ruby set atop them to keep them in place. She heard a whoop and followed the sound to find Lasaro stripped down to his shorts, a look of sheer delight on his face as he ran across an outcropping and flung himself into the water. The resounding splash echoed across her and sent small waves lapping at her feet. Lasaro resurfaced, shaking his head like a dog, water droplets flying as he grinned at her. His silver-blond hair had lost its ponytail and strands of it were plastered across his face. His blue-gray eyes shone with joy.

He was breathtaking. He was *happy.* And he was a boy, and she was a girl, and they were completely, deliciously, terrifyingly alone. She stood frozen on the shore, small waves lapping at her wet boots, staring at the prince she was beginning to think she might be very foolishly falling for.

"Swim with me!" he shouted, and the spell was broken.

She backed up a step, her eyes wide. "I don't know how to swim," she confessed, eyeing the deeper water where he was moving his arms and legs in some mysterious fashion that appeared to be keeping him afloat.

He paddled to the outcropping he'd jumped from and pulled

himself up, then came to stand in front of her. "That's perfect," he said, still grinning, that heady joy still bright in his eyes. It drew her forward against her will.

She swallowed. "Why is that perfect?"

"Because I'll teach you," he said, and held out a hand.

She eyed it. His hand was perfect—long, slender fingers, unblemished skin, square nails. The hand of a prince. Would it really fit so well in hers?

She wanted to find out.

She took a deep breath as if she was about to plunge underwater right this second. That was what it felt like: the unknown beneath her, and her deciding to surrender to it, a strange thrill shooting through her veins. It was the same mix of fear and fascination and excitement she'd been addicted to all her life, only now it was distilled, purified, and boiled down to its essence. A dragon stood before her, and he was a prince, and also the boy she thought she might like as more than a friend, and he was holding out his hand and asking her for *something*. Because this wasn't just swim lessons. This wasn't anything like the last time he'd offered her his hand, to seal a deal made between a dragon and his new tamer. This would be her and him, stripped down to their underclothes, in a vast secret lake made of gems beneath a magical school where he was her only true friend, however much he once might've claimed otherwise.

It wasn't wise to accept his invitation. She should maintain her distance. If they became close like this now and then later he went distant again, it would crush her. She wouldn't be able to perform her taming duties properly.

But he was still holding out his hand and waiting so patiently for her to decide, and she couldn't deny that happiness in his eyes or the excitement in her own heart.

"Okay," she said, and she slid her fingers into his.

CHAPTER 17

Lasaro led his tamer into the shallows until the water
floated around her thighs. Which he was *not* looking at.
He made himself focus on the water around her instead, the
way it glowed ever so slightly green, and tried to guess what
had given it that quality. Probably some of the phosphorescent
mineral veined through the rock above had leached into the
water. It was eerie and beautiful and warm and magical and
made even more so by Kaelan's presence. It renewed him. He
felt like the last few weeks—the last few months, really—of
hardship, of trying and failing to prove himself a good future
ruler and a perfect son, had washed away, leaving behind only
Lasaro.

Who was with Kaelan. Who was half-naked, and very wet,
and looking at him like he was the only boy in the world.

He swallowed and forcibly returned his thoughts to the phosphorescent mineral.

"This is amazing," Kaelan said, scooping up water in her cupped hands and marveling at it. "It's magical. I can *feel* it. It's like it's... I don't know—"

"Strengthening you? Renewing you?" He filled the words in for her, tugging her deeper until the water crept up to her waist.

She nodded. "It's like I had all these cracks in me that I didn't know about until the water filled them up."

"You're so poetic," he remarked, smiling.

She made a face and flicked water at him. "Are you going to teach me to swim or just butter me up? Because I'm fine with either, but you promised me a lesson."

Lasaro laughed and tugged her a touch further until the water came up to her shoulders. She looked nervous and stopped there. He leaned in. "Trust me," he whispered in her ear.

She shivered at his closeness, but didn't move away, and goosebumps rose across her arms. He felt suddenly powerful, invincible—that she would react to him that way, and that she trusted him in an unfamiliar environment.

He'd been in romantic situations before. He'd had a handful of flings, one with the stablemaster's daughter and two with palace maids, but none of them had ever made him feel like this. He knew nothing could come of it—he would eventually have to marry for political advantage rather than personal affection, especially if he became king—but right now, that wasn't what he wanted to think about. His mind was always so busy, so strained with trying to figure out what a good prince would do. All he wanted right now was to be here with Kaelan and not think about the future.

"Okay," Kaelan answered him.

He started with the easier maneuvers, teaching her how to float on her back when she tired, and then how to tread water. When she floated, he held one hand beneath her, fingers splayed across her lower back to support her until she was confident, and he knew he would dream of the curves and dips of her spine against his hand later that night. When she asked to learn the breaststroke and wanted him to hold her up in the water until she figured it out, he had to keep his eyes firmly fixed on the ceiling and his mind on counting the gems over-head—not on the way her stomach felt as she stretched—to avoid embarrassing himself.

She was his *tamer.* His subject. Not his girlfriend. This was a swimming lesson only. A friendly outing, an exploration of their shared environment. But Lasaro couldn't deny he felt more than just *friendly* when her fingers accidentally brushed his chest, and when she looked up at him with her eyelashes sparkling with water drops and her hair wet and plastered across her shoulders and chest. Her undershirt was thick enough for modesty, but it clung to her in a way that made his mouth dry, and her shorts covered far less skin than the robes he was used to seeing her in.

It was both a relief and a torture when she finally tired and the swimming lesson was declared over. They dragged themselves up onto the gem-strewn shore and flopped down on the smooth onyx outcropping he'd jumped from earlier.

"I should be exhausted," Kaelan said after a moment. "But honestly, now that I've caught my breath, I feel like I could jump up and run a lap around this whole place right now."

"Me, too," he said. The joy and attraction and uncertainty mixed together with whatever magic was in this place, making for a potent brew of emotion that had his dragon blood surging closer to the surface than it had since that day at the river. It felt suddenly so right and natural and perfect that, in a snap-second decision, he shifted.

His vision changed, disorienting him the way it always did. He thought this might be how a hawk saw things; he could take in many details at once, and could zoom in on impossibly faraway objects. But right now, there was only one thing he wanted to see. He lifted his head—grateful as he did that the ceilings in here were so high, since at his full height his head reached higher than most small buildings—and gazed down at Kaelan, who lay a few feet away. With his dragon vision, he could pick out the individual drops of water beading on her arms and legs, see each strand of black hair plastered across the onyx stone, note how her face had filled out a touch in the last few weeks and how her skin looked healthy now that she had better food. She had her eyes closed, and he wanted to memorize the peaceful look on her face and tuck it away for later.

"Don't fall asleep—Ragnhild will kill you if you miss your shift," he thought to her jokingly, and only when she jumped away and shrieked did he remember she was unused to dragons and hadn't seen him shift. Chagrined at his mistake and horrified to see the startled fear in her eyes, he tucked his head under one massive paw, peeking out at her from underneath it, trying to look harmless. After a moment, he decided to completely trash his dignity, and he rolled over onto his back like a puppy asking for a belly rub. If he looked ridiculous enough, maybe it would wipe that awful fear from her face.

Slowly, a cautious smile crept over her features. "Warn me next time," she scolded him, and then she edged closer.

"Sorry," he said telepathically, and lifted his head as she approached. He inhaled. His dragon form meant a heightened sense of smell as well as sight. She smelled like the kitchens— fresh bread and a tangle of spices—and like fresh air.

She raised an eyebrow. "Are you sniffing me, Lasaro?"

He rolled back to his stomach and ducked his head under his paw again, trying to look innocent.

She snorted, continuing her examination of him as she walked a little closer. "It seems like that shift was a lot easier for you than the others have been," she mused. Hesitantly, slowly, she put a hand on his shoulder, having to stand on her tiptoes to do it. He shivered at the feel of her fingers on his scales for the first time ever, and the quickness of her breath and the hitch in her heartbeat told him she felt the same way.

"It was," he said. *"I didn't even feel angry or have to push myself like the other times. It was just there. I think it's this place. It's strengthened our bond, strengthened my powers."*

But she was only half-listening, sliding her hand across his leg and side, attention riveted on the feel of him. "You're beautiful," she said quietly, and the lingering nervousness vanished from her features completely. It made Lasaro feel intoxicated.

He tried to pull himself together. He had no idea how to respond, so he channeled his annoyingly charming brother Freyr. *"I prefer devilishly handsome,"* he managed.

She chuckled. She'd reached his wings now, and a shiver overtook his whole body when she gently ran her fingers over the leathery membrane. Taking care to move slowly and not startle her, he lifted his wings and held them out for her inspection. "They're huge," she marveled, craning her neck. His wings stretched over the entire outcropping they were resting on, shadowing the edge of the lake. "But so graceful looking. You know... Embers breathe fire, and I've heard Terras connect with the earth through touch, but I wonder how Ariels reach their magic?"

A half-formed instinct came to him and, without giving it any further thought, he stretched his wings out to their full extent, then swept them swiftly upward. A whirlwind of air curled from his wingtips and he reached out with some instinctive, ancient sense and carved it, sculpting it into the shape and speed he wanted. He pulled his wings down and sent his finished creation toward Kaelan.

The gust of air caressed her, circled her, lifted her hair and fanned it out, and evaporated the moisture that had still been beaded on her skin. It didn't push against her the way normal wind would, but instead molded itself to her shape and curled around her like a house cat winding around its owner. When it faded, she was completely dry.

And, also, goggling at him like he'd gone mad.

"Oh," he said belatedly, *"sorry. I would've warned you, but it just sort of... happened."*

She held out a now-dry arm to marvel at the magic he'd formed. "That was amazing," she said at last, a little begrudgingly.

"That was the first time I've ever used my magic," he said. *"I didn't even really mean to do it, it just sort of happened. I think it's whatever magic is here that's letting me do all this so easily."*

Kaelan lifted her gaze to stare at the lake before them. "What *is* this place?" she muttered. Then, decisively, she wheeled around and marched back to her clothes. "Come on!" she called. "Let's go check out the library and see if we can find anything. We shouldn't come back here until we know it's safe. I'd hate to have you, I don't know, overdose or something."

"Same for you. You're part dragon, too," he pointed out. *"Doesn't it make you feel different?"*

She paused in the act of pulling her tunic back on over her undershirt. "Yeah," she said slowly, frowning as she pushed her arms through the sleeves.

He cleared his throat—which in dragon form sounded more like a coughing growl—and curled his tail around his feet. *"Um. You'll have to turn around, please. I wasn't wearing my uniform when I shifted, so…"*

She smirked and faced the wall. "Right. Of course."

He transformed back to human form—and he felt tired, but not nearly as shaken and exhausted as he usually did—and hurried to dress himself, sans underclothes, which were now in a shredded pile atop the outcropping. Kaelan tapped her foot impatiently the whole time, and as soon as he had his pants on, she was striding toward the exit, leaving him to tug on his shirt and hop into one shoe after the other as he tried to follow. "Ow," he protested. "Some of these stones are sharp!"

"Hurry up and get your shoes on and you won't have to worry about it," she responded.

"You know, some tamers revere their dragons," he called after her. She didn't respond. He rolled his eyes, but smiled.

And then, as they left the tunnel and entered the normal lighting of the library, with its familiar quiet taking the place of the Emerald Lake's echoing vastness, his smile fell away when he realized just how many bad decisions he'd made that night. He'd led Kaelan on. He'd led *himself* on, letting himself believe for a while that he and Kaelan could be more than just dragon and tamer. Something between them had changed, gone soft and sharp and electric all at once, and it should be making him very nervous, he knew. But as he watched Kaelan's retreating form, he couldn't bring himself to ruin tonight by reinstating their prince-subject roles. Tomorrow, he'd make things right, and put more distance between them.

Tonight, he just wanted to be Lasaro with Kaelan.

They searched through the library for an hour, but found only glancing mentions of the Emerald Lake. Finally, when they were both yawning and sleepy-eyed and Kaelan's dawn breakfast shift was growing dangerously close, an old leather-bound book floated over to them. The library, giving them a hint.

"What is it?" Lasaro asked, suddenly awake. The book had dropped itself into Kaelan's lap.

She held up a hand to forestall his questions as she cracked it open. She frowned, flipping through it. "This is just a treatise on Terras. The dragon quake they accidentally caused a few centuries back, the way they formed Mount Firewyrm—they *formed* Mount Firewyrm?!"

"Focus," Lasaro said.

With an effort, she kept flipping through the pages. "Right. I can study that later. Okay, famous Terra Masters, their methodology for weaving the tapestries…" Her head jerked up and she looked at Lasaro. "The Tapestry Room!" she said, and without another word, she leapt to her feet—tucking the book safely under her arm, of course—and darted across the library.

As soon as they reached the Tapestry Room, she put Lasaro to work pulling the corners of the heavy tapestries up so that she could search for one on the Emerald Lake. By the half-hour mark, he was panting with effort. He glanced at the skylight. The sky had lightened almost imperceptibly to a shade of navy rather than the indigo it had been when they'd first arrived. "We need to get back soon," he said. "You're going to have to start your shift, and I've got a class in a few hours. Refreshing as the lake was, I would *very* much like to get at least a little sleep before I have to face Master Henra again."

She shushed him, peeling up another tapestry for him to hold.

"Here it is!" she announced, her voice muffled as she burrowed deeper into the layers of fabric.

He maneuvered himself around so that his back sustained the weight of the top tapestries. The one Kaelan was looking at showed a gleaming green body of water surrounded by jutting gemstones—the Emerald Lake. Kaelan grabbed his hand in hers and laid both their palms against the fabric.

Instantly, his consciousness slipped into the tapestry. He was disoriented at first—he'd done this before with the magical tapestries in the palace's private collection, but it had been a while since then—but he still had Kaelan's hand in his, and that anchored him.

The woven Emerald Lake was beautiful. It couldn't quite capture the way the water glowed, but the fabrics had been well-chosen and well-dyed, and the magic of the medium allowed them to move throughout the scenes of the tapestry.

Ten minutes later, Lasaro pulled them out. They struggled out from under the tapestries and dropped to the floor, shaking and breathing hard from their exertion and the long night.

"So, it *is* magical," Kaelan said at last. "The lake, I mean."

He nodded. The tapestry had been clear about that much. Dragons could go there to bathe and absorb the energy of the water. The magic of the place was apparently even strong enough to transform a dragon who was on the verge of being stuck in human form, which explained why it had been so easy for him to shift. It replenished the magic of dragons and dragon-bloods and sometimes allowed them to access new abilities. It was impossible to overdose there, though, which was good news.

"It said the lake is particularly potent for Aquas," Lasaro mused. "You can't shift or control any of the elements, so we don't know what form of latent powers you might have, but what about your father? You'd have a good chance of being the same type of dragon as him. Do you know what kind he is?"

Kaelan's expression shut down into a blank mask. "No," she said shortly.

He frowned, taken aback by the change in her. She'd been exhilarated in the tapestry, thrilled to satisfy her curiosity, and even during the long night of research she'd only gotten mildly irritable. Now, though, it was like she'd cut herself off from him. He could even feel it through their bond—it was as if she'd pulled a curtain across her emotions, pushing him out.

So, she didn't want to talk about her father. He supposed that wasn't unusual, since she'd mentioned she lived alone with her mother and grandmother—she might dislike the father who'd apparently abandoned them, or perhaps he'd passed away and she grieved for him. Lasaro wished she'd trust him with her feelings, but maybe if he wanted her to open up to him, he'd have to take a turn first.

"Sometimes I think I might be scared to be a dragon," he admitted.

She glanced up, her blank mask falling away in surprise. "What do you mean?"

He looked up at the skylight, trying to find the right words to explain his feelings. "That first time when I transformed at the river, I couldn't stop thinking about the sky. I wanted to fly up into it forever, to… lose myself."

"Ah," Kaelan said, understanding dawning on her face. "You're afraid you'll be a rogue."

He lifted one shoulder, uncomfortable. "The same thing happened the second time I managed to shift. When you're there, I can control it more easily, but it's still hard. It's like the sky calls to me, and it's almost impossible to ignore it."

"Then don't ignore it."

He frowned. "What do you mean? I can't risk going rogue. My mother cares for me, but she'd do whatever she must to protect the kingdom. Including naming me a threat."

Kaelan's voice was soft when she replied, "You really think she'd give you to the dragon hunters?"

He sighed, running a hand through his hair. "I don't know," he confessed. "I want to think she wouldn't. But it's what a good ruler would do, isn't it?"

"Sometimes you have a very black-and-white view of morality," Kaelan said, "and you completely fail to consider how love changes the equation."

"It shouldn't," he replied stubbornly. "The good of the kingdom should take precedence over everything—love, tradition, any one person's ideals."

She scoffed. "Says the boy who's so afraid of his love of flying that he allows it to keep him from embracing his powers."

He blinked. Was that really what was happening? He'd thought of the way he felt about the sky as an obsession, a dangerous addiction, but could it really just be love?

Kaelan's voice softened further. "There are things you care about, things you enjoy doing, in your human form too, right? Maybe hobbies you enjoy so much you wish you could do them all the time?"

"I guess," he allowed, remembering how much he loved to ride Allfather across the countryside during his rare vacations away from the palace.

"It's probably the same for your dragon form. But since everything is so new and sharp and overpowering for new dragons, your love of flying is, too. I'm sure you'll get used to it, learn how to balance it and focus. But a love of flying isn't itself going to make you go rogue."

His lips tightened. He wanted to believe her, but the fear was powerful... and he wasn't sure he could risk her being wrong. He needed to make sure Kaelan would always be there to steady him, to tame him, to let him be absolutely sure he wouldn't go rogue. "Have you made any progress with getting the masters to officially admit you as a student?" he asked.

She made a frustrated sound. "No. Master Olga seemed like my best shot, but she said she can't go against the Council of Masters. I need to convince the rest of the masters, or at least a majority of them, that I should be a tamer. I've come up with a list of ways to do that, but nothing that seems like it would actually work. You?"

"I haven't come up with any good ideas, either." He grimaced, then glanced up at the sky. It had lightened and turned to pink at the eastern edge of the skylight. He'd barely have any time to sleep even if they left right now, but he found himself reluctant to end their adventure. Tomorrow, they'd have to go back to normal, and he wanted this night to stretch on forever.

But all things must end, so he climbed to his feet and reached out a hand to help Kaelan up. "We'll think of something," he told her, and he tried to believe it.

CHAPTER 18

D uring the weeks that followed, the few swimming
lessons she managed to snatch with Lasaro were the
sole bright spots in Kaelan's life. She paid for those long
nights dearly, though—her tiredness made her clumsy at work,
which Inga and her friends exploited to get her in trouble with
Ragnhild and even, once or twice, with the masters. Olga
intervened enough to keep her from getting fired and kicked
out, but not enough to shorten her shifts or stop the bullying.
And as the fall term approached its end, the tamer and dragon
students closed ranks, becoming more viciously competitive
than ever as the pressure mounted to form and strengthen
bonds before initiate testing began.

All while Kaelan was stuck in the kitchens.

She slammed a pot of tea down in front of a tamer student who
barely noticed as he was bent over a text and studying intently.

Kaelan's frown deepened. It must be nice to be allowed to study during the daytime and have the opportunity to sleep at night. Instead, she had to get most of her training from her scattered, rushed sessions with Drya, trading advice on bonding for sneak peeks at what the tamer trainees were learning. She'd also had to cram studying into her furtive evenings, cutting short her explorations with Lasaro and getting more exhausted with every passing day. She was willing to give up any amount of sleep for their infrequent visits to Emerald Lake, but she felt less enthusiastic about her long evenings of combing through the library in search of something, anything, that might give her an advantage in her quest to be made an official student. She'd caught Master Olga in the halls a few times and begged for her help, or at least some kind of hint about what more she could do to achieve her goal, but all Olga ever said was, *"Patience is required of tamer students, Pupil Younger."*

So, she kept her grueling schedule day after day, growing wearier and crankier with each new dawn, wondering how much longer she'd have to keep this up.

"Kaelan!" shouted Ragnhild, hurrying toward her with a mix of alarm and irritation showing in her expression.

Kaelan set the tamer student's roasted quail down next to his tea—being slightly gentler with the meat than she had with the drink—and turned. "What?" she asked, trying to rein in her own annoyance.

"You've got a squawker," Ragnhild said shortly.

Kaelan's irritability vanished in an instant and she darted after Ragnhild toward the crow that was perched in the corner of the kitchens. The other workers were striding away from it, giving it wary looks and keeping their hands free so they could cover their ears if it opened its beak. This particular bird looked ancient, a good quarter of its feathers missing or sticking out at odd angles. Kaelan slowed as she approached it, keeping her hands in plain sight and being careful not to make any sudden movements that might frighten it. It held a letter clutched in its claws, and she leaned in from as far away as she could to extract it. When she held it aloft, and the creature fluffed what feathers it had and hopped back up to the windowsill, everyone in the kitchen let out a relieved breath.

The bird jerked away at the sound and screamed out an ear-shattering *CAW-CAW-CAW*.

Everyone cursed and winced, most of them ducking away while a few made threatening gestures at Kaelan and the crow with whatever cooking implements they were holding. With one hand clutching the letter against the side of her head, Kaelan flapped her other hand at the bird until it shut its beak and flew off. The other workers wandered back to their tasks, sending Kaelan dark looks and muttered curses, but she ignored them as she turned the letter over.

The intrigue that had started to simmer in her faded. This wasn't from her mystery sender, the person who'd given her the parchment and coins and knife, who might or might not also be her traveling companion from her journey to the Akademy. The address scribbled in the corner of this letter was from Gladsheim, and the handwriting was unfamiliar.

Hands suddenly shaking, she tore open the envelope and read swiftly. When she finished, her fingers were numb, and the letter drifted out of them and settled slowly on the floor. A pot stirrer accidentally stepped on it. Kaelan made no move to retrieve it.

The letter was from Reida. She reported that Ardis had taken a turn for the worse and hadn't woken in three days. Longer even than that, now, given the days the letter would've taken to reach the Akademy. Reida had used some of her own money to hire a messenger to deliver this letter by the fastest means possible, and more money in order to move Ardis and Haldis into a room at the inn where they could be warm without Haldis having to chop firewood, but the move was a stopgap measure.

Her mother had entered the coma phase of the wasting sickness. Ma now officially only had eight weeks left before she died. And Kaelan was still helpless to stop it.

The students and most of the staff were granted a rare holiday the next morning, but Kaelan couldn't enjoy it. She'd locked herself in her room, ignoring her usual night of exploration with Lasaro in favor of pacing and studying, studying and pacing and worrying frantically that she was missing the one thing that might help her mother.

Lasaro might be able to heal her mother—eventually, after he harnessed his powers. But even though he was doing better at holding his dragon form since their talk in the Tapestry Room and their handful of visits to the Emerald Lake, he still hadn't been able to use more than a tiny bit of magic, and hadn't shown any healing abilities at all. Haldis herself had said that an untrained dragon could cause Ardis more harm than good. And Master Olga had already refused to help. None of the other masters would so much as give Kaelan the time of day, and according to what Olga had said, none of the dragons in the kingdom would go against their policy to heal the family member of a would-be student who wasn't officially personally committed to them yet.

She only had one card left to play. She had to tell the masters who her father was. Rogue or not, Mordon was one of the most powerful dragons to have ever taught here, and they'd *have* to honor that. At the very least, they'd have to let her out of the kitchens so she could become a real tamer and help Lasaro gain control faster, or maybe she could use her heritage as leverage to get one of the masters to heal Ma immediately. But, then… could she really risk them being petty enough, or scared enough, to turn her out entirely if she told them the truth? She'd be left with nothing, not even the future and stability she'd so tentatively started to hope for.

A knock sounded at the door. "Go away!" Kaelan shouted, certain it was Frigg, who was always forgetting things she was supposed to take with her to class.

"I could pull rank and order you to open the door, but then I'm fairly certain you'd poison my next mug of cider, so I'll settle for 'please let me in?'" Lasaro's voice was muffled and haggard with forced cheer, but suddenly, he was *exactly* the person she needed to see.

She took a sharp turn out of the line she'd been pacing across the room and opened the door. Lasaro's expression brightened when he saw her, then darkened again as he took in her features. She was practically vibrating with exhaustion, and worry had tightened her mouth and kept her shoulders high and tense.

He stepped inside and closed the door behind him. Then, as carefully and gently as if she were a fragile, crumbling thing that he was putting back together, he gathered her into his arms and held her. "I worried something had happened when you didn't meet me last night. Want to talk about it?" he asked quietly.

She clung to him, her hands fisting in his beautiful gray robes. "My ma," she whimpered, the words pouring out of their own accord. "She's... unwell. She caught a wasting sickness from a villager she was trying to heal last year. I just found out her illness has progressed. She's—she's dying."

"I'm so sorry," he murmured, but he didn't say anything else because there wasn't anything else he could say. Kaelan knew nothing would help. Nothing except her fulfilling her promise.

"I was going to make her better," she said helplessly. Her eyes were dry, but she wished she could cry, even if it had to be in front of Lasaro. She needed something, anything to release this terrible tension and pain. "I was going to find a way to fix her."

"The favor I promised you," Lasaro realized aloud. "You were going to use it to ask me to heal her."

She hadn't told him before because she'd known there was nothing he could do about it anyway, not untrained as he was, and not before she was officially committed to the dragons. And also—she'd thought it would hurt too much, to admit the truth to him. But now, she *wanted* to tell Lasaro. Wanted him to know about her, to see her, to understand how she was hurting so he could help ease it. Because he would. He was her friend. He'd proven it during the last weeks, no matter their original deal, and she realized now that it had hurt her much more to keep this from him than it would have to admit it. "Yes," she admitted. "Once you were stable enough to control your powers, I was going to use the favor to have you heal her."

He pulled back to look at her, his gaze intense. "We can still do that, Kaelan. We could go right now. The masters will excuse a short absence, and they'll probably forgive the breach of the magic-use policy eventually. There are *some* benefits to being a prince after all."

She shook her head, squeezing her eyes closed. "It means so much to me that you're willing to break the rules for me... but you know you don't have enough control yet to heal her. I can't risk..."

He sighed, drooping, and it took a moment for him to answer. "You're right. I understand. I'm sorry."

She opened her eyes. "It's not your fault."

"It's not yours, either."

"Yeah," she said, but she couldn't force herself to believe it.

"Is there... do you still have time? I mean, maybe if we really buckle down, we could strengthen our bond faster, make sure I master my powers by the end of the term. Is there a chance she'll be okay until then?"

Kaelan stepped out of his embrace and exhaled, tucking her messy hair behind her ears. "The wasting disease takes a while, most of the time, but it's already been over a year. She fell asleep a few days ago and won't wake up. My friend said she can still get some broth into her, and she's warm and safe, but at this stage in the sickness… she's got about two months left."

The words cut into her like glass shards scraping over her skin. She'd been wrong before, when she'd thought it might at least bring some twisted form of relief to know exactly how long her ma had left.

Lasaro put his hands on her shoulders. "Okay," he said. "Then we still have time. I'll train harder, put in some extra time with the masters; I'll even ask for some private tutoring." He hesitated. "I would offer to try to find a friend who could help your mother, but most dragons are loyal to the masters even over the royal family. There's a strong possibility they would report us rather than healing her, and then we'd risk getting expelled and losing any chance at success for trying to go against the dragons' policy."

She gave him a shaky smile. "I understand. Thank you for doing what you can."

"Of course." Then he dropped his hands, stepped back, and nodded decisively. "But today," he declared, "we are taking a break."

A frown slashed across her face. "What? You just said we need to work *harder*, not *less*. I should spend the day in the library and you should take an extra lesson, or go to the Emerald Lake."

"We've been doing all those things nonstop for the last month, and we're both exhausted. Sometimes a day off is the best thing you can do for your work."

She crossed her arms. "*Working* is the best thing you can do for your work."

Lasaro crossed his own arms and raised one eyebrow. "I didn't want to have to do this, but I'm willing to risk poisoned cider to stop you from killing yourself with your ridiculous stubbornness. Kaelan Younger, I, Prince Lasaro Afkarr of Alveria, your dragon and future king, hereby order you to accompany me into Bellsor for the holiday. We will look at all of the charming little shops. I will buy something for you to send home to your mother, and you will *rest*, and *eat,* and *relax*. Or else."

Kaelan gritted her teeth, her rebellious nature insulted by the order—but she knew he was right. She'd been up all night pacing with worry and getting nowhere, and she was too frazzled right now to study effectively or to be able to sleep. A day off might do her good and help her get into a stable enough state to actually do Ma some good later. "Fine," she said, dropping her crossed arms with a huff.

Lasaro smiled. "Excellent."

She leveled a finger at him. "I might still poison your cider."

"Duly noted."

"And also, *I* will buy something to send home to Ma and

Grandma. I do have some money, you know." Though, she still didn't know who had sent it.

"As you wish." He held out an arm. "Shall we, then? If we hurry, we can catch one of the supply carts on their return trip into town and steal a ride."

She sighed, grabbed Frigg's extra cloak from its hanger— Kaelan hadn't had time to buy one yet—and marched resignedly out the door with him.

Three hours later, Kaelan was less relaxed than ever.

She stood bewildered outside a store, holding a scarf that had been unceremoniously shoved into her hands. "I didn't even pay him yet," she said, staring at the door that the shop manager had locked behind them after he'd dumped them back on the sidewalk.

Lasaro was puzzled, too. "The whole town feels off today," he said, glancing around.

It was true. The passersby hurried on their paths, heads down, muttering darkly amongst themselves. So far, Kaelan had overheard grumblings about dragons not earning their keep and the looming war with Unger, and others suggesting the queen was growing too old to rule properly. When people looked at Lasaro and Kaelan, it was with a pointed glare or, in the case of the shop owners, a stare that went right through them as if they weren't even there. And when she'd tried to buy a new shawl for Grandma and this scarf for Ma, both shopkeepers had given her the first thing she'd stopped to admire and then had a sudden, mysterious need to close up shop in the middle of the day.

Kaelan remembered the law about dragons getting whatever they wanted without pay, but surely that didn't apply to mere Akademy students, and surely not in Bellsor—a city that had thrived in the very shadow of Mount Firewyrm for centuries. She knew the outlying villages were becoming more disgruntled about dragons of late, but could anti-dragon sentiments truly have spread so far, so quickly?

Lasaro tugged at his robes, agitated. "This isn't exactly the calming day I had in mind," he said with a sigh, but then he suddenly brightened. "But I have another idea."

"Wonderful," Kaelan said, barely straight-faced, but he smiled and scooped up her hand anyway, and she couldn't bring herself to pull away.

"Come on," he said, tugging her down the winding street toward the carriage taxis. "We'll hire a crow to send those gifts, and then I'm taking you to the palace."

CHAPTER 19

L asaro led Kaelan through the shining halls of his home, delighting in her poorly hidden awe. She was doing her best not to look like a gawking tourist, but she gaped at all of the golden frames, the carefully tended fountains and marble-tiled courtyards, and the tiny, delicate songbirds that trilled throughout the gardens. She'd gasped aloud when she'd seen the orchards, where the hedges were sculpted into long, stylized dragons. When he'd plucked an orange from a tree—magically enhanced to grow much further north than its usual environment—and tossed it to her, it had disappeared into her mouth so fast that he'd had to laugh. She'd turned haughty at that, but snatched three more oranges a few minutes later and devoured them all just as quickly as the first.

Lasaro's enjoyment faded as they wound their way deeper into the heart of the palace, though. Kaelan might see a beautiful display of power and wealth, but to Lasaro, this was his child-hood home—and his trained eye could make out the cobwebs in the corners of the windows, the silver sculptures that were beginning to tarnish at their bases, and the guards who didn't quite stand at full attention. The hair on the back of his neck prickled at their gaze as he passed. He turned around to match their stares one by one and, after a moment, they each pulled themselves up straight and turned back to their duties. Still, a lingering sense of unease wriggled deeper within him as he led Kaelan toward the family wing of the palace.

He paused in a corridor that dead-ended in a glass door leading to the palace's herb gardens. Kaelan made a face. "Don't I see enough herbs at the Akademy?" she asked, peering through the door. "I mean, these are laid out nicely, but once you've seen one sprig of rosemary, you've seen them all."

He just gave her a grin and pulled her to the far wall, counting his steps as he approached a painting of Thor. Four, five, six—there. He reached up to the wall and traced the nearly invisible seam of a door inlaid next to the art. "I've always liked to explore," he told Kaelan. "I found these secret passages one rainy day when I was seven. They lead up to the private areas of the family wing. Want to go meet my brother and sisters?"

Kaelan hemmed and hawed, backing away. "I don't know," she said. "I mean, this is the *palace*. Won't we get in trouble?"

"Not any that I can't get you out of," he promised.

The door yawned open. Kaelan leaned forward, fascinated despite her reluctance. "Are there spiders?"

"Maybe," he allowed. "But also, I'm a dragon. I'm certain I can take any spider that tries to lay a fang on you."

She snorted and moved toward the door, shoving him lightly on the shoulder as she passed. "You know, you've lightened up a lot since we first met," she told him with a smile.

"I live to please," he said archly, but he couldn't help feeling a little glow of happiness at her show of affection—and at the way her shoulders had finally relaxed, and the haggard lines around her eyes had softened. His plan was working at last. She deserved a break, and he was glad he was able to give her one. Especially since she'd helped him with his own fears. He'd been able to transform more easily ever since that night in the Tapestry Room when they'd spoken of his love of flying, and he'd even managed to take to the skies without being overwhelmed by his fear of going rogue. The sky had still called to him, and he'd allowed himself a few minutes to exult in flying, but he'd been able to keep ahold of himself and transfer his attention when he needed to. He wasn't where he wanted to be yet, but it was progress—and it was thanks to his tamer.

Who the Hel-damned Akademy still refused to recognize as a student. He wanted to throttle every master there, which was a feeling made worse by the fact that he technically *could*, if he wanted to alienate important potential allies in his quest for the throne. Oh, he couldn't force them to accept her—the royal line had a delicate balance of power with the Akademy—but he could certainly get by with some intimidation… except that he couldn't. Not if he wanted to prove his leadership skills and show himself capable of solving a problem without resorting to threats. And the threats would likely only backfire anyway, knowing the masters.

Lasaro eased the secret door shut behind them, plunging them into darkness until he pulled a chunk of glowing green rock from his pocket.

"Did you steal that from the lake?" Kaelan demanded.

He shrugged. "It seems you are a terrible influence on me."

"I'm not a *thief*."

"It's for academic purposes. I was studying what kind of mineral it might be and whether it's what gives magic to the lake, and whether carrying it with me will provide the same benefits the lake does."

"Okay, that does maybe sound like my influence," she admitted.

He led her into the tunnels, up a set of stairs, and through a dark hallway. A faint voice reached him and he paused, tilting his head and scanning the wall until he found a small screen that let dim light filter through. He dropped the glowing rock in his pocket and crept over to peek through the screen.

"...trust your spies?" a woman's cool voice was saying. Lasaro located the speaker quickly: his mother, sitting at the head of a long, cherry wood table. Her tamer, a tall, ruddy-cheeked brunette woman, knitted quietly in a corner behind her.

"Lasaro?" Kaelan whispered, and he motioned her to stand next to him. She squinted through the screen at his side and they both listened.

"Yes," said a man's voice. One of Alveria's top generals, judging from what Lasaro could see of his bald spot and distinctive uniform, which was so tightly pressed it would be a wonder if the thing couldn't stand up without him in it. "I trust them without reserve. And they're all giving me the same message: General Marque is on the move."

Queen Celede sighed and touched a hand to her temple, which meant she was getting a headache. Lasaro thought back to the murmurings he'd heard in the village about her being too old to rule. She'd as much as said the same thing to him before he'd left for the Akademy. But surely, she would be well for a while longer. Surely, she could keep the kingdom reined in and stable until he could manage to prove himself. He'd already managed to find his dragon form; now he just had to harness his powers fully by the end of the year and make his bond official, and then he could be named the heir.

"Did they offer any specifics? Avenues of attack, weapons, troop numbers, or locations?" the queen asked.

"I'm afraid not. Several of them risked their lives to tell me even this much. But the signs are becoming clearer every day that Unger's peace talks are nothing but a smoke screen for their true plans to overthrow you."

A new voice cut in: Linna, one of Lasaro's twin sisters. "Attack!" she ordered, throwing the word at the general like a weapon. "I don't understand why we haven't already. Gather all of our forces—every dragon, every soldier, every boy who can so much as hold a sword—and throw them all at Unger right now. Overwhelm them before they can do the same to us." At her side, the other twin, Linge, nodded her agreement.

Lasaro's jaw tightened. They hadn't changed a bit. Still advocating a preemptive war that would precipitate disaster.

"That option is not yet on the table," Queen Celede said firmly. She turned to glance down the table. "Freyr? Do you have anything to contribute?"

Freyr glanced up. He'd been reading a book and clearly hadn't even been listening to the conversation. Lasaro wanted to shake him until he saw sense. Freyr might very well be the next ruler of Alveria if Lasaro's quest failed. Couldn't he *try* to be a decent prince?

"I'll support whatever you decide," Freyr replied mildly, and then he went back to his book.

Fatalistically, Lasaro searched the faces at the table for his final sibling. Elda was leaned back in her chair admiring a gaudy new bracelet that circled her small wrist, paying no attention to the people around her just as they paid no attention to her.

His dragon temper rising, Lasaro pushed away from the screen. Kaelan scurried along behind him, alarmed as he took three long steps, threw open a secret door inlaid in the wall, and strode into the meeting.

Chaos erupted. Linna and Linge had their daggers out before they'd even had time to see who'd entered, and their tamers—a redheaded boy and a brown-skinned girl—had to step up and murmur calming words to them. Freyr set down his book and laughed. Elda screamed in surprise, knocking her chair over as she scrambled toward the far door to escape. The general shouted, shoving his chair back in his haste to rise and drawing his sword to defend his queen.

"Stand down," Lasaro barked as he strode past, barely looking at the man. The general gaped for a moment, his mouth opening and closing like a land-stranded fish before he sat back down in his seat so hard that it made the chair legs scrape against the floor.

Queen Celede raised one eyebrow coolly, gazing at the door that opened into darkness behind him. She raised a hand and, gradually, the room quieted. "Good of you to join us," she said mildly once silence had fallen. "Would you care to enlighten us as to the reason you never informed me there was a secret spy tunnel running behind my war room?"

He stopped in front of her, ignoring her question. "Surely, now you must see that the surgical strike I advocated is the only way to prevent war," he said, his words hard. He lifted his head and let his gaze sweep over his siblings, not bothering to hide his disgust. "And that my siblings' suggestions show they either have too little backbone or too much dragon blood to deserve a place in this room." His own dragon blood began to simmer, clouding his vision with anger.

Freyr dropped his eyes, but offered no rebuttal. Elda gasped in indignation at Lasaro's words, her hands fluttering. Linna narrowed her eyes in turn and Linge began to trim her nails with her dagger, which she had not yet put away.

Queen Celede kept her eyes on Lasaro. After a long moment, he realized she was still sitting and that he was standing, hands fisted, looming over her like a threat. He lowered his eyes and dropped to one knee in apology, showing the proper deference to the current ruler of Alveria.

"I would be happy to take your suggestion," his mother said at last, and his heart leapt until she added, "if you have gained enough control of your powers to secure the masters' approval and the Council of Nobles' respect."

His heart plunged. He glanced over his shoulder. Kaelan was standing in the doorway, half in and half out of the tunnel, her eyes wide as her gaze darted around the room. "I've made progress," Lasaro said, knowing he was grasping at straws.

"I've transformed half a dozen times and found my tamer. This is her."

Queen Celede looked at Kaelan, taking her measure in one quick gaze, and then lowered her eyes back to him. "Is the pairing official, then? Has the bond been tested, and the two of you made initiates?"

He gritted his teeth. His dragon blood writhed within him, his anger turning inward and growing. He would have to admit that he'd failed, that he wasn't worthy of her approval. "Not yet, Mother," he ground out.

Her expression was regal, with just a touch of sadness tugging at its corners. "Then I am afraid you are wasting everyone's time," she said. Her tone was gentle, but the words cut deep. A waste of time: was that how she still saw him? He'd disappointed her. He'd failed her, failed himself, failed his country. And it *hurt*. He retreated deeper into his dragon instincts, which were all fury and defensiveness, so he didn't have to hurt so much.

His siblings and the general were looking at him with varying degrees of pity and savage satisfaction, and the dragon in him snarled. He had to prove himself a strong leader. He had to win his mother's approval. He couldn't stand the way she was looking at him right now—like he was a disappointment, a failed experiment.

The dragon in him took over. Its anger pushed the words out

before he could even comprehend them. "My tamer has not yet gained admittance from the masters," he bit out. "She is a peasant and they require her to prove herself before allowing her into classes. Had she managed to secure their approval by now, she and I would have an official probationary bond already. Her failure is the only thing keeping me from fulfilling the bargain you and I made."

"What bargain?" snapped Linna from her spot across the table, but Lasaro didn't answer her. He had barely even heard her. All he could hear was the soft intake of breath from over his shoulder, from the place where Kaelan was still standing in the doorway. The sound stabbed through him like it was a thing made of glass and barbs, but he didn't look at her, couldn't let her pain undermine the righteous, draconic anger that carried him through this moment. He would be named king no matter what it might cost her. He *had* to be named king, to save his country from disaster. If that meant he had to sacrifice her feelings, so be it.

But was that really what he had done? Had he laid the blame at Kaelan's feet to serve the greater good... or because he couldn't stand to see his mother disappointed in him?

The thought speared through his dragon instincts, deflating his anger until he could finally begin to grasp what he'd done. He swallowed hard and then swallowed again, going back over the conversation, his shock growing as his words sank in.

"Please forgive me, your majesties," came Kaelan's strangled voice from behind him. "I will excuse myself, if I may. I don't belong here."

Queen Celede nodded her permission, not taking her eyes off Lasaro, and Kaelan's footsteps faded away into the tunnel.

His mother sighed, her regal expression dropping. "Stay," she said at last, sparing her youngest son a small, wan smile. "You're here now, so you may as well sit in on the rest of the session before you return to the Akademy."

But Lasaro was already standing, looking back at the tunnel. His chest hurt. Breathing hurt. He'd betrayed Kaelan, offering his tamer up to his mother like a sacrifice just to save himself. He'd given in to his dragon instincts—the one thing he'd been terrified of doing ever since his first transformation.

He'd been cruel. And worse, he'd tried to excuse it.

A true king took responsibility for his actions. A true king wouldn't have blamed a girl who'd done nothing wrong, and wouldn't have allowed his humiliation and anger and dragon blood to make decisions for him.

He'd made a mistake. And he had the terrible feeling that it would cost him more than he could bear to pay.

CHAPTER 20

Kaelan stormed out of the palace, barely caring if the guards saw her crying. Hel, goddess of the underworld, could take them for all she cared. She was glad when she found the exit and merged into the busy foot traffic of Bellsor, though, so that she could become just another nameless Akademy student on holiday rather than the girl Prince Lasaro had brought to the palace who had later left teary-eyed and alone.

She stopped, smacking her hand hard against the brick of a shop. Her hand stung and tingled, her palm white with the force of the blow, and she felt thankful for the distraction of the pain. It kept her from thinking about how Lasaro had completely, utterly betrayed her.

He'd called her a peasant in front of his mother. The Hel-damned *Queen of Alveria*, and all of her royal children to boot.

Kaelan knew she was a peasant, and her status was simply a fact and normally didn't bother her—but Lasaro had used it like a weapon. He'd flung the word out the same way most of the masters did, the same way Inga did on a daily basis: with the intention of hurting her. He'd betrayed her, *belittled* her, just so he didn't have to tell his mother that his failure fell on his own shoulders. He was still too scared of being a dragon to maintain his form for long, and he was still struggling to control his powers as a result—he only didn't want to admit it and had blamed her instead. And she would never forget that.

The tingling in her hand faded and her shoulders drooped. The truth was, she never should have thought he'd seen her as anything other than a peasant in the first place. Their nights at Emerald Lake, the way he'd held her when she'd told him about her mother—they were discrepancies. Aberrations. *Mistakes*. Perhaps he did care about her, but he would never allow anything to come of it. And neither should she. She knew now that he was capable of hurting her to protect his own feelings. She would never be comfortable with him again, not the way they'd been together before. Not now that she knew it was so easy for him to turn on her. Especially when she was feeling so raw after what she'd learned about her mother's condition.

She'd trusted him with the most vulnerable parts of herself, and he'd crushed them.

More tears slipped down her face. She wove into traffic, her steps feeling lifeless, not caring where the winding roads would take her. She wished she could be angry again instead of feeling so devastated. She *should* be angry.

Maybe she'd bonded with the wrong dragon. Maybe she should distance herself and try to find someone else while there was still even a little bit of time. But what if he wanted retribution? She'd sworn him fealty, after all. What punishment could he demand for her if she broke faith with him? She wanted to think he would never hurt her like that, of course. The Lasaro she'd spent weeks exploring the Akademy with wouldn't.

But the Lasaro she'd just seen in the war room? She had no idea what he was capable of.

She bumped into someone ahead of her who'd stopped without warning. She wiped her eyes and frowned, peering over the man's shoulder. *Everyone* who was walking ahead of her had stopped, and more people were cramming in behind Kaelan as well. There must've been about a hundred people gathered in this small square. She craned her neck and spotted the cause of the disturbance: a man standing on the edge of a fountain, talking to the people around him.

She frowned, her tears momentarily forgotten. She was sure gatherings like this happened all the time in Bellsor, but this crowd had an odd, edgy energy to it that made her nervous. She slipped between people and worked her way toward the fountain, trying to see what was happening. The people she passed were focused, their mouths tight and their eyes burning with interest. Some of them were yelling their agreement and raising their fists in the air.

Kaelan's unease deepened when she got close enough to the speaker to get a better sense of him. He was dressed like a peasant, but the way he carried himself—square-shouldered, chin up, eyes scanning the crowd and picking out details lightning-fast—spoke more of a soldier's bearing. He was stocky, with short brown hair and a scar on his cheek. He looked to be perhaps twenty-five, but he didn't *feel* like a young man. There was something in his eyes, something in his mannerisms, that spoke of age. The contradictions of him made her feel strangely anxious.

Then, she got close enough to catch some of what he was saying.

"For too long, the dragons have sat on their mountain, and in their palace, content to toss us a scant handful of favors in exchange for taking the rights to all we own. To them, we are nothing but beggars squatting in houses the dragons could take at any moment, living from hand to mouth on farms the dragons could burn to ash if it pleased them."

The people shouted. More of them rose and shoved their fists into the air, and a nervous energy wound through them, thrumming in Kaelan's bones like instinct. A woman jostled her, and Kaelan glanced up to find her frowning sharply at the Akademy cloak Kaelan had borrowed from her roommate.

The woman turned her eyes back to the speaker, but Kaelan spotted another person a few feet away who was also glaring at the cloak.

Anxiety winding itself tighter around her, she began to search for a path out of the crowd.

"Dragons are hoarders!" the speaker shouted. "And, for too long, it's been *our* power they've been hoarding. We work the land, till the soil, and break our backs to provide for our families and countries, while their thievery is protected by law!"

Kaelan found a narrow gap between two men and slipped through, but was hemmed in by the wall of a shop and a group of boys her age who had gathered to listen.

"Well, I say it's time to take our power back! The common folk should rule their own country!" yelled the man. The crowd stomped and shouted their support, nodding, nearly all of their expressions turning dark.

Kaelan squeezed through the boys, her breath coming shallower and quick as they jostled her. This was getting ugly fast, and she was wearing a target on her back. She slipped the cloak off and balled it up inside-out, but anyone who gave her more than a passing glance could still tell from the color and the fine fabric that it was part of an Akademy uniform. She could drop it, but then she'd have to deal with Frigg. Kaelan was weighing whether the situation was drastic enough to merit her roommate's rage when she spotted Lasaro.

The prince was standing at the edge of the crowd on the other side of the street, staring at the speaker, his face gone white and his eyes distant as if he were under some sort of spell. An elderly man pushed past him and Lasaro nearly fell, but he didn't take his eyes off the man at the fountain.

Kaelan stood motionless, torn. He must've come after her, to apologize, because he'd realized he'd been a colossal ass. Or perhaps he was simply returning to the Akademy.

Someone else pushed past him, shoving him off balance as the crowd grew more restless, but still he didn't move to extract himself. If he kept this up and the crowd became violent, he would risk being caught in a riot. She should help him—or leave him to his fate and wash her hands of it.

She sighed. Regardless of his cowardly actions earlier, *she* was still an honorable person, and she couldn't let him be trampled by his own people. Reluctantly, her heart curling further into itself with every step, she pushed through the crowd to reach his side.

"Prince Lasaro," she whispered, unwilling to call him by his name the way she had when she'd thought they were friends. "We have to go."

He blinked at her.

Someone pushed her and she fell into his side, but she righted herself and tugged at his sleeve, hating that she still craved his touch despite his betrayal, and still found his warmth familiar.

More than anything, she wanted to wrap her arms around him and pull him close and protect him. "You're wearing Akademy robes," she hissed, "and that man is spewing anti-dragon sentiment. If this goes south, these people will turn on you, and they may not recognize you as a prince in time to stop themselves."

Lasaro blinked again and shook his head. "I… right. Yes. Okay," he said thickly at last, and with that he allowed her to pull him away from the fountain.

A scream went up from the group. Kaelan ducked instinctively as a shadow fell over her, and she looked up to find three dragons hovering high above the gathering. She could just barely make out the tamers on their backs.

From the far edges of the crowd, guards mounted on horseback shouted for the crowd to disperse and people scattered like rats on a sinking ship. Not all of them, though. A few pockets of protesters were shouting curses at the dragons above, and others were stalking toward the guards with weapons in hand. One man spotted Kaelan and Lasaro, took in their cloaks with a glance, and spat on the ground and began moving toward them.

Needing no further incentive, Kaelan dropped her cloak on the cobblestones and drew her gold and silver knife. "Are you well enough to defend us if necessary?" she shouted at Lasaro over the commotion.

He shook his head again, like he was trying to jar his brain into working order. "I…"

She huffed, pushing through the fleeing people. "Never mind, I'll do it. Just stick the pointy end in the other guy, right?" She brandished the weapon at the people in front of her. "Move!" she barked at them, and they obeyed.

A mounted guard galloped past, one of his horse's hooves clipping Kaelan. She reeled, clutching her arm and wincing. That was going to bruise. She spotted an alley between shops and ducked into it, dragging Lasaro along behind her. It was shadowy and relatively quiet, and when they emerged into the street beyond it, the traffic was thin enough to allow them to escape toward the Akademy. Kaelan kept her knife out anyway, keeping one wary eye on the dragons still hovering overhead and one eye on the people around her.

She didn't relax until they'd reached the rest area at the foot of Mount Firewyrm. A handful of students were clustered around the space, shading their eyes as they stared toward the hubbub, talking in too-loud voices that were excited and fearful by turn. Kaelan tugged Lasaro to a bench and unceremoniously pushed him onto one end of it. "Are you hurt?" she demanded.

His eyes had finally focused, but he had to squint at her for a moment before he processed her words. "No," he said at last. "Well, I think a horse stepped on my foot at some point, maybe? But my boots stood up to it, so I'm mostly fine."

"Good," she said shortly, and sat down at the opposite end of the bench. Now that the adrenaline was wearing off, the terrible wrenchings of shock and betrayal were pulling at her again, and her eyes burned hotly. She turned her head so Lasaro wouldn't see any tears she couldn't hold back.

He saw anyway. "Kaelan," he said, his tone so helpless it almost pulled her gaze toward him despite herself. "I am so sorry. I came after you as soon as you left, but I couldn't find you, and then there was that gathering—"

"A horse clipped me, too," she said, staring straight ahead, "in the arm. I don't think it's broken, but I'd probably better visit the Akademy's healer just in case."

He swung off the bench and dropped to his knees on the ground in front of her. The excited conversations around them went silent as the other students stared at the prince kneeling before a peasant girl. "I was an ass," he said, ignoring the onlookers.

She raised her gaze to meet his at last. "Yes," she said, aiming for sounding snarky, but her shaking voice betrayed the tears she refused to shed.

He winced and seemed to shrink into himself. "I hurt you. I was wrong. I blamed you because I couldn't bear for my mother to blame me, and it was a cruel and terrible thing to do. I gave in to my dragon instincts, to my anger, because I couldn't stand to feel like a failure, but that was *wrong*. What I did back there, it was everything I've been scared of lately—that my instincts would take over, lead me to do something I'd regret." He took a breath, shook his head. "I'll do better, I swear. I'm so sorry. I hope you don't—I wish you could..."

The pain and sincerity in his tone tore at her, and her heart uncurled. Understanding more of what had driven him to say what he had about her—that it was his dragon instincts that had pushed him—helped clear things up, at least a little. And he sounded genuinely horrified by what he'd done. She let out a long breath and then raised a hand. "Lasaro," she said simply, and his whole body relaxed at the word. It meant he understood her tone, understood what she was offering. It wasn't forgiveness. Not yet. And it didn't mean things would be the same between them—he'd damaged that trust, and it wouldn't heal quickly. But it was a start.

He did care about her. He'd made a mistake, a terrible one, and it would hurt for a while—but the fact that he'd recognized it so quickly and was willing to apologize this way, publicly, kneeling in front of her the way he was only supposed to kneel in front of his mother, the queen... she dared to hope, just a little, for both their futures.

She motioned at him to sit beside her, ignoring the other students who were openly gawking at them. From the corner of her eye, she spotted Drya giving her a subtle thumbs-up before the tamer student turned away and loudly said, "What is everyone standing around here for? It's a holiday, isn't it?

Let's go order some cake and take a nap." She marched toward the trailhead up the mountain with no further delay. Aelx, a light-haired tamer student who'd had an obvious crush on Drya for weeks, trotted quickly after her. Def, who'd been gawking at the prince, snapped his mouth shut, shrugged, and followed. The rest of the students shuffled slowly after them.

Kaelan managed something like a smile, thankful for her friend's help—and for the signs that Def was starting to treat his tamer like a friend rather than a toy—and then she turned her gaze back toward the city. She tried to surreptitiously dry her tears on her sleeve, but stopped when she spotted the three dragons still wheeling high in the sky over the spot where the crowd had been gathered.

She cleared her throat, awkwardly breaking the silence. Things might be strained between her and Lasaro right now, but they had to talk about what had happened in Bellsor at some point. "I don't know who that guy was, but I don't like him," she said. "Or the trouble he was stirring up."

Lasaro glanced at her, apparently trying to process the change in topic. Then he seemed to absorb her words, and he tilted his head, his eyes narrowing. "I think there might've been some kind of magic at play," he said after a moment. "It did a number on me. And on everyone else in that crowd, probably. I admit that anti-dragon sentiment seems to be growing more quickly than I'd realized, but there's no way that man could've gathered that many people that quickly and whipped them into such a state without magic." He tapped his fingers on his knee, brooding. "It is worth noting," he said slowly, "that you didn't seem to be affected."

Kaelan frowned. "You're right. I don't think I was."

"Any idea why? It could be useful to know what it is that stops that sort of force from affecting people."

"No idea. Maybe because I'm a tamer?"

"I'm not sure. That could be it—I don't know that there were any other tamers in the crowd." They were both quiet for a while, watching the dragons wheeling above Bellsor and still trying to process the emotions from their earlier conversation, and then Lasaro stood. "In any case, I suppose things seem to be under control for now. I should probably go to the lake just to make sure I get fully recovered from whatever magic that was." He hesitated. "You'll… would you come with me?" he asked awkwardly.

She looked away. "Yes," she said. "I still need to help you control your powers so you can heal my ma." But she ached at the new awkwardness between them and at her own lingering unwillingness to trust him.

He lowered his gaze. "Right. Yes, of course."

They climbed the mountain quietly, side by side and miles apart.

CHAPTER 21

K aelan was scrubbing a soup pot when she heard the news about Inga.

"…so bad it cracked the cobbles and nearly toppled part of the Akademy wall," one kitchen worker was saying.

Another shook her head. "Stav better get ahold of himself. If he goes much further down that road, he'll be rogue."

"Inga's already paying for his mistake."

"Inga was his tamer?"

"Not anymore."

Kaelan dropped the pot and interrupted the discussion, frowning. "What's this about Stav and Inga?"

The other workers frowned at her—she was still an outsider as far as they were concerned, even though she'd worked with them for nearly three months now—but one of them shrugged and answered.

"Stav and Inga were undergoing some sort of test just outside the walls yesterday," he said. "Stav had a temper fit and caused an earthquake that tore up part of the Akademy's main courtyard and dumped Master Lars on his ass to boot."

Kaelan smirked at the image of Lars being thrown on his rear. Too bad she hadn't been there to see it.

"Stav was reprimanded and Inga got thrown out," the man finished.

Kaelan's smirk faded. "Thrown out entirely? Not just reprimanded along with Stav?" She wouldn't mind at all that Inga wouldn't be around to torment her anymore, but the fact that a tamer could be tossed out on her ear for what sounded like a relatively minor infraction boded ill for Kaelan who still hadn't even managed to become an official tamer student in the first place.

"Thrown out," the woman she'd been talking to confirmed with a sour look. "Didn't even let her consider staying on to join the staff. Said her failure to control her dragon through the bond meant she wasn't strong enough to be a tamer at all. Everyone's too tightly wound right now, if you ask me. The punishment wouldn't have been so severe last year."

"It still would've fallen on the tamer, though," muttered the other kitchen worker darkly. "Dragons get away with everything. That needs to change, if you ask me."

Kaelan stared at her. She wasn't wrong about the unfairness of the punishment—it sounded like Stav was the one who'd caused the trouble, and not Inga, for once—but that conclusion felt awfully similar to the one the man in the square at Bellsor had come to. It had been a week since the mob, but she could still recall every word he'd spoken with painful clarity.

The man interrupted her thoughts. "Hopefully Drya and Def will do better," he said as he grabbed a bowl of cake frosting and added a few drops of coloring to it.

Kaelan snapped upright. "Drya?" she asked in alarm. "What do you mean?"

"I heard they're doing some testing with the two of them right now. If Drya is struggling as much as I've heard, I'll bet she'll go the same way as Inga—"

But Kaelan was out the door before he could even finish, whipping off her apron and sprinting down the halls. She had most of the twists and turns memorized now, thanks to her nightly explorations with Lasaro—although she hadn't had many of those for the last week—and quickly found a balcony that overlooked the half-dozen training courtyards two stories below. She leaned out, scanning for her friend. Her only friend in this entire place, who might be thrown out just like Inga if she couldn't prove she'd improved her bond with Def. Kaelan had met with her twice more in the last week, and the other girl had reported progress, but maybe not enough.

She spotted Def. He was aloft above her, circling the Akademy as he peered down at Drya in one of the courtyards below. Master Henra stood next to the tamer, her sharp frown visible even from this distance. "...not enough control," she was saying, her normally smooth voice sharp as a whip, loud and irate enough to carry easily across the grounds.

Kaelan's hands squeezed into fists. If even Master Henra was riled up, Drya was definitely in trouble. Kaelan couldn't let her get thrown out. There was already a painful new gulf between her and Lasaro—if she lost her only other friend entirely, the Akademy would be even more miserable than it had been through those first few weeks, with Kaelan alone and homesick.

She took a deep breath and tried to calm herself. Maybe she could help. She'd been working with Drya on boosting her empathetic powers, so they'd worked together before—though only in practice, not on an actual dragon—and plus, Kaelan had the advantage of all the power boosts she'd gotten from the Emerald Lake. Maybe she could help Drya pass this test. She'd never heard of a tamer being able to strengthen a bond that didn't belong to them, but Kaelan was desperate enough to try, anyway.

She quieted her mind and gazed up at the blue dragon circling above. Her heart flopped as he dipped a wing and swung around, flying directly over her. She'd seen plenty of dragons lately, and she wasn't nearly as nervous around them as she used to be—but the sight of that particularly sapphire sheen instantly put her back on that riverside two months ago, when dragon-Def had nearly killed her. Those slitted eyes, fixed on her as he'd stalked forward. Those sharp teeth. She could still recall his roar, animalistic and earth-shaking.

She shook herself. *You're not on that riverside anymore,* she told herself firmly. *You're not even the same person as that girl now.* She was stronger. She knew herself a bit better. She could do this.

She took another breath, settling herself, growing roots. The sun was dipping into the hills now and she focused on the beauty of the sunset colors to ground herself, ignoring Henra's increasingly sharp commands. Then, when Kaelan was ready, she reached out to Def. She closed her eyes and opened her mind, pleading with her tamer senses to do... well, she didn't know what. Something.

And, after a moment, they did. It felt similar to how her healing instincts had grown when she'd touched the dragon eggs, but this was more like fumbling her way into a new sense altogether. It was almost like sight, but for her emotions —she could *feel* Def's frustration, his uncertainty and growing panic. Instinctively, she reached deeper with her new sense, searching for his bond. There—it felt like a thin tether, binding him to Drya below. She marveled at the feel of it, the way it twanged against her senses. Then she pulled up all the strength and steadiness that was in her and, somewhat clumsily, figuring out what she was doing as she did it, she poured it into the bond.

The connection between Def and Drya thickened, tightening. Kaelan could feel the very moment when Drya's intentions finally managed to reach her dragon. Kaelan opened her eyes and saw Def tuck his wings and dive toward the moat, magically pulling water up from the river in a twisting spout and raining it down over the courtyards. Drya cheered in victory and relief, and Henra narrowed her eyes, but grudgingly nodded. Kaelan sagged, grinning. She'd done it. She'd helped them strengthen their bond enough to pass the test—and had gained new insight into her own powers in the process.

But after a moment, her smile faded. Their bond would be tested more before it was approved, and Kaelan herself wasn't even *allowed* to have her own bond with Lasaro tested. With winter drawing nearer, she only had a matter of weeks to convince the masters to let her become a tamer before she and Lasaro both failed to get the things they needed most. Kaelan would have to return home to a life that no longer felt like it fit, to a dying mother she couldn't save. Lasaro would be paired with another tamer if he was lucky—and, if he wasn't, he'd be sent home in disgrace, never to be the king.

She tapped her fingers on the railing, trying to think of another way out of all this. Maybe she could use what she'd learned today about her tamer powers as leverage to convince the masters to accept her. She could help other students strengthen their bonds now after all. Surely, they'd see that that could be useful. She'd have to talk to Lasaro about it—but, as soon as she thought of that, she could already suspect what he'd say. The masters were set in their ways and wanted students to achieve things on their own merit. They were more likely to think of what she'd done as cheating than to find it useful.

Kaelan's earlier sense of triumph dissipated completely, leaving her more agitated than ever. The masters were foolish, self-righteous. They might believe in honor and tradition, but their honor was self-centered—they cared most about upholding their own goals, their own ideas of what was best for everyone else. The realization left her disgusted.

She wheeled around and strode back into the castle. It was nearly nightfall; maybe she could start her explorations a little early tonight. They always calmed her down—unless Lasaro was present, lately. She was working her way toward forgiving him for his betrayal, but their friendship still hadn't quite recovered, and she came away from their meetings drained rather than energized. She wouldn't meet him tonight, she decided. She needed an evening to herself.

She turned—then paused. In the strange, long shadows of twilight a story or two beneath one of the unused courtyards, she thought she'd seen something move. She squinted and frowned at the spot. After a moment, she made out three cloaked figures slipping along the outside of the Akademy walls, edging down the thin path carved out of the mountain, nearly hidden by the deep shade as they made their way toward the drawbridge. One of them walked with a sort of shuffle, his shoulder oddly slumped.

Students sneaking out? No. They didn't move like kids. They almost moved more like soldiers. Particularly the one in the front, with his square shoulders and long, sure strides. Unease stirred in Kaelan's stomach. There was something familiar about that figure. His hood was up, but he almost reminded her of the man in the square who'd nearly started a riot.

She hesitated. Three grown people sneaking around the outside of the Akademy, one of whom might or might not be involved in some sort of brewing rebellion, could only be bad news. She should probably tell the masters.

Unless… the figures below were masters themselves, and she was mistaken about one of them being the man from the riot. After all, plenty of people had square shoulders and walked like soldiers. She relaxed as soon as she had the thought. That had to be it. The Akademy was ancient and well-guarded by dragons and, she was sure, protective spells—no one nefarious would be foolish enough to be skulking around here. And if the people below truly *were* masters, then they were likely up to some secret dragon business that they apparently didn't want students to know about, which meant she might get in trouble if she admitted to having seen them.

And she definitely couldn't afford to get into any more trouble.

Decision made, she strode back into the castle to explore.

Even after an hour, she still couldn't get her mind off all of her worries. They ate at her so constantly that she ended up back in the Clutch Room where she thought at least she could brood about some worries that *weren't* hers. Because this room had been bothering her ever since the last time she'd been here— with the few dozen baby dragons who'd been too long in their eggs, and no eggs at all that felt recently lain. She'd stopped by the library before this to gather up books related to eggs, and sat cross-legged in the Clutch Room now, spreading the tomes out before her. She'd read through two or three other books already and had confirmed that eggs didn't usually take this long to hatch, and she had a few dark suspicions about what might be wrong, but hadn't yet had the time to do enough research to fully understand the problem.

She glanced at the egg nearest her. "Okay, Junior," she said softly. "Let's figure out what's wrong with you."

Two hours of research later, she had her answer.

She stood up, barely noticing how her spine popped in protest and her legs tingled from having been in one position for too long. She walked over to Junior's egg—or, the egg whose dragon she'd come to think of as Junior—and laid a hand on his shell, horror and sadness uncurling deep within her. "So long," she said softly, "and all alone."

"How long has that one been in there?" asked a voice from behind her.

She jumped and whirled around. Lasaro stood a few paces behind her, his hair messy like he'd been running his fingers through it, his hands stuck awkwardly in his pockets.

Kaelan glanced from him to the egg. It almost sounded like Lasaro might already have guessed the answer she'd just discovered. But then—he was the prince, after all. Perhaps he'd known all along. "Seventy years," she said, keeping one comforting hand on the egg.

Lasaro nodded, not moving any closer, but a trace of grief crossed his features. "They're all like that," he said, motioning at the nests further into the cave. "Every decade, they've been taking longer and longer to hatch, and fewer and fewer new eggs are laid. And hardly any of them are female."

Kaelan looked down at the egg under her fingers. "Dragons are going extinct," she said, voicing the conclusion she'd reached just a few moments ago.

Lasaro's grim nod confirmed it. "Soon, we won't have enough numbers to sustain the population. And I don't know if Alveria can stand without dragons. We've still got a few hundred right now, and we're long-lived, but we're still mortal. Even if we weather the short-term threat from Unger… in a matter of decades, Alveria might fall anyway."

She bit her lip. So, this was one of the "other worries on the horizon" he'd mentioned when they'd first met.

"Let's go swimming," he said suddenly, a strange light in his eyes.

She frowned. "What? Right now?"

"Yes," he said, stepping forward and capturing her hand in his, tugging her after him so quickly that she nearly tripped. "Sorry," he said, and he loosened his grip although he didn't let go.

"But my things—" Kaelan protested, twisting around to look at the books she'd left lying in a semicircle.

"We can get them later. I want to… there's something I need to tell you. Ask you."

Cranky now, Kaelan snatched her hand from his—it still felt too strange, too much like the way things had been between them before—though she kept following him. "And you can only tell me at the lake?"

"Yes. I mean, I'd like to."

Her frown deepened as she stared at his back. He was acting so strange, jumpy and even more awkward and strained than usual for the last week. "Is everything okay?" she asked cautiously.

"It will be. I think I've found the way to get the masters to admit you."

Her heart leapt. She sped up to match his steps. "Really?"

He shot her a quick sideways glance, giving her a small, cautious smile. The awkwardness that had lain thick between them lifted a little. "Yes. I was going to tell you earlier this evening, but you didn't meet me like we planned."

"Oh. Right, sorry. I just needed some alone time, I guess."

"Oh. Of course." The awkwardness settled back into place.

They navigated to the lake in silence. Hope twisted deep into her—could he really have found a solution? She waited impatiently for him to undress, but instead, he only took off his boots and socks and sat at the bottom of the outcropping, dangling his toes into the water. Like that, he stared down at his feet like they held the answer to the meaning of life.

Something was off.

Slowly, she sat next to him. "Lasaro?" she asked. "Are you sure everything's okay?"

He looked up and met her eyes at last. "Everything's great," he said, but the mix of uncertainty and hope and desperation in his eyes belied his words. "Now that I know how to make the masters accept you as my tamer."

Eagerness rippled through her again. "Well, don't hold back!" she said, impatient. "Tell me how."

He inhaled and then blew out the breath and turned fully toward her. "Kaelan Younger," he said, the words sounding wooden and formal in his mouth, "I need you to marry me."

The world went still, leaden. She stared at him.

It took two tries to make her mouth move, to make the word come out. "What?"

"Marry me," he said again, pulling his legs up so that he could scoot closer to her. That same desperation and hope and uncertainty shone brighter, almost feverish. "Then you'll be a princess, and the masters won't be able to deny you admittance."

She shook her head, then shook it again, trying to make his words make sense. "You want me to marry you," she said slowly, "so that the masters will accept me as your tamer? That's your plan?"

"Yes."

She couldn't find the words and couldn't begin to figure out what she was supposed to say. Her emotions were a snarled, tangled mess. She should be happy, right? A prince was proposing to her. But it was so sudden, and it felt so *wrong*.

I need you to marry me, he'd said. Not *I want to marry you.* Not *I love you.* He was doing this because it was the solution to a problem. Because it was the best thing for his country, and the only way he could see to achieve his goal of becoming king.

Her emotions untangled and merged into a shining thread of fury—at him, and at herself for stupidly falling for a boy who would always care more about his kingdom than her. She stood in one swift motion. "No."

Bewildered, he looked up at her. "What?"

"*No,*" she said, biting off the word.

"You're refusing to marry me?" His bewilderment sparked to anger. "This is the only way! You swore me your loyalty, didn't you? Didn't we make a bargain? We have to do this!"

She took a step back, unable to believe what she was hearing. "Your court would be in an uproar. It's against tradition as you haven't even presented me to them first; it'll dishonor them—"

He jolted to his feet. "I DON'T CARE!" he roared, and wind blasted out from him with the words. He took a deep breath and calmed his magic, but she could still feel it through the bond, prickling and restless. "Forget tradition and honor. I don't care what they think. I'll save my country no matter what it takes."

"Even if you have to sacrifice me to do it?"

"You see marrying me as a sacrifice?"

She leaned close to look him in the eye. "*You* see marrying *me* as a sacrifice. It's not something you want, it's something you think you have to do to save Alveria. And you don't care what that will do to my future—what marrying a prince who doesn't love me, in a country full of nobles who'll hate me even more than they do now for it, on the eve of war, will do to *me*. As long as your kingdom comes out ahead for it. Odin's eye, Lasaro. Are you really so heartless?"

She waited for him to deny her conclusions. He didn't.

Her anger dulled and turned to grief. First the betrayal last week, and now this. It was more than she could take. This was all so *wrong*. She could've wanted to marry Lasaro. She might even have let herself daydream about him proposing to her— but not like this. Not for these reasons and not in this way, not when he didn't even truly *want* to be with her. Was she really nothing more than a tool to him, something he could use to achieve his ends? Tears welled up in her eyes before she could stop them.

Lasaro fumbled. "It's not that I don't—I mean, I care for you…"

"Plus," she added, swiping angrily at her cheeks, "tamers and dragons marrying is forbidden. Dragons can only marry each other. And now we know why, don't we? Dragon blood is getting too diluted, I bet, and that must be why too few eggs are being laid. It must be such a terrible choice for you. Marry a dragon and help save your species, or marry me to save your kingdom."

He looked away, but then he nodded.

She straightened up again. "Well. Luckily, you don't have to make that choice," she said, the grief tearing at her voice and making it tremble. "Because, no, Lasaro Afkarr, I will *not* marry you."

She turned and fled.

CHAPTER 22

L asaro was on his feet before she reached the tunnel back out to the library. He'd learned his lesson from last time when he'd waited too long to go after her back at the palace.

"Wait!" he shouted, reaching for her arm.

"My oath was that I'd be loyal to you as long as you didn't ask me to do anything that went against morality," she spat back at him. "This qualifies."

"Marrying me is immoral now?" He couldn't help being bewildered, not to mention hurt and angry. Marriage was the perfect solution. The *only* solution. He didn't know if he was in love with Kaelan—he cared for her, certainly, but there was so much else at stake that he couldn't sort out his emotions— but he'd never expected to marry for love in any case. He couldn't understand why she saw his choice of marrying her as any more of a sacrifice than his marrying some haughty daughter of a baroness would have been. Yes, it might be a difficult adjustment for Kaelan at first. But she would be a *princess*, and later a queen. Why would she be angry about that? This was the only way her mother would be healed, too. It wasn't like she wasn't getting anything out of the deal. Did she think he would force himself on her once they were married? Surely, she knew him better than that. If she wanted, this could be nothing more than a business arrangement until she wished otherwise. Royalty often viewed marriage as such after all.

And as for his need to save his species—there wouldn't be any species left to save if Alveria fell to Unger. Every last dragon would be enslaved, forced into Unger's army to be used as living weapons. He needed to save his country from the immediate threat, which he could only accomplish if he became king, and then he could worry about the lack of new dragon hatchlings.

Kaelan whirled on him, reading his thoughts from his silence, or maybe through the bond. "We'll find another way to save our country," she snapped, "that doesn't involve your idiot sense of duty-at-all-costs choosing your wife for you." She turned and started striding away again.

His frustration came to the boiling point. He stopped in his tracks and shouted after her retreating form, "We don't have time to find another way! Master Lars is pushing the final testing of the probationary bonds forward. He just put up the list of tamers and dragons to undergo the test to become initiates, and neither of us were on it! Which means I'll be held back, and you, Kaelan, will be *expelled.*"

She froze. "What?" she whispered.

"Why do you think I decided to propose tonight? This is our last chance! Testing has already started, and you remember what happens to tamers who fail to bond. The masters are just waiting for a good excuse to kick you out, and this'll be it—and as for me, I'll have failed to fulfill my bargain with my mother, and I won't be named crown prince at all. I have to be strong enough to control my powers, and I have to have an official tamer by the end of term, and neither of those things will happen without you. Oh, they'll try to shove other tamers at me. They've already tried. But no one else is compatible enough. No one else is *you.*"

She stared at him. "Inga and Stav," she realized, "and Drya and Def. I thought they were just doing some sort of preliminary testing for individual courses, not bond testing."

He shook his head. "It's official. It lasts a week, and now there are only five days left. Getting married, and quickly, is the only way to force the masters to accept you. We've already tried everything else."

Kaelan's expression went thoughtful and distant. "Not everything," she said slowly.

"This is a terrible idea," Lasaro said the next afternoon.

"It's our only idea, or at least the only one that's not idiotic and potentially ruinous," Kaelan shot back.

"How would marrying me ruin you?"

"It would ruin *you*. Your court would make sure of it. Sometimes tradition is in place for a reason. If you want to change how your kingdom is run, you need to make sure your people trust you first, and marrying me secretly just so I can be your tamer isn't the way to do that."

Drya, who was standing between them, blinked. Her expression had gone rigid with the force of not goggling at the two of them—but Kaelan had said she could be trusted with the truth of their situation, and also, Drya was the backbone of their new plan. Which, in Lasaro's opinion, was ludicrous.

Drya had just finished dyeing Kaelan's hair blonde after having cut it as short as a boy's. The cut looked fitting on his tamer, wild and spiky and soft all at once. The plan was to dress her in the clothes of Aelx, some tamer student who reportedly had a crush on Drya—which, presumably, was the only reason the boy had agreed to this plan—and pass Kaelan off as him for the testing session today. While posing as Aelx, Kaelan would prove her ability to control Lasaro, their bond would be approved, and then she'd whip off her hood and reveal her identity, and the masters would be forced to accept her.

There were a thousand ways it could go wrong.

"They tried to test me with another tamer this morning already," Lasaro said. "I called up a windstorm that blew all the other dragons off the face of the mountain. If I hadn't felt your presence nearby to calm me, I probably would've brought down a tornado to wipe this whole Hel-damned place off the map. Everything is so much harder to control when I'm in dragon form. They'll probably only risk pairing me with one more tamer. Are you sure you want to take this chance?"

"Yes," Kaelan said, her lips tight as Drya rubbed some sort of powder over her cheeks to make them paler.

"Stav failed again this morning, too," Lasaro pointed out relentlessly. "Another tamer, Morr, got sent home because of it. The masters are so on edge, they refuse to even acknowledge that Inga should've been Stav's tamer. They kicked her out, and Morr too, for something so minor that they both would've been given the chance to re-test if it would've happened last year. I don't know why the masters are so much more uptight this year—they're worried about the threat from Unger and the unrest in Bellsor, I'm sure—but either way, trying to trick them like you're planning to could push them over the edge, backfiring on us in a big way."

"We have to risk it," Kaelan said stubbornly.

He sighed and flopped down on Drya's bed. It was obvious that Kaelan simply wasn't going to agree to his own plan, no matter how he tried to convince her. And her plan felt much, much riskier. If the masters found out he'd played a direct part in deceiving them—and even if everything went exactly as intended, they would have to realize he'd been a part of it—they might toss him out entirely rather than simply reprimanding him and holding him back. The chances of failure were abominably high. But there were only a few days left to get Kaelan approved, and it was obvious to him by now that no other tamer student would do when it came to controlling his powers.

"Okay," he said at last, running a hand through his hair. "If you're really willing to risk it all like this... I'll trust you."

Kaelan graced him with a smile. It felt like the first he'd seen from her in ages, and a tiny thread of hope tugged at him. "Thank you," she said.

Drya pulled out Aelx's tamer trainee cloak from the closet. "For what it's worth, Kaelan, I think you'll do fine. Judging by how you helped me and Def the other day, I'm pretty sure you're one of the strongest tamer students to ever study here."

Kaelan turned to her friend, her eyes widening. "I didn't know you knew about that," she admitted. "I hope you're not mad?"

Drya laughed incredulously. "Of course, I'm not mad! You strengthened our bond—I recognized the feeling of you from our practices together. If not for your help, I might've been kicked out right along with Inga." She shuddered.

Lasaro looked back and forth between them, trying to wrap his mind around what their conversation implied. "Kaelan," he said at last, "you... influenced another tamer's bond?"

"Yes," Kaelan said, "though I'm still not quite sure how. It was sort of instinct. I was worried, I just knew I couldn't let Drya flunk."

Lasaro shook his head. "That shouldn't be possible," he marveled.

Kaelan crinkled her brow. "Really? I thought it was just some higher-level skill I'd managed to unlock or something."

Drya pulled the cloak over Kaelan's head. "No time to wonder!" she said. "It's almost time to go. Make sure to keep your hood up and your hands down, Kaelan. You can pass as Aelx if your face is shadowed, but if anyone sees that burn scar on your arm, you'll be made."

"What if her sleeves fly up in the wind while she's riding me?" Lasaro asked, and Kaelan's head swiveled toward him again, her eyes widening with something like alarm. She hadn't thought of that. In fact, the dazed look on her face made him think she might not have realized that these last few rounds of testing involved a tamer riding their dragon at all.

"I'll be flying?" she asked, wonder laced through her tone. "On you?"

His lips curved up. "Yeah."

She blinked. "Okay," she said after a second. "That's… that's okay."

Drya clapped her hands. "I think this is as good as it gets! We have about ten minutes before Prince Lasaro and 'Aelx' are supposed to be downstairs. How do you feel?"

Kaelan put a hand over her stomach. "Sick," she admitted.

"Me, too," Lasaro chimed in. He stood and held out a hand to his tamer. "Shall we?"

CHAPTER 23

K aelan's heart pounded as she watched from the shadows of the fountain at the edge of the courtyard. She was supposed to lurk there until Lasaro switched to dragon form. That was the cue for her to walk out, quickly present herself to the masters, and start the test. Which she had to do without speaking. Or lowering her hood. Or letting any of them catch on through any of the hundreds of ways they might figure out that she wasn't actually Aelx.

She set her jaw. She had to do this. It was the only way to make Lasaro crown prince, to heal her mother, and to secure her own future. She and Lasaro had faced some tough times lately, but she still had faith that they were meant to be together as dragon and tamer. This was the future she'd finally chosen for herself, despite her fears and all the obstacles in her path.

Now she had to fight for it.

Lasaro strode up to Master Olga, who was currently in the form of a rail-thin, regal-looking dragon with shimmering whitish-gold scales. Lasaro's hair was tied back neatly, his steps were steady, and his gaze fell calmly on each of the masters in turn as he waited for them to announce the start of his final test. How could he be so still? Kaelan herself felt like she was about to have a heart attack. But then, she supposed he must be used to the pressure of being in the public eye, having every gesture and word weighed and judged like grains of wheat on a scale. If she became official tamer to the future king, would she ever grow used to that sort of pressure? She supposed she'd have to, somehow.

Master Lars—in dragon form, as well—jerked his head at Lasaro. Lasaro closed his eyes. He was trying to transform. Quickly, Kaelan closed her own eyes and reached out to him through her bond. They found each other in the darkness. She latched onto the agitation simmering beneath his outward calm and wrapped herself around it. It eased, and the shift rippled through him.

"Well done," boomed Master Olga's voice through Kaelan's head, sounding faintly surprised. *"Aelx!"* she called out.

Kaelan opened her eyes and stood. That was her cue. She took one last steadying breath, tugged her hood all the way forward, and marched out from the fountain's shadow toward her test.

"Fly!" Master Lars commanded Lasaro. Her dragon snapped his beautiful mist-gray wings open and whirled into the sky, graceful as an eagle, and soon he was no larger than a speck. Master Lars turned to Kaelan. *"Aelx, tell him to summon a light breeze that changes the direction the flag flies,"* he ordered, jutting his head at the Alverian crest that fluttered from the Akademy's tallest tower.

Kaelan's eyes widened, realizing belatedly just how unprepared she was. She and Lasaro had never tried to communicate actual maneuvers or orders through the bond—only emotions and general senses. And they'd never communicated anything at such a great distance.

She clasped her hands together, careful to keep her sleeves down. Nothing to do now but try. She turned away from the masters and looked up toward Lasaro, straining to feel her way along the bond, relaying the orders, but Lasaro only felt faintly confused. He was getting tenser with every passing moment, uneasy with their deception. And—Kaelan frowned. It was almost like there was some other sort of interference, as well, something that kept distracting her from her hold on the bond. She gritted her teeth and pushed harder, forcing herself to focus. She tried to send on the master's orders in pictures rather than words, but Lasaro only sent back a growing frustration.

Okay. Time to keep her cool. They'd communicated in the

past with feelings, right? She had no problem feeling his emotions right now. So, maybe those were stronger than words and pictures. She shut her eyes, ignoring the growing annoyance and disappointment of the masters arrayed behind her, and focused on the flag. She thought about how it made her feel—how the sound of it snapping in the wind reminded her of when a breeze tugged at the laundry on the clothesline back at home, how the red of the flag matched the red of her favorite book, that tattered treatise on dragons that she'd read so many times. Then she thought about the direction north—the opposite of the way the flag was flying right now—and how it brought to mind the chill of the mountains. She strengthened those feelings and sent them into the bond.

Lasaro's frustration melted away. Kaelan opened her eyes just in time to spot the flag flip over and flutter in a strong westward wind.

Behind the masters, a few tamer students—Drya included—cheered. She glanced over as Lars silenced them with a glare.

"Have him lower the temperature of the air enough to create a rainstorm over the courtyard," Master Olga ordered.

Buoyed by her joy at their success, Kaelan didn't even think about the difficulty involved. A few moves back, her family had lived at the foot of a glacier, and the thunderstorms there had been spectacular: the lightning reflecting off the mountains of ice, the rain freezing into strange shapes at the second drops hit the ground. She captured those feelings of awe, those thoughts of storms, and sent them to Lasaro. He tucked his wings and dove, and when he snapped them out again, clouds spun from his wingtips. They roiled and grew, shadowing the courtyard, and thunder cracked. Raindrops fell: just a few at first, and then enough to drench Kaelan. She grinned, delighted at what could only be considered a smashing success —until she realized the rain had washed away her carefully applied makeup.

She gasped, pulling her hood down more tightly, but it was too late. The tamers stared at her, pointing and murmuring, and Lars was snarling. Master Olga dropped her head, disappointment shining through her eyes.

Lasaro caught Kaelan's sudden fear and plummeted through the clouds to land at her side, lifting one protective wing over her—but even he couldn't protect her from this.

"You should not have done such a thing," Master Olga said, her tone aggrieved, but Master Lars surged forward and cut her off.

"Sabotage!" he growled, his eyes furious. His magic gathered in the air like static electricity, and the storm overhead crackled with lightning. *"How dare you deceive us!"*

Kaelan tried to protest. "No, I didn't—it wasn't meant to—"

"There must be punishment," Master Henra interrupted from

where she stood, her eyes and tone as cool and unreadable as ever. "This cannot be allowed to set a precedent."

"She must be expelled," Master Olga said sadly, and Kaelan stopped breathing. No. This couldn't be right. Master Olga was her defender, the one master who'd been on her side, the closest thing she'd had to an ally among the teachers.

"No," said Master Lars, his tone going suddenly cold and satisfied in a way that made Kaelan's skin crawl, *"that's not enough. She will be sent to the dungeons until we figure out what to do with her, and who else contributed to this deception."*

Lasaro's temper exploded. His wing caught Kaelan up, dragging her close to his side, and he crouched. His claws sparked against the courtyard's tiles. *"Absolutely not,"* he said, his tone sounding almost feral, ripping through Kaelan's mind with the ferocity of his will. The students at the edge of the courtyard winced and covered their ears. *"She is my tamer. I am your prince. You will not touch her."*

A sense of wonder settled over Kaelan. The warmth of his protection wrapped around her, holding her tight. She felt safe. She felt...

Loved.

Was that the emotion strumming through the bond right now? Underlying Lasaro's desperation, his fury, his fear? She put a hand on his scales, warm and hard and beautiful, and thought it might be true.

But his magic was prickling, rising, and boiling over. He was about to do something he'd regret in the name of protecting her. She pushed a calm she didn't feel through the bond which her touch had heightened. After a moment, he twisted his neck to stare down at her. The boiling magic began to fade.

"Kaelan," he said helplessly.

"I'll be fine," she whispered, though she wasn't sure it was true. Her heart beat hard in her ears. Everything had gone so terribly, desperately wrong, and she had no idea what would become of her now. What would become of her prince. Her mother. All the people who mattered to her were in trouble, and she'd done all she knew to do to help them, and she'd failed.

She'd *failed*.

"Stand aside," Master Olga ordered.

Lasaro and Kaelan kept their eyes on each other. After a long moment of wrestling with himself, the prince stepped back, leaving Kaelan to be led away.

Master Olga was silent during the long trip downward. Kaelan wished she hadn't had the whole journey memorized—the

Clutch Room was right next to the dungeons, so she knew from her visits there exactly how much closer to her doom each turn and staircase and hallway was taking her. Her dread grew, mixing with Lasaro's—even at this distance—until their tangled feelings felt like a sheet of glass in the middle of her chest, keeping her heart from beating properly and making her pant with the weight of it.

Failed. The word kept time with her stuttered heartbeats, repeating in a relentless drumbeat in her head. She'd failed. She should've realized the rainstorm would wash her makeup away, and should've done something to prevent it. She should've thought of a better plan in the first place. Maybe she should've simply accepted Lasaro's proposal. At least then her mother would still have had a shot at getting healed.

I'm sorry, she told Ardis silently, willing the words to travel somehow over the hills and mountains and villages and the vast, impossible distance between them. Would she even get to see Ma again? Or would there only be a grave waiting for her when the dragons sent her home, assuming she was sent home at all?

She stifled a sob, not wanting to cry in front of Master Olga. The white-gold dragon didn't look back as she stopped in front of a massive set of double doors. She swept one wing gracefully along their surface and they swung silently inward. She motioned with her head for Kaelan to go in, her gaze remote and even more unreadable than normal.

Anger bubbled up beneath Kaelan's grief. "I'm sorry I disappointed you," she said, and waited until Master Olga looked at her to continue. "But the masters forced us to this extreme. You should have just accepted me. What would it have cost any of you, except pride?"

Master Olga watched Kaelan for a long moment, then folded in her wings and motioned into the darkness through the double doors. Trembling, Kaelan backed through them, still turned to face Olga. *"You will stay here until our judgment is made,"* Olga said, sadness tinging her voice, and then the doors swung shut between them.

Kaelan squeezed her eyes closed. *I am brave,* she thought to herself, trembling in the darkness. *I am strong.*

But she didn't turn around.

Standing there with your eyes shut won't make the trouble go away, said her mother's voice gently in the back of her mind.

She opened her eyes, and she turned around.

There were only a few sconces scattered throughout the vast room, but they gleamed and reflected off a massive hoard of silver and gold. Treasure was heaped deep into the huge room like sand on the ocean floor. It gathered into drifts, sunken into glimmering valleys. Piles of it reached up toward the chimneys embedded in the ceilings high above. The dungeon wasn't full of cells and rats and torture implements the way she's feared—it looked more like a treasure room. She walked deeper into it, marveling, and nearly tripped over a hunk of emerald as big as her fist. Its shimmering surface reminded her of the Emerald Lake, and of her stolen moments with Lasaro, as well as the way she'd felt the first time she'd touched his scales there, and the way his hands had splayed over her stomach when he'd held her up in the water.

A tear splashed on the emerald. She fell onto her knees and curled up atop the hard, lumpy treasure, not caring that the dungeons weren't dank and terrible the way she'd imagined. She was still alone. She had still failed, and it had still cost the futures of all the people she cared about most in the world.

She couldn't think about it any longer. She couldn't face it and didn't want to process this whole terrible day. Weeping, she closed her eyes and willed sleep to take her.

She dreamed.

A black dragon unfurled itself and its shadow covered the kingdom. Horizon to horizon, black wings rose like vast tidal waves. Its scales reflected the orange and yellow of the burning cities beneath it. Its eyes—green, bright, and unreadable—watched only Kaelan.

Father, she thought, but did not say.

"Daughter," he answered, and his voice was the ocean

crashing through its boundaries, and the earthquakes that cleaved her country to rubble, and the roaring of the soldiers that swarmed through the cities beneath them.

She woke with a start, alone in the dark among the treasures of the dragons, and didn't have any tears left to cry when she realized sleep would provide her no escape.

CHAPTER 24

Lasaro was angry enough to transform right here in the middle of the Great Hall and go into full-on dragon combat with each and every one of the idiotic, short-sighted, pride-consumed masters arrayed before him. "You are making the wrong decision," he said through gritted teeth, for what felt like the hundredth time.

He could feel Kaelan in the back of his mind. Their bond had grown stronger during their test, but now they were separated by so many walls that the distance dampened everything except her fear and a dull, heavy grief. Her mother's life was at stake, as well as Lasaro's future and the future of the whole damnable kingdom—including the fates of the masters themselves—and all they could focus on was what punishment their best potential student should receive. Yes, she'd undergone the test under false pretenses—but she'd been *amazing*.

With no formal training and hardly any preparation, she'd done things no other tamer had been able to do for Lasaro. And he refused to allow the masters to punish her for that.

Master Lars looked down his nose at Lasaro. "We are making the only possible decision, *Pupil* Lasaro," he said, making it clear that Lasaro was nothing more than another student to him. "Kaelan will be cast out and, after we speak with the queen, likely banished from Alveria entirely. An example must be made. The other students must know that the Akademy's rules and expectations are not to be toyed with."

"You can't do that!" Lasaro shouted, his temper nearing its bursting point. "We're bonded! She must be at my side if I'm to take the throne." He bit his cheek. He hadn't meant to let that last bit pertaining to the bargain slip—his emotions were making it hard for him to control himself.

Master Olga frowned at him. "Yes, we're aware of the situation."

He froze. "You… are?"

She smiled thinly. "The Akademy has its sources. And as it turns out, we have as much desire for your success as you do. We have come to the same conclusions as you have with regards to who is the best heir for Alveria. As a result, we are willing to give you special consideration, extend the testing deadline, and try to pair you with one of the more experienced tamers."

He frowned, caught off guard. "I thought the more experienced tamers were all taken by other dragons already."

"They are."

He gaped at her. They were willing to take another dragon's tamer to bond with him, when Kaelan had already proven she was his perfect match? "This is ludicrous! I order you to accept Kaelan," he said. To Hel with the fragile balance of power between throne and the Akademy; he needed his tamer back.

But Master Henra was shaking her head. "That will not be possible," she said coolly, and Olga nodded sadly in agreement. "Our decision is final. You may accept it and remain until you have fulfilled the terms of your mother's bargain, or you may be ousted for your part in today's deception."

And, just like that, the masters all exited the room in a blur of white robes and colorful trim. Lasaro stayed where he was, staring into the distance, feeling like the world had upended itself below his feet.

He could stay, and try again—with a more experienced tamer this time, and perhaps one with enough knowledge and experience to make a new bond work. He could prove himself to his mother and, maybe, if he worked hard enough, earn back the trust of the masters who were after all valuable allies. Perhaps he might even gain enough control to heal Kaelan's mother after all… but she would never be a tamer.

She would never be *his* tamer. She wouldn't even be welcome in his country any longer. Not if he went along with the masters' plan.

He whirled around and marched out of the Great Hall. Out of the Akademy. He reached for his anger, reached for Kaelan, and—even with her as far away as she was—he rippled instantly into dragon form. He leapt off the end of the courtyard and spiraled skyward.

He didn't know how long he flew. He gave himself to his love of the sky for a long time, too angry to be afraid of his addiction to flying, and eventually the unending blue calmed him enough to allow him to think straight. And, in the space between one breath and the next, he knew what he had to do.

Lasaro marched into the inn, a determined fury held tight around him like a cloak. He scanned the tables and found the people he'd been searching for. When he pulled up a chair, all four of them turned to stare at him.

"Any particular reason you've called us here?" Inga asked blandly, the first to speak. Her porcelain skin was blotched, her eyes red from crying. It hadn't been too hard to track her down. And, once he had, he'd sent word back to the Akademy to get the other three people at the table to join them here for a clandestine meeting.

Stav leaned forward and put his hand over Inga's. His former tamer's fingers curled around his, accepting the comfort. "I'm guessing it's about Kaelan," Stav said, raising his brow.

The other two members of the group, Def and Drya, turned to Lasaro for confirmation. He nodded. Drya leaned forward, her eyes sparking with anger and eagerness. "We're going to break her out, aren't we?"

The table exploded into sharp exclamations of astonishment and denial, but Lasaro just let out a breath. This was the moment. The masters had given him a choice, and this was his last chance to take their offer before he took another direction. This was his last chance to go along with the flow of things and finally win his mother's approval, to be an heir worthy of her, to be the person he'd always wanted to be and save the kingdom he'd always wanted to rule. But all of that would require abandoning Kaelan—and that, he refused to do.

"Yes," he said, and he heard his whole future drop into that single word.

"You've got to be joking," Def said, gaping at him. "You want to go against the masters? They made their pronouncement right before you called for us—everyone heard it! Kaelan is *banished*. And you want to help rescue her and, what, hide her?"

"No," he replied. "I'm going to take her to my mother. The queen can overrule the masters' decision and make her my tamer. And I'll have her reinstate you, too, Inga, and order the masters to reevaluate how harshly they've been grading all the tamers." His mother would be furious, it was true. She'd support him, though—she'd have to, to save face. But it would be a long time before she forgave him.

Stav shook his head. "That's a bad move, Las. The masters are nearly as powerful as the queen. Is going against them really what's best for the country?"

No. It was what was best for Kaelan. He'd make it up to his country later.

Not as king, though.

He sighed. "Just trust me, all right? Kaelan doesn't deserve to be cast out of the kingdom just because some pigheaded dragons refuse to see past her peasant status."

Drya slapped her hands flat on the table and leaned forward. "I'm in."

Def turned to her, his eyes wide. "What? No way, you are *not* getting involved in this. You could get kicked out, too, and I'd have to start all over with a new tamer! Passing the tests won't mean a thing if you get expelled."

Her head swiveled around and she leveled a glare at him. "This is important to me," she said. "If you want my respect, I need yours. I understand if you don't want to help, but you have no say over what I do and do not choose to involve myself in."

Stav gawked at her. Inga raised one eyebrow, coolly impressed.

After a long moment, Def sagged, defeated. "Yeah," he said, "okay. I get it. I'm sorry. I guess I'm in, too."

Inga shrugged her agreement, the intensity in her eyes belying her casual gesture. Stav held his hands palms-up, appealing to them to see sense, but when no one budged, he sighed and nodded.

Lasaro leaned forward and smiled, though his expression felt fierce and joyless. "Good," he said. "Now, here's the plan."

They started at the kitchens. Lasaro pulled his distinctive silver-blond hair up under a cap and donned some street clothes he'd picked up in Bellsor, tucked beneath an apron. Inga was at his side in similar attire. They waited around the corner from one of the kitchens' side entrances, plastering themselves tight against the wall of a staircase to avoid being seen. Any second now, Stav and Def would start the disturbance that would be their cue to move.

A crash clattered through the hall. A loud male voice shouted, and then a dragon snarled and roared in response. In the kitchens, yelling erupted, the sounds panicked and excited by turns as the workers rushed out to either calm or watch the fight. Someone shrieked, and the ground beneath the hall rippled in a localized earthquake. Sconces rattled and portraits clattered off their hangings to crack against the floor.

Inga huffed. "Do dragons have to overdo *everything?*" she muttered, easing out of their hiding spot.

Lasaro didn't answer, too busy scanning the low bar that divided the kitchen from the main hallway. There. A tray of bread and soup. He snatched it up and handed Inga a water pitcher and a cup. They darted down the hall, unnoticed by the crowd and narrowly avoiding Stav's lashing tail.

"This way," Lasaro whispered, taking a sharp turn that led past the Clutch Room. His heart clenched when he remembered the empty nests, the unhatched eggs. Yet another problem he couldn't solve.

He refocused on the stairs beneath him, on the tangle of Kaelan's emotions growing stronger in the back of his mind, on the problem he *could* solve. *I'm coming for you,* he tried to tell her.

They finished descending and listened quietly at the bottom of the staircase. No sign of anyone nearby. Lasaro stepped out into the hallway that led to the dungeons—and nearly ran face-first into a guard.

Inga swooped to his rescue. "Master Olga sent us to deliver a meal to the prisoner," she said, smiling shyly at the man. Lasaro cursed internally. The guard might believe their lie and let them through, but his presence alone was enough to put a damper on their plan. If he alerted the masters before Lasaro could get Kaelan out of the Akademy, everything would be ruined. They'd probably put her on a dragon's back and fly her out of the kingdom this very day if they realized he was trying to overrule their decision, and then she'd be as good as lost to him.

But Inga, already ahead of things, was looking bashfully at the ground and blushing. "Haven't I seen you around before?" she asked, and then she dared to look up, tossing her hair over her shoulder and biting her lip.

The guard, young and inexperienced enough to fall for her ploy, smiled back at her. "Probably," he replied. "There aren't many guards at the Akademy—I guess the dragons tend to keep everyone mostly in line. But they like to keep a handful of us around as a show of good faith to Queen Celede, or at least that's my best guess. It's not like we really get to do much."

"What are you doing right now?" she asked coyly.

He cleared his throat. "Uh. I'm... supposed to be guarding the prisoner. A girl."

Inga's eyes widened with false alarm. "She must be a rogue dragon for them to need to send you to guard her."

"No, just some tamer who played a prank on the masters."

Inga scoffed. "That's all? Is it an insult for them to send you down here to babysit her, then?"

The guard frowned like he hadn't thought of that.

Inga bit her lip again, glancing up and down the hallway, and then grinned. "I actually have a confession. Could you help me out with something? I have this bet going with my friends about which of us can make out with the most guards, and I thought maybe you might be just the guy to help me win."

He grinned back. Sensing victory, Inga shoved her water pitcher and cup at Lasaro and he accepted them, scowling and rolling his eyes like he was put out. Silently, he thanked her for her sacrifice—though, from the wink she tossed him as she tugged the guard away, it didn't look like she considered it much of a sacrifice. Good for her, he supposed.

As soon as they were out of sight, he left the water and the tray on the floor and hurried to the double doors of the dungeon. He examined them for a moment; it looked like they only required a dragon's touch to open. He frowned. That didn't seem very secure. Nevertheless, he pressed his hand against one of the inset carvings and the door swung silently open.

He stepped into the dim light. "Kaelan?" he called, squinting. His eyes widened when he spotted the treasure and then understanding washed over him. The masters might call this the dungeon, but it wasn't an actual prison—this was a school, not the palace, and this was a dragon hoard, not a place to keep lawbreakers. He knew that treasure such as this could often help heal a wounded dragon; this must be where the masters went when they needed to restore themselves. They'd probably sent Kaelan here because it was the most secure place they could think of.

Coins rattled across the floor. Kaelan stepped out from behind a treasure dune. "Lasaro?" she asked, her tone sounding as ragged as she looked. Her short hair was messy, the olive skin under her eyes smudged purple with exhaustion. Unable to help himself, he hurried to her and wrapped his arms around her in a fierce hug.

"I won't let them send you away," he said firmly.

Her arms lifted to wind around his back. She laid her head on his shoulder, and his heart broke with the fragile way she held herself—like she could fall to pieces at any moment. "They want to send me away? As in… exile?"

"I won't let them," he repeated stubbornly.

She pulled back, tilted her head, and frowned. She could probably read something that was off in his voice. "How exactly will you stop them?" she asked cautiously.

"I'll go to my mother. She'll overrule them. She'll be angry, and so will they, and there will be consequences—but you'll be accepted into the Akademy, and you'll be my tamer, and I'll heal your mother."

Realization dawned in her features. "Consequences. Your mother will take the kingdom away from you for this, won't she?"

He closed his eyes. "The kingdom was never mine," he finally acknowledged. Maybe it never would've been his, anyway. All that work, all that *trying*, all those years of proving himself to a family that refused to truly see him. Would becoming a dragon in full control of his powers really have changed that? And if it had—would he have made a good king anyway? Good kings weren't constantly trying to prove themselves or always seeking approval. They simply did what needed to be done and accepted the consequences. How ironic that he had finally learned that just in time to give up on being a king forever.

"You can't," Kaelan said firmly.

He opened his eyes. "I can and I will."

"You *cannot* give up your kingdom for me. I forbid it."

He laughed humorlessly. "Who swore fealty to whom, again? I'm breaking you out, and you can't order me to do otherwise."

Her lips pressed together, and then her gaze went over his shoulder. Her features shifted into shock, then alarm—and then they hardened into something unfamiliar. She looked back at him. "You won't," she said quietly, an unnatural calm permeating her words. "I've got one card left to play, and it's high time I played it."

An uneasy chill snaked through him. Before he could answer, she raised her voice.

"Master Lars, Master Olga," she said, "I'm so glad you've joined us. I have something to tell you."

Horrified, Lasaro spun around. The two masters stood in human form next to the guard from earlier, who was holding Inga's hands behind her back. A sheepish-looking Stav and Def—who had a bloody gash across one shoulder—stood at her side. Drya stood in front of Lars, her short hair twisted messily upward like a flame, looking like an incandescently angry pixie. Apparently, her plan to keep Master Henra occupied had been successful, but Lars and Olga must've guessed she was up to something.

"And what is that?" Lars boomed, glaring down his nose.

Kaelan lifted her chin and squared her shoulders. In a flash, Lasaro remembered her as she'd looked at the river: facing down her potential death, fearless and refusing to look away. The chill of premonition that snaked through him tightened and squeezed, and he lifted a hand to stop whatever she was about to do, but before he could, she spoke again.

"When I first came here, you questioned who my dragon

father was," she said, her words ringing clearly across the heaps of treasure. "I'll tell you his identity now, so that you'll know I have as much right to be here—and as much potential as a student—as anyone you've ever trained."

"Kaelan—" Lasaro tried to cut her off, sensing something terrible was about to happen, but she ignored him.

"My father is Mordon," she announced.

Silence blanketed the unmoving tableau. Her words echoed inside Lasaro's head, bouncing off his skull, refusing to make sense. Mordon. Enemy of the throne and fugitive of the country, rogue and monster.

And the father to Lasaro's own tamer.

CHAPTER 25

The quiet that surrounded Kaelan was profound. It dug into her bones, burrowed deep in her blood, and wrapped her up like a fly caught in a spider's cocoon. It trembled, and she trembled with it.

She had made a bad choice. She understood that. It was why she'd waited so long to tell them the truth. But this was the only choice she'd had. She couldn't let Lasaro give up everything for her.

The masters were all staring at her silently, frozen. Stav and Def stood stock-still ahead of her, incredulous. Drya was just as stunned, her eyes full of unshed tears. Even Inga looked shaken.

None of them spoke. Somebody needed to speak.

"I said—" Kaelan started, but Lars cut her off.

"We all heard what you said." His voice was cold and dead, which shook Kaelan more than his fury would have. "That name is not welcome here. Nor is anyone who bears it."

The world tilted beneath her. "But I don't bear his name!" she cried. "I'm Kaelan *Younger*, daughter of Ardis Younger. I may have inherited some of Mordon's powers, but that doesn't make me automatically rogue like him. I don't even know what he was named a rogue for!"

Master Olga's gaze shifted to her. "He was named a rogue for his attempts to take the throne of Alveria," she said softly.

The back of Kaelan's neck prickled. *Usurper.* Her father was a would-be usurper.

And her dragon was the prince.

She whirled around, searching wildly for Lasaro. He was a few steps behind her, his eyes vacant with shock, with his face pale and bloodless. She reached for him.

He stepped away.

"Lasaro," she whispered, unable to form whatever it was she wanted to say to him. She could *feel* his withdrawal, his sudden fear of her, and it made her sick with desperation. She couldn't lose him. He had to trust her. They'd been through too much for this to be the thing that tore them apart.

She'd made a mistake to tell them all who her father was. She could see that now. But surely, this was still fixable. Surely, she could make them—him—see sense.

"I would never be like him," she said, her voice thin. "I wouldn't—I'm not..." she couldn't form the words.

Lasaro looked back at her. His beautiful eyes were empty, iced over, and his feelings of betrayal and shock churned in her mind. He turned his back on her.

She gasped, feeling like she was drowning. He didn't believe her. He'd come to save her, to give up everything for her, and he'd been willing to do all of that—until he'd learned who her father was. And now, suddenly, he was willing to abandon her to the so-called justice of the masters.

She had had so much faith in him. So much *belief*. He'd betrayed her once before, but he'd worked so hard since then to win back her trust, and then today he'd traded his future to ransom her own. For one shining moment, they'd been together, wholly and completely. And now... this.

A fissure cracked through the bond, resounding inside her skull. Some of Lasaro's feelings vanished from her mind as if a void had sucked them away. The fissure widened, more threads of Lasaro's emotions snapping away like a fraying rope in a heavy wind. Then, with one final, thunderous *snap*, the bond broke under its own weight.

A sob was wrenched from her. It echoed off the walls and bounced off the treasures, mocking her. She couldn't feel

Lasaro at all anymore. She was blind and deaf, trapped in an airless, windowless room, and she couldn't feel her way out.

Master Lars shook himself and transformed into a dragon. *"Kaelan Younger,"* he said, his voice ripping through her mind. *"You are banished from Alveria."*

He snatched her off the ground, claws wrapping tight around her chest, and launched upward toward the chimneys.

Master Lars dumped her on a hill south of the Akademy. *"You have one week to leave the country,"* he snarled into her head, and then he left.

The hill around her was quiet. No—not quiet. It sounded like her mountain back home. Like solitude. The wind whistling softly across the austere landscape; the cry of an eagle circling overhead. A few months ago, she would've given anything for these peaceful surroundings. But now, it was only a cruel reminder of the future she'd finally come to desire... just in time to have it stripped away.

She couldn't cry. She refused to. The masters didn't deserve her tears. Nor did Lasaro, not after what he'd done. This new betrayal was so much worse than the old one. Its consequences were unfathomable. By turning his back on her when she'd needed his support the most, he'd shattered her trust completely. And a bond couldn't sustain itself without trust.

Her head felt so empty now. Impossibly empty. She wanted to curl up and weep, but she'd already decided she wouldn't do that, so instead she drew the gold-and-silver knife that had still been sheathed at her waist and hurled it away from her with all the strength she could summon.

Thwump. It was the soft sound of her blade hitting something that gave beneath its force. There was a soft, startled *caw*, and then silence. Kaelan turned in the direction she'd thrown her blade. A crow lay on the ground, wings splayed, her dagger through its chest.

She gasped even as she ran to the bird and dropped to her knees. Something rolled out of the folds of her cloak: golden coins. They must've gotten caught in her clothes when she'd been sleeping on the treasure. Ignoring them, she tugged her blade out of the crow and picked the little creature up. Its head flopped lifelessly in her hands. Those familiar, beady eyes were shut, its onyx feathers still instead of ruffled with irritation. It was the crow who'd delivered the first package—the one that had contained the knife she'd just killed it with.

Grief tore through her. It was just a bird, she tried to tell herself, just a small thing, only a crow, nothing compared to what had already been robbed from her today. But it wasn't true. It was a life, and she'd taken it.

Tears blurred her eyes. She was a *healer*. She was supposed to fix things, not break them. And the crow was so little and helpless in her hands, its blood sticky and still warm, its feathers soft. It was too much. She wept, tears dripping down her face and spotting the feathers.

And with them, the crow stirred.

She froze, afraid to take a breath. It wasn't dead, but dying. And how much worse was that when she couldn't help it? But, no, her healer's instinct told her it wasn't dying at all. In fact, it was... fine.

The bird hopped up. It peered down at itself, at the sticky, bloody mess on its chest. It peered back up at her, its eyes wide again. Then it fluffed out its feathers. And then it flew away.

She stared after it, amazed. Her hands were still covered in blood and bits of down. Her healer's sense had confirmed the crow was as good as dead. And then it had just... fluttered off.

She'd stopped crying, but tears were still streaked across her face. One dripped down onto her hand.

And glowed.

She blinked, but the glow didn't go away. There was a dim, but undeniably golden gleam emanating from the teardrop. And suddenly she remembered the tapestry of Mordon, the voice intoning, *He had great healing skill, highly unusual for a dragon.* And the gleaming golden beams of energy emanating from him as he'd stood over an injured dragon.

Kaelan had inherited healing abilities from her mother. Was it possible she'd inherited them from her father, too?

She stood up all at once, her hands—still covered in blood— shaking. Ma's form of healing was one thing. It was finding the right herbs, mixing good potions, and calming those who were dying as they slipped into the afterlife. But Mordon's healing, the magic of a dragon and the power to *actually heal* the sick and dying... that was something else, and vastly more powerful.

She stared after the crow which had disappeared into one of the Akademy's towers above. She'd healed it. It had been dead, or nearly dead, and she'd brought it back to complete vitality.

Could it be possible that she didn't need a dragon to heal her mother?

Her breath quickened. That wasn't possible... was it? Why would she suddenly have the ability to miraculously heal like that when she'd never shown any sign of it before?

The coins.

She scrabbled for them, running her fingers through the grass around her, and picked them up. Three heavy golden half-weights. The seal on them was old, the face of Alveria's then-ruler unrecognizable. She hadn't had the presence of mind earlier to wonder much about why the dragons kept a hoard of treasure in their dungeons, but now that she thought about it, she remembered how much the masters loved their gold and silver, and how there were rumors that treasure was able to heal dragons and restore their powers. Was it possible it had brought out latent healing abilities in her also? And maybe all of the gems in and around the Emerald Lake were part of what made its magic so potent as well. Between that and her stay in the dungeons, it appeared she'd finally gained access to powers that had lain dormant in her blood all this time.

She hurried to the crest of the hill. She was on the far side of the Akademy. Bellsor lay between her and the way home. She had a week before she'd be an exile, and that was barely enough time to get back to Ma. And she wasn't even sure if her magic would work on a human yet.

But she had to try.

She started down the path that would lead her home.

CHAPTER 26

Kaelan walked through the capital of the country that had just exiled her with her head held high. She'd used one of the coins to buy herself new clothing so that she wouldn't look like a tamer—and to have Aelx's clothes sent back to the Akademy. Because she wasn't a tamer. Not anymore, and not ever again. It still broke her heart, and she didn't think she would ever stop mourning what she'd lost, but at least she was no longer keeping secrets and denying her identity. It gave her a strange sort of relief to walk through Bellsor now, having taken ownership of her heritage and her powers, knowing that the worst had already happened. She'd once been so fearful of this city and its loudness, the way people stared at her. But now, she knew nothing could hurt her more than she'd already been hurt.

She didn't look at the Akademy, even when the city's winding streets curved back toward Mount Firewyrm. She refused to wonder what Lasaro was doing right now. If his head felt as barren and his heart as broken as hers. If he had disavowed her entirely, and if he'd already paired with a new tamer.

Her throat tightened. She'd calmed enough to be able to put his response in perspective: he'd been shocked when she'd named her father, and Mordon was apparently a direct enemy of the throne. Of Lasaro's family. Perhaps what had happened in the dungeon felt like a betrayal to him as much as it did to her. She *had* been keeping secrets from him, after all—not that she had known it would be so personal, or that it would matter so much.

But it did matter, of course. Lasaro had turned his back on her because of Mordon. She had lost her faith in him as a result, and it had broken their bond. All because of her father, a dragon she'd never even met.

She lifted a hand—she'd washed them at a fountain at the edge of town—and turned it over, staring at the spot where the glowing tear had landed. She wondered if she'd inherited any more of Mordon's abilities. He'd been the most powerful master to ever teach at the Akademy; if she was half as talented as him, perhaps she could make something of herself after all. Maybe she could find a teacher, someone like Reida's cousin who'd been to the Akademy, and find out more about what she could do. She could become a healer like Ma and Grandma. She'd have to hide her dragon blood—dragons were even more disliked in neighboring countries than they were in rural Alveria—but maybe, someday, she could become something other than Lasaro's tamer, and learn to love it.

A group of people jostled her as they passed and she came back to herself. There were suddenly a lot more people on this street than there had been a few moments ago. Maybe there was a knattleikr game going on? But most of the people moving in tight groups around her wore sharp, serious expressions. A strange energy hummed through the air, in fact, winding around them, stirring her blood and drawing her forward. She clamped down hard on the urge to follow the crowd instinctively, taking a step back and knocking into a woman behind her.

"Watch it!" the woman snarled, but she wasn't looking at Kaelan. She was craning her neck to peer at the square up ahead.

A sinking feeling spiraled through Kaelan's gut. This energy— it felt familiar. It reminded her of squared shoulders, a scarred cheek, and old-souled eyes in a young face. She moved forward, allowing herself to be tugged along by the current of people and energy, and when she came to a statue, she hopped up on its pedestal to see above the crowd. People were gathering up ahead, cramming themselves into a square to listen to a man who stood on a bench. It was the man who'd been fomenting rebellion last time—the one who spoke like a peasant but stood like a soldier. She could only make out a few of his words from this distance, but the raised fists and the ripples of angry murmurs around her told her all she needed to know.

Torn, she glanced around. Surely, the palace knew about what was happening here already, or the Akademy did. With her powers stronger than the last time she'd been in this situation, she could feel the energy binding the crowd together, and pick out the strands of magic that stirred up their dissatisfaction into something darker and more dangerous. But there were no guards in sight. This had all happened too quickly.

She hopped off the pedestal and squeezed between bodies, her heart pounding as she edged closer. She jumped onto the ledge on the side of a shopfront, close enough to hear more now.

"Dragons and humans were never meant to live together!" the man cried out. "If the queen continues to advocate this madness, then she is unfit to rule! We must oust the dragons if we are to return Alveria to greatness!"

The crowd shifted around her like waves in a sea that was growing more turbulent by the second. Someone knocked Kaelan from her ledge and she caught herself, scraping her palms against the ground. She shoved herself back to her feet quickly to avoid being trampled, her heart racing now as the tension tightened around the crowd.

The man on the bench lifted both his fists into the air. "If those in power won't act to protect us, we must protect ourselves!"

The mob responded with a collective roar of agreement. The magic woven around them tightened like a net with the sound —and, as one, the crowd turned north.

Toward the palace.

Kaelan gasped, her gaze flying back to the man on the bench —and he was staring right at her. She could *sense* that it was him holding the magic, keeping the people enthralled and attuning them to his message, turning the rest of the world down around them until all they could see was him. It was magic. No, it was even more familiar than that. It was *tamer* magic.

Then she was caught in the tides of the crowd, her eye contact with the man broken. She bobbed through the mob like driftwood caught in a storm, trying to push past the wall of bodies but being forced to move along with them to avoid being overrun. Someone shoved at her shoulder, and someone else grabbed an arm. She tried to pull away, but then a man came out of nowhere and latched onto her other arm, and she was carried swiftly to the edge of the crowd. Realizing something was wrong, she kicked and struggled, but whoever was carrying her didn't even react. They dragged her into an alley between shops and then dropped her.

She scrambled to her feet—and came face to face with the man who'd been standing on the bench.

He gave her a courteous nod. "Hello," he said, his words laced with the faint trace of a foreign accent that she couldn't quite identify. "You are a tamer."

Her hands shook. The gold and silver knife, she still had it, so she could—ram it into his side, or his throat, or attack one of the guards nearest her? No, that would be foolish, as she was no good with a blade, and there were three of them and one of her. Best to try to talk her way out, then.

"I'm not," she protested, her voice wobbling with her fear. This man had been fomenting anti-dragon sentiment in a city *full* of dragons. If he was that bold, what might he do to her, one lonely dragon-blood in a town that was about to be torn apart by rebellion?

The man lifted his brow. "You are," he said, "and I know that because I was one, too."

Kaelan froze. She'd guessed he'd been a tamer, but why would he admit it to her? Whatever his motives, she was in big trouble. He'd made her, and she was more alone than she'd ever been in her life, defenseless and surrounded. "I'm not a tamer anymore," she replied quickly, hoping that might win her some points. "I was thrown out."

His smile looked like a wound, his startling white teeth

gleaming like bone beneath his lips. "Then we have even more in common. They threw me out, too. Although, I'm sure they'll come to regret it." He held out a hand for her to shake. "I'm General Marque of Unger. Nice to meet you."

She gaped at him. Unger. He was from *Unger*. A general from the country Lasaro had been certain was chomping at the bit to overthrow Alveria, disguised as a peasant and fomenting rebellion right under the palace's nose. She had to do something. She had to stop him. She couldn't let him hurt Lasaro, and hurt her kingdom. But what on Odin's green earth was she supposed to do?

"From the way you're looking at me, I can tell you think I'm some sort of monster," the man said. He pulled a small knife out of his pocket and began cleaning his fingernails with it. "I can assure you I'm not. In fact, I'm here to make everyone's lives better. You've been to the Akademy, been up close and personal with dragons. Do you really think they're what's going to make Alveria great? Do you really like how you're living, under their thumbs? I can tell you're a peasant, so I know you must have even more insight than those pampered nobles out there as to how unjust your society is," he said, motioning with the knife at the mob that was still thundering past their little alley.

"What do you want from me?" Kaelan demanded, trying to sound brave. Trying to *feel* brave. This man was talking to her when he could easily kill her. Surely, that meant she might still have a way out of this.

"Our cause could use people like you," he replied, confirming her suspicions. "People who the Akademy has used up and thrown away. People they're too afraid of to tolerate. You're powerful—I can feel it. You, Kaelan Younger, are meant to be a catalyst. Just like me."

"How did you know my name?" she demanded. Maybe someone from the crowd outside would see her, and save her. If she could just make the general keep talking for long enough.

He only shrugged one shoulder. "The dragons, they're all about tradition, loyalty, honor. But those things are holding the world back from true progress. I'm here to change things. That's what catalysts do. That's what *you* could do, if you helped me. And, when it's all over, you can stand in the ruins of the Akademy that betrayed you and smile."

She stared at him. Deep inside of her, something stirred. It felt a little like courage. Like certainty. Like something she hadn't realized she'd been struggling to find. Her hands stopped shaking. "That's what *you* want. Not me." Her words were calm, even. "Right? They turned you out—wouldn't even let you stay on in the kitchens, apparently—and now you want revenge. I bet that's what's behind your whole 'the common man should rule' act. You don't want what's best for Alveria. You want to ruin the dragons because they ruined you."

He pointed the knife at her, his smile going sharp. "You only know how I feel because you've felt that ruin yourself."

"I have," she acknowledged, accepting the pain that still weighed her down, "but that doesn't mean I want to turn against them. I want to make Alveria *better*—not by upending tradition and honor and loyalty, but by restoring those things. The Akademy is too harsh because their honor is false. Their loyalty is to themselves. True loyalty and honor, worthwhile traditions, those are what will restore us."

He quirked an eyebrow. "And as for you?"

She took a deep breath. "As for me," she said, knowing she was probably sealing her own fate, but too stubbornly honorable to do otherwise, "I can only be loyal to myself, to what I am, and to those I love. So, no, General Marque. I will not join you."

Those I love. Ardis. Haldis. Lasaro. They were a tangled web of emotion inside of her, but the danger she now faced made her other troubles seem so small. She hoped Lasaro could forgive her, and knew that she would have forgiven him, given more time. She hoped he would heal her mother. She hoped Ma and Grandma would know she'd died bravely.

The general sighed, sheathed his knife, and motioned to the two men behind her. "Very well," he said, regret in his tone. "Deal with her, would you? I have urgent business at the palace." With that, he turned and walked away into the crowd.

Kaelan held up her knife, determined to at least go down fighting, but the men easily took it away from her and tossed it aside. It clattered into the gutter as they grabbed her arms. She drew breath to scream—no need to die bravely if there was a chance to not die at all, right?—but one of the men clapped a dirty hand over her mouth. They dragged her into the building next to the alley, an inn. It was closed up and abandoned. The furniture was in disrepair and one of the walls sagged inward as if it would collapse at any moment. The men released her and she flattened herself against a wall, her breath coming fast.

One of the men drew his sword and shuffled forward, limping slightly on his left side. His eyes were bored, businesslike. He would murder her in cold blood and not care at all.

All of the air in the room seemed to vanish and she panted, trying to pull enough oxygen into her lungs. Sudden terror squeezed her like a vice. A moment ago, she'd been so brave. So calm. So ready to die for what she believed in. Now, all she could think about was what that sword would feel like when it went into her. She stared at the man who held the sword, memorizing what he looked like. Maybe Hel would allow her to come back as a ghost and haunt the bastard. But her gaze snagged on his stooped shoulders and brought back a sudden memory of three cloaked figures sneaking out of the Akademy. One of them had walked like a soldier and had reminded her of the man she now knew to be General Marque. And one of the others had had stooped shoulders and a shuffling gait just like the man in front of her.

The men she'd seen that night had been rebels. Unger spies. Why would Unger spies have been sneaking into the Akademy? They had to know it was incredibly well-guarded. It would have been all but impossible for them to get in.

Unless there'd already been spies on the inside to help them.

Her breath went still. Her panic was white-hot now, turned to something that felt like lightning inside of her: potent, electric, and waiting to be released. There were spies in the Akademy. Everyone inside was in danger. Especially the hopeful heir to the kingdom.

And she was the only one who knew.

The man who was standing back waved a hand. "I want to see what's happening at the palace," he said. "Can you hurry it up?"

She gathered up the lightning in her chest, wound it tight, and drew it back like an arrow on a bowstring.

The man with the sword smiled. His eyes went from being bored and businesslike to contemplative. He would care about killing her, she realized. He would *enjoy* it. "No need to rush," he said, keeping his eyes on Kaelan.

Kaelan bared her teeth at him. "That's where you're wrong," she said.

She released the energy. It streaked out of her in a scream of raw power, arrowing straight for the Akademy, containing a single word.

"LASARO!"

CHAPTER 27

L asaro was in the Tapestry Room. He wasn't sure why he'd come to this place, or how long he'd been here. An hour? A day? It didn't matter. Only one thing did, and she was gone forever.

He slumped. He was lying to himself when he told himself he didn't know why he'd come to this room. This was *her* room. Kaelan's. All those nights they'd snuck out together to explore, she'd always ended up here. She was so curious, so driven, and so intelligent. And so obsessed with finding out more about Mordon. Now he knew why, he supposed.

He shook his head. It still hadn't quite sunk in. His tamer, his friend, the girl he might have been in love with—how could she possibly be the daughter of that monster? He didn't know a lot about Mordon, but all royal children knew enough to understand that he was their greatest enemy. He'd been incredibly powerful, and then one day out of nowhere he'd gone rogue and sworn to make himself king. The cost of his betrayal had been great. Many had sided with him even after he'd disappeared, and the rebellion had nearly torn Alveria apart. It was still tearing the country apart, resounding through the years with the backlash of anti-dragon sentiment—people resented him, and by extension all dragons, for what he'd done to the kingdom.

How could Kaelan have lied to him about something so important? Even if she hadn't known all the details about Mordon, and even if she wasn't willing to trust the masters, surely she might have trusted *him* with the secret of her heritage. But, then, what would Lasaro have done if she'd told him the truth? He'd been shocked today, distraught and betrayed. The rift that had opened between them had torn their bond apart—he still winced, to think of how awful it had felt. If she'd come to him sooner, maybe he might have adjusted better. Maybe they could have worked through it.

But it was too late now. Lasaro would be put through another trial with a new tamer in a matter of hours. He'd had no choice but to agree to the masters' plan. It made him sick to think of sharing the bond with someone other than Kaelan and having that level of intimacy with anybody who wasn't her. But if he couldn't save his tamer, at least he might still be able to save his country.

A few weeks ago, it might have been enough. A few months ago, it would have been all his dreams fulfilled. But now all he could think about was what he'd lost.

He stood and went to the wall. He lifted up the layers of tapestries and found the one of Mordon that Kaelan had been looking at when he'd first found her here. He brushed his fingers over it quickly in goodbye, remembering that moment when she'd hugged him. Then he stepped back and turned to go meet whoever the masters had assigned to be his new tamer.

A bolt of magic careened through the walls of the room like they were made of air. Lasaro gasped when he sensed the crackling power but barely had enough time to turn before it crashed full-strength into his chest.

"LASARO!"

He snapped upright, his eyes going wide. Kaelan was in trouble. Kaelan was calling for him. No, she was *screaming* for him. She was afraid. She was helpless, and she needed him.

Without another thought, Lasaro accepted her magic into himself. It rippled across him, touching his mind, transforming his body into its dragon shape instantly. Something bloomed inside of him in reaction: a ball of emotions... fear and fury and desperation and need and love.

Kaelan. She'd restored their bond. And it was so *strong,* impossibly strong, tugging him urgently toward Bellsor.

Without hesitation, Lasaro leapt off the floor of the Tapestry Room and launched himself through the skylight with a roar. Glass shattered around him, bouncing off his wings and scraping against his scales. He spiraled into the sky and then hovered, shaking the glass off as he scanned the city below. The capital looked like an anthill that someone had stomped on. The streets were flooded with people and mounted guards and general chaos, though no other dragons were there yet. Rivers of humanity washed down the streets, screaming in a mad stampede as they rushed toward the palace.

He kept searching. The palace would have guards, and his formidable twin sisters. Kaelan only had him. He could deal with whatever was happening out there once he'd rescued her from whatever danger she was facing.

There. That run-down inn in the eastern quarter of the city, that was where the bond was strongest. He tucked his wings in and dove, her fear and helpless fury screaming in his mind, obliterating all other thoughts. People scattered beneath him, but he paid them no mind. He tipped one wing and did a barrel roll, crafting a funnel of wind, and then hurled both it and himself through the roof of the inn.

He tore the building apart with his teeth and claws and wind and magic. Bricks and boards shrieked through the air around him as he ripped down the wall separating him from his tamer. There: she was plastered against the far wall, two men in front of her, one with his sword drawn to strike her.

The world went black with Lasaro's rage. He roared again, and it sounded like the world coming apart. He tucked his wings and hit the ground. The funnel that had torn the building to shreds tightened to a small, deadly skewer of a tornado, spinning across the floor and heading straight for the men who would hurt the girl he loved.

A warm hand slid across his scales. *"Lasaro,"* whispered a familiar voice into his mind. Pinpoints of light broke through the darkness of his rage, and he came back to himself. He looked down.

Kaelan's hand was on his chest. He could feel her heartbeat, and sense the strength and calm she was feeding him, and hear her thoughts. The two of them had bonded, wholly.

"Kaelan," he said softly, and he carefully wrapped his wings around her. The tornado shuddered and died, leaving the two petrified men to flee across the piles of debris and into the street. He ignored them, focusing only on his tamer. *"I'm sorry,"* he told her. *"I should have stood with you. I should have supported you. I don't care who your father is, I belong with you regardless. I know you're not like him."*

"And I'm sorry I lied to you. I should have trusted you with the truth."

He shuddered with pleasure at the emotions emanating from her. Acceptance, love, relief—her feelings were like a drug.

The full bond made what they'd had before look like a shadow, a pale, lifeless imitation.

She looked up at him. The wind he'd created had died down enough for her to speak aloud and be heard. "There's a rebellion," she told him, her emotions tightening into dread. "Those men were from Unger. They were with General Marque—he's the man who was stirring up the mob last time we were in Bellsor, and he did even worse than that today. Half the city is on their way to the palace right now, and I think the general has spies he's been meeting with in the Akademy, too."

The news settled inside Lasaro, cold and hard. *"We'll have to worry about the Akademy later,"* he said grimly. *"If the palace is under siege, they'll need all the help they can get."*

"I'm with you," she told him, the strength of her determination underscoring her words.

He gazed down at her. *"Then be my rider,"* he said softly.

It was the last step of the probationary bond. The finishing touch of a blooming relationship between dragon and rider, meant to be taken during the last stage of a successful test. It meant they were one, bonded, wholly together.

Kaelan's eyes shone. Then she lifted her head suddenly like she'd remembered something. "Just a second," she said, backing away. "Don't move." She darted out into the alley, kicked a few loose boards and bricks around, and came back with her gold and silver knife, tucking it into her waistband.

"Just in case I run into either of those two soldiers again," she muttered darkly.

"I'll hold them down for you," Lasaro replied, his tone just as grim.

Then Kaelan was smiling at him and the moment shifted like dawn cutting through the mist. He could feel her curiosity, her shy eagerness, her shimmering joy as she approached him again.

"Ready?" she asked.

In answer, Lasaro lifted one of his front legs for her to step onto. She hopped onto his knee, then slid from there onto his back. She felt right there. She *belonged* there. If his city was in trouble, he was glad she would be the one to help him put it right.

He spread his wings and lifted off, slowly this time, giving her a moment to adjust. She whooped from her spot on his shoulders, clinging tight, her joy resounding in his mind. His happiness wound around hers and he rose higher, their joined strength buoying him as he searched for the best way to help stop the riots.

A shadow fell over him. Then it slid over the block below him, and covered the one next to that, spreading like ink over his city. His joy dimmed as he realized how massive the shadow was. Kaelan saw it, too, and her unease mingled with his.

A shiver of premonition rippled over him. Slowly, dreading what he would see, he looked up.

A vast black dragon was hovering over his city.

CHAPTER 28

Kaelan stared up, her heart stumbling in her chest. Last night's dream flashed through her mind: Mordon, his wings unfurled like immense sails over the city, blocking out the sky as the Alverians destroyed each other. It was happening—right here, right now. The return of Mordon. And the destruction of her country.

She shook herself. The black dragon was too high above them to offer much detail and there had to be more than one black dragon in the kingdom. It could very well be someone from the Akademy, a master she hadn't met or perhaps one who had retired, come to help with the riots. It was much too big to be anything but fully grown and possibly even ancient, but there was no reason to jump to the assumption that it was her father. It could be someone else. She desperately wanted it to be anyone else.

But there was a thread of familiarity tugging at her when she looked at him. When he swept those colossal wings down, the wind and magic that buffeted her felt almost like he knew her. Like he was greeting her.

She shuddered and tore her gaze away from the black dragon. Whoever he was, he wasn't attacking, just sitting up there in the sky watching. Which meant she and Lasaro should be dealing with the more immediate problem of the attack on the castle.

"We'll have to deal with him later," she said, forcing herself to refocus on the streets beneath them. There—the crowd had almost reached the palace. Running at the very front was none other than General Marque.

Lasaro swooped down. The general glanced up and spotted them. Suddenly, Lasaro hesitated.

"What's wrong?" Kaelan asked, feeling his sudden uncertainty.

"Those are my people down there," he said, spreading his wings wide to slow his descent, gliding above the streets. *"They're only rioting because he's compelling them, using his magic to grow a little dissatisfaction into acts of violence. I don't want to hurt them."*

"Then don't! But if you don't stop them somehow, they're going to hurt your family, and even if they don't get to the royals, they're still creating an opening for Unger. All General

Marque has to do is wait for the soldiers and the citizens to do each other in, and then he can just stroll in and take control. That imminent attack you were worried about? This is it!"

Still, he hesitated. *"I don't know,"* he said at last. *"I can't explain it, but I don't want to. Something feels... wrong."*

Her hands tightened on his neck. What was he talking about? Didn't he understand what was at risk?

General Marque was looking up at them, his eyes narrowing as he slowed. The mob parted to stampede around him like a river parting around a rock. His magic kept him safe, kept them in his thrall, and made it so that none of them trampled him.

Realization dawned. He was a tamer. He had the ability to connect to dragons and influence them. She remembered the dragons who'd hovered above the conflict the last time he'd brought a mob together in Bellsor—they hadn't stepped in to help the guards break things up, probably because of General Marque's influence. What if he was using that same ability on Lasaro?

What if he could use it on the *queen*?

She shuddered with disgust and anger. How *dare* he touch her dragon. How *dare* he put his filthy, honorless magic anywhere near her. *"I'll fix this. Hold on a second,"* she told Lasaro, and then she closed her eyes. She reached through the bond and found the foreign tendrils of Marque's power, just as she'd expected. She wrapped her anger tight around them and tore them to shreds. They fell away from Lasaro instantly.

She opened her eyes. General Marque was staring up at her— not with fury, but with speculation. It made her feel itchy all over, but she bared her teeth at him, hoping he could sense her determination to tell Lasaro to squash him like a bug if he ever tried to mess with their bond like that again.

"What was that?" Lasaro asked, startling at the sudden change in his own emotions.

"General Marque has tamer magic. I guess it's like mine—he can use it to interfere with other tamers' and dragons' bonds. He was using it on you, but he won't do it again," she said.

"Unless he feels like losing a few limbs," Lasaro replied, his tone low and dangerous.

The rush of people was almost upon the palace now. Kaelan bit her lip, frantic, having no idea how to stop the chaos that was about to take place. Lasaro was right; these people were Alverian citizens, only turned into Marque's pawns through magic that drove them to do things they wouldn't have been doing on their own. Lasaro and Kaelan couldn't harm them, and they couldn't allow the soldiers that were now arrayed at the palace's entrance to harm them, either. But they *did* have to stop them, and quickly.

"Hold on tight, I've got this," Lasaro said, and he dove. She yelped and clung to his scales, caught by surprise, and she

was nearly unseated when he plummeted to the ground. He pulled up at the last second for a whisper-soft landing, aided by a bit of his magic that cushioned him with a quick updraft.

The palace's guards were on their right, bristling with swords and lances, their armor polished to a blinding sheen. To their left was the mob, brandishing makeshift torches and broken-off broom handles and chunks of bricks. There were seconds before the two small armies collided—and Kaelan and Lasaro were caught right in the middle.

A sudden anger rose in her. These people—everyone on all sides of this conflict—they were infuriating. The mob hated dragons mindlessly, and the soldiers were ready to murder their own people. She should raze them all to the ground, use her power and Lasaro's to end this once and for all, and leave no one standing. Everything would fall at her feet.

She jerked away from the thought, suddenly coming back to herself. That urge… there was no way that had come from her. But, for a moment, she had gone along with it. She could still feel the compulsion, the dark, tempting desire to destroy, and she shuddered, wondering how far it might've taken her if she'd let it. As the mob hurled itself closer and their time ticked down to the endgame, she closed her eyes, reached inward, and latched onto the traces of destruction lingering in her mind. She followed the magic out and up. It was much stronger than Marque's, more expertly woven, and thinner but much harder to break. She found its source, hot with magic like the sun itself, and turned her face toward it.

When she opened her eyes, she was looking at the black dragon.

"Kaelan!" Lasaro shouted, his alarm jolting her back into the moment. They had seconds before the mob threw itself on the army. Quickly, she sent a telepathic shout toward the Akademy, making it as loud as she could. Normal tamers couldn't communicate with other dragons, but then, normal tamers couldn't influence other people's bonds the way Kaelan had with Drya and Def, either. She would have to hope she might be able to break other rules as well because they were going to need back-up. Then she took a deep breath, drew up all her magic and strength of will, and shoved it all into Lasaro, trusting him to know what to do with it.

Lasaro reared up, lifting his front legs off the ground, and Kaelan tightened her grip to stay atop him. Something was building in him. He waited, spun it and fashioned it, and then released it with a vicious, powerful downward swipe of his wings. Wind roared out from him, blasting over both forces. The soldiers staggered backwards, pushed off their guard as their weapons were torn from their hands. The first few rows of the onrushing mob flew through the air and away from the conflict, landing on cushions of air a few feet above the ground before dropping back to the cobblestones.

Something tickled at her mind—a tug of foreign magic.

Friendly, familiar magic this time. Kaelan looked up, squinting at the skyline above Mount Firewyrm. A blue dragon was racing toward them, a girl with flame-twisted hair on his back.

"Drya!" Kaelan called out, throwing her magic at the other girl like a rope to reel her in. Def immediately course-corrected, aiming for them.

"Kaelan!" Drya answered, sounding shocked. *"How are you doing this? This magic, it's—I've never felt such strong—"*

"No time for that," Kaelan cut her off. *"General Marque from Unger is here and he's using magic to influence Alverians to attack the palace. We have to stop everyone from killing each other. Send for reinforcements. We need everyone you can bring—students, masters, anyone! Tell them not to hurt anybody. These people are under the influence of foreign magic. We need to show them that they can trust the dragons, that we'll protect them. Search for General Marque."* She pushed an image of the general into Drya's head and received back a still-startled acknowledgement. Drya went silent, her focus elsewhere as she had her dragon call for help.

Lasaro dropped heavily back to the ground, panting. He'd used up a lot of magic and his strength was waning. Quickly, Kaelan patted him on the shoulder in reassurance, squeezing her legs to nudge him to move forward to where part of the mob was recovering and rushing at the army again.

He snorted at her. *"I'm not a horse,"* he said, sounding half-annoyed and half-amused.

She smiled. *"At least you won't bite me like Allfather did. But seriously, get a move on; you've got to do your hurricane thing again up there before people get hurt."*

"Your wish is my command," he said sarcastically, but she sensed his focus and effort as he gathered in a breath and then expelled it in a roar. Wind blasted outward from the sound, less powerful than his earlier wingbeat, but still blowing the front line of the crowd back and making them stumble. *"I don't know how much I have left,"* he said, his voice thin. *"Taking down the inn and then doing this, it's taken a lot out of me."*

Taking down the inn. Such a simple phrase for what he'd done. She flashed back to the maelstrom he'd created when he'd rescued her, the bricks that had spun around her like leaves in the wind, and the ferocity with which he'd shredded through a wall as if it had been made of paper. She'd felt his rage, the depth of his feelings when he'd seen her helpless—and the gentleness with which he'd wrapped his wings around her when she'd calmed him.

"Thank you for that, by the way," she said softly.

He twisted his head to peer up at her. *"That's what dragons do. Protect their tamers,"* he replied soberly, and it sounded like a promise.

"Lasaro!" rumbled Def's voice. Kaelan looked up; Stav hovered behind Def, Inga on his back, and two other young-looking dragons were behind them. *"We've got some back-up for you. Sorry this was all we could gather. The masters wouldn't believe us."*

"Four is plenty. Get down here and help us find General Marque," Kaelan sent back grimly. *"Once we put him out of action, his hold on the crowd will wear off and they'll be more willing to listen to reason."*

Def hesitated.

Lasaro spoke up. *"Kaelan is calling the shots,"* he said firmly, his voice even more tired than before. *"She's my tamer and has my full trust, and if you call me your prince, then she has yours, as well."*

Def dropped to the ground in front of them, hesitated a moment longer—and then, at a not-so-subtle nudge from Drya, shrugged. *"Okay,"* he said. *"Kaelan, what do we do?"*

"Stav, make it harder for the mob to get to the palace. Can you cause some small earthquakes, make the ground tougher to cross? Think ditches, low walls, treacherous fields of rocks."

"Yes, ma'am!" Stav called, and the earth around them started to tremble.

"Def, call up a storm to flood the ditches Stav makes, and see if you can get some mini-moats set up. Get some lightning in

here, too. Don't hurt anyone, but make sure they know that if they try to get past you, they're likely to get blasted."

"Got it!" The sky above the palace began to darken and rumble.

"The rest of you, and Lasaro, get up in the air and search for Marque from above. Anyone who finds him—and that includes you, Def and Stav—knock him out. That should cut off his magic and get these people sane again. And watch out for urges to be violent or turn against one another! Marque has tamer magic, and that black dragon above us tried to influence me a moment ago."

Alarm rippled through the other dragons. One of the tamers gasped. *"Is that—"*

"I don't know, but as long as he's just sitting up there, we don't have the resources to waste fighting him," Kaelan said firmly. *"Everyone to your duties!"*

Lasaro lifted off with less energy than normal, hovering just above the rooftops as they started searching for Marque. Kaelan squinted, trying to make out individual faces in the angry mob, but people were starting to riot and it was hard to make out any details in the midst of the chaos. Smoke trailed up from a stage that had been lit aflame, and some of the rioters were taking advantage of the confusion to break shop windows and make off with the goods inside. Small fights had broken out where one group had turned on another, blood splattering bright against the black cobblestones.

Kaelan cursed. She'd never find him in this mess.

"Look for a gap!" Lasaro shouted.

"What?"

"A gap! When he was standing still earlier, everyone just kind of parted around him instead of running him over. His magic is protecting him. Look for a gap, a quiet spot—that'll be him."

"Yes!" Kaelan exclaimed. Of course, that was the perfect strategy. She leaned over Lasaro's neck with renewed concentration, this time sweeping her gaze in broad strokes across the chaos below rather than trying to pick out individual faces. She searched for a pattern, a spot where no one fought, looking for the steady blankness of cobblestones—

There!

General Marque was moving against the tide of the crowd, striding briskly down a side street, everyone moving mindlessly out of his way even though they hardly even seemed to see him. It looked like he was headed for one of the less-protected side entrances of the palace.

"Oh no, you don't," she muttered, mentally nudging Lasaro toward the spot.

"I don't think I have enough magic left to fight him," Lasaro admitted. *"But I could chew him up a little, if that helps."*

Kaelan frowned. *"Let me try something first,"* she said slowly.

Lasaro sent her a sense of agreement through the bond, too tired to even muster words. His flight path dipped and wobbled.

"Go ahead and set down," she told him. *"Just focus on keeping everyone away while I do this."*

Gratefully, Lasaro swooped down to the road a few shops behind General Marque. People gave him a few dozen yards worth of space, but hefted their homemade weapons, eyeing him. They began clumping into larger groups after a moment and gained courage, some of them even beginning to edge toward him. She'd only have a few moments before they attacked.

She closed her eyes and cast her magic out around her. She quickly found the threads of Marque's power and followed them back to their source. He was like a spider sitting in the middle of the web, and the people around him were all trapped flies. With just the twitch of his fingers, he could make them dance—and they'd think it was their own idea.

Kaelan's mouth shaped into a snarl. Righteous fury rose up in her. Her whole life, she'd been forced to obey men like this, who thought nothing of trampling over the will of people they considered somehow lesser. Corrupt soldiers, bullies like

Bekkr, the tax collectors who demanded an extra ten percent to pad their own pockets. Well, now it was *her* who had the power. And she planned to use it.

She gathered up all the magic she had and Lasaro pitched in, sending her all the magic he could spare, as well. She pulled together all of the threads of Marque's telepathy, feeling them go taut like fishing lines. Then, wielding her power like a knife, she sliced through them. They went limp and fizzled out like sparklers.

She let out a triumphant yell and opened her eyes. Marque had frozen in place, feeling his telepathic control rebounding. He turned and looked across the people who, just a moment ago, had been under his control. They were slowing down, looking at each other, confused. But others who were still under Marque's control barreled faster toward the palace—Kaelan had to do more. She had to finish the job.

"Get me closer to Marque!" she told Lasaro.

"Are you sure you have enough left to do that again?"

She was bone-deep tired from all of the magic she'd already performed, but she didn't have a choice. *"Yes,"* she said, trying to make herself believe it. *"But just in case, call for back-up."*

Her dragon was silent for a moment, sending out a call to the other dragons. *"They're all occupied,"* he reported back. *"The front of the palace is still under heavy siege—those people are still under Marque's power."*

It was up to them, then. *"Let's go,"* she told him.

Lasaro lurched forward, mowing through the mob of people between him and Marque. The rioters shouted and fell back, still confused, some of them clustering behind wary soldiers for protection. Kaelan pulled together all that was left of her power. It was dregs, pitiful. She was untrained, young, and had only recently discovered her powers. But, right now, she and Lasaro were Alveria's only hope.

Marque spotted her. One of the men next to him—the Ungerian soldier who had nearly killed her earlier—drew his weapon again and made to charge toward them. Lasaro reared back and roared, and although it was much less impressive than his earlier blast, it was still intimidating enough to knock the man back. Quickly, Kaelan found a nearby line of Marque's power and, rather than cutting it, started to follow it toward the general. If this was going to work, she needed to take this problem out at its source.

Marque's eyes met hers. He sensed what she was about to do. Quicker than a thought, he drew his knife and threw it straight at her heart.

Lasaro spotted the weapon just in time and flared his wings wide. The knife glanced off the edge of one, throwing up sparks, but its course wasn't altered enough. Before Kaelan could so much as draw another breath, the blade plunged hilt-deep into her shoulder.

She looked down. Blood seeped out in a red bloom around the wound. She took one ragged inhale as the corners of her vision began to darken. Her legs and arms went numb, and her grip on Lasaro slipped.

She didn't feel it when she hit the ground. Her vision was tunneling. She was fading out. A shadow fell over her: Mordon? No, Lasaro. He stood over her, roaring with a sound like an avalanche, his fear and anger ripping through her mind.

Her gaze shifted. Marque was running. He was fleeing toward the palace, and Lasaro wouldn't pursue him, not with his tamer down. This was her last shot.

With the remnants of her quickly draining energy, she picked a line of his magic back up. She traced it out and up. She followed it past shopfronts, rioters, screaming soldiers—and into General Marque's mind.

He met her there. They squared off, and his power was huge, immeasurable compared to her dwindling magic. But she didn't need to defeat him. Didn't need to pit herself against him. She just needed to slip under his guard…

Marque stopped, frozen in place two blocks away.

…find the place where his energy stemmed from…

He turned around. Staring at her, eyes wide, mouth open.

…and turn it off.

Marque dropped like a rag doll.

Instantly, everyone around them stopped what they were doing. They backed away from the fights, stared down at the goods they'd been stealing, and stammered out embarrassed apologies. At least, that was what Kaelan guessed they were doing. She couldn't quite tell because she couldn't hear anything. She was fading out, the last of her energy drained by knocking Marque unconscious.

One of Marque's soldiers rushed to him. He shouted and several other men came out of the crowd, converging on the spot. Then a shining hole of some black magic opened in midair and sucked them away, disappearing the next second as if nothing had happened.

Lasaro dipped a claw carefully beneath Kaelan and turned her. He shifted, dropping to his knees at her side in human form, lifting her head and shouting something. The purple beneath his eyes looked haggard, and his skin was paler than she'd ever seen it. He would need awhile to recover from this. Then again, so would she. If she was going to recover.

Her gaze went distant. Floating above them, sail-like wings blocking out the sun, was the black dragon. He reached down and touched her mind.

"Daughter," he greeted her. His mental touch was gentle, but his voice like a rockslide or a tsunami or some other

inevitable, unstoppable force of nature. *"I am glad to see you coming into your powers."*

She tried to respond, but found she didn't even have enough magic for that. The darkness crept in veins and rivulets over what was left of her vision. Everything went black then, and between one breath and the next, she fell back into nothingness.

CHAPTER 29

L asaro paced.

He had been pacing for a long time. Hours, he thought, probably—and then he passed a window and noticed that the night sky had turned pink at the eastern edge. Dawn. So, he'd been pacing this single palace hallway the whole night.

He pivoted at the end of the corridor and started back toward the far side.

"You'll wear out the carpet," chided a mildly cool female voice from an adjacent hallway. He slowed down and turned. Queen Celede stood below the arching entryway, her hands folded demurely, clad in a blue gown that cascaded from her shoulders and made her look beautiful and aristocratic and nothing like the formidable dragon warrior he knew she was.

"Mother," he said with a stiff bow, itching to get back to his pacing. He'd been well past exhaustion for hours now, but his brain wouldn't stop running in frantic circles. Keeping on the move was the only thing that distracted him enough to stop him from knocking in the door to Kaelan's room and demanding the healers save her, right *now*, and medical science be damned if it tried to stop them.

Queen Celede's lips pursed. "You're worried," she observed.

"Yes." His reply had been short, his tone curt.

"I was on lockdown when everything happened, but I was told you and your tamer performed admirably," she said. "Come, sit with me." She motioned to some low couches against the wall.

Reluctantly, Lasaro dropped into one and rubbed his face. "Have you heard anything from the healers?" he asked. The Akademy, chagrined by their failure to make an appearance during the earlier battle, had sent their best dragon-blood medic to attend Kaelan. The deceptively diminutive woman had immediately huddled with two of the palace's best healers in Kaelan's room, and they'd all kicked the hovering prince out. He'd been stranded in the hallway ever since, and since his tamer's suite had several other exits, he couldn't even try to ambush the healers for news on their way in or out.

"She's still sleeping, but she will be well," his mother said, and tears sprang to Lasaro's eyes with sudden relief. He blew out a long, shaky breath as the depths of his exhaustion hit him. But he couldn't sleep, not yet, not till she woke up. He needed to hear her voice before he could rest if only to reassure himself that she was really okay.

"I'm glad," he replied roughly.

"You two are fully bonded?" the queen guessed, one eyebrow raised.

"Yes, but it's not official. The masters have still refused to admit her." Quickly, he summed up the revelations of the day. Mordon, his parentage of Kaelan, the personal appearance of General Marque, the strange magic with which the Ungerians had vanished when their attack had failed. Having summed up the forces arrayed against his country, he felt even more overwhelmed than before.

When it was over, his mother sat still and serene in a way that told Lasaro she was planning to rain down fire and brimstone on whoever had let Marque and Mordon into her city. "I see," she said simply. He knew what she was thinking behind those easy words, though: that Mordon was a threat to her family and all of Alveria, and there would be no easy way to stop him. And if he was somehow allied with Unger… their kingdom was in even more desperate trouble than they'd thought.

The queen looked back at him. "This tamer of yours. You trust her, regardless of her heritage?"

"With my life. With all our lives," he added without hesitation.

She nodded. "Then, as far as I'm concerned, you two are officially bonded."

He dredged up a smile. "Thank you, Mother. That means a lot to me."

She reached out one hand and placed it atop his, offering what was as close to open affection as she ever had. "I'm afraid it won't mean much to the masters," she warned him. "You may have made some powerful enemies at the Akademy."

He grimaced. "I suppose that means I've left the terms of our bargain unfulfilled." He tried to feel something—pain, regret, anger, disappointment in himself—but nothing came. He'd feel all that and more later, he was sure, once the situation was settled and Kaelan was awake, when he could think about anything but her recovery.

Queen Celede tilted her head thoughtfully. "I'm not sure," she said. "You've certainly made some missteps. You've cost us some of our most valuable allies. But you also saved the city and showed your people that you are able and willing to fight for them as a dragon." She considered things for a long moment. Lasaro tried not to hope, already worn emotionally ragged by the events of the last twenty-four hours. At last, his mother waved a hand. "I suppose we shall have to consider our bargain voided. I can't name you heir right now, not with the masters opposed to you, but I won't name any of your siblings, either. And maybe once the threat from Unger is taken care of and you've won back the goodwill of the

Akademy, we can talk about your inheritance again. In the meantime, you and your tamer still need to finish your training there, I'm afraid."

Lasaro exhaled. It wasn't much, but it was better than he'd hoped for. "That sounds agreeable to me."

She smiled at him—a real smile, the corners of her eyes crinkling in a way he hadn't seen in years. "For what it's worth, I am proud of you," she said, patting his hand. "You acted like a real king last night. It gives me hope for our kingdom's future."

"Thanks," he replied, stunned. His mother's approval settled over him like a warm blanket.

She raised a hand. "But I hope you know that my love for you is not based on your performance. It has come to my attention of late that that may be the impression I give, and I... dislike that any of you children may have thought you needed to earn my affection." Without waiting for a reply, Queen Celede rose, elegant and graceful as always, her cool mask slipping back into place as she prepared to return to her duties. "I hope your tamer recovers well and quickly. Goodbye, Lasaro." She turned to walk back down the hall she'd arrived from.

"I love you, too, Mother," he said softly.

She turned her head just enough to let him see her smile, and then she strode down the hall and disappeared.

Someone was shaking his shoulder. Groggily, Lasaro swatted them away and muttered a threat, his thoughts muddled.

"I beg your majesty to refrain from 'popping off my head and using it as a knattleikr ball,'" said the dry voice of the palace's healer.

The healer! Lasaro sat bolt upright, grabbing the man by the lapels. "What news of Kaelan?" he demanded, his voice rough and creaky from sleep. He blinked away his fogginess, trying to focus. Someone had brought him a chest full of treasure from the Akademy dungeons, and that plus the Emerald Lake rock he'd had Stav bring up from his room at the school had helped Lasaro recover from his overuse of magic. He felt like he'd slept for years. His thoughts were still murky, but he felt refreshed and renewed, ready to take on the world.

The healer cleared his throat. Lasaro still had hold of his lapels, and the poor man was twisted over Lasaro's couch in an awkward position as he tried to free himself.

"Oh. Sorry," he said, and he released the man. The healer huffed and straightened his clothes. "Kaelan?" Lasaro prompted, standing up with alacrity.

"She is awake," the healer reported, but he didn't manage to get out another word before Lasaro was on his feet and running for the door to his tamer's suite. "She has remarkable healing abilities, and appears to be nearly fully recovered, but she needs rest!" the man shouted at his prince's receding back.

Lasaro shoved through the door which had been left ajar, though he'd been ready to tear it off its hinges if it was still locked. Kaelan was sitting up in her bed, combing her hair with her fingers and yawning.

Lasaro stopped dead in the doorway. She was staring dazedly out the window and hadn't noticed his entry yet. She was in a nightgown, a thin scrap of silk that barely covered anything. It hadn't occurred to him that she wouldn't be fully dressed, but of course, she'd been sleeping. He quickly turned his back, blushing and clearing his throat, resisting the impulse to turn back around and stare—only to make sure she was really okay, of course. Not to… look at anything. Although he really, really wanted to look at things.

His emotions, still slow and foggy from sleep, curled into a confused mess. Yesterday—had it been yesterday? How long had he slept?—he'd finally admitted to himself that he loved Kaelan. But what exactly was he supposed to do about it? She'd reacted badly when he'd proposed marriage, and he could understand why. They both had other priorities at the moment. But where did that leave them now? A dragon marrying a tamer was still forbidden by his own mother, and his court would be thrown into chaos if he announced he was courting a peasant. He'd already gone against the Akademy for Kaelan's sake. And, truth be told, he would be willing to make as many more enemies as he needed to for his tamer—but with Alveria at the mercy of Unger as well as Mordon, throwing his court into disarray would only weaken his kingdom when it needed to be stronger than ever to avoid annihilation. He didn't know what he should do. Dishonor his family and break with traditions—some of them foolish, others vital—to be with the girl he loved? Or somehow find a way to be her dragon but nothing else, and keep his country, if not his heart, in good shape?

Kaelan spotted him. "Lasaro!" she cried, and the bond lit up with her relief and happiness. Unable to keep his back turned and unwilling to keep pondering a question he had no answer to, he hurried to the side of the bed and lifted her up in a fierce hug. She'd wrapped the blanket around her shoulders, and she felt sleep-soft and warm. His emotions uncurled and stretched out, coalescing into joy and a shattering relief at finally being certain she was okay.

"Don't scare me like that ever again," he ordered her, stepping back.

"I'll do my best to avoid knife-throwing Ungerians in the future if you promise to do the same," she replied dryly.

His mouth thinned out. "No promises there, I'm afraid," he said, but he left it at that. They could discuss the forces mounting against Alveria later.

Right now, they had something more important to do.

He found some clothes that would fit her draped over a chair. He picked them up and tossed them at her. "Get dressed," he said.

She blinked at him. "If you're dragging us back up Mount Firewyrm to yell at the masters for not showing up, I'm on board, but can I get some breakfast first? And maybe brush my teeth? This is for your benefit as much as mine, trust me."

He cracked a smile. Gods, but he'd missed her. "Yes to the breakfast and the teeth-brushing; no to the masters. They can wait a few days."

"A few days? What do you mean? Where are we going?"

He went to a window and looked out at Bellsor. The fires had long since been put out, and dragon-bloods, soldiers, and citizens alike were helping to clean up the mess. The sight gave him hope.

He turned back to Kaelan. "The capital is safe enough for now," he told her. "So, we're going somewhere I wish I could've taken you a long time ago."

CHAPTER 30

The wind had tangled Kaelan's hair into an impossible mess, she was freezing, and her breath was short from being at such a high altitude, but she had never in her life been happier.

She smiled down at her dragon. Lasaro was gliding now as they neared their destination, flitting through the scattered clouds, his pearlescent silver wings stretched wide to catch the air. He was magnificent. *They* were magnificent. She was feeding him energy and calm right now, and in return he wrapped her in security and a quiet, serene joy. The trip—which would have taken nearly a week on foot, but had only lasted the span of a single morning on dragon-back—was the most exhilarating experience of her life.

And also possibly the most confusing.

She was in love with Lasaro. She was honest enough with herself to be able to admit that. But from there things started to get... problematic. A few days ago, he'd proposed marriage even though he had seen marrying her as a sacrifice. She'd refused because it wasn't what she wanted for herself. Plus, it would've been dishonorable for him to go against tradition so thoughtlessly. Now, though, she thought his feelings might've changed. The way he'd felt in her mind when he'd burst into her room earlier had implied that. But even if they had changed, what could there ever be between the two of them? Would he really go against everything that was best for his kingdom to marry her? Should she allow him to?

"You okay?" Lasaro asked, sensing her distress.

She snapped back into the moment and shook herself. She was flying in the clouds with a dragon she'd officially bonded after having saved the royal palace of Alveria from invaders. She deserved to enjoy herself. She could figure out what to do about their relationship later.

"Never better," she replied sincerely, grinning. She spotted a tiny huddle of buildings tucked into the ripple of mountains below them and pointed. *"I think that's it!"*

Gladsheim. Her home, which no longer felt like her true home at all. It looked so small from up here, so insignificant and petty. But also, somehow, like a rightful part of something much bigger than itself. She was grateful for her time there and in all of the other villages where she'd lived. Those years had shaped her, given her strength, and taught her sympathy for those who were powerless. Now, though, her life was vastly changed. She wouldn't fit in that village anymore. It would never be home again. The thought at once felt both sad and profoundly right.

Lasaro glanced down. *"Shall we come in for a gentle landing, or make an entrance?"*

A slow smile spread across her face. *"Definitely make an entrance."*

He roared. The sound blasted down into Gladsheim, and the villagers below—who looked like specks from this distance—froze. Then he folded his wings in close to his body, nudged Kaelan to wrap her arms tight around his neck, and dove.

Tears streaked from her eyes. Her stomach flipped over, weightless, as the wind screamed in her ears and tore at her clothing. It was like falling and flying and dying and *living* all at the same time. The rippling mountains grew into behemoths. They passed the topmost peak, grazing so close to it that one of Lasaro's feet knocked a bit of snow off. The village grew bigger and bigger, rising toward them so quickly that she felt certain they were about to make a dragon-shaped crater right in the middle of the town square —and then, at the very last second, Lasaro snapped his wings out, stretched his legs, and pulled up for a landing. His claws scraped trenches in the frozen ground for the length of nearly a knattleikr field before he came to a complete stop.

He stretched up to his full height, shook himself out, and yawned.

Quietly, Kaelan snickered. *"Perfect,"* she told him.

The villagers were huddled in doorways and under the protection of the covered market, gaping at Lasaro. Kaelan slid down from Lasaro's back, revealing her presence. "Where's Reida?" she asked loudly.

No one answered. A few people goggled openly at her.

Someone pushed through the huddle of bodies in front of the inn. "Kaelan? Is that you?" came the familiar, shocked voice of Reida.

Kaelan grinned widely. "Reida!" she cried, a rush of happiness going through her at the sight of the girl who'd once been her only friend. And how strange was it to think that she might have more than a single friend now? Judging from what Lasaro had told her on the way here, Drya, Stav, Def, and a handful of tamer students had all checked in with her healers while she'd been sleeping, just to make sure she was okay. And although she had argued that they were just making sure she hadn't suddenly transformed into an evil mini-Mordon, Lasaro had insisted they respected her for her actions during the battle.

Reida approached with gingerly, careful steps, her gaze flitting from Lasaro to Kaelan and back. "I see you were successful in your quest to become a tamer?" she asked. Fear and excitement warred in her eyes. Kaelan knew the feeling well.

"Yes," Kaelan said proudly. "Everyone, meet Prince Lasaro."

Everyone gasped in a deeply satisfying fashion.

Reida was hiding a grin now. She curtseyed low. "Nice to meet you, your majesty," she said.

Lasaro inclined his head, looking regal and imposing. The hundred-foot-long trench behind him didn't hurt either.

"Reida, where's Ma and Grandma?" Kaelan asked. Last she'd heard, they'd had a room at the inn.

Reida's smile faded. "They went home."

"Home? What? Why would they do that?" Kaelan asked, alarmed. It was early winter already here, and the ground in the mountains was iced over. She couldn't think of any reason they would go home—unless Ardis had wanted to be there when she passed.

A sudden panic overtook her. No. That wasn't why they'd left. It couldn't be. Maybe Ardis had woken up. Or maybe they'd had to take care of the animals. But then, why would they both go, and not just Haldis?

"Kaelan…" Reida started, but Kaelan couldn't bear the look of pity on her friend's face. Without another word, she swung back up onto Lasaro. He rose into the air and, following her directions, raced toward the cabin on the mountainside. She dropped from his back almost before he landed, hurrying toward the door. No one was outside. The garden was overgrown, the stalks of toad's tongue frozen and shining with a coating of ice. Fearing the worst, Kaelan threw open the door without even knocking.

The cabin was warm. The rocking chair was creaking as Grandma pushed herself back and forth, her knitting clutched in her hands, eyes squinted to see the threads. And Ma was lying on her bed, bone-thin and shivering but blessedly alive.

Kaelan went limp with relief. Lasaro, in human form now, entered the hut behind her and closed the door, then stood awkwardly to the side, nearly glowing with the leftover magic of his transformation.

Grandma stared at them. "Child," she said at last, "what on Odin's earth is going on?"

Kaelan smiled through suddenly watering eyes. "Grandma. This is Prince Lasaro, my dragon. Together, I think he and I have enough magic to heal Ma."

Grandma's gaze flitted from her granddaughter to Lasaro and back. Holding her breath, Kaelan waited for her judgment. "Well," Haldis grumbled at last, "I suppose he looks strong enough." Which was as close to approval as the old bat ever got.

Kaelan huffed out a laugh and went to hug her. She felt thinner and frailer than ever. "How are you and Ma?" she asked. "Why did you leave the inn? I feared..."

Grandma pursed her lips. "So did I," she said quietly. "I thought it might do her some good, being out in nature again."

Kaelan frowned severely. "Nature is freezing. And you have hardly any food here."

Grandma huffed. "Don't lecture me, little miss. What're you wasting time for? Get over there and heal your ma." The harsh words were laced with affection, as always, and Kaelan was happy to obey.

She motioned at Lasaro, and the two of them knelt by Ardis' bedside. Kaelan put her hands on Ma's back, focusing all of her healing ability on the woman. What she sensed was troubling. Ma was in bad shape, her body fighting hard, but overwhelmed by the sickness and fatigue. She hadn't been truly well for a long time before she'd fallen ill—with so little good food available, and having to work so hard to earn such a meager living, that was no surprise. Kaelan bit her lip, uncertain. She was in such dire condition, and Kaelan was so new at all of this. What if she couldn't help? Or what if she made things worse?

Lasaro put his hand on her shoulder, pouring strength and magic into her. "You can do this," he told her.

She took a deep breath and nodded. Then she closed her eyes, called up her magic, and began to heal her mother.

It was careful, painstaking work, like searching out all of the loose threads in a tapestry and weaving them back together in exactly the right pattern. But slowly, bit by bit, Kaelan chased the sickness out of her mother's body. Lasaro stood by her the whole time, giving her every drop of power he had, and it took all of it to finish the job. When Kaelan sat back nearly an hour later, they were both sweating and gasping—but the wasting illness was gone from her ma. She was still thin, but her cheeks had healthy color in them now, and she wasn't shivering.

"She was ill for so long," Kaelan said, wiping her brow, uncertainty swirling painfully through her. "I don't know if she'll pull through, even with the sickness being gone."

Grandma's touch was gentle on her shoulder. "You've done all you can do," she said. "If she's going to wake, it likely won't be for a while—healing takes a lot out of both parties. Or, in this case, all three parties." She guided Kaelan over to her old cot. "Rest. I'll wake you if her condition changes. Get some sleep, both of you." Then she narrowed her eyes at Lasaro. "Though not in the same bed."

Lasaro smiled when she had gone back to her knitting. "I like her," he whispered to Kaelan as he stretched out on the floor next to her cot.

Kaelan smiled, but her eyes were already drifting closed, and she couldn't manage a reply before sleep overtook her.

Kaelan woke to her mother's singing.

She thought it was a dream at first. Ma hadn't sung for over a year; she'd been too short of breath and weak, though not too unhappy. Even on her deathbed, Ma had always found something to be happy about. But she'd never sung—and now, the light, lovely strains of a familiar lullaby sung in her mother's melodic voice curled around Kaelan, tugging her back toward sleep.

Groggily, knowing something important had happened but not quite remembering what, Kaelan opened her eyes. The cabin was drenched in starlight. Motes of dust danced in slow motion through the room, caught in the beams of light from the full moon. Outside, snowflakes mirrored the dust's dance, giant flakes drifting daintily toward the ground. The air felt like magic. Not the dragon kind, not the kind Kaelan had now over-used twice in as many days—but the breathtaking, impossible sort of magic where you're doing something normal and then suddenly wake up and realize how magnificent your normal, everyday life is.

Ma was tucking her in.

Kaelan raised a hand and trapped her mother's. Ardis stilled. She hovered in the starlight above Kaelan's cot, her feet carefully placed to avoid getting tangled in the legs of Lasaro, who was currently snoring and dead to the world.

Ardis smiled at her daughter. She kissed her forehead. She lifted the kicked-off covers back up to Kaelan's chin and tucked in her daughter for the first time in a year.

Kaelan's eyes watered. Her mother's hands felt warm and full of memories, and she wanted to say something—*I love you* or *I don't know what I would've done without you*, maybe—but she knew that to speak would shatter the spell, and the starlight would become just normal starlight, and the night would go from magical to mundane, and this moment deserved better than that. So, she just turned her head to kiss her mother's hand, closed her eyes, and drifted back to sleep as she listened to the quiet whistling of the wind on her mountaintop and the soft humming of her mother's beautiful, impossible, everyday lullaby.

Kaelan was the first one up the next morning. She was still tired, but her magic had recovered a bit, so when she passed Haldis' haggard form in the rocking chair, she brushed a hand against her grandma's forehead and gave her a boost of power. Not much, not enough to fully heal her eyesight—that had already faded beyond complete repair—but enough to revitalize her, to wipe away the strain and worry of the last year. Kaelan smiled. Couldn't have the old bat keeling over on her. She dropped a kiss on Haldis' forehead, and the old woman grunted and pulled her feet up, snoring softly.

Kaelan picked her way over to the teakettle and carried it to the door, ducking outside long enough to scoop up some of the freshly fallen snow to boil for tea. When she came back in shivering, Lasaro was awake. She smiled at him as he yawned and stretched but didn't go to him. The early morning silence felt peaceful, almost holy. She glanced over at her mother, who was in bed sleeping again, and at her grandmother curled in the rocking chair, and at Lasaro, who was blinking drowsily at her from his spot on the floor. Her family, all three of them. Her home, too—not this cabin, which felt more like a long-lost memory than her true home—but them. Home was something that was carried wherever these people went.

She gathered kindling and stirred up the embers of last night's fire. When she had it crackling merrily again, she put the teakettle on its hook above the flames and went to sit next to Lasaro.

"We did it," she told him, breaking the silence at last. The sun had risen and was beaming across the floor like molten honey, just touching their toes as they sat side by side.

Lasaro put his arm around her. "I knew we could."

She snuggled into him. It felt good here. Right. She still had no answer to the question that hung between the two of them, but for this moment, whatever they had was perfect.

"What now?" Lasaro asked after a moment.

She heaved a sigh. "Now," she answered, "we go back to the

Akademy and tell a couple of dragons where they can shove it if they ever try to separate the two of us again."

Lasaro laughed softly. "Good," he said. "I wouldn't blame you if you wanted to stay here with your family, but I'm selfishly happy you want to fight the masters for the right to be an official tamer trainee. Plus," he added, more grimly now, "you're one of the most powerful tamers there, and I think we're going to need that in the coming months."

"You're headed back, then?" came the voice of Ardis.

Kaelan jumped to her feet as her mother sat up. She ran across the cold wood floor and wrapped Ma in a hug—gently, careful of the fragile, still-healing form under her arms. Ardis felt like a bird, all bone and angles. But she would heal. That was the important thing.

"Is that okay?" Kaelan asked her mother, pulling back. "Can I go back to Bellsor?"

Ardis laughed. "As if you've ever needed my permission to do anything," she said, playfully smacking Kaelan's hand. Then she grew sober. "You are a grown woman as far as I'm concerned. I'm sure you've had to prove yourself plenty over the last few months." Her eyes slid to Lasaro. "Enough to bring home a prince, anyway," she said, a question in her voice.

Lasaro gave her a bow. "Kaelan is quite talented—not to mention stubborn—" Kaelan snorted but didn't deny it, "and has made herself invaluable to me. I'm afraid there may be some conflict coming Alveria's way, and I would be greatly indebted to you if you could spare her."

From her chair, Haldis snorted. "Nicely put," she said. "Are you sure he's royalty, asking for something instead of just taking it?"

Ardis slanted her grandmother a look, but didn't chide her. They all knew she'd only spoken the truth.

But Kaelan had another truth. "Lasaro will be the best and kindest ruler Alveria has ever had," she said, certainty making her words firm.

Lasaro smiled at her gratefully, then turned back to the two older women. "Actually, I also wanted to offer you some compensation. In return for Kaelan's services, and for the hardships you've had to suffer, I would be happy to give you a suite of permanent rooms at the palace."

Kaelan's mouth fell open. That was incredibly generous—and likely to upset a load of nobles—but both Ma and Grandma were shaking their heads.

"That's very kind of you, your majesty, and it would be lovely to be close to Kaelan," said Ardis, "but we much prefer the solitude and freedom of our own home. Although, I do hope you'll visit often," she said to her daughter.

Lasaro tried again. "A gift, then, from the palace. Whatever you want, it's yours."

Now Haldis laughed. "We don't need *things*, boy." She cackled so hard that she then coughed. "Things own you. We enjoy being free."

Kaelan glared at both of them, the ninnies. "Do you enjoy not being able to afford medicine and eating broth for dinner every night?" Ma started to protest, but Kaelan tugged her gold and silver knife out of her belt and drove it into the table, splintering the wood. "You'll take this and sell it," she ordered. "It'll give you plenty to buy a cow and even a horse, and to fix this place up, and to eat well every night through the winter. This isn't a gift from the palace, it's a present from your daughter. You *will* take it."

"Fine, bossy girl," Haldis grumbled. "But you didn't have to put a hole in our table."

Kaelan rolled her eyes, exasperated.

Lasaro shifted. "Um," he said, clearing his throat. "I hate to interrupt this, and, Kaelan, I'd be happy to come back for you later if you want more time with your family, but I left Bellsor in the middle of a developing crisis, and I should probably be heading back to it."

Kaelan glanced between the three figures before her. "No, I'll go, but—give me a moment with Ma, would you?"

Grandma hobbled forward and grabbed the prince unceremoniously by the arm. "Come on, boy. You want to compensate us so badly, chop some firewood."

Kaelan watched them leave, smiling. Then she turned to Ma, who was leveling a gaze at her that seemed to see right into her soul.

"You understand now, don't you?" Ma asked softly. "How I could've fallen in love with Mordon."

Kaelan let out a breath. "I suppose I do. Dragons are..." She stopped. She didn't want to lump Lasaro in with dragons in general—whatever power he held over her had been hers to give, and not due to the normal magnetism and charm of his species.

"They are," Ardis agreed, a wistful tone in her voice. "But he's not just any dragon, is he? You love him."

Helpless beneath her mother's knowing gaze, Kaelan spread her hands. "I don't know how it could ever work, but I can't help loving him anyway," she admitted.

Ma enveloped her in a hug. "You two take care of each other, understand? And you take care of your heart." It was a warning, but lightly given. Kaelan embraced her mother in return and then kissed her on the forehead.

"I will. I love you," she told Ma, and then she went to find her dragon to return to the Akademy.

CHAPTER 31

The Akademy gates opened at Kaelan's touch. She traded glances with Lasaro. "I guess that's a good thing?" she asked dubiously. "They haven't locked us out, anyway."

Lasaro, remaining in dragon form, pushed the doors open more widely. He moved heavily, still a bit clumsy from his over-use of magic. Both of them needed a dunk in the Emerald Lake as soon as possible after healing Ardis and stopping General Marque before that.

Kaelan turned to glance back down at Bellsor. Thin trails of smoke still drifted up from the fires that had been put out but were still smoldering in the rubble. The streets had been mostly cleared, and normal afternoon traffic moved through the city, but the atmosphere of the town was changed now—it felt wary, worried. Most of these people had found themselves under the control of a foreign usurper, and the ease with which they'd nearly destroyed their own city frightened them. And they still had those seeds of dissent, of dissatisfaction, growing inside them. That was how Marque had been able to manipulate them, because they truly were unhappy with the way they were being ruled. Kaelan pursed her lips. Before Lasaro and the queen could go to war with Unger, they'd have to make peace with their own people.

She turned back to the Akademy—and came face to face with Master Olga.

Kaelan yelped and leapt back in surprise. A faint thread of Lasaro's amusement filtered through her mind. She glared at him.

"Pupil Younger," Master Olga said coolly. "Prince Lasaro. You've arrived just in time." She turned without another word and motioned them in, clearly expecting them to follow.

Kaelan and Lasaro traded a glance. Just in time for what? A full formal trial? A sentencing? Beheadings? She shook herself, taking her fears firmly in hand. She was the daughter of Mordon, heir to the most powerful master who'd ever taught here, even if she didn't hold to his same ideals. And Lasaro was a prince and her dragon, as the queen herself had proclaimed—or so Lasaro had told her, anyway. There was nothing the masters could do to them. Except, perhaps, expel her once and for all, right when she'd finally realized this was where she wanted to be.

Her mouth was dry as she followed Master Olga into the recesses of the Akademy. After a few moments, they emerged into the Great Hall. Blinking at the bright light cast off by the massive fireplaces, Kaelan spotted the newest class of tamer and dragon students arrayed in the middle of the room, with the masters perched on the beams crisscrossing above. Master Olga turned, smiled at Kaelan, and motioned to a servant who'd been standing against the wall. The man hurried up to the two of them, pushed a bundle of fabric at Kaelan, and then returned to his place. Kaelan frowned down at the bundle and turned to ask Master Olga what was going on, but the master just rippled into dragon form and flew gracefully up to her own perch.

"Kaelan," Lasaro whispered. *"Look at their clothes."*

The students were wearing their uniforms, but something was different. Where the tamer students had once worn black trainee robes, they were now clad in a rainbow of colors. Kaelan frowned, glancing through the group, and picked out Drya. The girl grinned widely and gave her a quick thumbs-up, then motioned at her to join them. Still uncertain of what was happening, Kaelan advanced. Lasaro transformed into human shape—luckily, he was still wearing his leather-like under-suit—and then an intake of breath told him he'd figured something out.

"This is the graduation ceremony. They've been officially bonded," he whispered.

Kaelan's heart dropped. Why would Master Olga bring her here? It was cruel to make her watch if they still meant to try to kick her out. Or maybe they were putting her on probation or something, and this was meant to be a carrot dangled before her, to tempt her into good behavior.

"The clothing," Lasaro whispered, nudging her to look at the bundle of fabric she was still carrying. It was soft, a lovely mist-gray color that reminded her of fog. She realized what it was: Lasaro's uniform.

Her dragon was graduating to initiate status.

Numb with warring emotions, she lifted the cloak toward him and tried to smile. She was happy for him. She could be happy for him. But he laughed quietly and unfolded the bundle, separating it into two pieces and handing one back to her.

Two uniforms. The masters had given them two uniforms, both the misty gray of Ariels.

She gasped and looked up at the masters arrayed above them. "I'm—I'm to be an approved student? I'll be Lasaro's official tamer, an Akademy initiate?" She'd thought she'd have to fight tooth and nail to force them to let her prove herself, to give her a future here. She hadn't expected to simply be handed an official bond as soon as she walked in. The uniform was beautiful, too, draping over her hands like silk, and she shoved it over her head as quickly as she could manage. No sense giving them time to take it back after all.

Master Olga wrapped her tail around herself. *"Kaelan Younger, Lasaro Afkarr, for your service to our country, you have been promoted to initiates and your bond has been made official."*

"For now," intoned Master Lars, who eyed them both from his own perch.

"Put on your uniforms and join the others," another master added, his tone flat. *"This is already taking long enough."*

But even the master's crabbiness couldn't dim Kaelan's sudden joy. She was to be a tamer. A real one, acknowledged by both the Akademy and the queen. She belonged to Lasaro. He belonged to her. And now everyone knew it.

Lasaro pulled on his own uniform, took Kaelan's hand, and went to stand by Def and Drya. Def smiled and bumped shoulders with Lasaro. Lasaro, looking surprised and then thoughtful, bumped shoulders back. Kaelan grinned. It looked like the prince had found his first real friends, too.

The ceremony was quick. The masters praised the students' hard work, especially noting the services performed by the dragons and tamers who had assisted with the battle of Bellsor, and warned them of even more tests to come. The thought of Unger's invasion and Mordon's return hung heavy over the gathering for a moment, but it was brushed away—

for now—by the students' loud cheering. The masters dispersed to their duties then, and the students spread out to congratulate each other and make their plans for the winter break. Only Stav was left alone, wandering slowly toward the exit.

Kaelan frowned. "They didn't reinstate Inga, it looks like."

Lasaro jogged to catch up with Stav, and Kaelan followed. "Stav, thank you for your help the other day," Lasaro said.

Stav struggled to smile. "Thanks."

"So, they didn't pair you with a tamer?"

The other boy shrugged one shoulder. "I refused to accept anyone but Inga. I'm headed to Bellsor now, to check on her."

"I'm sorry," Kaelan said, understanding exactly how he was feeling. She'd have to see what she could do to help him. She didn't care much for Inga, but she'd seen her flying with Stav in the battle, and Lasaro had told her how she'd helped free Kaelan from the dungeons before that.

Lasaro patted Stav's shoulder and let the boy go. And then it was just her and her dragon left in the silent Great Hall. The fires crackled, and when Kaelan leaned against the Wall of Names, it felt warm and happy at her back. She spread a hand across it and smiled. *Thank you,* she told the Akademy silently.

Lasaro cleared his throat. He raked a hand through his hair

and looked up at the ceiling as if for inspiration. "Kaelan," he said at last, his tone signaling a shift to a more serious topic.

Kaelan looked down, fingering her beautiful brand new robe. She didn't want to talk about what she knew he was going to talk about. She wanted to stay in this moment forever, with a friendly Akademy at her back and a warm, fuzzy feeling in the pit of her stomach.

But Lasaro turned to her anyway. "About what I said at the Emerald Lake a few days ago. When I proposed."

Her heart took off at a gallop. She didn't know what she hoped he would say. "Yes?" she asked, her mouth going dry again.

He shifted from foot to foot. She could feel how hard this was for him through the bond, but he forced himself onward. "You were right."

"I was?"

He nodded. "It was foolish of me to try to gain the throne by force, without caring what traditions I broke or who I dishonored in the process. There are many things I want to change about the kingdom, but to change those things and have them *stay* changed, I need to have the support and respect of my people. To win them over, I'll need to tread carefully—to fight for what matters most."

And is that me? she wanted to ask. The words tore at her, but she sealed her lips and beat them back. She would let him say whatever he needed to say.

"Alveria is in crisis right now," he went on. "Besieged on all sides. We need every ally we can get for the coming fight, especially if Mordon's returned. And... one of those allies will probably have to be my wife."

She stared at him for a long moment. "What are you saying?" she asked at last.

He grimaced. "I always knew I'd have to marry for political advantage. I didn't mind. Not until I met you."

Her heart twisted.

He went on, pushing the words out even though each one hurt him—and, through the bond, hurt her. "But as much as I might like to find out what more could grow between you and me, I fear that Alveria would tear itself apart if I began courting you at a time like this. When I marry..." He stopped, cleared his throat. "When I marry, I think it will have to be... to a noble. Or foreign royalty if it will forge us a new ally in the fight against Unger and help protect our borders."

Not you. The words screamed between them, unspoken. *I cannot marry you.*

And, just like that, she finally knew what she wanted.

What's more important? her grandma had asked her once. *Loyalty to yourself, or honoring promises to others?*

For a long time, Kaelan would've said honoring promises. It was ingrained in her being. But lately she'd found herself torn, and now, finally, she was faced with a stark choice between the two. Honoring her promise to Lasaro would mean seeing him on the throne and securely married to someone else. But loyalty to herself would require something else entirely. Because she didn't *want* him to marry someone else. She wanted him to marry *her*, court *her*, and only ever love *her*.

Wouldn't you rather look to yourself than a promise? her mysterious traveling companion had said. *What is it that you want, Kaelan?*

Lasaro. She wanted Lasaro. But she couldn't have both him and a secure country.

She shook herself and stood a little straighter, shoving her grief away. She couldn't have both him and a secure country with the way things looked right *now.* That didn't mean the situation couldn't change. Who knew what might happen tomorrow?

She waited to speak until she was sure her voice was level. "I understand."

She loved the prince and couldn't have him. But a few weeks before, she'd wanted to be a tamer and had been told she couldn't have that, either. She would find a way to keep her promise *and* be loyal to herself—a way to have Lasaro and keep the country intact. She didn't know how or when, but she'd do whatever it took to make it happen. And, in the meantime, she had a school full of new friends, a country full of challenges, and a dragon at her side.

She was a tamer. She was Kaelan Younger, daughter of Mordon, daughter of Ardis. She was bonded to Prince Lasaro of Alveria—the boy she loved, regardless of what might lay in their future. And, together, there was nothing they couldn't do.

END OF THE DRAGON TAMER
ALVERIA DRAGON AKADEMY BOOK ONE

The Dragon Tamer, 31 October 2018

The Dragon Sickness, 26 December 2018

The Dragon Throne, 27 February 2019

PS: Keep reading for an exclusive extract from **Dragon Raider (Sea Dragons Trilogy Book One).**

THANK YOU!

I hope you enjoyed **The Dragon Tamer**. Please don't forget to leave a review.

Receive free books, exclusive excerpts and be kept up to date on all of my new releases, when you sign up to my mailing list!

ABOUT AVA

Ava Richardson writes epic page-turning Young Adult Fantasy books with lovable characters and intricate worlds that are barely contained within your eReader.

Her current work is 'The First Dragon Rider' Trilogy.

She grew up on a steady diet of fantasy and science fiction books handed down from her two big brothers – and despite being dog-eared and missing pages, she loved escaping into the magical worlds that authors created. Her favorites were the ones about dragons, where they'd swoop, dive and soar through the skies of these enchanted lands

Stay in touch! I'd also love to connect with you on:

      f facebook.com/AvaRichardsonBooks

      g goodreads.com/AvaRichardson

      BB bookbub.com/authors/ava-richardson

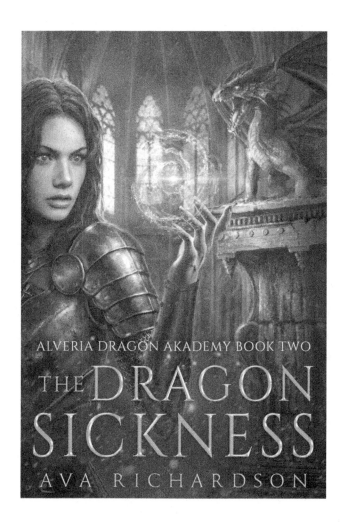

BLURB

As Kaelan Younger begins her training at the Akademy, her bond with Lasaro, Prince of Alveria, grows stronger each day. But even though she's become his tamer, their bond remains as powerful as it is unpredictable—with the potential to become too much for them to sustain. Until they can find some sort of balance, their partnership remains in doubt.

However, more than just the eyes of the Akademy's masters are watching Lasaro's performance. The fate of the crown depends upon the development of his powers and his control over the elements. Now, treachery already at work in the Akademy threatens to destroy everything, and as a deadly illness sweeps over the dragons of the kingdom, Kaelan must learn to call upon her skill as a healer to help save them even as she works to become a more adept tamer.

With so much at risk, and her own powers beginning to surprise her, Kaelan finally realizes there's more to her lineage than she ever expected, and that she may have to become something far greater than a tamer if she is to save herself and those she loves.

Get your copy of *The Dragon Sickness*
Available 26 December 2018
AvaRichardsonBooks.com

EXCERPT

Chapter One

Kaelan Younger fitted her tight leather helmet over her black hair, refusing to notice the way her hands trembled when she buckled its strap. She took a deep breath and rolled her shoulders. When that didn't help settle her, she resorted to hopping in place a few times, trying to get herself calm and in the right frame of mind for the upcoming training exercise—the first one she'd been allowed to participate in since officially being accepted as an initiate tamer student at the Alveria Akademy.

Luckily for her, Master Olga—the only master who was at all friendly toward Kaelan, though "friendly" was a relative term —would be overseeing today's class. She was currently pacing behind the row of students lined up on the parapets, slow and serene and as intimidating as always in the form of a white-gold dragon. Kaelan wanted to be glad it was her who'd be judging Kaelan's performance, but really it only made the stakes feel higher. Because, if she screwed this up, she'd risk losing Olga's support. Which she could not afford to do. Kaelan had had to go to some pretty extreme lengths to get accepted to the school, and she felt fairly sure that most of the teachers would be happy to have any excuse to toss her out in the cold again.

*"Tamers, prepare yoursel*ves," Olga called out, her cool, telepathic voice ringing in Kaelan's h*ead. "Dragons, move for*ward."

The dragons had been waiting on the opposite side of the balcony. At Olga's order, they fanned out across the edge of the parapet, their wings loose and ready, ferocity and eagerness shining in their eyes. They ranged from being brilliant Ember orange to a rich Terra brown, with a spattering of sapphire Aqua dragons and a single pale Ariel. The Ariel was, in Kaelan's opinion, the most beautiful—and she didn't just think that because h*e was* her dragon. Lasaro was majestic in his dragon form, and a literal prince in human form. Right now, he stood in front of her, his scales a soft, pearlescent silver that matched Kaelan's official tamer robes, with a black spine and pale blue eyes. He was watching her, concerned and also a bit amused at her worry. His emotions thrummed through the bond between them: he thought she was going to do great. He believed in her. He cared for her. He loved—

The bond snapped shut like a curtain had been drawn between them, and Lasaro turned away to look at the horizon, the lines of his body going rigid as he forced down his feelings.

Mentally, Kaelan curled in on herself, protecting her own emotions. She was in love with Lasaro and he was in love with her, but either of them giving in to such feelings could only lead to disaster. She was his tamer, after all, and nothing more; he would have to marry some carefully chosen noble girl for political gain someday, and that was as it had to be. And *she* *w*as fine with it.

Or, at least, she would force herself to be fine with it until she thought of some honorable way to change it.

Kaelan inhaled deeply and tried to refocus. Any second now, the training exercise would start. She shouldn't be so nervous about it. She was more than ready for whatever Master Olga might throw at her. She and Lasaro had already fought in a high-stakes battle just a few weeks ago, and plus, her dragon was a prince, and she herself was the daughter of the most powerful dragon to ever teach at the Alveria Akademy.

It didn't matter that her father had turned out to be a rogue with a scheme to steal the throne. Or that her princely dragon still had trouble holding his form after he'd shifted, and that today he was especially distracted, feeling tense and closed-off now at the other end of their bond.

And it went without saying that Kaelan and Lasaro were both constantly preoccupied by their efforts to put him on the throne of Alveria. He was the queen's youngest son, and the only one fit to rule, but he had yet to prove himself to his people. Without their support and the support of his mother, Alveria would be doomed to fall under the leadership of one of his inept or war-loving siblings.

Just a few months ago, Lasaro had made a deal with his mother that if he learned to control his dragon powers enough to be officially bonded with a tamer, he would be named her heir, but that bargain had gone up in smoke after Lasaro had lost the goodwill of the politically powerful Akademy masters during his attempts to have Kaelan named his tamer. And now the kingdom of Alveria was in turmoil, accosted by enemies without and threatened by a potential civil war brewing within it, and the throne was being seen as weak and unstable. It was a huge mess, and it wouldn't be easily fixed.

It was no wonder Kaelan and Lasaro were both so distracted lately. But they had to move past that, had to *focus, had* to—

"Begin!" Olga called out.

The row of tamers hurried to mount up, and one by one the dragons swept up into the air. Caught unprepared, Kaelan was a few seconds behind everyone else. She scrambled onto Lasaro's back, wishing not for the first time that there could be some sort of saddle provided for tamers. She supposed that would be a bit undignified, but it would have made things easier. Still, she knew tamers needed to be ready to ride their dragons at any moment and not just when everything was prepared for their comfort.

Lasaro was still tense, but he opened himself to the bond a bit more now, knowing they needed a strong connection to fly together. The second she was seated on his shoulders, he magically called up a huge updraft that launched him into the air. Kaelan yelped at the sudden speed, clinging tightly to his back. His smooth scales didn't give her much grip, so she had to use pretty much every muscle in her body to stay atop him. And if she fell...

She squinted down at the quickly receding mountaintop that the Akademy sat on. That was an awful long way to plummet.

But then she looked up at the sky, and her fear and uncertainty dropped away, just the same as always happened when she was flying. Instead of the terror she should probably have been feeling, the thrill that raced through her now combined a strange mixture of excitement and abandon and utter peacefulness. The updraft died out around them, and then it was just her and Lasaro, spiraling upward, his steady wingbeats and the softly whistling wind providing the only sound. He rose and fell with each stroke like a ship crossing the sea. She always felt at home on his back—and at his side, when he was in human form—as she never had anywhere else in her entire life. Sometimes when she flew with him like this, she almost felt as if she were a dragon herself. As if the two of them were so close they were a single being, one with powerful wings and a calm mind and a heart that *beat for* the sky.

"There!" Lasaro shouted suddenly, this coming as his only warning before he tucked his wings in tight and dove toward the forest below. Kaelan yelped again, belatedly tightening her grip as her stomach surged. She'd nearly managed to forget that this was a training exercise, a mock battle meant to teach tactics and strategy. Today, it was Terras and Aquas matched against the plentiful Embers and the lone Ariel. Lasaro's job was to circle the battle from above, pick out the enemy force's location and movements, and send that information *to his* teammates. He wasn't supposed to be dive-bombing toward the ground so fast that it made Kaelan's eyes stream with tears as the wind screamed over her, twisting her *robe and her hair.*

"What are you doing?" she shouted telepathically. Though she could hardly see, she'd spotted what had to be his target—a Terra flying low over the forest, not even looking up at *them. Her alarm grew. "Lasaro, he doesn't ev*en see us. Pull up!"

But instead, Lasaro tucked his wings in tighter. Still trying to

433

distract himself from his earlier emotions, he'd given himself over to *the thrill of battle.*

"Continue your attack," Olga projected to them both, watching from her spot on the parapet.

Kaelan gritted her teeth. She shouldn't contradict the only master who was even willing to consider liking her, and during Kaelan's very first real *exercise to boot, but... "It's dishonorable. That Terra won't even be able to fight back—"*

"*Honorable* doesn't win battles!" Lasaro shouted back at her. She reached out to him tentatively then, trying to feel what was going on in his head. He didn't want to think about honor. Didn't want to think about anything. The dragon instincts in him wanted to take over, and he wanted to let them because, when he did that, he didn't have to think about his worries for Alveria's future and the feelings he shouldn't have for his tamer. The power of his instincts roared through their bond, the sheer animalism of it nearly drowning out Kaelan's own thoughts, making her feel sick and dizzy. Once upon a time, not too long ago, Lasaro had been terrified that his instincts would take over when he was in his dragon form and make him go rogue. She was glad he'd apparently gotten past that fear, but this was taking things a bit far.

They were nearly upon the Terra, who still hadn't looked up. Kaelan struggled with herself for a moment. She wanted to do *well* at this exercise—she had to do well—but it was wrong to strike an opponent who was so unprepared. The Terra would be knocked right out of the air with Lasaro coming in at this velocity. He might even get injured. And, even worse, she could feel Lasaro's draconic excitement at the thought: he was anticipating the moment when he'd slam into the other dragon, the visceral joy of it, the sweetness of victory afterward. He wouldn't hurt the other dragon too badly, of course, but catching it unprepared would likely put the Terra out of the exercise for good. Lasaro would win—and he knew how badly Kaelan needed them to win today. As much as he was doing this to distract himself, he was also doing it for *her*.

She swallowed. She did want to win, it was *true,* but not like this. "Stop!" she said to him through the bond one last tim*e, unable to help herself. "You're supposed to stay above the battle; you don't need to do this. I know you're trying to avoid your f*eelings, but—"

"I'm fine!" Lasaro snapped, projecting the telepathic words widely instead of through the bond—the equi*valent of shouting o*ut loud.

"Don't lie to me!" she snapped right back, her words also "shouted" ou*tward, her emotions boiling. "Now you're dishonoring our bond as well as this battle. We're partners. We should always* be honest with each other!"

Olga cut into the argument, her c*ool whisper as hard as stone. "You love your honor, Pupil Younger, but it isn't always easy to know the honorable thing. Sometimes a lie can be more honorable than the truth."*

"*A*nd honor doesn't win battles," Lasaro repeated, and then he crashed into the Terra.

The Terra's tamer had looked up at the last second. Kaelan had seen his eyes go wide and his mouth open for a shout, and then the two dragons had collided, and a shock juddered through her hard enough to nearly unseat her. The Terra crashed to the earth, its tamer leaping off and rolling aside just in time to avoid being crushed. The dragon snarled up at them, shaking itself and limping toward the Akademy as Lasaro rose back up into the sky. His emotions cooled a touch, satisfied by the attack, but Kaelan had only grown sicker and dizzier— from the shock of the collision, maybe, though somehow that didn't quite feel right.

Lasaro sensed it. He wrestled with his animalistic instinct, brought it under reluctant co*ntrol, and came* back to h*imself. "Are you* okay?" he asked.

"I don't know," she confe*ssed, hunching low over h*is back. "Something feels wrong."

He reached the height where he'd been circling before and resumed his patrol. The emotional tension from earlier rose up in him again, tw*isting its wa*y through their bond. "I'm s*orry,"* *he said after a long pause. "But I meant what I said earlier. About honor not winning battles. With the Kingdom of Unger beating down our door, we're going to have to do anything we can to gain the advantage. King Lothan won't show us any honor, nor will General Marque—he proved that before winter* *break. We can't afford to show them any, either. And these* *simulations, these training exercises, they're to prepare us for* *what we're going* to face out there in real battle."

Kaelan shuddered, remembering the way Marque had infiltrated the capital city of Bellsor and stirred up a rebellion, using his tamer powers to take control of the citizens and make them riot. That certainly hadn't been honorable. But was the solution really to return dishonor for dishonor? How would that make them any better than General Marque?

Sickness stirred again in Kaelan's gut, making her feel like she might throw up. She didn't want to mull over these thorny questions anymore. She didn't even really want to fly anymore. That, more t*han anything, was a little alarmin*g. "I think I might be getting ill," she told Lasaro.

He banked, *dipping one wing to take a wide turn. "It is winter. Maybe you picked up a c*old. Do we need to quit for the day?" His reluctance tugged at the bond—the dragon part of him craved the thoughtless freedom of the battle practice—but she could feel him fighting valiantly to focus on his tamer's needs.

She hesitat*ed, gl*ancing back at the dista*nt Olga. "No," Kaelan* repli*ed finally. "W*e have to do well. Keep—"

"Watch out!" Lasaro shouted, suddenly snapping his wings wide to slow to a near-stop in midair. A bright orange Ember dragon tumbled past them, her scales flaring in the sunlight and her wings fluttering uselessly above her as she fell toward

437

the ground. A tamer clung to her neck, screaming. Kaelan stared at the pair in shock. The dragon—Dagma, if she remembered correctly, the daughter of palace courtiers—had been way too far up. This wasn't anything like whenLasaro had slammed the Terra to the earth; Dagma was falling much too quickly, and had had time to gather enough speed to end her life, and definitely the *tamer's,* when they hit the forest below.

"Dagma!" Lasaro shouted, his confusion and worry *thrumming* in the back of Kaelan's head. "Pull up!" But the other dragon didn't answer.

"Can we help them?" Kaelan yelled, too shaken to even use telepathy to transmit the question. But Lasaro was already tucking his wings and diving. He wouldn't reach Dagma in time, though—*not with how far t*hey'd already fa*llen. "Use air currents!" Kaelan shouted.* "Try to slow her fall! Catch her wings!"

She felt Lasaro's focus tighten. A moment later, Dagma tumbled sideways as the air buffeted her, but it only slowed her fall slightly, and now her tamer's grip looked even more tenuous. Panicked, Kaelan peered around them, trying to see through th*e mercil*ess wind of their own dive. There! "Inga!" she shouted.

The other tamer who Kaelan had been addressing—a muscled blonde girl—turned. She was seated atop Stav, a dark brown Terra a ways below them. Kaelan reached out to her telepathically, ignoring the other girl's dislike when she sensed it—the sentiment was no surprise, and even though Kaelan had been responsible for making the masters grudgingly reinstate Inga as a tamer after her failure *last month, the fe*eling was still mutual. "Dagm*a is falling!" Kaelan yelled into her mind. "Have Stav soften the earth where she's going to fall. I'll help Lasaro* call up a stronger updraft to cushion her."

Inga's attention snapped below and, after a brief pause, so did Stav's. Kaelan would've reached out to the dragon himself, but Stav was among those who'd been wary of Kaelan ever since she'd revealed she was the daughter of the most infamous rogue dragon in the country. At least it seemed that he still trusted her enough to help with Dagma. That was all that mattered right now.

Bel*ow them,* Dagma had nearly rea*ched the ground. "Ready?"* K*a*elan ask*ed Lasaro.*

*"You'll have to help me," he said. "I'm... ha*ving trouble focusing today."

"I've got you," she said, and she closed her eyes. She felt for the bond that flowed between them and tethered them to each other, grasped it hard with her mind, and poured her strength and determination into it. Lasaro's concentration sharpened. She felt him channel magic into the air beneath Dagma, felt it catch at her wings, and felt her tumble slow. Kaelan pushed more strength at Lasaro, giving him everything she had.

And then she opened her eyes. She needed to see for herself whether it had been enough. Her breath caught in her throat as Lasaro's wind buffeted Dagma, blasting her back upward a few inches so that she seemed to hover momentarily just above the treetops before she finally crashed down. Powder—fine sand, maybe?—exploded into the air around her.

Kaelan let out a breath, sagging down as Lasaro spread his wings, pulling out of his dive to drift to a landing. Stav and Inga were spiraling above, and Master Olga was flying swiftly toward them. Kaelan slid off Lasaro, rushing to check the tamer, but the boy was already staggering out from under his dragon. Thank Odin, he was alive, and at least well enough to walk.

Kaelan hurried over to him. "Does anything hurt? Here, let me check you, I'm a healer—"

But the boy—Trem, she thought his name was—put his hands up, his eyes wide. "Don't touch me!" he gasped out. "I'm fine."

Kaelan stopped short. "But... you should let me check you first. You're much more fragile than Dagma right now, and you could have internal injuries—"

He was already stumbling away. "Master Olga will take me to the Akademy healer."

Anger rose up in her, but it was swiftly replaced by a wrenching humiliation. He was scared of her. Because she was the daughter of Mordon. He wouldn't even let her try to help him because of it. She'd thought that the students would be more accepting of her now, since they'd been friendly enough toward her during the trainee-to-initiate graduation ceremony they'd all shared, but apparently, in the handful of weeks since then, that camaraderie had faded into wariness.

"Fine," she snapped, trying to cover up her humiliation as s*he put her hands on Dagma befor*e anyone could stop her.

"Did anyone see what happened?" Olg*a called out, touching down* at the edge of the clearing. *"Who struck her?"*

*"No one!" Trem said, his voice shaky. "We were up even higher than Lasaro, about to try to dive-bomb like he did. No one was anywhere nea*r us."

"Maybe she went up too high and couldn't breathe?" Lasaro suggested, following Kaelan to Dagma's prone form, shadowing his tamer with a protective wing. His support nudged her through the bond—he knew how Trem's lack of trust had hurt her, and thought Trem was a fool for it.

"No," Kaelan said aloud, closing her eyes to send her healer's senses into Dagma. "Trem wouldn't have been able to breathe either in that case, and would've passed out and fallen—" She stopped short as her senses flared. Something was wrong inside Dagma. It bubbled thickly, like soup left on the burner too long. Gently, Kaelan delved deeper, unease sliding through her. The... sickness? She wasn't quite sure if that w*as the* *ri*ght label for whatever it was she was feeling, but something was twisted deep into Dagma's cells, corrupting them from the inside out. She gasped as she drew her healer's senses back and saw the magnitude of the destruction that had been wrought. Every single cell tingled with wrongness, every bit of Dagma overtaken by it.

Kaelan had felt something like this before. Once, she'd helped Ardis ease the passing of a woman who'd had tumors throughout her whole body. There had been the same sense of corruption, of a body so thoroughly invaded that it could no longer fight back—but this felt subtly different, strange and unnatural. "I think she might be badly sick—" Kaelan started, and then she was interrupted by a massive thud and a rush of wind. She opened her eyes and jumped to her feet, dodg*ing away by ins*tinct, and nearly stumbled over Dagma's tail.

"Stav! Inga!" Olga cried out, her voice showing a thread of emotion for once. Shock. Kaelan steadied herself and whirled around. A cloud of fine sand had risen into the air again. Through it, she could just make out the form of another fallen dragon. Stav. He was groaning, his wings flopping weakly.

At his side lay Inga—one leg trapped beneath him, her eyes closed, and her body as still as death.

Get your copy of ***The Dragon Sickness***
Available 26 December 2018
AvaRichardsonBooks.com

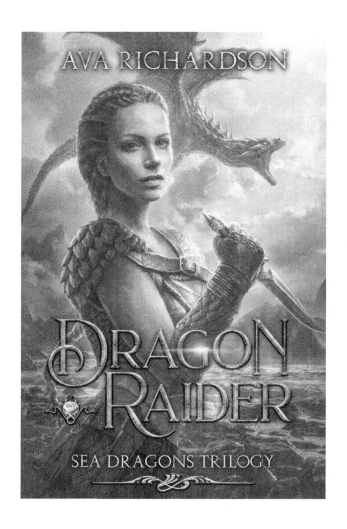

BLURB

Will adapting to a changing world make one young woman lose touch with where she came from?

Far from the kingdom of Torvald, on the Western Isles near the coast, Sea Dragons rule the skies. Lila is the daughter of the Raider leader, destined to take his place one day aboard their plundering ships. Her people value only what shiny trinkets they can get their hands on, but she aspires to much more than that: Lila wants the Raiders to become Dragon Mercenaries, dragon riders who help protect merchant fleets and navies from attack. Her father Kasian is skeptical, but a young monk named Danu—with a quest of his own—comes bearing a prophecy claiming that Lila is the lost heir of Roskilde, a born Dragon Rider.

With Danu's guidance, Lila finds the unruly dragon she's destined to bond with—but the mismatched pair soon learn that much more than just their futures is at stake.

Get your copy of **Dragon Raider** at
AvaRichardsonBooks.com

EXCERPT

Chapter 1: Lila, dragon-thief!

The claw print in the sand was huge. *Much* larger than even I had expected. *Hang on a minute. I thought that fisherman had told me that this island was inhabited by the sea-greens dragons?* I bit my lip, glad at least that I didn't have my foster-father here to watch my moment of fear. Chief Kasian of Malata was known as a harsh man, even amongst us proud Sea Raiders of the Western Oceans.

444

The sun was starting to burn off the sea fog that clutched onto this bit of rock where I'd directed my little skiff, revealing that, in all other ways it was just as I had been told: a tiny, rock-topped atoll with a smattering of trees and a golden beach skirting its northern side. This little islet had no name other than a designation, "the last bit of rock before you get to Sebol" the old sea-salt fisherman had told me, and it was on this beach that I had found my first evidence of the dragons.

A track of claw prints, each almost the size of my little boat. Not that the skiff was very big – I had chosen the skiff from my father's flotilla for its speed rather than strength. But still, I calculated quickly – if this foot was that big, then that meant that the leg would be as big as a tree, and the body it connected to… I shuddered. The beast would be, even at the very least, larger than most of the huts and houses on my father's island-rule of Malata.

"You *did* say that this was a bad idea," I murmured at my father, far away and doubtless angry at the fact that I had gone off *again* to try and find the dragons.

And their eggs.

Still, there was little that I could do other than press on. I was Lila of Malata, adopted daughter to the chief of the notorious Sea Raiders of the Western Isles. I did not shirk from a challenge. I *was* the challenge.

The tracks led to the head of the beach and the rocks beyond.

The white stone was crisscrossed with lines of black – Bone-rock, my people called it. Notoriously hard to shape, it formed the core of many of these little islands that speared the Western Seas. Moving as lightly and as quietly as I could, I passed into the rocks and started climbing, toward the dark cave openings where this dragon must have made its lair.

It's a long way down from here. I pushed away the thought as I climbed. Why did dragons have to make their dens on the tops of things? Why couldn't they live in nests on the ground? The soft goatskin leather of my gloves was already scuffed and torn, and I could feel the edges of the rock beneath. The heat was making me sweat, and I was glad I had managed to argue my difficult hair into the warrior's braid this morning. *Just a few more feet—*

"Ach!" My foot slipped, and instantly pain tore along my shoulders and arms as I hung from the rocks. *Don't look down. Don't look down…*

I looked down. Beneath me, the rocky walls jagged and snarled out, with the occasional tuft of scrubby sea grass, all the way to the frothing grey-blue ocean below.

Sweet Seas… I breathed, my stomach lurched and my limbs trembled in that way they always did when I was forced to be anywhere up high.

"Don't overthink! Do!" my father would have shouted at me. He had tried to drum this fear of heights out of me ever since he had found it in the child he had rescued after the raid had taken her parents. I closed my eyes, gritting my teeth as I tried to remember the lessons he drilled into me. "You're a Raider, Lila! The most fearsome thing on the four oceans! Nothing stops you. Not a bit of wind under your feet!" And then he would tell me to get up that rigging and tie off that knot, or secure the sail anyway. I had to do it.

"Think of your crewmates waiting for you! What if we had one of that brute's Man-o-Wars on our tail? Your crew are depending on you!" He would shout, which would spur me to get up there and do what I had to do anyway, admittedly with shaking fingers and taking twice as long as any other of the Raider sailors.

Just like I had to do this.

Because if I don't do this, the Raiders are finished. I gritted my teeth, opened my eyes, and pulled. My back screamed in pain, but I managed to bring myself up to the height of the cave opening, my boots kicking on the Bonerock until I found a purchase and – "Ugh!"— I flopped over into the shallow depression before the dragon's lair, panting and wheezing, and waiting for my heart to slowly calm down to just a dull roar, rather than a thunder.

Slowly, the world came back into focus. I was Lila Malata. I was alive. And I was here because my father's Sea Raiders were getting themselves decimated by the self-styled Lord Havick of Roskilde. The Roskildean ships were larger and stronger than ours, and they always seemed to know which shipping routes we were heading for. They would be out there already as if expecting us, ambushing our smaller, faster boats with fire and catapult, and slowly my father's mastery of the seas was being whittled away. I didn't think that we Sea Raiders had another generation in us if this plan didn't work.

The darkness of the cave beckoned. Disturbingly, there was a litter of bones on the front "porch." Small bones as long as my finger, which I guessed were the spines of the marlin fish that the sea green and blue dragons adored so much. I hoped they were that, anyway.

"Lady Dragon... Great Dragon...?" I called out hesitantly, my voice, used to shouting orders from the decks piers as it was, sounding small and hesitant in the darkness. *How are you supposed to talk to dragons, anyway?* I had no idea. We Raiders didn't exactly have a big library, although I had tried to get through the collection of scrolls that my adopted mother Pela of Malata kept. Each one had been stolen from the captain's quarters of some merchant ship or another, and only a few had talked about the great Dragon Academy of Torvald.

And Queen Saffron, I thought, feeling a flush of borrowed courage. The tales said that she was like me, almost. Not a Raider of course, but she was a Western islander who had managed to tame a sea green and blue dragon, and ride on her all the way to the citadel of Torvald, where she defeated the evil King Enric, and there reinstated the Dragon Academy with Lord Bower.

If she can do it, so can I, I thought – and I wasn't even dreaming of flying off to take over a city far from home. I just wanted to raise an egg for my father, and save my adopted people from being wiped out.

Thankfully, however, that old fisherman who had told me that there was a dragon cave here on this atoll had also told me that the dragons go off hunting early in the morning, meaning that their nest would be unprotected. I wasn't *quite* so foolish as to attempt to steal a dragon's egg with an angry mother still sitting on it!

No noise from inside. Good. The footprints I had seen couldn't have been fresh. The last thing I wanted to do was disturb a mother dragon as it sat on its eggs! I crept forward, letting my eyes adjust to the gloom before I could make out the deep piles of dried twigs and grasses making a rough nest. It was warm in here, and made me want to yawn. But what if there was *more* than one dragon in here? What if the old fisherman had been wrong?

Focus, Lila! I told myself. Don't overthink. Do!

Cautiously grabbing onto one edge of the nest, I pulled myself up around the edge and stared inside.

Three eggs. Three, glorious dragons – each the size of my

head, fat and round, and heavy with the life that they contained inside. One was blue, one was yellow-orange, and one was a speckled turquoise.

Which one? I hadn't been prepared for this. I had thought through every eventuality on the way here – how I would drag the skiff up to the line of scrub trees and hide it in case any of Havick's scouting vessels were out, how I would race down the beach if I was disturbed… But not which type of dragon I should choose to save the Raiders. In fact, it was faintly baffling *why* there were three completely different eggs here in the first place. I thought dragons might be like the sea birds of the cliffs: one set of parents, one egg – but what if they were more like the sturdy little island goats – all of the nannies and kids together in one warm place? *Could there be multiple dragon mothers laying eggs in one nest?*

The danger had just escalated three-fold, if that was the case. I would need to be quick.

Could I take all three? I patted the canvas sack on my back and knew that it wouldn't hold more than one. I could feasibly put one down my shirt and *maybe* be able to climb back down one handed—

Ugh. No. A sudden wave of vertigo just at the memory of that awful climb swept over me. "Okay then, not three…" I whispered, wondering just *how* angry a mother dragon would get if she lost two of her eggs rather than just one.

Pretty angry, I guessed. An angry mother dragon was the very *last* thing that we Raiders needed on our heads. *But one egg? Surely, she won't miss one out of three, right?*

But which one? I looked at the blue, the orange, the turquoise. The blue dragons were long and thin, right? And the sea-green turquoise where the commonest sorts of dragons we had around here. They flew in flocks, small but fast, sharp beak-like snouts as they dove into the water and out.

But what about the orange? Did they even *have* orange dragons way over in the Dragon Academy? Wouldn't it be something when word reached the court of Queen Saffron that a Raider girl had managed to train a rare orange?

Didn't they have orange dragons down in the southern king-dom? I cursed the fact that, not for the first time, we Raiders had to rely on rumors from passing travelers or stolen bits of knowledge and lore we could get from our plunder. If only I knew more about dragons!

The blue will be quick, but they have notoriously difficult tempers, I thought as my hand hovered over the blue egg. The orange dragons of the deserts haven't even been tamed yet. My hand wavered over that one. It would be a great accolade, but I had no way of knowing if it would be a disaster. At least with the speckled turquoise – which had to turn into our more local sea green and blue, right? – at least with that one I had seen them flying, I knew a little bit about them?

I grabbed the warmth of the egg, and at that exact moment two things happened.

The egg *pulsed* with a beat, as the creature inside hammered on its thick shell. "Huh!" I gasped, and the air about the cave was split with the trumpeting call of a returning mother dragon.

"Skreyar!"

Get your copy of **Dragon Raider** at
AvaRichardsonBooks.com

WANT MORE?

WWW.AVARICHARDSONBOOKS.COM

Made in United States
North Haven, CT
27 May 2023

37051550R00254